Penguin Bo

Myra Hook Cwac

The Cattleman's Daughter

Rachael Treasure lives on a farm in Tasmania with her husband, John, and her children, Rosie and Charlie. They run sheep and cattle along with a new venture producing hydroponic stock feed with their company T&T Fast Grass. Rachael has an exciting, ever-changing website at *rachaeltreasure.com* featuring stories from her life on the farm and working-dog training information.

PRAISE FOR RACHAEL TREASURE'S BESTSELLERS

Jillaroo

'Rebecca is a wonderful character being both feisty and fallible ...
The author's solid and believable characters and plot ... make *Jillaroo*
a widely appealing read. In short, a real treasure.'
Australian Bookseller & Publisher

The Stockmen

'I loved this honest and heartfelt tale of life on the land – it captures
the very essence of being Australian.'
Tania Kernaghan

'This is a terrific book – compelling, gritty, sexy, moving and funny –
with some vibrant characters, set against heart-stoppingly
beautiful Australian countryside. It's so well depicted you'll
want to flee the city and find your very own stockman ...'
Australian Women's Weekly

The Rouseabout

'A heartwarming look at women on the land'
Who Weekly

'A rollicking good read'
Brisbane Courier Mail

The Cattleman's Daughter

'A moving Australian story of landscape, love and forgiveness'
Weekend Gold Coast Bulletin

'Treasure writes with true grit, wit and warmth'
Australian Women's Weekly

RACHAEL TREASURE

The Cattleman's Daughter

Penguin Books

PENGUIN BOOKS

Published by the Penguin Group
Penguin Group (Australia)
250 Camberwell Road, Camberwell, Victoria 3124, Australia
(a division of Pearson Australia Group Pty Ltd)
Penguin Group (USA) Inc.
375 Hudson Street, New York, New York 10014, USA
Penguin Group (Canada)
90 Eglinton Avenue East, Suite 700, Toronto, Canada ON M4P 2Y3
(a division of Pearson Penguin Canada Inc.)
Penguin Books Ltd
80 Strand, London WC2R 0RL, England
Penguin Ireland
25 St Stephen's Green, Dublin 2, Ireland
(a division of Penguin Books Ltd)
Penguin Books India Pvt Ltd
11 Community Centre, Panchsheel Park, New Delhi – 110 017, India
Penguin Group (NZ)
67 Apollo Drive, Rosedale, North Shore 0632, New Zealand
(a division of Pearson New Zealand Ltd)
Penguin Books (South Africa) (Pty) Ltd
24 Sturdee Avenue, Rosebank, Johannesburg 2196, South Africa

Penguin Books Ltd, Registered Offices: 80 Strand, London WC2R 0RL, England

First published by Penguin Group (Australia), 2009
This edition published by Penguin Group (Australia), 2010

13 5 7 9 10 8 6 4 2

Text copyright © Rachael Treasure 2009

The moral right of the author has been asserted

Cover design by Laura Thomas © Penguin Group (Australia)
Text design by Anne-Marie Reeves © Penguin Group (Australia)
Photography copyright © Peter Stoop
Photography concept by Heath Harris and Rachael Treasure. Credit to Hawkesbury River
Saddlery Company for equipment, and thankyou to Glenworth Valley Station
'Naked' written by Sophie Clabburn, lyrics reproduced with the kind permission of Jimmy Forte Music
Typeset in Sabon by Post Pre-press Group, Brisbane, Queensland
Printed and bound in Australia by McPherson's Printing Group, Maryborough, Victoria

National Library of Australia
Cataloguing-in-Publication data:

Treasure, Rachael
The cattleman's daughter / Rachael Treasure
9780143203186 (pbk)
Ranches – Victoria – fiction
Victoria – fiction
A823.4

penguin.com.au

For my main men: my husband, John, my son, Charlie, my brother, Miles, and the two grandpas, Valentine and Douglas

Author's note

I grew up using fire as a land management tool on our Tasmanian farm, and I experienced the 2003 and 2005 fires in the Dargo High Plains, so it's no surprise that fire became a theme of my novel. I wrote this book before the devastating 2009 fires, but I hope it may offer hope or healing to those affected and create new thoughts on how we manage this landscape with balance and common sense.

PART ONE

One

When Emily Flanaghan hit the tree and her heart slammed out of rhythm, she didn't hear the rush of hooves as the other bush-race riders belted past her. Nor did she hear her silver-grey mare, Snowgum, roar in agony, screaming out a hideous guttural sound. As the mare's hooves, like dark river-stones, flailed the air, Emily was lost to the smell of blood of both horse and human. Instead, she felt herself drifting up through the filter of gumleaves, her panic subsiding. She marvelled at the imperviousness of gum-tree trunks, how solid they were, in all their silvery beauty.

Gone was the surge of fear she had felt when she and Snowgum had taken the full force of the big chestnut gallop-ing beside them, hitting them broadside. Silver stirrup irons clanked, the horses grunted punch-drunk, and Snowgum was shunted off course. As the tree loomed directly in front of her, Emily had for an instant wished she'd never fought with bloody Clancy. She wished she'd never entered the race just to claim some ground back from him out of pride.

Images of her two girls, Meg and Tilly, flashed in her mind. They had been down at the marquee with their mob of little friends, running amok. Both girls were lean country kids, with messy, sun-kissed ponytails and grubby faces, now waiting nervously to see their mum race her horse across the line.

Her youngest, Meg, had clung to her whispering, 'Mummy, don't go in that horsey race. Please,' her freckled nose scrunching up. She'd felt Meg's tears on her neck, prompting the sting of her own.

Then, in the seconds before she hit the tree, she thought of her dad, Rod, and the pain it would cause him to lose her at just twenty-six. She felt the weight of guilt in leaving him alone, now of all times, when a stroke of a pen in a faraway parliament could soon take their family mountain cattle runs away from him. Then she had a flash of her brother, Sam, on the other side of the world in a Nashville recording studio. Or, more likely, in a bar with a bourbon in his hand, wearing irresponsibility on his face along with his too-cute grin.

Finally, she saw Clancy. In the last split-second of life as she had known it, Emily felt the horror of Clancy's rage towards her. As she hit the tree, she felt an overwhelming sense of regret that she'd mucked up her life so badly. She had allowed herself to be stolen away – from herself, from her family and from her mountains.

Then came the pain of impact. As Snowgum gave way beneath her, Emily heard the sound of running water, and wondered why that water was slowing to a trickle. She didn't realise it was the sound of the blood in her veins moving slower and slower. She listened to an axe falling somewhere in the distance, quickly at first, then slowing to a few lazy haphazard strikes. She didn't know it was her heart, beating slower. Then slower. Then almost still. Just one . . . lazy . . . hack . . . at . . . a . . . time.

Emily's body lay crumpled and still on a dry rocky creek bank while a frenzy erupted around her. Race officials in fluoro orange vests clambered over tussocks and scrambled through shallow rocky waters. One of them punched words into a two-way radio as he ran.

'We got a rider down! We need an ambulance! It looks bad, real bad.'

On the golden river flat, where the makeshift tent city of the mountain cattlemen's get-together sprawled out for the two-day celebrations, people were still watching the race. The commentator, oblivious to the fall on the other side of the rise, continued to call the Mountain Cattlemen's Cup as the field of horses half slid down the jagged slope towards the finishing straight.

Horses were sheened with sweat, riders gripped tight with denim-clad thighs and, with gritted teeth, hissed their horses on. Adrenaline surged through the veins of horses and riders alike. The two leaders hugged the curve of the track tight. One rider's boot struck the fluttering triangular blue-and-yellow flags strung between star-pickets as his horse was bunted and shunted home. They flew past in a blur, belting for the line. Only three people in the crowd were ignoring the neck-and-neck finish.

Rod and his grandchildren, Meg and Tilly, searched desperately for Emily on her grey mare. As the rest of the field raced home with Emily nowhere in sight, Rod felt panic rising within him.

'Where's Mummy and Snowgum?' Meg said, squinting up at her grandfather.

Rod gripped both girls on their shoulders. 'I'll go find her. I promise. You stay here.' He tried to sound confident as he saw Meg's eyes fill with tears. A friend in the crowd stepped forward and guided Meg and Tilly away. Rod nodded his thanks to the woman and then he was gone, sprinting towards his ute.

A pretty bush nurse was doing up the silver press-studs of her blue overalls in the back of the ambulance. She pulled her long, chestnut hair back into a ponytail and smoothed the rumpled sheets of the stretcher bed, her rosy lips still raw from his stubbly kiss. She could still taste the beer, cigarettes and dust on his lips. Penny felt dizzy and giggly all at once, recalling the full force of his lust. Their encounter had been fast and furious.

She knew he had been watching her all day, like a predator stalking its prey. The very moment that Kev, her ambo crew partner, walked away to get a drink, Clancy had run to her, curved his arm around her waist and dragged her into the ambulance.

He'd kissed her hard on the lips and reefed open the studs on her overalls to clutch at her breasts. Then he'd lifted her onto the stretcher bed as she swiped aside the drip stands and oxygen equipment. He had wrenched down her overalls, tugged at his own leather belt and unzipped his jeans, revealing hips as snake-thin as a bull rider. He'd set at her in a flat-out gallop, the rhythm of his thrusts rising in crescendo as the commentator called the mountain race outside the ambulance. As Penny thrust her hips against his, she threw her head back and gripped his perfect backside tight. She felt like a sweating, blowing horse, and he, her rider. The ambulance rocked and she wanted to scream, but she had pressed her hand over her mouth and bitten down hard into the flesh of her palm.

When it was done, Clancy lay on her for a time, breathing heavily. Penny had shut her eyes and stroked his muscular shoulders, already beginning to long for the next encounter. They could only ever steal moments like that. She hoped no one had seen – he was not so subtle when he was drunk. But she'd smiled coyly as she smuggled him out from the ambulance and jammed his big black hat back on his head. Thankfully, everyone's eyes had been on the race.

In the lead-up to the Mountain Cattlemen's Cup, Kev had been watching Penny in the side mirror flirt with that selfish bugger, who acted as if his wife and two kids didn't exist. Disgusted, he'd turned the mirror away and eventually taken himself off to find a cuppa. He couldn't bear to watch.

Now, back in the cabin with his feet up on the dash, Kev was relieved to see the mongrel husband had gone. But suddenly the radio was alive with urgency and Kev knew immediately that it was a bad one.

'Penny!' he yelled. 'Get your arse in the front!'

*

In the creekbed, Rod knelt beside a course official, who had gingerly loosened Emily's protective vest. Rod cried out in anguish when he saw his daughter's twisted broken body. The translucent white glow of her normally tanned skin, the blood trickling from the corner of her mouth and the deathly stillness of her limbs injected fear through him.

The official bent over Emily's face, listening desperately at her pale lips for breath. Next to them, others were hauling on Snowgum's reins, pleading with the mare to stand so they could move her away from Emily's body. Snowgum's cries were so excruciating Rod wished the mare would just lie down and die. He couldn't bear to see Snowgum's white flanks coursing with blood and the way she twisted in pain. He heard someone scream out, 'Does anyone have a gun?' Rod's world spun. This couldn't really be happening. He looked at the lifeless body of his daughter, whispering, 'Please, God, no.'

She simply could not die. Not his Emily. Before Clancy had stolen her away, Emily had been the lifeblood of their family and of their whole mountain community. This beautiful girl somehow represented their future. For years Rod and his sister, Flo, had battled to keep the mountain cattleman traditions alive in the face of sustained attacks by politicians, bureaucrats and environmental idealists, mostly with the hope that Emily would one day come home to them. Each time Rod had trudged to another meeting to negotiate his grazing rights with the ever-changing guard of government men, he had held Emily there in his heart as a reason not to give up. Emily's presence revived him and kept the weary older generation of cattlemen laughing and hoping. But then she had moved away with Clancy. Rod had watched, heartsick, mute, as Emily's marriage ground down her soul and eroded her spirit. The bright flame of her youth began to dull.

Now, here she was, all but extinguished, and Rod felt the sting of guilt. *He'd* been the one to encourage her to ride in the Cattlemen's Cup. He had thought somehow it was the start of having her come home to him. He lay his hand on her cheek. Now here she was leaving him in the worst way imaginable.

'We're gunna have to start CPR,' the official said, glancing fearfully at Rod. 'She's not breathing and I can't get a pulse.'

Rod squinted down the track, looking desperately for the ambulance. As the man gently eased Emily's helmet off and bent forward to breathe life-giving oxygen into her mouth, Rod was shocked to see that her long, dark hair had been chopped off, the scissor hacks still angry and angular against the softness of her heart-shaped face.

'Emily?' he cried. 'Emily, stay with us. Emily!'

Two

Somewhere through the haze, Garth Brooks was playing. Sam Flanaghan rolled over, dragging with him all the pain from last night's Budweisers, downed after his gig. He'd been in honky-tonk heaven when he'd stood on the Nashville sidewalk and gazed up at the giant neon-red cowboy boot and flashing guitar of Robert's Western World.

As he strode into the bar carrying his guitar case he was immersed into a rowdy nocturnal den of burgers, boots and booze. He was heady from the crush of rhinestone cowgirls done up to the nines in tassels, tight jeans and lairy two-tone dress boots. The smell of deep-fried chicken mingled with the odour of spilled beer and the sickly sweet scent of the perfumed and peroxided women. Sam sucked in a breath. Right from the start, he had known he was going to get carried away.

Now, in his newly rented bedsit, Sam's gummy, long, dark eyelashes peeled themselves apart. The first thing he saw was his guitar case, open. Next to the Conargo Pub sticker that was faded to a mottled text, he saw a hot-pink bra hanging carelessly over the metal clip of the case. His eyes roamed further towards the bedside table, where the sound of 'Friends in Low Places' was coming from. There he saw a large black bra curled up beside his bed like a sleeping cat. Not one but two sorry-looking condoms lay on the floor like bedraggled windsocks. Eyes wide open now, and with a slow, wicked grin, Sam extracted his limbs from those of the two naked Texan girls sleeping on either side of him.

One girl was dark and lean and lay on her back with her forearm rested over her brow, as if she were having a crisis. Her mouth was open and she was making gentle snoring sounds from the back of her throat, her breasts sagging a little too much either side of her sturdy ribcage.

The other, a blonde, lay on her stomach with her knee turned out on the bed, her bent leg mimicking the position of her arm. She was dribbling slightly. The peaches-and-cream complexion that had caught Sam's attention from the stage now looked dimpled and pasty. Ellen and . . . ? He couldn't recall. He did remember they were both soldiers. Home on leave from fighting their 'war on terror' and holidaying in Tennessee, sinking whisky as if there were no tomorrow. Brassy, boastful women in uniform, though clearly not in uniform now, he thought dizzily. Sam looked down now at the blonde's breasts. He had so wanted them as a pillow last night, so far from home, but his cheek had met not the soft yield of flesh but stubborn plastic. Implants.

Sam frowned. Garth was still playing. He remembered that

it was his phone – a different country-legend ringtone for every day of the week, just to motivate him. To get him through the humiliation of suddenly being a nobody in Nashville. He'd come here because there were music legends in every recording studio who could be hired to play on new albums. If his Aussie hit song, 'Jillaroo Junky', about a bloke who couldn't keep his hands off the rural chicks, was picked up, his dream of making it Keith Urban-big in the States could come true. But so far every single producer had drawled, 'A Jilla-*what*?' It seemed he'd jumped the gun – just like his manager said he would.

'Sam Flanaghan,' Ike had said, tapping Sam's dinner-plate rodeo buckle before he'd flown out of Sydney. 'You're a cowboy from the bush – you're just not ready for Nashville. You need some professionalism under your belt before you do this. It'd be best to grow up a bit, kiddo, before making a trip like this.' Ike had knocked his knuckles on Sam's head. 'But there seems to be no one listening inside there.'

And Ike Johnson had turned out to be right. Sam had been in Nashville doing the rounds for months now but no record company people had called. Only the dodgy rabble of mates he made in seedy bars ever phoned.

He reached over the blonde, knocked a glass of water onto the grimy brown carpet, swore, then fumbled to find the silver form of his phone. He flipped it open.

There was crackly static on the line.

'Hello?'

'Sam?'

'Dad?'

'Sam! Oh, thank God. Sam, there's been an accident. It's Emily.'

Suddenly Sam's world back home came hurtling towards him. Not Emily! The big sister he'd idolised all his life. He sat bolt upright, his mind firing.

'What kind of accident? Is she going to be all right?'

'I don't know, Sam. I don't know. It's pretty bad. They're going to chopper her out.'

Sam heard the raw fear in his father's voice, then the line went dead. When he tried to redial, it went straight to messagebank.

'Dad! Call me back when you're in range!' Sam threw down the mobile and sank his head in his hands just as the Texan girls began to groan their protests for waking them.

Sam was transported back to Dargo Primary School with Emily by his side, her long, dark hair in lopsided pigtails. They sat at scratched wooden desks just as their father had before them. Sam and Emily adored their teacher, Mrs Dongeal, who had also been their father's teacher.

She may have had wattles like a bush turkey hanging from her neck and what looked like a single overripe watermelon for a bosom, but motherless Sam and Emily craved female attention, and Mrs Dongeal was all for giving it to them. She'd taught in the district for forty years, and sometimes Sam and Emily would fake a few tears just to be drawn into the soft pillow of her bosom, ignoring the prickle from the sharp hairs on her chin.

No, it was inconceivable that Sam could lose Emily too.

Everything revolved around Emily, like the sun. Sam didn't know how he'd have survived the loneliness of his childhood in the rugged mountain country without her. Nor would he have found his heart-place in music.

Emily and Sam were fifth-generation cattlemen, descended from a line of determined, hardworking, resourceful people. Sam had grown up on stories about their great-great grandparents, who had bush-bashed their way to the remotest part of the high country on horseback with the kids strapped into armchairs on either side of a packhorse. His great-great grandmother, Emily, who had barely ridden before that trip, carried Sam's great-grandfather, then just a nine-month-old baby, on a hired horse.

He had heard how his forebears had pit-sawn timber and carved out a living from the mountains using both brains and brawn. Tirelessly they built their dreams in the most rugged country in Victoria. In the early days, when the Flanaghans weren't packing goods over the mountains with a team of work-fit bush horses, they were supplying miners with food and equipment from their hut on the King's Spur, or droving mobs of cattle over the mountains in search of sweet summer grass. Even on rare days of rest, the Flanaghan boys were tearing off on adventures; searching for gold, digging mine shafts, climbing cliff faces, leaping horses over too-high logs.

While stories abounded about Sam's long-gone relatives, Sam just didn't seem to ache for those kinds of adventures. With no mother to anchor him, Sam found himself wandering far from home, whichever way the wind blew.

It had been the women in the family that kept the men

in line. Family folklore told of old Emily always dishing up a meal or preparing a bed for anyone who needed hospitality in that wild, sometimes bitter place. It was Emily who encouraged her boys to dabble in poetry and write stories, painstakingly etching out their letters in the dull glow of a candle flame in a mountain hut, amidst snow storms. Emily who encouraged them to sound out a tune on a harmonica beside a summertime campfire, to take an interest in hymns and the word of God.

The strong mountain women of the past were still present in his sister. Emily had a quiet strength that seemed somehow rooted in the mountain rock on which she stood. Sam knew he had missed out on the hard-work gene that Emily had so firmly ingrained in her. At least he had a good dose of the musical gene, but the mountains were no place for a dreamy, lazy boy, and every day of their lives Emily had covered for him in some way, and made him feel okay about himself.

Sam pictured the snowgrass plains where the cattle grazed for four months of the year. Beautiful when fine, frightening when the weather came in savage. But always that country had a kind of majesty that even Sam felt running through his blood as a spiritual part of him. If he needed to escape for bright lights and action, it was a comfort to know he could always return to the mountains.

For his family, it was a duty to care for those high-country grazing runs that also served them as a kind of insurance policy against drought. Even in dry times, cows that had struggled on winter pastures on their lowland property at Dargo would become glossy with health and rolling fat once they'd grazed on the high-plains government land.

The snowmelt and the rich soils that had been spelled for seven months always did the trick for both the horses and the cattle. But without access to the high-country runs, the six thousand acres on the lowlands, split roughly three ways between Sam's father and his brother, Bob, and sister, Flo, the lowlands simply could not support them all. Why did they continue to slave every year for a meagre, sometimes absent, income, when life could be far easier? Sam just couldn't see how their struggle was worth it. The whole grazing enterprise hinged on the land up top on the Dargo High Plains, and Sam well knew the government could take that away overnight. It had been a noose around the family's neck for generations – ever since the conservationists had come as bushwalkers from the city and begun to make noises about the inappropriateness of grazing cattle in the high country. Now with the massive campaign in the Western world that 'meat is murder', who wanted to live like a man sentenced to hang, reasoned Sam, when you could get on anonymously in a city doing your own thing?

As Sam thought of his gorgeous, funny sister, he suddenly felt totally lost. Somewhere on the other side of the world she was fighting for her life, or worse, and here he was acting like some loser using grog, drugs and wild women to distract him from a neediness he couldn't seem to quench.

Looking around the Nashville dive, Sam realised how much he missed home – not his flat in Sydney, but home, in the mountains. Sure, he had loved his road crew on his Australian tours.

The tour bus with the ice chest that was always kept topped up with beer. The pub crawls from state to state. The bright-eyed Aussie country girls with a thirst for beer and music and a good-looking bloke. But now all he wanted was to be jamming in the Dargo pub. To have life back to normal. An awful dragging fear for Emily gnawed in the pit of his stomach. He had to go home. If he stayed and carried on the way he had been, Sam knew he was headed for trouble. He'd get himself in deep. Schapelle-Corby deep.

Three

Flo Flanaghan ran her fingers over the ears of her wiry-haired mongrel working dog, Useless, to stop her leathery hands shaking. She was completely rattled after the call from Rod. Through the crackling line of the mobile, she'd heard Emily was in a helicopter on her way to a Melbourne hospital. She jammed a finger in her ear to block out the sound of the Hereford calves bellowing for their mums. Something about a collapsed lung putting pressure on the heart, or cardiac concussion, or some bloody thing. Flo didn't know. All she knew was that it was bad, and she was worried sick for her niece.

She squinted beyond the yards where her cat, Muscles, sat on a post licking his white paws, and looked towards the timbered rise. She pushed back her cap, searching for signs of a truck or a float. Rod had said they were sending Snowgum home, for Emily's sake. He had told Flo the mare would either make it or not, travelling doped on painkillers after being patched up by a vet. Flo prayed Snowgum would come back to Tranquillity alive. Illogical though it was, she, like her brother Rod, somehow felt that if the mare lived, everything would be all right and Emily would come home to them too.

In the cattle yards her other brother, Bob, came to stand beside her and followed her gaze along the dusty gravel road.

'You could have a good feed for the dogs tonight if that horse carks it,' he said. Flo shot him a glance. He was a sarcastic bastard at the best of times. Flo wanted to knuckle him right there in the cattle yards and in their younger days she probably would've.

'Ah, piss off, Bob,' she said. He always pushed her buttons. Deep down, she knew he was masking his concern with masculine bravado, for even he had a soft spot for Emily and her mare. But couldn't he go a little gentler at a time like this?

She'd put up with him for the best part of the afternoon as they tagged cattle. It was rare for Bob to offer help, so she had reluctantly accepted in the hope he was turning a corner. For the past eight years she'd fought hard not to resent him for inheriting the most and the best land when their parents died. He was the eldest son and that was his entitlement, as was the old-fashioned way, but looking at Bob now, with his belly pushing out his bluey singlet and his raspberry-red nose from too much grog, Flo wondered yet again how her parents could have left their land and livestock to a man like him. Tradition, she thought huffily. Blind, stupid tradition that said the farm must be left to the eldest son.

At least her parents had been sensible enough to will her and Rod a third of the lowlands to scratch a living from, and they still shared the high-country licence. As long as Flo could pay the bills, have a counter meal now and then and maybe buy a new vehicle every ten years, she was happy. The Flanaghans had never carried themselves like landed gentry. They were workers who had over generations become the largest graziers on the mountains.

Each generation increased the comfort of their lifestyle from hut to homestead, but no Flanaghan would spend money on grand furnishings or cars, instead choosing to splurge on the best bulls and stockhorses. Their Dargo property, Tranquillity, had a beauty all of its own: six thousand acres of grassy hillsides and bush-covered ranges flanking rich river flats that meandered along the Dargo River. Creeks had carved their way through granite cliff faces and fed life-giving water into the clear bubbling river. It was a waterway alive with trout and tiny native aquatic creatures and gave the whole place a heart and soul.

Because Rod was the only one of them to have children, he had been left the white rambling weatherboard homestead that had been built in the early 1900s. It was set above a river flat, cooled by breezes running over a large spring-fed dam and sheltered from fierce sun and icy winter winds by a deep bull-nosed verandah. It was a lovely old home but now had a ragged air about it, like a beautiful woman past her prime. Every year Rod said he would paint it, and every year, with money tight, the job slid down the list.

The same could be said for Flo's home. She lived further along the track, near the cattle yards. Flo had made the former workman's cottage cosy with her parents' treasured old things. She was settled and happy there with her working dogs and her fat tortoiseshell Muscles, her animals taking the place of the children she had never had.

Spectacularly above the houses rose the mountains that made up the other part of the Flanaghan property. Eighty kilometres along a sometimes dusty, always rutted mountain track, the family owned another nine hundred acres of the best alpine meadows to be found and a handsplit-timber homestead that had survived a hundred snowy winters. Surrounding the Flanaghan land were the stunning Dargo High Plains. A licence of a hundred thousand acres, secured by Flo's great-grandmother Emily one hundred and fifty years before, had set the family pattern of droving cattle from the lowlands to the high plains every year as the seasons changed. Of course, not all of the mountain run was suitable for cattle, but it gave the family access to summertime grazing when the snow had melted and the native grasses, rested and revived, shot up from the fertile soils.

Flo and Rod loved the land, both the riverside country on the lowlands and up in the mountains, but Bob seemed only to endure it. He rarely stayed at the homestead they all shared up on the plains. In fact, since he had inherited the family's alpine country and over a third of the best lowlands country on Tranquillity, Bob had felt more and more cheated. He had all that land, all those cattle, but no money to show for it.

Instead of working like a dog, Bob began to drink like a fish. As he unravelled, so too did the farm, the fences slumping, land crumbling from overgrazing, the cattle's coats looking dull and undernourished from depleted soils. His high-country runs were slowly overtaken by weeds and looking sour from overgrazing. Bob was the type who gave cattlemen a bad name. No matter how often Flo and Rod tried to help him, so as to help the land that their parents had once kept in top order, they were always stung by Bob's arrogance.

As Flo drew her hand away from Useless's ears she realised the dog had rolled in a fresh pat of cow dung.

'Ah shit, Useless.' She frowned and wiped her hands on her grimy jeans.

'Shit's right,' Bob said, rolling a smoke. He lifted his leg, scrunched up his purple face and let out a long, noisy fart as he lit up. 'Christ,' he said from the corner of his mouth, 'I'll blow meself up if I'm not careful.'

'Please, just rack off, Bob,' Flo said. She realised now it wasn't tea he'd been drinking out of his thermos that afternoon. She could tell by the way he narrowed his eyes as he drew deeply on his cigarette, wobbling slightly as he did so. No wonder he was being a prick. Grog and Bob were a bad mix.

'What's up your bum?' he said, blowing smoke out.

Flo shook her head and surprised herself when she began to cry. 'Emily,' she said, as tears washed rivers of dust down her cheeks. She moved over to a rail and leant on it, resting her head on her forearms and shutting her eyes.

The image of her niece came to her easily. Flo had practically raised Emily with Rod. The little dark-haired girl with the shining cocoa eyes had toddled into Flo's life pretty much full-time after her mother, Susie, had died. Flo had never been a mothering type, so she'd been uneasy when Rod had silently placed the screaming newborn baby boy, Sam, in her arms and ushered Emily to Flo's side. Flo had stood there, panic and grief swirling within her, watching her broken brother turn away to take care of Susie's funeral arrangements. Now it was all happening again. How unfair that their family was once more entangled with tragedy and the remoteness of the medical world. While Susie had bled to death in a bush hospital with no doctors within cooee, Em was now fighting for her life in a chopper on the way to a city hospital.

'Aw, geez, Flo! Don't go acting like a woman on me, cryin' like that,' Bob said. 'She'll be right. She's a tough nut, that little Emily.' He clumsily thumped a hand on Flo's shoulder. She sniffed and nodded, relieved he was showing some sympathy, then she swiped her nose with the back of her hand. She laughed at herself and at Bob. Yes, she thought, looking down at her wiry body clad in man's clothes, she was more bloke than sheila.

Flo Flanaghan wasn't unattractive, she was just wiry and steely, as if metallic plates ran beneath her weathered skin. Her bones were angular, giving her face a striking look with her glowing almond eyes, yet she swaggered like a man, sat like a fella and held a teapot as if it were a spanner. Some people who didn't know her well said she was half bloke, and that she must have a set tucked between her legs. She looked funny in a frock and whenever she wore one couldn't seem to find the walk to match it. Her sinewy legs bowed out from years in the saddle.

But every now and then she'd throw her bandy leg over some stock agent or overweight dozer driver, just to prove to all the bloody rogues at the pub that she wasn't a lezzo.

'You're right,' Flo said. 'Emily's tough. But I still want you to piss off. We'll finish the tagging tomorrow.'

Bob shrugged, sucking the last of his smoke before treading it into a cow pat. 'Suit yourself. I'll be off home.'

Flo watched as he ambled like Shrek, all shoulders, no bum and skinny legs, over to his mud-splattered ute. On the back, his rust-coloured kelpie DD, short for Dickhead Dog, began barking like crazy as soon as Bob fired the engine and revved away.

Home for Bob was the new brick house built for their parents' retirement. It was not far from the original homestead but at least it was out of sight. Flo's mother's garden had once been welcoming and green but now it was a tangle of long-dead grass and twists of wire. There were broken bottles on the front porch and rubbish blowing in the yard.

Flo was letting go the last of the cattle from the holding yard when the truck rolled in, rumbling to a halt outside the sheds with a loud choof of air brakes. Flo braced herself for what she might see in the back. Old Baz Webberly jumped out of the truck.

'Thanks for bringin' her across,' Flo called to the old cattleman.

'You mightn't thank me if she's not made it,' he said, limping as he always did. 'No one held out much hope for her. But we decided we'd try and keep her goin' – for Em's sake.'

The mention of Emily's name left a cloud of fear and uncertainty hanging in the still evening air between them. Flo knew Baz would be thinking of Emily's quick smile and easy way with everyone. They walked to the back of the truck and dropped the door, expecting to find the mare keeled over dead.

'I'll be buggered,' said Baz.

Snowgum stood with her legs splayed and head hanging so her nostrils touched the rubber matting of the truck's floor. Her breathing was laboured and her flanks looked as if a cheese grater had shaved the skin away. Her white snowdrift sides were now bloody, weeping and raw. As the light found her, she turned her head gently and half whickered and half groaned at Flo.

Tears filled Flo's eyes at the sight of the broken, bloodied mare.

'Good ol' girl. You're home, you're home.'

They settled Snowgum into the skillion shed with a deep bed of straw and thumped a needle into her neck to inject more painkillers. Flo sighed from the stress of it all and was suddenly surprised to feel Baz's arms about her. She had to stoop a little to rest her head on his shoulder but was glad of the comfort. Then she pulled away and swiped her face with her big hands.

'I'm good now, Baz. All good.'

'You'll be right, love.' He patted her hand.

Suddenly not wanting to be alone, Flo forced a smile.

'Fancy coming in for a cuppa? Maybe you could stay the night. Drive your truck over the steep pinch in the mornin'. If you like.'

'If I like? Aw, come on, Flo,' Baz said, eyes glistening. 'You know me. I'm a mount'n man who loves mount'n women. Course I'd love to stay.' He sidled closer to her. 'And how 'bout a little touch and feel for a sad old bugger like me too, eh? A fella gets lonely on my side of the mountain now the missus has passed.'

Flo laughed. 'You dirty ol' fart,' she said, thumping him on his arm.

He looked up in a parody of dejection. 'Oh, all right then, if I can't tempt you with me body, we'll just have tea. And I'll stick in the spare room, I promise.'

As they walked back to the house, arms linked, Barry wobbling slightly on dicky hips, he muttered, 'No harm in asking though, eh, Flo? When you get to my age, you know what they say . . .'

'And what's that, Barry?'

'Never trust a fart and never waste an erection.' He wheezed with laughter.

'Oh, Baz,' Flo sighed. 'It's gonna be a long night either way I go, I can just see it. Stuff the tea, let's just get straight on the whisky.'

Four

Emily saw herself being carried across a mountain clearing. She turned her eyes away and drifted up into the sky, hovering over the canopy of gum trees. A narrow stream of black clouds pulsed towards her. The intensity of the approaching storm sent electricity through her very being. The world around her seemed to vibrate and shimmer into a blur just as she felt the frightening rush of storm clouds on her face. But once Emily found herself immersed in the eye of the storm, she knew not to be afraid. She knew to be calm; that she was everything, and everywhere, and had nothing to do but feel love and peace. For the first time ever, she had a clear understanding of the spiritual. The truest notion of what those on earth called God. She saw beyond the word that had confused her all her life. She was entire and complete and it was a joy to simply drift as an energy of life.

But suddenly, the clouds pulled back and Emily looked down to see a valley spread out below, its tall green grass dotted with cattle. Weaving through the valley's centre was a silver river, flanked by lush trees. She recognised the landscape as Mayford, but somehow it was different. On a small rise above the valley, in a clearing, Emily saw a hut and a woman standing beside a smouldering fire.

Emily knew she must go to her. She drifted downwards. As she neared, she saw that the woman wore a high-necked navy work dress that was worn and faded. Her skirts fell all the way to the ground, dusty at the hem and resting on the toes of her scuffed lace-up boots. Her grey hair was parted at the centre and pulled back into a bun piled atop her head, but her deep-set dark eyes were bright and youthful. She had a long, strong nose and a kind expression on her oval face.

The sturdy hut to the woman's right was made from thick logs, laid horizontally, topped with a steep shingled roof and a thick square chimney. Behind the woman stood a man, his arms folded across his broad chest. His braces hung in loops beside his thighs and his open woollen work shirt was stained with sweat. He too had grey hair, balding across his brow. His eyebrows had remained dark, as had his bushy moustache, but his trimmed beard was snowy white. His deep brown eyes also looked youthful and alive. Emily noted his hands, huge and square, a contrast to his short stocky stature. Her own father had these hands. To the man's right, a glossy chestnut horse with white socks dozed on a hitching rail. A black shaggy dog with a sliver of white running the length of its nose and across the dome of its head stood on the verandah and barked once at Emily, but then wagged its feathery tail before settling down at his master's feet.

Not far from the hut Emily noticed a planting of tall, floppy-leafed corn, and next to it a stone enclosure holding a lazy sow dozing prostrate in the sun. Somewhere in the bush high above the hut she heard the tinny jangle of a bell and the bleat of a goat. With her hands on her hips, the woman watched Emily.

'What are you doing here, Emily?' the older woman asked. 'It's not your time.'

'It's not?' Emily said, searching the woman's face.

'Are you looking for your mother?'

'Should I be?'

'Go back,' the woman said gently. 'You have work to do.'

'Work?' said Emily. 'What work?'

'Mother Nature's work, maybe.'

Emily frowned. 'What do you mean?'

The woman laughed softly.

'Go back, Emily, and perhaps you will find out.'

'But I want to stay here. That's a beautiful horse. This is a beautiful place. It's our place, isn't it?'

'Go back to your children.'

Emily frowned and the woman gently urged her again, 'Go back to your children, Emily. I'll be there for you.'

The woman stooped and threw a few sticks on the lazy fire, gathered her skirts and turned away. She walked over to the man and together they went inside the hut, letting the heavy curtain of canvas fall shut. Emily somehow knew the woman was her great-great-grandmother, Emily Flanaghan. And the man her great-great-grandfather, Jeremiah. They were the ones who had carved out a life in the rugged mountain terrain and had remained after all the goldminers left. They were the ones who had begun her family's journey. She wanted to follow them inside the hut but she suddenly felt a shock of pain, as if someone had clasped her ribcage with steely claws. Pain ripped through the red string of her muscles and gripped her bones so hard they snapped into shards of white. She felt herself being dragged backwards through the sharpness of the fallen branches of snowgum limbs that had speared the ground around her. Then a pain so strong it blinded her.

Emily could hear voices shouting over a rhythmic whumping noise.

'She's gone again!'

'Clear!' someone shouted.

A pulse of electricity spasmed through Emily's body, her legs jerking straight, her spine pressing hard onto the stretcher where she lay. Gone were the smells of eucalypt and horse sweat and fear. Now there was only the scent of engine fumes and a roaring in her head. She tried to fight to see where she was but the pain was too much. There was no way known she wanted to come back. Not to her life. Not to Clancy, anyway. All she wanted was to find her valley in the mountains and to find her family again.

Emily blacked out.

Five

In a dark old cottage in Fitzroy, Luke Bradshaw stepped from the shower and slung a towel around his hips. His shoulder-length black hair curled in loose ringlets, dripping water onto his broad brown shoulders. He swiped away the mist on the mirror with the palm of his hand. The reflection of his dark, almost black, eyes met his own gaze. He opted not to shave. All he was doing today was going to the uni gym. Without lectures, tutorials and exams, this city life was stupefyingly boring, he thought miserably. But until he got a job, he was spending a lot of his time pumping weights or swimming laps of the pool.

It wasn't out of vanity, more a frustration of not knowing what to do with the energy zinging through him. His was a farm boy's body, used to doing, used to moving, used to being stretched with hard physical work. For the past three years, while studying his environmental management degree, all Luke had used was his head. Not his hands, nor his brawn.

Sometimes, when the lectures drifted into esoteric intellectual drivel, he even doubted whether he was using his brain.

Now Luke itched to get out of the city. But to where? He swiped more mist from the mirror, turned side on and tried to push out his belly. Nothing. It was sculpted to perfection, his skin dark caramel, his body carrying no fat, a throwback to a dash of indigenous ancestry. His colouring was not a good look for the son of a western wheatbelt boy. At the tiny local primary school where he'd grown up, his peers, other farmer's sons, repeatedly called him 'coon' or 'boong'. At least here in the city no one seemed to give a damn about skin colour, Luke thought. Melbourne was made up of all types.

Opening the bathroom door, he emerged from a waft of steam and sauntered down the cluttered hallway, squeezing past road bikes, kayaks, backpacks and camping gear. In the kitchen, his girlfriend Cassy was eating organic nine-grain toast smeared with tahini. She was reading *The Age* and didn't look up when he came in.

'Good morning,' he said.

She grunted and went on reading. Luke wondered for the umpteenth time why he put up with her. He shut his eyes, lashes long and dark resting on his high cheekbones. He knew. What else was there to do? Now that his dad had sold the farm, what else was there? Cassy Jacobson made the time fly. She was one out of the box and she had pushed him out of his comfort zone.

'Suck shit,' she at last said after finishing the article.

'I'd prefer Weet-Bix, thanks,' Luke said, eyes glinting cheek-ily at her.

'Huh?' she said, glancing up.

'You asked me to suck shit,' Luke said smiling, the dimple showing on his cheek.

Cassy gave him a dirty look. 'No, not *you*. *This*.'

She tapped her skinny index finger on the paper. Luke propelled himself away from the bench and leant over her to see the article better.

'A mountain cattleman's daughter was involved in an horrific race accident at the Victorian Mountain Cattlemen's Cup on Jumble Plains yesterday,' he read in his best anchorman newsreader voice. 'Emily Flanaghan, 26, of Brigalow, hit a tree whilst riding in the Cup. Ambulance officers revived her at the scene and she was flown to Melbourne with suspected internal injuries. She remains in a critical condition. Race officials were unable to comment on the outcome of her horse.'

Luke looked at Cassandra's intense blue eyes. 'You're saying suck shit to this?'

'Yeah. Stuff 'em. Bloody cattlemen. Serves them right. That tree was trying to tell her something. Get off the mountains!'

Luke nodded. 'Maybe, but you can't help feeling sorry for the girl. Pretty rough to hit a tree.'

'She's not getting my sympathy. I'm more worried about the horse. Poor thing didn't have a choice, did it?'

'Oooh, Cassy, you're so harsh! You are so mean, especially to me.'

'Am I?' she said, spinning round and running her fingernails down his bare torso.

'Ow!' He pulled away from her but she had hold of his towel.

'C'mon, pretty boy. Let me bite you.'

He felt her pointy teeth on his neck and he turned to bite her back, nibbling at her long thin neck that was now starting to bristle in the weeks since her Demi-Moore style buzz cut. She smelt of lavender and sandalwood oil. The scent had remained on her skin from their slippery lovemaking by candlelight the night before, when she'd emptied a whole bottle of massage oil over him in the bath. She'd still only halfway cleaned the bath, giggling as she bent over naked before him wiping the towel over the oil-smeared enamel surface.

'What's Karla going to say when she gets back from her bushwalk? She'll go ape.'

Luke had shrugged. He didn't really give a toss what Karla thought. He watched Cassy, nude. Her small, pointed breasts swinging down like a bitch in pup and the waggle of her tiny white backside. She was so uninhibited about her body. Luke had seen more of a female form in the past two years than he'd ever thought he'd see. There were still times when Luke was confronted by her aggression and selfish ways. It left him wondering if she was a really gutsy and intelligent girl – or just fucked in the head. Still, she made life exciting and she'd turned his farm-boy ways inside out since he'd met her two years earlier.

When Luke had first come to Cassy's house, after they'd skipped a tutorial at uni, he'd been confronted by a bookshelf filled with feminist theory. As Cassy whipped up a vegetarian risotto for him, the boy who'd been raised on chops and three veg on a wheat and sheep farm in the west ran his fingers over the spines of her books: *Stone Butch Blues*, *Cunt*, *Lesbian Ethics* and *Herland* were just some of the titles.

'Whoa,' he said to himself, as if steadying a nervous green-broke horse.

After their 'first-date risotto', washed down with cask wine, Cassy became like a predatory lioness. Her eyes focused intensely on Luke, as she pounced, and he felt her nails dig excitingly into his skin. She made him go down on her that first time they made love. Her body had patches of thick, dark hair in places most Australian women waxed, shaved or hid, and Cassy seemed culturally exotic at first. None of the girls from Luke's hometown in the wheatbelt had been this uninhibited. They all had long hair and shaved legs and played sex by the rules. Country girls, although fun, liked a little bit of romance.

Unlike Cassy, who, in the first five minutes after they met at the uni library, said, 'Fancy being my flatmate, and fuck buddy? We can save on a room and rent.' It turned him on and turned him off and challenged and excited him all at once. So for the past two years, uni life with Cassandra had been interesting in the extreme. She was the antithesis of the type of girl his mother wanted him to bring home. And at the time, that suited Luke perfectly.

He recalled the day he led Cassy into the Bradshaw family kitchen – it was as if he'd brought a footrotty sheep onto the place. Luke had been delighted by his old man's reaction. His father was in the process of gradually selling off the farm to a tree plantation company and Luke felt his old man was literally selling the farm out from under him. As each title was sold Luke felt more bereft, as if he was in limbo, with nowhere to go in life. Luke figured his parents deserved a dose of Cassandra.

It had been so funny to see Cassy drying the dishes for his mother while lecturing her on feminist theory and how most men were 'terrified of being swallowed up by the vagina'. His mother nearly dropped her china teapot. It was Cassy's refusal to stifle her screams during sex, on the basis that she was entitled to 'self-expression' no matter where she was, that had undone his mum and dad. His parents had suggested they not stay the second night, and would be better off going straight back to their share house in Melbourne. And a haircut would be good too, his mother had suggested. For Luke, that was, not Cassy.

Cassandra pulled away from him now and glanced up at the kitchen clock.

'Shit,' she said suddenly. 'My batik course. It's on in fifteen. Can I borrow the Datto? You can get the tram later, can't you? Please!' She slipped a cool small hand inside Luke's towel and twirled her fingertips in the hair there. 'Pretty, please?'

'Okay.'

'Great! But make sure you're in the city by one. The rally's on.'

'Rally?'

'Yes, I told you about it. Remember?'

Luke looked guiltily blank.

'The wind turbines. They want to put them on the Prom. Right where the parrots fly. It's just plain wrong.'

'Parrots? Yeah, that's right! Parrots.'

'You'll be there?'

'Yeah, sure.'

She grabbed her satchel made from recycled tyres and turned to go.

'But just one thing,' Luke said. 'Couldn't the birds just learn to fly *around* the wind towers?'

Cassy looked at him as if he had just vomited green slime.

'Shit, Luke. *Shit!*' she said, as she exited the kitchen with the irritated stomp of her Doc Marten boots. 'You *are* taking the piss. Geez, I hate that.' She slammed the door and Luke smiled and looked again to the newspaper. Next he heard the door open again and Cassandra pelted an orange at his head.

'Ow!' he said. 'That really hurt!'

'Well, imagine how the parrots feel, running into those bloody great spinning blades!' And then she was gone.

The house fell silent, apart from the constant drone of traffic on the freeway behind the back fence. Luke rubbed his head as he listened to the stream of trucks, sedans, utes and vans making their way to work or the shops or somewhere. City life, pulsing on in its own constant, ever-hungry energy system. Luke sighed. He missed the country. Here he was, a graduate in Environmental Management. But what environment could he manage? Where? He didn't know. Back out where his home had once been, the farm that was now managed-investment-scheme trees as far as the eye could see? He thought not. It broke his heart knowing all that land that had once produced food was now being taken over by blue gums demanding nutrients and water in great hungry monocultures. Land that no one loved any more.

He glanced again at the newspaper article and silently wished the cattleman's daughter and her horse well, then turned the page gloomily, wondering what other horrific stories the media was dishing up for breakfast this morning. Then an advertisement caught his eye.

Department of Land Sustainment, Conservation and Environmental Longevity (DLSC&EL) requires a Victorian People's Parklands (VPP) Ranger for the Heyfield–Dargo Plains region. University qualifications essential.

He'd often heard about this region from his grandmother. Gran's genes were responsible for Luke's dark colouring. She and her people had come from that place. Luke felt a tingling sensation on his skin.

The mountains, he thought. Yes, he loved mountains. Perhaps the excitement now coursing through his veins was a sign he was being called back to a home-place. After loving then losing the flat landscapes of the family wheat farm, and then being absorbed in the buzzing energies of a big city, the idea of living quietly in the mountains was like a tonic. Luke had never been to the high country, despite Cassandra's plans for a bushwalking trip that had never eventuated. But the Victorian Alps sounded so rugged and beautiful. Luke looked up at the clock. The government office phone lines would be open by now. He would ring right away.

Six

Emily was sure she could see angels. The blue-white light before her seemed to drift and shimmer. She tried to drag something from her face but could barely lift her arm. She could hear a slow hiss, in and out, repeating itself over and over, and feel something tugging her skin, just below her heart. It felt like she wasn't breathing at all. She wondered whether she had died. From far away she heard a voice.

'Emily?' Was it her great-great-grandmother again? 'Emily.' A cool hand on her arm and a bright light in her eyes. 'You're in hospital. You've had a fall off a horse. Emily?'

Horse? Snowgum! Emily thought with a jolt. Then she foggily remembered she had left her girls somewhere. She grappled to recall where.

'Meg, Tilly?' she mumbled, agitated, her words lost in the mask that covered her nose and mouth. Again the woman soothed her.

'Your girls? Yes, they've been here to see you. Look.' The

woman held up bright paintings. Emily recognised Meg's familiar wild brushstrokes in vivid colours and Tilly's neat pencil lines in pastel shades. Relief flooded her.

On a trolley near the bed sat an unruly bunch of everlasting daisies and roadside flowers the girls must have brought from the mountains. Emily watched the nurse move to the end of the bed, the room spinning and coming in and out of focus. It terrified her. She frowned and made a small murmuring noise. The nurse came and laid a cool, comforting hand on Emily's arm.

'You'll be fine, sweetie, but very tender for a while, and a bit groggy. You've broken ribs and there's some internal bruising. The doctors had you under sedation to make sure your heart is tracking right. That heart of yours must be pretty smart and strong – it just got right back on track beating for you. You're a very, very lucky girl. You've been given a second chance, darling.'

Second chance? Emily tried to fit all the pieces together of how she'd come to be here. She thought of Clancy and felt a lurch of despair – the memory of him was a cruel one.

'I'll go find doctor to tell him you're back with us. Won't be long.' And the nurse was gone.

As Emily lifted her arm gingerly she noticed a needle taped to the back of her hand with clear fluid running through it. Pain ripped through her. She panicked. She just wanted to see her dad and her girls. She just wanted to go home. But where could home be now? There was no way she was going back to the squat brick house in Brigalow she had shared with Clancy.

No, she thought, home was one hundred and fifty kilometres away in Dargo. But not just Dargo. The Dargo High Plains.

As she stared at the back of her hand, Emily thought of her mountains. Her little finger became the Long Spur, her ring finger with the plain gold wedding band became the main Dargo Spur. Her middle finger, the one she raised at Clancy's back, was the White Timber Spur. Her index finger, which she also pointed at Clancy accusingly, was the Table Spur, and her thumb the Blue Rag Range. The back of her hand was the Dargo High Plains, where the Flanaghan homestead nestled on sub-alpine meadows, surrounded by white-grey snowgums. Her beloved mountain run was mapped out on her hand. Gingerly she lifted her hand further to scratch her scalp that itched and burned. She was shocked when her fingertips met with the short tufts that stuck up at all angles. My hair, she thought! They've cut my hair! But then she remembered . . .

It was the day before the Cattlemen's Cup. She had been sitting on the edge of their marital bed, gazing at herself in the mirror, waiting for Clancy to come back from his truck run to take them away for the weekend. Her long, dark hair looked lank and greasy, even after a wash. Her jeans felt too tight and her tummy rolled out over the top of her leather belt.

She poked at the fat roll with her finger.

'That's no muffin top,' she said to herself. 'It's more like a bloody double-sponge cake.'

She looked around the room, bored with it. She'd slept

here every night for six years but it had never felt like home. The bedspread fell neatly to the clean carpet, a delicate clock, a wedding present, ticked in a civilised fashion beside the bed. Stacked on her side were Hereford cattle and Australian Stockhorse magazines. On Clancy's side were truck and girlie mags. A tacky, tempting headline read 'Boobs Galore!'. Emily glanced down to her own breasts, which had sustained both her children for the first fifteen months of their lives. Breastfeeding had been the most natural thing for Emily, but for Clancy it was not. His brain was wired to think tits were for blokes not children. And he was jealous of the attention Emily gave the girls. Over time, he stopped touching her. He rolled away from her in bed every night and his back became a wall.

She flicked open one of his magazines to see a girl pouting, lips parted in a suggestive 'O'. Emily looked at the girl's pert, round and surgically enhanced breasts. Her blonde hair tumbled down over her shoulders. She imagined Clancy wanking over her. It made Emily shudder. As she flicked through a few more pages a piece of paper suddenly fluttered out like a butterfly, landing on the floor. Emily picked it up. It was a receipt, from a truck stop near Brisbane. As Emily read through the items it became clear that dinner wasn't the only thing dished up for truckies on the long haul. Prostitutes were also for sale.

Emily's cheeks reddened as she read the bill Clancy had clocked up. *Room hire and a Cherie sweetheart special with doubles, plus extras.* Extras? Emily's heart began to race, her skin prickled and she felt like she would throw up. She stared at her image in the mirror and gritted her teeth, stifling her cry of pain so the girls wouldn't hear. Bastard!

She had suspected Clancy. She'd seen the magazines of big rigs with their dodgy ads at the back, and part of her had known. The sensuality she and Clancy once shared in their marriage was all but gone. She felt the fury course through her, fury at herself as much as anything. She had given herself over to Clancy in marriage, given him her body, given him two beautiful children and given up her cattleman's life – and for what?

Even in the first wave of shock and anger, Emily could admit that, immersed in motherhood, she had also withdrawn from Clancy. She saw that she had been black with depression. In the past year, to keep herself cheery and a little sane, she had loaded the kids in the stroller and trawled the big ugly shopping centres hunting down amusing underwear for herself. It was also a kind of test for Clancy, to see how much or how little he noticed her.

In the mornings she'd pull on pink, frilly, ruffled undies with cloth cherries hanging from them or slip on a purple and black pair that read, *Enquiries Welcome But Knock Before Entering*. Not once did he say anything. Not once did he notice. The months wore on. Her silly underpants collection grew and so too did her conviction that their marriage was dying. No wonder Clancy didn't notice her knickers, she thought as she clutched the receipt in her fist. His mind was on other women, freer than her.

She stripped off to her bra and Kmart 'Hot Stuff' undies, and stood looking furiously at her ridiculous self. Her once work-fit body had softened from motherhood and inactivity. Six years she had been here! It shocked her that time had closed in on her so fast. In the ever-expanding town of Brigalow she was immersed in a world of washing and daytime TV, with only an occasional trip to a bigger town twenty minutes away, where she felt stupefied in shopping centres and suburban ugliness, while her husband was off with truckstop whores. For years she'd been living like this, or rather, dying like it.

Her brilliant stockhorse, Snowgum, was squashed into a weedy one-acre block amidst Clancy's truck-trailers. Her highly trained working dog, Rousie, was confined to a kennel in a backyard, listless with no view. These days both creatures rarely got a glimpse of work on her father's cattle farm. Since the birth of her second child, Meg, Emily had found it too hard to pack them all up – kids, dog and horses – and cart them out to Grandpa's farm. There, behind the high weatherboard fence and beneath the Hills hoist that seemed to span one side of the yard to the other, Emily felt stifled. Trapped. Like her soul had come unstuck.

Looking in the mirror at her soft white belly and pudgy arms, Emily was amazed at what she had become. It didn't make sense. In the Flanaghan family, women held the same status as the men. Sometimes the Flanaghan women held even more clout in the family than the men. They may have provided domestically, but they also rode alongside the men, camped out in the mountains, mustered and salted the cattle and worked the dogs. They were raised that way. The kids were the work-force, whether you were a boy or a girl. There was no room to be sexist up in that wild mountain world. Everyone had to be capable, everyone respected as equal. But in Clancy's world, women were objects for men or domestic servants.

Within their marriage, Clancy had never hit Emily with his fists. Instead he punched her mercilessly with his words and negative energy. He pummelled Emily with his put-downs. *Stupid woman. Fat hag. Surly bitch. Nag.* When he talked to his mates he called her 'The Missus' or 'The Boss'. And he talked about her in front of her as if she wasn't there. His words as sharp as arrows stuck, barbed, in her skin.

The Emily Flanaghan who had smiled readily, laughed loudly, galloped horses, cut out cattle and chainsawed fence-posts had gone. But, looking into her eyes in the mirror, Emily vowed that this weekend, at the Mountain Cattlemen's Cup, she would find that girl again. She tossed the receipt in the rubbish.

'Stuff you, Clancy,' she said. 'You won't beat me.' She rummaged in the bedside drawer, pulled out the scissors. Crying silently, Emily began to hack away her long, dark hair.

Seven

Luke Bradshaw checked his watch. He was early. He combed his long, curly hair behind his ears and inspected his face in the rear-view mirror. He'd wanted to cut his hair before the job interview, but Cassy had told him no.

'Keep your locks. It's a government position. The more indigenous you look, the better,' she had said as she lay naked on their bed, watching him dress.

Luke looked up now to the tall, sleek building with the striking green logo that someone had no doubt been paid a squillion to design. He got out to feed coins to the parking meter and, as he did, watched the government staff slot their cars into their allocated spaces and bustle into work. They all looked like fairly down-to-earth types, and their cars were middle of the range. Nothing too flash. Still, Luke wondered whether he'd fit in here, raised by his farming father who was far from approving of the bureaucrats – what farmer was? But if this job was his ticket of leave out of Melbourne, he'd be happy. Besides, he'd love to see his father's face if he did get a government job. Giving his dad the shits would be icing on the cake. Pissing his father off was one of the reasons he'd done the environmental degree in the first place. But what did the old prick expect, Luke thought bitterly, selling off the farm like that without any kind of consultation?

A brand-new white diesel Land Cruiser chugging into the car park caught Luke's eye. It was really flash. It had a snorkel for river crossings, electric winch, automatic diff-locks and, judging from the aerials, three different styles of radio and satellite communication wired into it. The driver had obviously just driven it through the car wash and the bright-green logo on the door was slick and shiny.

Luke watched the skinny, ginger-haired man at the wheel steer the cruiser to a spot nearest the building. He reached into the back seat to grab his briefcase, then hit the auto-lock button on the key ring. The cruiser made a little *peeyou-peeyou* noise, like a bird, and flashed its indicators twice. That man clearly loved his new government four-wheel drive, Luke thought. Luke found it funny that the man had parked in the head sherang's spot in the middle of a dirty great city, yet was dressed in khaki shirt and shorts and lace-up boots as if he was going bush-walking with Bindi the Jungle Girl.

Luke checked his watch again and decided to go in. He caught a glimpse of himself in the automatic sliding doors as he followed the man into the government office building. His long hair, combed back Antonio-Banderas style, looked slightly at odds with the grey suit and red tie he'd dragged out of the

47

cupboard, worn once for his grandmother's funeral. All he had to wear with the suit were his Blundstone boots. He felt like a dork. At least his boots were polished to shining, he thought.

In the airconditioned cool of the foyer, Luke offered up a smile to the girl behind the desk, but she was busy with the man who'd walked in moments earlier. Luke stood politely to one side, pretending to browse the brochures on the desk advertising how well the government was doing in all areas.

'Good morning, Kelvin,' she said brightly. 'I believe you're walking a different track today.' She gathered up a bundle of mail and newspapers and passed it to him. 'Down the corridor. First door on the right, I believe,' she said with a wink.

'Yes, Kylie, a new track. A new track. Thank you.'

'Congratulations,' she said.

As Kelvin made his way along the corridor, Kylie lifted her gaze from behind neat light-framed glasses to Luke.

'Yes? Can I help you?'

After signing in, Luke looked at the slip of paper handed to him that had the same flashy logo as the building itself. The fine print asked him to observe all safety signage and occupational health and safety requirements, and told him to follow the instructions of the fire wardens or management in the event of fire or emergency. He smiled to himself. The wording was so 'government'. If he got the job, he knew there was an entire language within these walls he'd need to learn. He clipped his security pass to his jacket and waited to be ushered along the hall by Kylie, who, once walking and talking, didn't stop to draw breath. She clearly relished her job.

'This is the first time Kelvin, er, Mr Grimsley, has been in his brand-new office with his brand-new title of acting region manager for the VPP within the DLSC&EL,' she said, looking at Luke expectantly, as if waiting for him to be as excited as she was.

'He's taken over from Ted Deagan, who's away on long service. Kelvin might seem a little distracted this morning as he hasn't had time to unpack. Human Resources stuffed up the advertising dates and have got you in a week too soon, but you and he will be fine. Normally we have a panel, so you're getting off lightly.'

Luke nodded at Kylie's monologue as she guided him along corridors and past offices that were as yet empty but would soon slowly fill up with the less-punctual staff.

'It's great to see Kelvin step up a notch. He's been dedicated to his job forever. I think he's had over thirty years in the department. No wonder they gave him a new work vehicle, even if it's just for a short time while Ted's away.'

'Will he ever get to drive it on dirt?' Luke asked quickly.

'Sorry?'

'Will he get out with it much?'

'Oh, no. Ted spends ninety per cent of his time in the office, but every region manager is entitled to a vehicle, aren't they? Now that Kelvin's acting region manager for the Victorian People's Parklands as part of the Department of Land Sustainment, Conservation and Environmental Longevity, he automatically gets a vehicle and a mobile phone.'

'Oh, I see,' said Luke, not seeing at all.

When they arrived at Kelvin's new office Luke was ushered in front of the man he'd seen get out of the Land Cruiser in the car park.

'Our job applicant,' Kylie announced brightly, offering Luke a chair in front of Kelvin's desk.

Kelvin Grimsley eyed the strikingly handsome young man before him as he shuffled through his application forms.

'I've noted you've ticked yes when asked if the applicant is of Aboriginal or Torres Strait descent. Where are your people from?'

'Well, it's just a dash of indigenous blood,' Luke said, blushing, 'on my grandmother's side. She was originally from the East Gippsland region, but I don't have any contacts there.'

Kelvin nodded, sliding his glasses onto the end of his nose.

'That's good. We need people with a connection to the land.'

'Yes, it's something I've lost since Dad sold the farm.'

'Oh, I don't mean a farming connection. I mean a spiritual one.'

'I see,' Luke said, a little perplexed by Kelvin's implication.

'Yes, I read in your application that your father grew wheat and sheep. But the farm is now sold. A sensible move, given that our arid land is not suited to these pursuits.'

Luke nodded, wondering if he should mention that most of the land had gone into government-supported pine production and blue gums that would rob the soil more than their farming ever had. He decided not to.

'I think my very practical upbringing will stand me in good stead for a job as a remote ranger,' he said instead.

'Yes, but agriculture is so simple when compared to the job we do. Your father was only managing a small area. Our department manages a vast expanse and we use science as our backing, not like farming.'

Luke was about to point out that they used science extensively in their farming practice but Kelvin continued on. 'I remember being like you. Coming in to apply for a job as a ranger. I thought it was so simple. I was a wide-eyed Melbourne lad, seeking boy's-own adventures in the bush!' He laughed at the memory, then leaned forward and laced his fingers together, resting his elbows on his desk. While his blue eyes looked directly at Luke, his attention seemed to drift far away.

'Of course I had many hours of practical experience in the bush. I bushwalked, backpacked, camped in huts and skied all my life – well, at least in school holidays. And when I was a young uni student, I had a bit of daredevil in me. I had a stint riding motocross bikes in the bush until I broke my leg coming off on a sharp bend in the Licola mountains. Oh, crazy times! In fact,' he said, snorting laughter, 'I sat my biological diversity exams with my plastered leg propped up on a chair. The examination supervisors had to check that none of the signatures on it held cryptic answers to the paper.' Kelvin was chuckling now. Luke wondered if the cheery man was socially inept or just a complete nerd.

'As a young bloke I loved to escape the city and get back to nature, so it was no surprise that when I finished my science degree I joined the government VPP service.'

'No surprise at all,' chimed in Luke, almost feeling sorry for this man who had clearly never conducted a job interview before and hadn't even had time to move into his new office. Still, he earned points for conviction in his own cause, Luke decided.

'I've devoted all of my working life to the thousands of hectares of natural bushland managed by the DLSC&EL,' Kelvin proclaimed proudly. 'Although, the department wasn't called that back when I started.'

'Oh?' said Luke.

'Yes, back then it was the Land and Forestry Department and the land was measured in acres and the vehicles were pretty rough. You don't mind roughing it, do you?'

'Me?' said Luke. 'Not a bit. I love sleeping out.'

'Well, you would, with your Aboriginal heritage. You know the place you're going is pretty remote? We've advertised the job internally for weeks, but so far no one within the department has applied.'

'Really?' said Luke, amazed.

'Oh, don't let that put you off. I can see why people don't want to move that far into the bush – especially family men. You'll be working mostly alone. And Dargo can be a hostile township full of shooters, loggers and rather aggressive cattlemen. The social life is zero for young people and the small school would probably be inadequate by the standards of governmental employees with families. It's good to have a young single man apply. You *are* single?'

Luke swallowed. 'Yes.'

But Kelvin was already standing to look at the map on the wall, his mind on another path.

'It's a big, difficult and complex job.' He pointed to the map with his pen, as if giving a geography lecture. 'The Alpine Park territory is some 465,000 hectares.' He ran his finger down the straight angular lines that divided Park from Government Forestry land and private land. Luke looked at where the township of Dargo lay and the massive expanse of mountain country that rose up from the town's fringes. It was out in woop woop, but that made it all the more appealing to him. Luke was glad they had a hard time filling the position – he couldn't care less if Dargo was a redneck town.

'If you do get the job, Mr Bradshaw, I'm sure you'll come to share my same principles and values of conservation of natural land. You'll also need to learn how to cope with the sometimes dangerous job of a ranger. Basically you're doing the job of a policeman, but without the uniform that speaks to the same level of authority. We also advise rangers not to become involved with the local community. Given the inflamed debate raging over alpine grazing, it would be best to steer clear of the locals, especially the cattlemen.'

He pushed today's newspaper forward on the desk and Luke read the fresh headline: *Grazing Bans on Political Agenda*. Within the text of the story was a breakout piece. Luke looked at it with interest. *Bush Rider Still Critical*. Kelvin stabbed his finger on the articles and shook his head.

'The thing that irritates me the most in this world is these damn mountain cattlemen. I've spent my entire career trying to oust them from their grazing runs. They profess to be the true conservationists,' Kelvin scoffed, 'but that's a ridiculous notion. All it's about for them is making money. They don't care for the high country. How could bushmen question what science has shown? That grazing and annual burning off are detrimental to the fragile, natural ecology of the Alpine region!'

Luke thought of the girl who'd been injured on her horse and shifted in his seat uncomfortably, but Kelvin failed to notice. He was clearly relishing his captive audience.

'It's only a matter of time before the government, based on the department's recommendations, passes legislation that will not renew the grazing licences in all the Alpine regions. Perhaps this accident will spell an end to the ridiculous get-togethers they insist on having each year in remote mountain areas. Surely the OH&S and insurance would now make that event prohibitive for their organisers. Not to mention the environmental damage such events inflict upon the land.'

Luke nodded.

'Yes,' Kelvin said, 'the cattlemen have caused me nothing but headaches. The day grazing is banned from the high country will be a happy, happy day. And it's coming soon.'

Kelvin Grimsley huffed as he stood, grabbing up his cup.

'Coffee?' he asked Luke.

'No, thanks.'

'Ha!' Kelvin laughed. 'No coffee? You're definitely the man for the job. Finding good coffee at Dargo would be like finding hen's teeth. Oh, what am I doing? I'm the acting manager! I don't have to get my own drinks.' He buzzed Kylie.

Smiling at Luke, he said, 'You could get to the top of the tree like me, son. If you work hard.'

As Kelvin continued his monologue Luke looked again at the newspaper article and wondered what 'critical condition' meant. Would the cattleman's daughter make it through, or die, or perhaps be hideously injured for life? He felt sorry for her, whoever she was. But his wandering mind was jolted back on track when Kelvin perched himself on the desk in front of him.

'I like you, Luke Bradshaw. Of course there'll have to be a formal offer, but I think you're the perfect man for the job. What do you say?'

Eight

'Congratulations,' beamed the pint-sized Indian doctor as he sailed into Emily's room, his white coat billowing behind him like sheets on the line. 'You've been moved off our critical list and you can now vamoose onto the regular ward.'

'Can't I just go home?' Emily said.

The doctor shook his head. 'No, my dear. You'll be in for a long while yet.'

Emily looked dejected as the doctor signed some paperwork and handed it to a nurse.

'Come on! Don't look so down,' he said. 'Rumour has it your gorgeous girls and your handsome husband are in the building and on their way. You've plenty to smile about.'

He exited the room as quickly as he'd entered it and Emily was left bracing herself. Clancy? Here? With the girls? How could she tell him it was over with the girls right there? But how could she wait? She couldn't bear to think life might go on as it had before the accident.

And suddenly they were there in the room, Meg and Tilly, with Clancy standing tall behind them, apprehension on his face.

'Mummy's awake!' shrilled Tilly and both girls ran to her, clambering up on the bed and covering her with kisses, the collection of drawings they'd brought for her getting scrunched and torn.

'Ow, ow, ow!' said Emily. 'Careful. Shift your leg, Meg. Gently! Mum's a bit sore. Oh, my girls! My little legends!' She glanced at Clancy and cautiously said, 'Hello.'

'Hello, babe,' he said gently, waiting for the girls' excitement to subside before he came over to the bed.

Emily focused her attention on the girls, stroking their hair, hugging them as best she could through her pain. Tears rose in her eyes as she realised the gift she'd been given to be able to hold them again. How easily it might not have been this way. The thought of them travelling through life without her was unbearable. She had endured her own motherless childhood, grateful for Flo, but there had always been such a void in her life.

'Mummy, there's a cupboard down there with food in it and Daddy said if you put money in it the cupboard opens!'

'A cupboard? Really? Oh! You mean a vending machine.'

'Yes. Why do they have those cupboards in the hospital?' Meg asked.

'So people can have a snack,' she said.

'Like grabbing an apple?'

'Yes, just like that. It's city snacking because they don't have apple trees much here.'

As the girls fired questions at Emily and she answered as best she could, she began to take in Clancy. He was hovering a distance away, wearing the same checked shirt she'd ironed for the Cattlemen's. Now it had been washed but was crinkled, the chest pockets of it turning up unevenly, like a pup with one ear up, one ear down.

At the cattlemen's bar, the night before the race, she'd spotted Clancy easily in that shirt the moment she'd walked in. He'd been standing under the sheen of the spotlights in a crush of sweat-stained hats and singlets, hairy backs and tats. He looked like a peacock in the colourful green and blue checks and she had felt so much like the plain pea-hen in her oilskin, her brown hat hiding her dull, cropped hair. Underneath her jeans she wore her aeroplane undies with little red and green biplanes buzzing on them and the words, *Landing Strip Under Repair; Proceed with Caution*. She knew now that Clancy wouldn't be getting the joke tonight.

With resentment, Emily drew in the smell of spilt beer. Summer rain careened off the marquee and she was angry at Clancy for not helping her set up camp before the storm blew in. Meg was slung on her hip, sulking, and Tilly clung dripping wet to her coat.

She could see Clancy was talking to an Amazonian bottle blonde. Her boobs were plumped up in a low-cut top so that her cleavage formed an inviting line down her chest. Her eyes were sparkling. Emily didn't know much about make-up but this girl was coated in it. Black stuff round her eyes and shimmery stuff on her lids and lips that glowed red.

Now she knew more about the inner workings of Clancy's mind, she knew the woman's red lips would remind Clancy of the parts of her he'd really like to know.

Emily felt jealousy and inadequacy spike within her. The discovery of the receipt for the prostitutes was still raw in her and it simmered beneath the surface like a volcano that could erupt at any time. She held onto the knowledge like a loaded gun, ready to fire at Clancy. Sprung. Despite her jealousy, Emily acknowledged the girl looked awesome. Slightly trashy, but totally at one with her far from magazine-perfect body. She was almost as tall as Clancy, with shoulders as broad as Lisa Curry. She was big and curvy, Wonder Woman in jeans and a tank top. Her wrists jangled with gold bracelets and glassy baubles and her white-blonde hair was caught up in swirls on top of her head. She looked like she'd snap a man in half in the sack, thought Emily, and perhaps if Emily hadn't come along, that's what she was planning to do with Clancy.

Emily looked at the men and women behind the bar who were busy topping up the booze baths with bags of ice to keep the cans cold. They tossed them down from the truck like army volunteers threw sandbags in a flood. It was the same scene from when she and Clancy had met at the get-together seven years ago. Clancy Moran stood at six foot tall, and was so impossibly good looking, women of all ages found it hard to draw their eyes away from him. He was something like a cowboy from a Wrangler jeans catalogue. In Melbourne, with his manly jaw line highlighted by flecks of stubble, his indigo-blue eyes and short dark hair, he'd been 'spotted' several times and asked to be in photo shoots, but Clancy had always responded the same way.

'Modelling's for poofters. No way.'

But when Clancy'd first hit on Emily, she made sure she wasn't going to be like the other women. She kidded and joked along with him like she would a big brother and stirred him mercilessly. It had driven him mad to meet a girl he hadn't won over in an instant with his looks.

'I swear you'll end up infertile with dacks as tight as that,' she'd said to him dryly as she leant, drinking legally for the first time at the cattlemen's bar. 'They're so tight I can near see your goolies. Did your mum shrink them in the wash or did you plan it that way to pull the chicks?' Clancy had met his match.

Ever since she was sixteen Emily Flanaghan had filled out a pair of jeans like only a fit, strong country girl can, the thick brown leather of her belt hugging her tiny waist. She often wore checked shirts with press-stud buttons that Clancy had liked to rip right open in one hit. He'd also liked the way she wore the buttons part way undone, so that there was always a glimpse of blue singlet and a hint of the gentle rise of her sun-kissed breasts.

He'd told her that he'd always had his eye on her. Even when she was a little tacker. The way, years ago, she claimed the junior cattlemen's cup on her nuggety little buckskin by a whisker to a big loping thoroughbred bay. He'd seen her each year as she blossomed and grew, cracking stockwhips like a pro in the junior whip crack. Her mouth set firm in a determined line, a soft frown on her face beneath her wide-brimmed hat as the crackers flew back and forth. The sound, mimicking a train rolling away from the station, echoing around the hills. The way her tanned and grubby hands stroked the snake of plaited leather of her stockwhips as she expertly curled them and hung them over her caramel-coloured shoulder when she was done. How she swung lithely on the back of her stockhorse and rode off like an exotic princess with her dark, wavy hair falling down her back. He had treated her like one and she had fallen for it.

Now, here they were again at the cattlemen's bar and he was treating her not like a princess but like shit. A rage surfaced in Emily. She pushed her way through the crowd, kids in tow, to Clancy.

Before she could fling angry words at him, the girl turned towards Emily and beamed a smile at her.

'Emily!' the girl said.

Emily looked blank.

'You don't remember me?' She laid her ringed fingers on her chest. 'Bridie. Bridie McFarlane. From Dargo Primary?'

'Bridie McFarlane! Oh my God!' Emily said excitedly. 'Course I remember you. I just didn't *recognise* you!'

'Yeah, well, the boys did call me pudden guts back in school. A total dag.'

'Come here!' And with that both girls hugged for a long time, the memories of their friendship in the tiny school flooding back. Emily bent down to introduce Tilly and Meg.

'This is Mummy's best friend from school!' She stood again. 'My God, what are you doing back here? I thought you'd moved to Tassie.'

'Mum and Dad are still there, but I've been away in Brizzie at *bewdy* school. You know, facials, waxing, tints. That kinda stuff.'

'Good for you!'

'And you?'

Emily shrugged and inclined her head. Clancy was standing beside them with two drinks in his hands, looking uncomfortable.

'Just being a slave to my husband. But I see you've already met.'

'*Husband*?' Bridie said, her eyes narrowing at Clancy. Bridie took both the cans from him without thanking him and very deliberately handed one to Emily, keeping the other for herself.

'Is he looking after you well in Dargo?' she said pointedly.

Emily shook her head. 'We're not in Dargo. Clancy runs a trucking business out of Brigalow and we've got a house there.'

'Emily Flanaghan in Brigalow! Geez!' she said, turning to Clancy. 'How'd you get her out of the mountains?'

'Looks and charm,' he said with a nervous wink.

'Wouldna worked on me,' Bridie said dryly, then turned her back to him and faced Emily and the girls. 'That's a shame you don't live there now, just when I'm movin' back. Settin' up me own beauty business.'

'In Dargo? Geez, why set up there?'

'A broken heart makes a girl do funny things. I guess I wanted somewhere familiar for a bit.' She swigged on her drink. 'You'll have to stop by.'

'I'd love to! I could do with some TLC.' Clancy looked put out. Emily realised how much he'd quashed her other friendships with women over the past few years. Suddenly Emily saw clearly how her life was not her own. She remembered the receipt. Hurt spiked again in her.

The clouds by now had drifted away in the wake of the storm, and the evening star in the east was shining brightly. The white silhouette of a new moon was on the rise as the pale sky began to fade to ink. Purple and pink rays fanned out from the setting sun, illuminating the western sky. The warmth was back in the air again, but this time it was steamy like a jungle.

'Oh,' Bridie said, ducking her head to look out from the marquee, 'would you look at that sunset! It's bloody beautiful up here. C'mon.' She linked arms with Emily and grabbed Tilly's hand. 'Let's take a walk, girls, and leave old Dad here to get sozzled on his own.'

Clancy looked pissed off, but Bridie held such command he didn't protest. Emily gave him a sideways look for good measure before moving away into the crowd.

Emily relished walking beside her childhood friend again. She and Bridie shared a past of wild girls going feral in the creeks, rivers and all about Dargo on their bikes and ponies. Bridie had been a blob of a kid, but now her wide blocky shoulders were tanned to a tasty cinnamon colour and she carried her weight well. Her tight-fitting aqua tank-top defined her waist that was wide but strongly curved enough in an hourglass shape to be inviting. She moved her ample arse like a slinky cat, which Emily guessed she'd learnt at beauty school. Despite her heaviness, she walked like she was sex on a stick. Emily wanted to take a leaf out of her book. Bridie oozed confidence and strength. But despite the broken heart she spoke of, she also seemed full of the joy of life. How Emily used to be.

They sat on a steep grassy bank lit by generator floodlights. Beside them Meg and Tilly joined the pack of kids who had taken to tobogganing down the slippery, dry incline on flattened beer cartons.

As they laughed at the kids' antics, Bridie leant her head towards Emily's and rested it against hers.

'It's so good to see you again.'

'Likewise.'

'Sorry I never wrote.'

'Same. I'm crap at letters. Thumbnail dipped in tar kinda stuff.'

Bridie stopped and turned to Emily suddenly, 'Can I get up close and personal again?'

Emily nodded, unsure what she meant.

'It looks as if you need some sorting,' she said, lifting Emily's hat and surveying the hacked hairstyle.

'I do?'

'Your husband just tried to pick me up at the bar.'

Emily felt tears rise in an instant. Of course he had.

'Doesn't surprise me,' she said, her voice cracking.

Bridie squeezed an arm about her shoulders.

'Hey! Shush! Don't worry, Auntie Bridie's here! Beauty consultant by day, trained counsellor and drinking partner by night.'

Emily nodded gratefully.

'I've been thinking about leaving him.'

'When?' Bridie asked. Emily shrugged, too choked up to answer.

'I know I've just met him, but he's an arsehole, Em. And I know 'em when I see 'em.' She tried to read Emily's reaction.

'Geez, sorry,' Bridie said. 'Tell me if what I've said is way too rude.'

Emily smiled. 'No, you're absolutely right. He is an arsehole. I'm gonna ride in the race tomorrow. After that, I'm telling him I'm leaving.'

'Really?' Bridie asked.

'Yes, really.'

'Good for you, girl!' she said, toasting Emily. 'There's no turning back!'

Later that night, as Emily quietly unzipped the tent, she felt Clancy's presence behind her.

'You think you're so fucken smart, don't you?' he said, grabbing her arm. 'Pissing off with that fat bitch and treating me like shit.'

She shook his grip away.

'Shh!' she said, aware of the other campers and the girls she'd just settled in the nearby tent. She moved away to the creek.

In the darkness she looked up at the stars through the river gums and tried to summon up the courage to tell him that she knew about the truckie prostitutes. That their marriage was over. But no words came. Clancy slid down the bank in his cowboy boots towards her. She could smell the grog on his breath and the pungent stench of his sweaty underarms. Still in her boots, she splashed through the shallows away from him.

After that her memory was fractured. Blotted out like shadows in the night. She remembered his fingers biting into the soft underbelly-white of her upper arms. His grip too tight. His fingers burning her as he shoved her back onto the jagged creekbed. She tried to cry out but he put his large hand over her mouth. The strength of him was frightening as he tugged her jeans down and grunted into her like an animal. Her eyes were scrunched tight, her head held by his big hand to one side. The press of rocks into the aching muscles of her back. She remembered the angry bite of ants against her thighs. Then the stillness afterwards, when he had rolled off her and swayed drunkenly away. The smell of his warm semen trickling out of her made her want to retch. She remembered crying, hugging her knees to her chest in the dust beside the creekbed, wondering how she could ever go on from here.

Emily looked at Clancy standing before her in the hospital.

'Have you got any money?' Her voice cold and matter-of-fact. He frowned.

'What sort of a question is that? What do you want money now for?'

She inclined her head towards the girls.

'Send them down to the vending machine.'

'What for?'

'Couldn't you go get them something so they can sit and eat it in the corridor? We need some time alone. We need to talk.' She knew they were the words he most hated to hear.

'Talk?'

'Yes, talk, Clancy. Talk. About us.' She cast him a look so filled with sadness and distress, he couldn't argue. He dug his big square hands into his pockets.

'C'mon, rug rats, let's go to the food machine.'

Meg and Tilly danced around their father, giggling. Emily watched him usher them out and despair swamped her. Clancy loved his girls in his own way. Here she was about to break up their family – no matter how fragmented that family had been. Would separation be too hard on the girls? Was it the right thing to do? Should she stay with Clancy and give him another chance?

She fanned Meg and Tilly's drawings out across the bed, looking at them closely for the first time. Matilda had painted a picture of Mummy and her horse. Snowgum had bandages around her legs and head. Emily grimaced before shuffling to the next one in the pile. This was by Meg and it pulled Emily up short. Her hand flew to her mouth as she stared at the picture.

It was a drawing of a house – but not a house. A hut, with a crude chimney, just like the one in her dream. Meg had drawn trees too, lots of them, and among the clumsy crayon slashes of a four-year-old there was a woman with grey hair wearing a long dark dress. Hovering above the hut was an angel. She had short dark hair, like Emily, and she was holding onto a horse that had wings too. It was all there on the page. Meg had depicted Emily's near-death experience. Emily shivered. The mountains, she thought. She was being shown the mountains.

There in her mind's eye was the original hand-split timber Flanaghan homestead – the one they stayed in when they took cattle up to the high country in the summer. The billy buttons would be out in full force now, dotting the meadows like thousands of little yellow fairy lights at dusk. The lupins beside the house would be standing tall in a burst of colour, and the old twisted trees in the orchard would be drooping from the weight of tiny, bite-sized fruit. All around the bush would be alive with summer insects. She could see her family riding through the groves of lush trees on the south-facing slopes, where bellbirds chimed like magic, and hear the low of a mother cow calling up her calf, the clop of the horses' hooves on the gravel track, the sound of the wind high up on a mountain ridge . . .

She kept her eyes closed.

'Well,' came Clancy's voice, 'I thought you wanted to talk. Meg's almost through her M&M's so you'd better spit out what you're going to say.'

Emily opened her eyes and looked at him so directly Clancy took a step back.

'I know,' she said.

'What?'

'I know about the truckstops in Brisbane.'

'What are you on about?' he said, the muscle in his jaw flinching, his eyes sliding away to the floor.

'The girls. Girls you paid for. Hookers.'

Clancy shook his head.

'It was a mate. He went there. I just waited in the truck.'

'Liar.'

He flinched. A blonde nurse with an upturned nose and spectacular breasts came into the ward. Clancy tried to avert his eyes but both Emily and he caught her perfume. Oblivious to the tension, the nurse moved over to the bed. 'I'm Simone. Once your visitor has gone I'll be moving you to a new ward.'

'He'll be going very soon,' Emily said coldly. Clancy blew out a breath, knowing he was sprung.

When the nurse was gone, Clancy looked anywhere but Emily's eyes. She had expected him to yell, to rant at her, but deep down Clancy Moran knew he had broken her trust, and broken their marriage forever.

'It's over, Clancy,' Emily said calmly. 'When I get out of here, I'm going home to Dargo. You can keep the house, you can keep everything. But I'm leaving and I'm taking the girls.'

'No,' he said, moving over to her. He put his hand on her arm and held her wrist firmly. In an instant Emily felt as if she couldn't breathe. A wave of nausea hit as she recalled with a blinding flash her trip in the mountains in an ambulance. It must've been on the way to the helipad. But, how could she remember, she reasoned? She was unconscious! Still, in her mind's eye she saw Penny's gloved hands ripping tubing from medico-packets. She could hear the voices around her. Kev in the front coaching Penny as he drove. A barking, urgent tone coming from the two-way as well. Then, Clancy's voice. Angry and drunk – too loud in the ambulance. Penny shouting at him to calm down. Then the whispers, the secrets that stabbed hurt through her.

Emily shot a look at Clancy, her face white.

'You right? You're not gunna puke?' he said, loosening his grip.

Emily swallowed. 'You slept with her too.'

'Who?'

'That nurse. In the ambulance.'

'Get a grip,' Clancy said. 'They need to change your medication. What are you on about?'

'I remember! I remember you talking. You were standing over me, talking.' Emily was shaking her head. She didn't want to recall but the images kept coming and she had this strange sense of knowing. The way Clancy's body tensed and his eyes narrowed she knew it was true. He'd not only been sleeping with prostitutes, he'd been having an affair. And he had raped her. She had been raped by her own husband. The room spun.

'Get out!'

'Calm down,' he said.

She lowered her tone so it was almost a growl.

'*Get. Out.*'

He began to back from the room.

'Meg? Tilly?' she called with a voice that sounded falsely bright.

The girls came in from the corridor, doe-eyed, still chewing on their lollies.

'Give your daddy a kiss goodbye and come sit up on the bed with Mummy now.'

'No, Emily,' Clancy said, his voice breaking.

'Can we stay? In the hospital?' Meg was jumping for joy.

'Just a little while, sweetie. You can help me move wards. Then I'm going to ring Grandad and he'll come get you. You can stay with him again for a while. Give Daddy the holiday he's always wanted.'

The girls let out a cheer, oblivious to the goings-on in the adult world. They nonchalantly kissed their father goodbye and clambered onto Emily's bed.

'Em,' he said again pleadingly.

'Clancy,' she said calmly, 'just go.'

Nine

Luke watched Cassandra drag off the head of her bilby suit and dump it on the grass.

'You *what*?' she screeched.

Luke sighed. Cassy, awkward in the suit, tipped herself sideways so she could sit on the park lawn. Her bottom lip began to quiver. Oh, God, Luke thought, panicked. She was bloody well going to cry! In the two years he'd known her, he had never seen her cry. He dropped to his knees beside her and held her paw that was worn and threadbare. He leant his head into her shoulder and for a moment wished the Wildlife Society would dryclean the bilby suit. It stank of marijuana and a rank cocktail of hippy, student and backpacker sweat.

'I thought you *wanted* me to be an environmental protector,' he said.

'Yes,' said Cassandra furiously, 'but not move to the country!'

'I thought you'd be happy I got the job.'

Cassy was fumbling with her paws for her mobile in her bag.

'What are you doing?'

'I'm calling Mum.'

'But you haven't spoken to her in two years. You said you hate your mum.'

She shot him a look. 'Well, at the moment I hate you more.'

Luke shook his head, suddenly angry. This job in the mountains was going to change his life more than he had thought. She was all bloody talk, this girl. Environmental crusader, his arse.

'Cassy, this is something I really want to do.'

'How could you do this without telling me? Taking off to bloody woop woop.'

'How was I to know they'd offer me the job straight away? C'mon, Cassy, give me a break. It sounds like a really great job. Besides, Dargo's only five or so hours away. Eight hours tops in a train and a bus.'

By now Cassandra was crying.

'C'mon,' Luke soothed. 'You can come up and camp out under the stars with me. Get back to nature. Use your new Trangia.' For a moment Cassy sank into his arms, the bongo drums of the other protesters echoing around them. Sniffing loudly and using the back of her furry paws to wipe her nose clean, Cassy nodded. He could feel her coming round, but in truth he now realised he was longing for a clean break.

'Cassy, please be happy for me. It sounds like a perfect job for someone like me.'

'But what about me? What about us?'

'Maybe you'll find a job somewhere in the region too? You can fight for all your causes at the grassroots level.'

'What?' The frown was back. 'Move out there? But my home is here. In Melbourne. What could I do out there to make a difference when all the lobby groups are based here? Honestly, Luke, you're so bloody stupid. And selfish!' The tears were back.

Where had she gone, Luke wondered? That angry, strong, young woman who fought for everything known to man. She was anti-battery-hen, anti-live-export, anti-dairy, anti-meat-eating. He'd loved the way she ploughed over ground she knew little about with such self-assurance. The people he'd known had always been so balanced. So polite. Compared to her, so boring. She was rock-solid in her opinions. Unashamed. It had helped him ignore his own uncertainty. His dad told him, 'There's no future in farming,' and his peers joked that leaving your farm to your son was a form of child abuse. So he'd set out to the city, with farming in his blood but nothing in his heart to replace it. He was lost and adrift in his life. Cassandra had given him something to cling to.

Now, as Cassy buried her face in the bilby head and sobbed, he realised she was lost, too.

He made his voice gentle. 'I'm going, Cassy. Whether you like it or not.' She looked small and pathetic slumped there in her ridiculous costume. 'If you love me, and you love the earth, you'll come,' he said, not at all certain he wanted her to come with him, but guilt driving the words. He reached out a hand to clutch her paw. Angrily she shook off his touch.

'If *you* loved *me*, you'd stay!' Then she was up and waddling over to her pushbike. She jammed on her bilby head and awkwardly swung her leg over the bike.

'Cassy!' Luke said. 'Don't be stupid.'

He couldn't tell what she said back, her words muffled by the bilby head, but with a mighty heave she pushed the pedal down with the oversized foot and steered her way out onto the footpath and away down the street into the traffic.

Ten

'Hooly dooly!' said Emily as she watched a girl wearing what looked like a rat suit sitting up in the back of an ambulance that had just arrived at the hospital. Through the opened doors Emily could see she had a near shaven head, numerous piercings and one of her legs had an inflatable splint on it like a giant floatie. She was yelling into a mobile, 'Trust you to have your phone off. When you get this, get your arse to the hospital. *Now!*'

This place was a madhouse, Emily thought. She had to get out of here! For the past few days, she had made herself walk laps outside the hospital no matter how much her body complained, trying to come to terms with a new idea of herself. Single mum. Separated. Divorcee-to-be. None of the words reflected the depth of fear she felt about her future and her sense of loss.

She craved fresh air and sunshine, but it was debatable how fresh the air was in this big city and sometimes walking outside made her feel more depressed. She had to hold her breath each time she walked past the cluster of smokers hanging about the front door. Patients in pyjamas trailing dripstands as they hoovered on their fags. Even nurses and other hospital staff loomed around ashtrays sucking the life out of cigarettes.

Today she'd bypassed the smokers' area and walked a little further, to the hospital's emergency entrance. Her bones ached, her muscles were tender, and her skin was blooming with bruises in an ever-changing palette of colours from black to purple, brown to yellow. Each time she lost her breath, the earth beneath her feet swayed and her vision was obscured momentarily by tiny lights.

But Emily was determined to get out of hospital as quickly as she could, so she kept on with her walks. She leant on a wall near the ambulance and watched the medico trying to pacify the girl, who was surely on drugs or just plain nuts.

'Now, you just sit back there,' said the officer, 'while we get you into the hospital and nice and comfy. They'll take you for X-rays first.'

Through gritted teeth the girl said, 'The Wildlife Society will be billing you for the suit.'

'I had to cut it. You can't be too careful with suspected breaks,' the officer said wearily. 'Besides, that rat suit has definitely seen better days. You could do with a new one.'

'Rat?' said the girl horrified. 'It's a *bilby*. A sacred animal.'

The medico clunked the trolley down from the ambulance with a thud.

'Ouch! Careful,' said the girl.

'Sorry, darls.' He spun the trolley bed about and pinned his dark eyes on her. 'It looks like a rat to me.'

'The bilby is a threatened sacred species of the Anangu people and it needs protecting,' she said, crossing her furry arms over her bilby belly and jutting out her chin.

'Really,' said the ambo flatly.

'That's the problem with the world!' the girl yelled. 'People like you, who don't care! What sort of patient treatment is this anyway?'

Emily could see the ambo was really annoyed now. He folded his arms across his chest, matching the girl's body language, and tilted his head as he spoke. 'You want me to go out to the Tanami Desert, do you, darlin', for the little bilby? Plant some habitat for him? Or maybe you think dressing up like a rat and riding a bike through peak hour is making all the difference? Makes sense to me!' He struck his forehead with the heel of his hand, then reached in the back of the ambulance and tucked the head of the costume under his arm. 'You can hardly count that as a helmet, Missy,' he said. 'And it sure does look like a rat.'

'Don't you Missy me. It's Mzzz, and for the last time it's a bilby!' the girl said emphatically, before turning her angry gaze on Emily. 'And what are you smirking at? I'm in pain here.'

'Oh, I can see that,' said Emily. 'Lucky you're not a horse. They would have put you down. At least you can be thankful that the staff here are great. You'll be right.' The ambulance officer gave Emily a wink and she smiled and began walking back through the hospital gardens, wanting to be away from this place more than ever.

A few hours later, Emily sat sunning herself on a bench in the hospital grounds beneath a beautiful white-trunked gum. That was when she first saw him – a dark-haired boy, about her age, in an old Datsun. She watched him driving past in his noisy bomby car several times as he tried, without success, to find a park. There was something about him that drew her attention to him and held it there. She didn't know what it was.

Eventually he skilfully reverse-parked across the road from the hospital and came jogging over the busy road, weaving through traffic. He wore faded denim jeans low on his hips and an olive green T-shirt that read *Save the Tarkine* rolled up at the sleeves to reveal perfectly formed biceps. His Blundstone boots were city clean, and the thin leather bracelet on his wrist gave him an aura of cool. His longish hair was a rich mass of black curls and framed a manly, clean-shaven face, and his big eyes were the colour of dark chocolate. He caught her watching him and flashed her a smile. It wasn't vain or flirty. Just friendly. She looked away, embarrassed, but he kept jogging towards her.

'Excuse me,' he said, 'which way to emergency?' Emily pointed. 'Thanks,' he said and she watched his broad shoulders and narrow backside as he jogged away from her.

Emily tilted her head back and looked up to the gumleaves above her. She was amazed by how this grand gum had survived, squashed as it was into this concrete landscape. Beneath the city's crust, the tree must've found generous soil to sustain it. Emily thought she needed to be strong, like the tree, though she was in a place that lacked the essence of what the bush brought to her soul. She shut her eyes, wondering why she was even thinking of such things. She wasn't one to sit and ponder. The accident had changed her somehow, and she wasn't sure how she fitted inside her old skin. Eyes still shut, she reached into her dressing-gown pocket and pulled out Meg's drawing of the woman at the hut.

'Excuse me,' came a voice, gentle enough not to startle her.

She turned and saw that the good-looking man was back.

'Mind if I sit here for a bit? Hate hospitals.' He shivered.

'Sure,' Emily said, smiling self-consciously, dragging her dressing gown over her cow-print shortie pyjamas. She pulled her feet in under the bench, shy that she was wearing R.M. Williams dress boots with no socks, the only footwear her family had thought to pack her, along with the worst of her collection of stupid undies. She wished she could put on a bra. She felt exposed and raw next to this man.

She looked away, up at the blue sky beyond the tree, noticing a puff of white cloud shaped like a horse. She wasn't sure what to say.

The man inclined his head towards the hospital. 'My girlfriend . . .' he began. Phew, thought Emily. That eased the tension. He wasn't back to pick her up or anything.

'. . . she got hit by a bus, on her bike.'

'Oh, that's terrible. I'm sorry.'

He shook his head. 'Oh, no. Luckily it wasn't anything serious. It would've been much worse if she didn't have all that padding. They've done X-rays. Just a fracture in her foot. They're plastering her up now. She'll be out soon. She told me to wait outside.'

Emily nodded and smiled, all the while thinking how mean he was to talk about his girlfriend's extra padding. Clancy often picked on Emily for getting fat. It seemed so many men were the same.

'How about you? It looks like you've had a rough ride.' He pointed to her arm that was heavily strapped across her chest in a sling.

'Me? Yeah. Horse accident.'

'Ouch.'

Emily nodded. 'Luckily I have a bit of padding too. So I lived.'

The man looked at her puzzled, then asked, 'How long have you been in hospital?'

'I was kept unconscious for the first five days and I've been here five days awake, although it's felt like fifty, and now they're saying I have to stay longer, worst luck.'

'So it was pretty serious, then?'

'They tell me I'm lucky to be alive. And so is my horse.'

A glimmer of something passed over the man's face.

'Hey,' he said gently, 'you're not the girl I read about in the paper, are you? The one from the cattlemen's race?'

Emily smiled in surprise, half-turning to face him.

'Yeah. That's me.'

'Wow,' said Luke. 'How amazing is that? I've been thinking about you.'

'You have?' she said, thinking how lovely he looked, but at the same time perplexed by him.

'I dunno why. It was just one of those snippets you hear that sticks with you. I suppose I just wondered how you'd got on.'

'Well, here I am.'

'Here you are! That's great. That's *really* great. I'm rapt to see you alive and well.' He was looking at her fully now, taking in her pretty smile and stunning dark-brown eyes with the long curled-up lashes. Emily stared back at him and for a moment she felt a zing. Then, just as suddenly, a wave of self-consciousness. They both laughed nervously.

He looked down at the drawing in her hands.

'Do you paint?'

Emily laughed. 'No. But my daughter does.'

'Oh, good! If you'd done that, you'd be crap, but seeing as your daughter did it, it's great. She's got talent. Is that your home?'

'Sort of,' Emily said.

'Just the one kid?'

'I have another little girl.'

'Two girls. Nice.'

Emily nodded and they both fell silent. Nothing more to say then. That will be the story of the rest of my life, Emily thought, resigned. Man meets girl. Girl has two children. Man loses interest. She glanced back up at the tree. The man was about to speak again, when they heard someone calling.

'Luuuuke!'

He jumped in his seat and looked around. Emily turned to see a skinny girl wearing shorts and a singlet being helped through the sliding doors on crutches by a nurse, who was carrying a large bag with the rat head sticking out of it.

'That's her. Gotta go,' said Luke, who sprang up and began walking quickly away. He spun around, walking backwards over the small patch of lawn. 'Nice to sort of meet you.' He shot her another heart-melting smile and then he was gone.

'Hooly dooly,' Emily said again. His girlfriend was Ratgirl. Her costume was the 'padding' he was talking about. She thought about his smile. His interest in her wellbeing and Meg's drawing. What a lovely, lovely bloke, she thought. And he went out with Ratgirl. The world was a funny old place.

That night, Emily woke suddenly, without knowing why. She propped herself up and looked around the darkened ward. Light from the corridor spilled a slanted rectangle over the floor. She glanced at the clock. It was eleven p.m.

'Bloody oath,' she said, sinking back into the bed. If the days were long at the hospital, the nights were worse. In the silent eerie space of the night ward, Emily saw the hut on the high plains and again felt the call of the land itself. She didn't even have to be asleep for the visions to come. What did it all mean, she wondered? She knew her life had been spared – but for what? And she knew, now, that she was being guided home.

Meg's paintings had shown her that. But why her great-great grandmother? Why wasn't her mother up there in the cosmos, being her guardian angel?

Emily went over and over these thoughts. For too long, married to Clancy, she'd shut out what her future might be. Now she was going to reclaim it. She was a cattleman's daughter, with a proud heritage of caring for the land. She was going to teach her girls the same bushman skills she had learned – and teach them the old-fashioned values that had so far been lost in their suburban lives of too much TV and junk food. She thought of the high plains now and wished herself and her girls there. She wondered though if it was all too late. The government was again being pressured to evict the mountain cattlemen. A sinking feeling besieged her. What if they lost the runs? What then of her life?

'Hurry up and heal,' she muttered now, looking down at her body. Then she heard a noise, a shuffling, that she was sure came from beneath her bed.

'Hello?' she said nervously.

'Shhh!' It was a voice in the darkness, directly beneath her.

'Holy fuck!' said Emily, grappling for her lightswitch, the nurse button, anything.

'No, no, no, you don't!' A man's hand reached up from beneath the bed and grabbed hers. 'Don't let anyone know I'm here!' She heard a familiar chuckle.

'Sam?' Emily breathed. 'Sam? Is that you? What the . . . ?'

With a clatter and a clank, her brother emerged from under her bed clutching a pillow and a hospital blanket.

'Sam! What are you *doing* here?'

Just seeing him caused emotion to well up within her. Emily flung out her arms as best she could and he fell into them as gently as he could. She took in the smell of him. A mix of hard booze and wacky tobaccy, but that same earthy smell that was him. Her brother.

'Shhh! Shhhh! I'm on the run from the law, sis. Keep a lid on it,' he said in a dreadful phoney Nashville accent.

'Oh, Sam, you big dumb idiot.' They were hugging, giggling and crying all at once. 'I thought you were in the States.'

'Had to come home and make sure my big sis was okay. I like the butch look,' he said, scruffling her hair.

'Shut up,' she said. They fell silent.

'I thought I'd never see you again,' said Sam eventually, giving her hand a squeeze. They sat silently contemplating how it could've been. Sam back for a funeral, not a reunion.

Emily held him at arm's length and took in the prison-style buzz cut, so different from the last time she'd seen him with his sandy blond hair all long and floppy. She saw he was still boyishly handsome with his five o'clock shadow and cute heart-shaped face, a mirror of her own. His jawline was fringed with dark stubble. He had that cheeky smile that turned up at one side and blue-green eyes like the sea on a mild day.

He was wearing the coolest tan cowboy boots, unpolished and scuffed about the intricate stitching on their pointed toes. His jacket looked like an inside-out sheep – the sort Marlboro Men wore when they rode horses and smoked cigarettes. But there was an air of detachment, even desperation, about him.

'What the frig were you doing under my bed, Sam?'

'I wanted to surprise you.'

'Surprise me? You scared the crap out of me!'

'You looked so comfy sleeping when I snuck in I didn't want to wake you. I thought I'd get some shut-eye too – it's a long bloody flight from LA, you know.'

'Does Dad know?'

Sam shook his head. 'Not even Ike knows.'

'But your music? Shouldn't Ike know you're home?'

He shook his head again. 'I need to lay low for a bit. Get my shit together.'

'Are you okay?' Emily asked gently. Sam shrugged, looking down at his lap.

'You've got yourself a little bit lost, haven't you?' Emily said, noting the pallor in his skin and the dark circles under his eyes.

'Seems like you have too,' he said.

Emily hung her head. 'I've split up with Clancy.'

'I kinda thought you might.'

'You did?'

'Uh-huh, one day.'

They sat in silence for a moment together, the moan of an old lady in the ward next door underlining their sadness. They had both felt a gap in their lives without their mother, so vast it felt like an ocean.

'Hey?' Emily said.

'What?'

'Want to do me a favour?'

'Name it.'

'Kidnapping.'

'Kidnapping?'

'C'mon,' Emily pleaded, 'you've got to get me out of here. Please.'

Their eyes met and brother and sister grinned.

'Are you sure you're well enough? You look like shit.'

'So do you,' Emily shot back.

'Gee, thanks. Well, where to?'

'Where do you think!' Emily jerked her head in what she thought was the direction of the mountains and the Flanaghans' old summer grazing homestead.

'The high plains. The perfect hideout,' Emily said.

'Yeah?'

'You've got your ute?'

'Yeah,' said Sam.

'Well?'

Sam grinned. 'Okey-dokey, let's get out of here!'

As Sam helped her out of bed, Emily noticed how slowly he moved and the way he kept vaguing out. He helped her pack her things, holding up a pair of pink underpants that had a cartoon elephant on the front with a stitched-on trunk and, on the back, a tail.

'These are truly woeful!'

'Shut up,' Emily said, grabbing the undies from him and shoving them in the bag with the others Flo had brought down from Brigalow. 'You're really stoned.'

'What if I am?'

'Only losers get stoned.'

'I'm a loser then.'

'That makes two of us,' Emily said, thinking of the mess she'd made of her life.

Eleven

'You can be Thelma and I'll be Louise,' said Sam as he helped Emily into the front seat of his sporty royal-blue Holden ute.

'No, I reckon I should be Louise. Lou-wheeze. Get it. Wheeze. The ribs!' They both spluttered with laughter. 'Ouch! It hurts to cack myself.'

That sent them careening sideways into the ute, in hysterics, before shushing each other. Sam glanced around to see if anyone from the hospital had come after them, but sneaking out had been easy. Anyone who was about seemed too busy to notice or care.

In the shine from the streetlights, he looked over at Emily. 'You sure you're right to do this?'

'Sure as sure.' Sam fired up the engine. 'No funny buggers,' Emily said. Sam could be a lead foot, particularly behind the wheel of his boy's toy V8 ute. He shot her a Jack Nicholson smile.

On the Monash Freeway, lit to glowing by endless rows of

lights, Emily was grateful to be heading away from this fast-paced world. Even in the middle of the night, the freeway was still buzzing with cars, trucks and vans, all hurtling along in a four-lane vortex of speed. This concrete shuttle-way was so impersonal, the landscape so artificial, Emily thought, as she looked at the tussocks and silver grasses planted beside the road. Designer nature. She hated it. Freeways frightened her.

Emily shut her eyes and suddenly a picture of her forebears came to her. They were travelling across the foot tracks in the high country, dressed in heavy felt coats with their hats pulled down low, their packhorses making slow progress through the snow drifts, guided only by the moonlight. Just enough to illuminate the snowpoles and the blazes on tree trunks that marked the way.

Emily knew how the miners in the region looked out eagerly for the Flanaghans' packhorse team to arrive from Harrietville loaded with supplies and mail. They travelled no matter what the weather and shared food and a campfire with whoever was about. There was always time to pull up and have a yarn.

Travelling through this city at 110 clicks in Sam's flashy V8 ute was not what Emily wanted her life to be. She felt the presence of her great-great grandmother, and suddenly Emily longed to live like her; busy with honest, meaningful work, yet in the heart of a world that turned slowly and held a rich silence, save for the sounds of nature. How hard could it be, Emily wondered, to stay on at the old homestead as the world turned white? She shook the thought from her. Ridiculous, she told herself, looking down at her weak and overweight body.

She looked out of the window to Melbourne's sprawl that glowed with electricity. Row after row of huge houses had swallowed up what were once dairy paddocks and orchards. Emily looked distastefully at the houses that had neither solar panels nor water tanks to sustain them, and no room in their tiny gardens for vegetable patches. These houses turned their backs to the sun and, together with the vast areas of concrete, collected thousands of litres of water that was channelled down drains and eventually spat out to sea, as if water was some kind of inconvenience. Airconditioned homes, their giant garages housing airconditioned cars, petrol-guzzling four-wheel-drives that never left the suburbs.

The city was a massive display of cars and consumerism, a system that used vast amounts of energy, yet gave very little back to the earth. Emily shook her head.

'How can you stand this place?' she asked Sam.

'Oh, I love it. Bright lights, noise, excitement. Different people.'

'This is exciting?' she said, indicating the urban sprawl beyond her window.

'Well, not this part. I mean the inner city. Especially Sydney. It was so cool.'

Emily frowned. 'Some of the people living in these houses are the ones calling us the environmental rednecks. They're the ones voting to kick us off the mountains. But look at these houses!'

'Yeah, I know,' Sam said. 'But they're not all bad.'

'They're so out of touch with, with . . . I dunno.' Emily

struggled for words. City people thought they were immune to Mother Nature, complaining when the airconditioning was bung or water restrictions were on, not realising that bushfires threatened power stations hundreds of kilometres away, or that irrigation water was being shut off to farmers to keep the city thriving.

'It's so hypocritical to see people live this way,' she said, gesturing to the houses, 'and yet they're always slamming us.'

'There's no point getting upset about it, Em. People will think what they think.'

'But can't we do something about it? What if they do revoke our grazing licences? What then?'

Sam shrugged. 'When you hear stuff on the radio and hear blokes like Bob being dickheads, I can see a city person's reasoning. I understand how they come to think the country's better off in the hands of a well-spoken scientist than a cattleman with no obvious credentials, other than the fact he was born and raised in the area.' Sam paused, the streetlights chasing shadows across his face. 'Look, I didn't fly all the way round the world to stir up this old conversation again. Let's move on, Emily. Have a laugh, be glad we're on the road and on the run. Cheer up!'

She looked sullenly out the ute window as another massive, fluoro-lit billboard loomed, advertising a new country housing estate. She turned to her brother and smiled in the darkness. He was right. The grazing debate had consumed enough of their lives already. What would be would be, she thought.

She breathed as deeply as her tender ribs would allow and

smiled. Suddenly, she was very grateful she had a mountain retreat to go to. So many of these people seemed to her stuck amid squares. In the boxes of their cars, the squares of their homes, cornered in the right-angles of their fences and streets, and this cornered their thoughts, just as she had felt in Brigalow. But now she was free.

'Are we going straight to the high plains? Or shall we call into Dad's and get the girls first?' Sam asked.

'I don't want to disturb them tonight. And I know Dad'll be furious. He'd probably try to send me back to hospital.'

'Okay, straight there?'

'But I really, really want to get Rousie tonight. I know Clancy won't be looking after him properly.'

'What if Clancy's there?'

Emily shrugged. 'You'll have to sort him for me.'

The sight of the Brigalow house prompted a flood of memories. Emily had to clamp her lips shut so she could slow her anxious breath. She began reliving the past: the day they'd first brought Matilda home as a tiny baby; the night feeds, Clancy fuming because the baby had woken him and he had an early run in the trucks. The way he'd joked about her stretch marks when she was eight months gone with Meg. Emily saw herself, her weight ballooning, her body clad in shapeless T-shirts and sagging tracksuit pants. She couldn't believe what she had become.

Sam pulled up and backed the ute into the drive. He turned to her with a cheeky grin. 'For a fast getaway, Louise,' he said.

Round the back, Rousie was going nuts on the end of his chain. His barks prompted the lights to flick on in the house.

'Shit,' Emily said. 'He's here.'

Sam got out. 'Don't worry.'

He ran behind the house and Emily swallowed nervously. She saw the bedroom curtains being drawn aside. She saw Clancy's naked torso. Then she glimpsed another form in the bedroom. A woman. In their bed.

Emily felt a strangling sensation in her throat. Her body tensed and every muscle contracted with hurt and anger. She sat in Sam's ute, holding back tears, trying to be strong. It was to be expected, she said to herself, chanting it like a mantra. The curtain fell on the scene.

Then Sam was back and Rousie was bounding around the ute, standing up on his back legs and sniffing the air for scents of his mistress. Her faithful dog. Emily smiled and wound the window down. Rousie, too polite to jump up on the ute door but too excited to contain his joy, bounded on the spot and whined with delight, his whole body wagging along with his tail. Sam commanded him onto the back of the ute, flipping open a gap in the tarp for him to nestle into.

The front door opened and there was Clancy.

'What do you think you're doing, Sam Flanaghan?'

'G'day, Clancy,' said Sam. 'Just helping Em pick up a few things. Clothes and that.'

'Fuck her.'

'Hello, Clancy,' Emily said mildly, trying to contain the tremor in her voice.

'You can take your stinkin' barkin' dog, but you're not setting foot inside this house. You chose to leave – so leave!'

'Well, could you just chuck a few of Em's things in a bag, mate, and then we'll go,' Sam said.

'No friggin' way, *mate*. Stuff you.'

'Clance,' Emily tried to soothe, 'please don't be angry. We've got to get on. For the girls' sake.'

Clancy roared like a wounded animal and came hurtling off the front steps towards her. She flinched as he started pummelling his fists on the roof of the ute.

'Just piss off! Get out of my life!'

Emily could smell the grog on his breath. Spit was foaming on the sides of his mouth as he yelled and she hunkered down in her seat clutching her head in her hands. Then Sam was dragging Clancy away, eventually flinging him to the lawn.

'Leave her alone!' Sam yelled as he stood over him. Clancy stumbled forward, but Sam was already in the driver's seat, revving the V8 and fishtailing it away down the street.

Six years' worth of distress began to tumble from Emily. She sat crying with her brother's hand on her knee. The tears wouldn't stop. Sam kept saying over and over, 'We'll be right, sis. We'll be right. We'll get to the plains and we'll be right.'

In the darkness as they drove, Emily looked at the glow from the dash. It reminded her of the first time she'd ridden in the truck with Clancy. She remembered the rush of excitement when he'd pulled up at the Tranquillity drive and she'd climbed up the steps to open the truck door. It had been five-thirty in the morning and still dark. The moon in the dawn sky was gently illuminating frosted paddocks. The first thing Clancy had shown her on the complicated computerised dashboard of dials and buttons was his sleeper light.

'I call it the sexy light.' In the dimness, he had cast her an inviting look. 'Do you want my sexy light on?' With a teasing smile, his finger jabbed the tiny cherry-red square with a half moon on it. The light above their heads gave the cab a seductive red glow. On that first trip, they'd barely travelled five kilometres down the road before Clancy pulled over and was kissing her. Emily had shuddered as he kissed her softly above the lace of her bra. The sensuality of that first time in the truck with Clancy was intoxicating.

As he undressed her in the cab, she had seen the cattle prodder propped behind his seat, the prongs of it looking as if they belonged to Satan himself. She'd never met a boy as bad as him. It thrilled her. All her life she'd been so good. So responsible. The glue holding her family together. Now here he was, this wicked man, who made her laugh and cry and lose herself in the sexual sway of lust. 'Want to get lucky with the truckie?' he had said, helping her up into the sleeper and drawing the curtains shut.

On that first dawn trip, with her body zinging from Clancy's lovemaking, Emily had loved seeing the other trucks coming towards them, all lit up like Christmas trees. She was falling in love, lost in the gentle sway of the cab, the modern interior snug and clean. For the entire trip she had longed for Clancy to reach over and touch her again. She watched his sexy hands draped over the big round steering wheel and the way his middle finger teased the split-shift button on the gearstick. As he double-clutched round bends, the sigh of the air-clutch reminded her of her own desires. Everything within that truck was plush and phallic. From the purple polish the men used to shine their silver stacks to the way the truck let out a sound like a whoosh of steam when Clancy pulled up at the truckstop. She was addicted to him. And back then, he had treated her as if she was the only one in the world for him.

Slowly, though, the truck had begun to take him away from her. More and more he left her alone with the babies. On the rare occasion she rode in the truck in the later years of their marriage, she found herself staring into the giant side-mirror, watching the white line fall away behind her. It felt like her life was going backwards, their love slowly turning into something toxic. Now, on her way to the plains, Emily realised she was free from Clancy. But with that freedom also came a great sadness, for what their marriage might have been.

PART TWO

Twelve

On the Dargo High Plains the snowgums glowed white in the light of a full moon. The gumleaves glistened liquid-silver, like a million tiny fairy lights in the treetops. Long grasses shone in the stillness of the night. As Sam hit another rut in the meandering gravel road and scudded over corrugations in the bend, Emily reached out for the door handle to steady herself, wincing with pain.

'Oi!' she said, casting a glance at Sam, who was happily swinging on the wheel.

'Sorry, mate.' He braked and swerved suddenly to miss a Hereford cow and calf that were dozing on the road. 'Oops!'

Emily glanced in the side-vision mirror to see Rousie dig his claws into the tarp of the ute, as if surfing the crest of a wave. She smiled at how happy he looked to be off that suburban chain and in the scrub again, nose to the wind, where a kelpie should be.

After they had sped through Dargo, and began the journey

past the Cherry Tree yards and up the Long Cutting, Emily began to feel better. She felt lighter, stronger, happier as the mountain air grew thinner and the vegetation, caught in the headlights, changed from straight-trunked woolly butts and Brown Sallees to twisted snowgums on rocky basalt.

Over a cattle grid and they were there at last: the Flanaghan High Plains Station. They veered off the main gravel road and parked at the station's front gate. Few people, save the locals in Dargo, knew this was the gate into the homestead. It was just a regular farm gate set among the snowgums, except it was far from straight. Its pipe frame carried a bow, where a panicked young horse had once hit it at a bolt in Emily's grandfather's day. No one had ever thought to straighten or replace it. Sam looked at Emily.

'Home sweet home,' he said, jumping out. Emily wound down the window and breathed in, savouring the smells of summer grasses, cooling after a day in the late-summer sun, fat-leafed clovers, eucalypts and clean mountain air. At last, joy rose within her. For now, her pain was forgotten, the memory of Clancy's anger buried, the stagnant sadness banished. She was home. All she needed now was her girls and her horse and her life could begin again.

The old track to the homestead was like a tunnel, lined with silver snowgums. The moon filtered through the canopy of gum leaves and illuminated the yellow everlastings and billy buttons and white paper daisies. The scene was so beautiful, Sam and Emily sat in contemplative silence as they rumbled slowly over the hillocky track towards the handsplit weatherboard homestead.

Sam left the ute idling and got out.

'You sit in the warm while I get a fire going.'

'No, bugger that. I'm tough. I'll help.' Emily did her best to ignore the stab of pain as she clambered out of the ute. The dressings on her wounds tugged and itched and she felt faint. She focused on feeling the solid core of ancient basalt soil and rocks beneath her feet. She found herself asking the place to ground her there, so that she would never leave again. The earth seemed to pulse through the soles of her feet and as she shut her eyes, it felt for a moment like time had stopped altogether.

Then a gust of wind raced through the trees and pressed its breath against Emily's face. With the moon above and the dark earth below, she felt both giddy and purposeful. She was meant to be here. But she didn't completely understand why. What was the old Flanaghan woman asking of her? Emily stared up at the icing-sugar dusting of stars in the velvety black sky. Suddenly her trance was broken when Sam threw a swag onto the deep old boards of the verandah and Rousie leapt joyfully from the ute.

As they opened the front door and walked inside, a rush of memories came to Emily of summer droving days. Just the creak and bang of the old wooden flyscreen triggered images of all the comings and goings from the place. Used only in the summer and autumn months as a base for tending their cattle on the mountains, the homestead was like a living museum of Flanaghan family history.

In the hallway, under a rustic bench seat, there was a line of old boots shaped by the feet of several generations of

Flanaghans. Old coats, still worn when unexpected snow came in at Easter time, made Emily remember her grandfather. She thought of him wearing one of those coats as he slid down a rain-soaked embankment to help a calf up out of the scrub, and how her five-year-old self had stood watching, rain running off her cowgirl hat, her fingers red and cold as ice. As she walked on the old lino, Emily felt the house stir itself awake to their presence.

In the kitchen, Sam reached up to the mantel for matches. The crack and fizz and smell of the match gave Emily a feeling of comfort as Sam lit a row of candles that had been stuck in Auntie Flo's whisky bottles. Sam heaved open the door of the old woodstove and tilted a candle inside so the flame caught the corner of newspaper.

'Sit tight,' Sam said. 'I'll go turn on the gas and get a load of wood for the night.'

Emily nodded. Gingerly, she pulled out a chrome and red vinyl chair that had been all the rage in the sixties, sat down at the kitchen table, and stared through the crack of the stove door, watching the bright flames dance. She listened to the roar of air in the flue and stretched her fingertips towards the growing heat. She ran her hands over the heavy wooden table. Etched on its surface were all the stories from the past. The dull light from the candles tipped tiny dark shadows onto the table's pockmarked landscape. Her great-great-grandmother had had the table brought up from the original hut in the Mayford gully, and here it had remained ever since. Emily felt a flash of energy run through her, the tiny hairs on her arms lifted and a tingle ran over her skin as she saw an image of olden-day Emily, her sturdy boots treading a dirt floor as she stuffed a rabbit at the table and turned to place it in a camp oven for baking. Emily blinked and the image was gone, just as Sam came through the door.

'Bit quieter than Nashville out there,' he said.

'Do you good,' Emily said.

'Do you good too.'

'I just want my girls with me and then I'll be set.'

'We'll ring Dad first thing.' Sam raised the old kettle in the air. 'Cuppa?'

Emily shook her head.

'No, thanks. I'm going to crash.'

As she carried the candle along the narrow hallway, cupping her hand about the flame, Emily felt the comfort of the house wrap around her. She was aching all over now, and part of her was scared, but she knew leaving the hospital had been the right thing to do. *This* was the place to heal. Wanting to shed her pyjamas that reeked of the hospital, she opened the old wardrobe and held out the candle. Whenever the Flanaghans came up to the homestead, they lived out of their bags, never staying more than a week at a time. It had been different in her grandparents' day. The clothes in the wardrobe had been there since they had lived up here full-time in the summer months to salt and muster cattle, fix fences and combat summertime weeds. It was easier than making the winding eighty-kilometre journey back into Dargo in their little old spring-suspension utility, or on horseback as they preferred. Pa always chose horses over cars. Part of his routine had been riding out and dropping a match here and there along the tracks to trickle fire through the landscape when the weather was just right, in the way the Aborigines had done. But over the years this ritual of burning had been reduced and eventually banned by the government, and the landscape had gradually changed. The beautiful open-treed country of Victoria's Alps had become a mass of bone-like fallen limbs from trees weighted down with snow. On the lower slopes dogwood and wattles, once kept in check by the cattlemen burning patches of bush in a mosaic pattern across the mountains, now choked the landscape. Places that were once gently cool-burned and periodically grazed were now inaccessible.

Life gradually changed for the Flanaghans too. The once isolated family living on the plains had become a thorn in the side of the government men, who did not believe the Flanaghans should profit from pristine wilderness. As the roads improved, the interference from the city increased. The more bushwalkers, skiers and rubberneckers arrived, the more rules the cattlemen faced. Emily's grandfather had died a sad man. Sad for his mountains. Sad for the loss of a simple life and for the loss of his privacy and freedom. Emily ran her fingertips over the coarse woollen dressing gowns – her grandfather's brown check, and her grandmother's soft blue one. An image came to her of her grandpa and grandma sizzling chops in a pan in the pre-dawn light, while a pot of strong tea sat on the kitchen table wearing a woollen brown-and-yellow tea-cosy – the one they still used. At the very back of the cupboard, Emily found a nightie she didn't remember at all. It was long and white, with intricately stitched blue flowers and tiny buttons at the scooped neckline. The sleeves were long, ending in a thin ruffle. Emily giggled. The nightie was so old-fashioned compared to the gauzy negligee Clancy always wanted her to wear. The angrier he had got over her cosy flannelette pyjamas, the more she'd dug her heels in. She'd only ever slipped between the sheets blissfully naked on nights Clancy was away, enjoying then the sensual feel of her skin.

She pulled the nightie off its hanger, which was stitched with the same tiny flowers, and decided to put it on. She did so slowly and painfully, then stared at her ghostly reflection in the mirror. The candle's light did not reach far, the lower half of her body, her legs and her feet disappearing into blackness.

'Bloody Joan of Arc!' Emily said, taking in her cropped dark hair, the shadowy sockets where her eyes were and the nightie's creamy glow. She sniffed at the sleeves but smelled only mothballs – not a trace of her grandmother's scent was left. She looked again at her reflection and carefully took a twirl, fancying herself as an old-fashioned heroine. Ignoring the crunch of pain, she tried to make a flourishing move towards the bed.

Emily clambered between the icy sheets, feeling so relieved to be out of hospital and strangely happy to be 'on the run'. She lay for a time twirling the hospital wristband around and around on her arm, looking at the ornate cast-iron work of the old double bed and thinking again about her grandparents. They had lived so self-sufficiently, with God and Mother Nature and the spirits of the land as their guides. She thought of the simplicity of their lives, and the core of happiness they carried within themselves. She'd felt it as a child, and she was sure she could see that same trait in her girls. Particularly her youngest, Meg. She would lay her hands on her mother's skin and Emily could feel something special in her touch. An odd child, Meg had never seemed to fit with others, preferring to play alone and talk to imaginary friends, making no sense to anyone but herself. Tilly, on the other hand, was less dreamy, and got on with the practicalities of life. In the hospital, it had been Tilly who got water for her mother and plumped her pillows and straightened sheets, while Meg had sat with her warm little hands on Emily as if trying to heal her. In the darkness Emily longed for her girls.

'Goodnight, Tilly and Meg,' she said to the empty room, conjuring the image of them peacefully asleep in her old bedroom at Rod's house. As she drifted off to sleep, Emily thought again of her vision of bringing her girls up and living here full-time, even when the snow came. Was it possible? Even the Flanaghans from three generations ago had retreated to their winter homestead on the lower valley of Mayford when snow draped itself over the mountains in thick blinding drifts of white. Was she strong enough to endure a winter here?

'Emily,' came the whisper.

In her sleep Emily frowned and stirred a little.

'Emily.'

The voice again. Suddenly Emily's eyes flashed open. She sat up in the pitch-dark room. The candle stub was extinguished. The moon had slunk away behind the tree tops and gone was the glow it created behind the old lace curtains.

A faint, eerie light came from the hallway, and she could hear music, gently playing. It couldn't be Sam. There was no radio here. No power to run anything. Before she had time to find fear she got up, her feet pressed cold against the lino. She struck a match and the skerrick of candle that was left offered up a pathetic, wax-drowned flame. She tiptoed along the hall and gently pushed open the door to Sam's room. Just as the candle petered out, she saw him sleeping soundly beneath old grey woollen blankets. Emily caught the sound of music again. Fingertips pressed to the wonky horsehair walls of the old house, she blindly felt her way along the hall to the kitchen, where the fire still glowed. The music was clearer now. Emily could hear an old piano accordion, and voices, too, being carried along with the tune. The voices were both male and female, and they were singing a hymn. As she walked through the kitchen to the old dining room, she saw a cluster of rough working men in their well-worn Sunday best. Emily stood in the doorway, holding her breath.

They didn't look up from their leatherbound hymn books as they stood in front of makeshift pews of flat slab-cut timber propped on bricks. At the front of the congregation stood a handsome young minister, his dark hair slicked back with a straight side part. He was wearing a three-piece suit, his brilliant white priest's collar catching the light from the oil lamps. Could this be the Flanaghan son, Archie, who had eventually left his preaching and returned to the plains to work with his young bride Joan, Emily wondered? She looked around. Next to them sat a cluster of children of various ages – Flanaghans, Emily somehow knew instinctively, for at their side were the same two people she had seen in her vision of the Mayford hut: Emily and Jeremiah. Together with a group of wayward goldminers, they were singing songs of thanks to God.

Without fear, Emily stepped into the room, wanting to join the gathering. As she did, the woman with the greying hair looked up. She tilted her head to one side and smiled gently at her. Emily smiled back. Then she, too, began to sing the hymn, the words foreign to her, yet somehow known . . .

'Emily. Emily,' came a voice in the darkness as she felt the press of hands on her arm.

She woke suddenly to see Sam above her, his face caught in the shine from a small kerosene lamp.

'What?' she said, sitting up.

'You woke me up.'

'But I was in the dining room.'

'What? No, you weren't! You were here, talking in your sleep. Well, not actually talking. You were singing. Trust me, *I'm* the singer in this family. Sounded like two cats in a bag.'

He held the lamp up to her. 'Geez, what are you wearing? You look like flamin' Julie Andrews from *The Sound of Music*!'

'A nightie. One of Nan's.'

'A passion-killer more like. It's a wonder she had *any* descendants!'

'Get over yourself,' she said. 'I'm not that bad a singer. And what would I want with passion anyway!'

'So, you're okay? You don't need more painkillers?'

'Why do you keep asking me that? I'm fine, really I am. I reckon it's you who needs the pills. Are you hooked on them or something?'

'Nah,' said Sam, but Emily felt a stab of concern for her brother, who'd clearly been pushing things too far in his life.

'Don't you go and do a Heath Ledger on me, mate,' she said. Sam looked off into the darkness of the room, his big, blue-green eyes reflecting the glow of the lamp. He said nothing. Instead he turned back to Emily.

'He's really hurt you, hasn't he?'

Emily felt unshed tears sting her eyes. 'I've let it happen, though. It's not all him. I let him . . .' her voice trailed off.

'It'll be all right. We'll both be all right,' said Sam as he gave her a quick squeeze, but she could hear the doubt in his voice.

She knew Sam had really struggled since his smash single had hit the charts like a storm two years earlier and then blown itself out to silence. It hadn't given Sam enough momentum to walk away with a Tamworth Golden Guitar that year, a crucial victory for any young up-and-comer. His disappointment had been tangible, and it seemed to Emily as though his life had begun to unravel from that night. Sam had drifted far away from the life they had once shared. He'd gone to the city and lost himself in the hullabaloo of beautiful people, parties and hype. He'd not written a song in two years.

'What are you going to do, Sam?'

'Clean up my act.'

'What are you on?'

'Just the weed.'

'You're lying.'

Sam shrugged. 'I tried some heavier stuff in LA. It's really messed with me.'

'Have you any with you now?'

'Just some weed.'

'Give it to me. I'll burn it.'

'No, you won't!' His eyes flashed panic.

'Sam,' Emily said firmly, 'do you want to get sorted?'

'Yes!'

'Then give it all to me in the morning. All your party pills, your dope and smokes, the lot – you're going cold turkey.'

Emily looked at her little brother. She'd seen women of all ages pressing themselves to the front of the stage at his concerts and staring up at him as if he were God's gift. He might act like he was ten foot tall and bullet-proof, but she could still see the little boy in him.

Emily could also see Sam did have a very special gift at his core. When he was younger, music seemed to pour out of him. Outside in the dark, Emily knew there was a circle of blackened rocks that made up the campfire the family had shared meals around in the summer droving days. Emily pictured a younger Sam, in his flannie shirt, sleeves rolled to the elbows, the campfire illuminating his handsome chiselled features and strong arms as he belted out a tune on his guitar.

The droving team, made up mostly of family, had sat on fold-out chairs, stumps, Eskies and rounded basalt boulders and gazed at him, mesmerised, as Sam's music vibrated through their bodies. His voice seemed to channel from the black sky above, sifting down through stars and campfire smoke. It was the voice of a strong, bold angel, singing pure country.

'Tomorrow, you start writing songs again,' she said. 'You write enough for an album. Write about this place, about the cattle, about the fires we panic about every year, about the snow, about the bloody bureaucrats threatening us all the time. Then we contact your company and you cut the best album yet. Okay?'

'I'm not writing about this place, Em. You know exactly what'll happen if I do. I'll be a bloody pin-up boy for the mountain cattlemen – and the whipping boy for the Greens.'

Emily shook her head. 'So what? This is your heritage.'

'Well, fuck my heritage!' Sam said, clenching his jaw. 'I'm not jumping through the hoops Dad and Flo have gone through all their lives just so they can graze a few cows up here.'

'It's not just about grazing cows and you know it. It's about looking after this land the way it deserves. Grazing it. Burning it. Caring for it. Not locking it up and leaving it and classifying it "pristine", like some untouchable thing or giant science experiment.'

'You just won't give it up, will you? You're flogging that same dead horse!'

As kids, Emily and Sam had been taught about the country that had been torn apart by frenzied goldminers in the 1800s, and how it had healed itself over. The same way grass grows over battle-scarred lands to cover forever the bones of fallen soldiers. They had seen how the land had reclaimed its balance over time. But the introduced weeds were the greatest worry. Each year the Flanaghans, with the exception of Bob, helped keep check of the most ruthless of weeds – blackberries. Sam and Emily knew the land on the runs in their care was in great shape, and the light stocking of cattle in the summer months helped the land.

They knew they didn't get it right all the time. In tough times, when cattle prices were down and drought bit, the family's environmental works took a slide because there was no money. They would see their father up to his ears in paperwork applying for funding assistance so they could fence streams or control more weeds. They saw his frustration when the use of their cheapest tool for managing the land, fire, was outlawed. They came to learn that signing the name Flanaghan on your application forms usually meant your application was rejected. The Flanaghans, their name synonymous with cattle grazing, had felt the sting of judgement and been branded as environmental outlaws – people who destroyed precious wilderness areas, bogging up peat swamps and trampling delicate flowers with their cattle.

Sam found it hard some days, being a Flanaghan, and his time in the city had made him bitter about his heritage.

'You know none of us cattlemen have the education to take

on that gigantic bureaucracy,' he said more gently. 'Our skills are in the care of land and animals, not media machines and political debates.'

'But your music, Sam! A song can open people's minds if it's sung from the heart. That's why you have this gift, so you can show from your heart that what we do up here is sustainable and even good for the plains.'

Sam laughed. 'I'm happy to become an urban cowboy and leave the protesting to the other tired old cattlemen.'

Emily sighed. 'Then you're a bloody quitter and a piker.'

'Yeah? So what if I am?' Sam shivered. 'I'm going back to bed. I'm freezing my nuts off here.'

Just before he shut the door of her room, Emily called out, 'Hey, Sam?'

'Yeah?'

'That dream I was having when you came in – what was I singing, anyway?'

Sam paused, his head bowed in the lamp light as he thought.

'Dunno, really. I was half asleep. But it sounded like a hymn.'

'A hymn?'

'Yeah. Weird, hey? I didn't think you knew any hymns.'

'I don't.'

Thirteen

From his chain near the woodshed, Rousie let out a deep bark that told Emily someone was at the front gate. Emily flung back the sheets and threw her legs over the side of the bed. A stab of pain knifed through her and for a moment the room wavered. She shut her eyes waiting for the giddiness to subside.

'C'mon, c'mon,' she willed herself. She was determined to remain strong. In the kitchen Sam looked up from an old newspaper.

'Why didn't you wake me?'

Sam shrugged. 'You must've needed the sleep.'

'What time is it?'

'Nearly eleven.'

'*What!*'

Emily trod the well-worn verandah boards in bare feet, scanning the track through the trees that were framed against a perfect blue sky. She caught a glimpse of her father's dusty white four-wheel drive, followed by Flo's red Hilux ute and horse float. A broad smile lit her face.

'*Yes!*' she said as they neared, ecstatic to see Tilly and Meg in the first vehicle and then the dark curious eyes of Snowgum looking through the float window, her ears flickering back and forth. The girls tumbled out of the four-wheel drive and ran towards their mother.

Emily stepped from the verandah and crouched to scoop them into her arms. She shut her eyes with relief. Here they were, together, at last. She ran her hands over the crowns of their heads and pulled back to look into their perfect eyes, which held the greens, greys and browns of the bush in their depths. Then she drew them in again for a warm hug. She looked up over their heads to meet her father's gaze.

'I'm sorry, Dad.'

Rod stepped forward to hold her. 'Are you okay?'

'Dad,' was all she could say as she buried her face in his rough woollen work jumper.

'I phoned the hospital and explained,' he said sternly. 'They're not happy. It was a very stupid thing to do.' His eyes travelled to Sam, who stood a little way off. Rod released Emily and his body stiffened for a moment, seeing his son's prison-style haircut and the dark circles under his eyes. Then his face softened.

'I'm glad to see you, boy,' Rod said, opening his arms out wide and embracing his son in a man-hug. 'It's good to know you're both safe and to have you both home,' he said, clapping Sam's back with his big, square hand.

Flo stepped forward, squinting at Emily.

'What the hell are you wearing, girl? You look like an escapee from a bloody mental institution!'

Emily looked down at her long white nightie and self-consciously ran her fingers through her short cropped hair.

'Good to see you too, Auntie Flo,' she laughed.

Flo hugged her warmly and muttered in her ear, 'Glad to hear you've ditched him, the mongrel bastard. If I can help you, darlin', you sing out.' Emily was shocked. She knew the family had bitten their tongues on the subject of Clancy for years. Now, Emily realised, that silence would be broken, albeit out of the girls' earshot. But before Emily could respond, Flo flicked her head in the direction of the float.

'There's someone else here glad to see you,' she said, and as if on cue, Snowgum pawed the float floor with her hoof.

As Flo slung down the door and Snowgum backed off the float, memories of the race rushed back to Emily. She saw the tree flash before her and smelt the fear. Cringing, she inspected the raw proud flesh of Snowgum's wounds on her shoulder and nearside legs. The ugly, brown-and-pink meaty welts dug deeply into her perfect white hide and were fringed with purple antiseptic spray.

'Oh, Snow,' Emily said, resting her forehead on the mare's neck. The others watched as Emily, in her long white gown, spent a quiet moment holding Snowgum around her neck, silently taking in the energy of the beautiful grey mare. They saw how beautiful both creatures were, but also how damaged.

'Thanks so much, Flo,' Emily said, tears in her eyes.

'No wuckers,' Flo said, her tone belying the anxiety of

nursing Snowgum back from the brink.

Flo disappeared into the truck, swung back the divider and there in the front of the float were the girls' two small ponies, Jemma and Blossom.

'Had to bring her mates,' Flo said. Tilly and Meg beamed at their mother.

Emily felt tears of relief sting her eyes. She had imagined her family berating her for leaving her husband, for bailing out of hospital, for coming here to the high plains. She imagined them dragging her back down to the lowlands to fulfil her role as a wife and mother. But here they were quietly supporting her – like they all knew that she was meant to be here.

In the warmth of the kitchen, Flo unscrewed the lid on the brandy bottle and poured a neat shot into a row of teacups.

'Purely medicinal,' she said, passing a cup to Emily.

'That'll go down well with her Panadeine Forte,' Sam said.

'Well,' Flo said, narrowing her eyes at him, 'from all reports, Johnny Cash, you'd know what mixes best with what.' There was an awkward silence as Sam realised the whole family somehow knew of his slide into drinking and drugs. His dad must've been on the phone to Ike that morning.

'C'mon, Flo. I'm good, I'm all good now,' Sam said.

They looked at him. 'Liar,' they chorused.

'But you'll be right now?' Rod said, more as a question than a statement. Sam shrugged, smiling nervously. He just needed a little more time to ease himself down.

Rod lifted his teacup to his lips, took a sip and winced.

'Tastes like medicine! Which reminds me, the hospital is sending discharge papers for you to sign and return *on the condition* that you check in at the Dargo bush hospital each day for the next two weeks, to see the nurse.'

Emily felt her skin bristle. She thought of Penny, Clancy's little nurse. She thought of the person she'd glimpsed in the bedroom at their house last night. She was sure it had been Penny. Though she wanted to be free of him, Clancy's infidelities still stabbed her.

'I'm not going to Dargo hospital,' she said.

'You have to,' Rod said.

Emily shook her head. 'I'm not! And I won't!' The girls looked up from their game, hearing the angry tone in their mother's voice. 'I'm fine up here.'

'But they need to change your dressings.'

'Then I'll travel into the Sale hospital. But I won't go to Dargo.'

The family, gathered round the table, looked at Emily in silence, pity in their eyes. She suddenly realised that they all *knew. They knew about Penny and Clancy*! Word had certainly travelled fast round the town. Emily felt utterly humiliated.

'I dunno what we're going to do then,' Flo said. 'I'm no nurse. Snowgum would tell you that if she could. And your brother's not up to the job – he needs a nurse himself.' Sam flinched and hung his head as Flo went on. 'Rod's flat out with the cattle and who's to run round after the girls until you come right? The only option is to send Bob up!'

'No! Anyone but Bob,' Emily said miserably.

'C'mon, Em.' Flo put a hand on Emily's shoulder. 'I was joking about Bob.'

An awkward silence followed as they each contemplated how life might move forward from here, until Rousie woofed his loud 'someone's coming' bark.

From the verandah they watched a little blue Suzuki four-wheel drive struggle over the track with a small grey-haired woman in the driver's seat.

'That's not Evie Jenner from down the road, is it?' said Flo. 'What's she wanting here?'

'Evie who?' asked Sam.

'You know. That woman who moved into the Gows ruins a few years back.'

'Yeah, I remember,' said Sam. 'Isn't she a loop-the-loop?'

'As nutty as a Picnic bar, so they say,' Flo said.

'A few roos loose in the top paddock, eh?' said Emily.

'A stubby short of a six-pack,' Tilly added earnestly, and they all looked at her and laughed.

Still, whatever her mental capabilities, Evie Jenner had slowly transformed Gows, a former hotel, from a state of sagging decay to one of homeliness. Stone by stone, she had resurrected the house that lay twenty kilometres from the Flanaghan homestead. A garden now thrived and a newly hung cast-iron gate invited visitors along the pathway. One time, droving the cattle past, Emily had seen Evie in the garden, fixing up a trellis of ti-tree sticks on which snowpeas could twine themselves upwards. Evie had looked up and smiled. She wore a floppy

121

straw hat, a long purple dress and a red striped pinafore. Giant black gumboots and loose green gardening gloves finished her look, which wavered between hippy and dotty old lady. At the sight of the cattle, the woman's little Jack Russell had made a beeline for the old stone fence. It clambered up, front paws spread wide, and stood yapping at the cattle.

'Jesus!' the woman called. 'Jesus Christ! Jeee-sus!' she called again. When Emily realised the dog was actually called Jesus Christ, she laughed out loud. Was the woman a nut or did she just have a wicked sense of humour?

The cattle stopped to look curiously at the small white dog barking canine obscenities at them. An older cow tossed her head in annoyance, then they ambled on again. In the past, the cattle had liked to walk over the rubble of the stone wall to graze on what was left of the old garden and scratch their backs on the low branches of the walnut tree. Emily had often scooted around them on her horse and sent a dog over to hurry them on. They were lazy beasts when they got the chance and the shade of the walnut in summer had always been so inviting. But within a year Evie had fixed the fence, so the cattle could no longer make use of the giant tree and the lush green grass now growing unchecked beneath it. Emily had looked at the pretty, productive garden and the sunny seat on the porch. Nutter or not, the woman was a goer. From astride Snowgum, Emily waved, but rode on with just a brief, shy hello.

Now, the entire family watched intrigued as Evie Jenner got out of her little blue car and hauled a large bag from the backseat. Her dog tumbled out, lifted its lip at Rousie and proceeded to piss on anything it could find.

'Jesus! Jesus Christ!' Evie cried. 'Come here, you little mongrel!' The dog ignored her. As she walked towards them, they saw Evie was tiny, but beneath her oversized clothing she was fit and wiry. She wore her grey hair in two braids, which framed her small tanned face. She came to stand before them all.

'I'm Evie,' she announced. 'I hear you folk could use a nurse?'

They stared at her, as amazed as if Mary Poppins herself had arrived.

'Cuppa?' was all Flo could manage and before they knew it they were ushering Evie through the screen door. On her way, Evie gave Emily a quick wink, with eyes the colour of new-spring growth. There was such a life force in her gaze that Emily felt the hairs rise on the back of her neck. The intensity of those green eyes! In a split second, that look had connected with something deep within Emily, something she had never felt before. It was as if Evie was *meant* to be here. As if Emily had known her before somehow.

Emily shook the feeling away and told herself the local rumours were probably right. With her long grey plaits, hippy skirt and homespun wool cardigan, Evie was probably one of those right-on organic types. The ones who made meat-eating and cow's-milk-drinking humans feel guilty for even breathing. Definitely anti-cattlemen. Emily decided there was no way she wanted to be nursed by her.

At the kitchen table, Flo did a poor job of being mother. She slopped boiling water into the teapot and noisily clanked an old tin of stale-looking biscuits onto the table.

'We've got brandy if you'd prefer.'

'Tea's just fine,' Evie said.

'Here,' Rod said, 'sit. Please.' He pulled out a chair and gestured to it.

Evie sat at the head of the table and the girls came to stand beside her, gazing at her long plaits.

'Is that your real hair?'

'Meg!' said Emily.

'Why is it white like Mum's horse?'

'Tilly!'

'Are you a witch?'

'*Meg!*' they all chorused.

Evie smiled. 'It's all right. Most people think I'm a complete nutter. It's just because I'm a woman and I choose to live alone on a mountain. At least I don't have a house full of cats and share their food with them.' Her smile warmed not just her face but the whole room. The Flanaghans laughed, relieved. She seemed like a very nice, *normal* person.

'How did you know we needed someone to help Emily?' Sam asked, still a little suspicious of her.

'Oh, word gets around,' Evie said vaguely. 'Which reminds me . . .' she reached into her bag. 'Today's paper.'

The headlines loomed large. *PARLIAMENT BILL TO OUST CATTLEMEN.*

'It's not looking good for you,' Evie said.

They huddled round the article. A Bill to ban the renewal of grazing licences, which had been in place for over a hundred years, would be debated in parliament the following week. If the Bill was passed, there would be a statewide blanket ban on cattle grazing on government parkland. The Flanaghans would be one of many high-country families affected.

Emily glanced at Evie. Had she come to gloat?

'We're going to have to get onto this,' Flo said. 'We haven't got much time.'

Rod looked up at Evie. 'Thanks for letting us know. We'd better get back down to Tranquillity and crank the computer up again.'

Sam rolled his eyes. 'Oh, God. Here we go again. Bloody groundhog day!'

'This is different, Sam!' Emily said, jabbing her finger on the article. 'In the past they've only threatened bans. Now, if this thing gets through, it'll become law. They'll kick us off for good!'

'And what if they do?' Sam said bitterly. 'At least we'd be done with this endless fight.'

'It'll be the land that suffers. They do it every time. Make one rule for an entire region. It just doesn't work that way. Not all the mountains are the same! You don't think we should be kicked off?' Emily turned to Evie, almost pleading.

'No need to shoot the messenger,' Rod said.

Emily slumped back in her chair and muttered an apology to Evie. But the news that the Bill could become law in a matter of weeks unhinged her. To be locked out forever was too much to bear. This was the only place she wanted to be – where snowgums flowered like frothy lace, the summer meadows growing thick with tiny star-like daisies and purple orchids as pretty as fairy skirts nestled at the base of grey-streaked, twisting gums, where billy buttons dotted yellow across the snowgrass, and around the soft edges of secret springs, moss grew in swathes of green magic beneath the ferns.

They had all worked hard to fence the cattle out of creek crossings that might become bogged. They had split trees and slung the heavy timber into deep postholes, straining wire and pulling taut barbs. If the snow melt was too soon and the country seemed drier and delicate, they lightened the load and took fewer cows up – sometimes well below the light stocking rates stipulated by the National Parks, if the land deemed it so. Wherever they could in the rugged country, Rod and Flo put in a snaking trail of underground poly-pipe to create gravity-fed trough systems to keep the cattle from the creeks that ran over the tufted snow plains.

'You don't need to convince me,' Evie said, holding up her hands. 'There's no right and wrong in anything in my world. Life just is as it is.'

Emily took in Evie's gentle words. She thought of the landscape across the fenceline, which told a very different story about the cattlemen. Uncle Bob's country, where the paddocks were flogged bare, where he let the cattle wander where they may into creek crossings. He'd spray weeds one year but then, on a booze bender, have no money for spraying them the next. He was rude to the Parkies, vocal with the media and caused all kinds of trouble. It was that kind of hypocrisy within her own kind that sometimes made Emily shy away from the whole debate. But then she thought again of her family's history, and the fact that city bureaucrats were planning to put a blanket grazing ban across the entire Alpine area.

'But how can you not question this?' Emily asked. 'It's a decision based on lines on a map, not the land itself. What kind of management regime is that? We'll be allowed to graze the forestry areas but not the Park, but how do you fence an area as steep as this when it's an imaginary line on a map? It's bureaucratic crap.'

Flo was getting fiery now and joined Emily by her side. 'We're being targeted as environmental scapegoats so as to distract people from the real issues – like fossil fuel, water shortages, global warming, mass consumerism. It has nothing to do with the land. It's all about getting votes. That's why we're getting our arses kicked!'

'Ladies!' said Rod, holding up his hands. 'We can talk about this later. But Evie came here for other reasons, and, for now, we need to find out what kind of care she can offer Emily.'

'Yes, you're right, Mr Flanaghan,' Evie said. 'I'm here to nurse Emily back to health. And anyone else who may need it,' she said, directing a mild look at Sam. He folded his arms across his chest.

'Who sent you?' he said.

Ignoring him, Evie rummaged in her bag.

'Here are my nursing qualifications and here are my fees, though I expect you can claim a percentage on that with your government health care.' She pushed a piece of paper over to Rod and Emily.

'It'll be easy for me to cook, too, as I'm not far down the

road. That'll be no charge for meals. Just neighbours helping others.'

Rod surveyed the documents, looked across to Emily and said, 'Sounds like we should give it a shot, eh, Em?' When Emily didn't respond Rod clapped his hands together like an auctioneer. 'Done! You're hired.'

Before Sam and Emily could question Rod's decision, the dogs outside began to scrap, to the sound of growls and teeth snapping.

'*Jesus Christ*!' cried out Evie.

'My sentiments exactly,' muttered Sam to Emily.

Fourteen

Two days later, with Jesus Christ lying on her lap and Rousie sleeping at her feet, Emily nestled contentedly in a comfortable lounge chair on the verandah. She sat in gentle sunshine, watching Sam and the girls grooming the ponies. Her grazes and wounds looked ugly and raw in the daylight, but Emily could feel the air on her skin doing them good.

In the kitchen Evie was humming to herself and even though the unfamiliar cooking smells emanating from the open window were disconcerting, Emily was strangely comforted by Evie's presence.

The peace and quiet was shattered momentarily as the old green phone shrilled from the kitchen. It was happening again, Emily thought sadly. The frantic phone calls flooding in for Rod and Flo as they planned the cattlemen's media campaigns to defend their right to alpine grazing. Ever since the eighties it had been this way, a long, drawn-out battle that left them depressed and depleted.

'Do you want me to get that?' Evie called, but Sam was already sprinting to the house.

'Could be my agent,' he puffed.

'Don't get your hopes up. It's probably someone from the Mountain Cattlemen's Association looking for Dad,' Emily called.

The girls wandered over to Emily. They looked with fascination at their mother's scars, grazes and fading yellow bruising. She felt the gentle zing of their fingertips and flinched when their touch strayed too close to a sore patch.

'Careful,' she cautioned.

'I'm glad Evie's here,' Meg said.

'Oh? Why's that?' Emily said absently.

'She's an angel.'

'She is not,' said Tilly, hands on hips. 'She doesn't have any wings.'

'She is too,' said Meg, and so they began to squabble until Emily guiltily raised her voice to quieten them and then coaxed them to go and gather some kindling for the campfire that night. It would be great to sit out under the stars and talk Sam into playing a tune.

Just then he came banging out the door with a tray in his hands. On it was a steaming pot of tea and their grandmother's ornate teacups, the ones from the back of the cupboard that they never used.

Sam set the tray down and leaned towards Emily as he said, 'She's a whacko, all right! You should see all the herbs in there.' He curved his index fingers in the air when he said 'herbs'. 'I've never seen a bigger stash of hooch. She's probably put it in your tea, in these biscuits she's cooked and in the stew she's making for dinner. We'll all be off our heads by sundown.'

'Well, you'd know, wouldn't you?' Emily sniped, then regretted it. 'I'm sorry, Sam. I'm a bit over it all at the moment. Clance, the parliament thing, my body. I've got too much time to think.'

'Drink your tea to start with,' said Evie as she came from the house. 'Chamomile for calm,' she said. 'And yes, Sam, I have a lot of herbs, but they're purely medicinal.'

'Yeah, *sure*,' said Sam, winking. '*Sure* they are.'

'Nothing of mine can be smoked or used to get high, I'm sorry. It's either blackfella bush medicine or European herbs. I've got a bit of Chinese stuff, but I find I can't grow a lot of that where I am.'

'I can get you a deer penis, if you like,' Sam said. Emily whacked him hard on the arm.

'Don't be disgusting, Sam,' she said.

'He's fine,' said Evie, settling down on an old chair. 'I love bum and dick jokes. You go for it.'

Emily pulled an amused face at the statement from a seemingly innocent old lady.

'It's medicine that's bought me up to the mountains. That and my own personal crud that I don't need to explain to you. But it's healing I'm interested in. Health and healing.'

'Really?' said Sam. 'I thought you were the local hooch grower. That's what they say at the pub.'

'Do they now? Well, they've never asked. And I've never said. Let 'em make up stories. It's fun for them and it does me no harm. Most of them say I'm mad. But aren't we all in some way?'

Sam and Emily glanced at each other.

'But why live on your own on the mountain? And not in the town and work as a nurse at the bush hospital?' Emily asked.

Evie shrugged. 'I'm a loner. Like you Flanaghans, I love the mountains. Anyway, I've moved past that conventional medicine stuff so the hospital has no place for me. It serves its purpose well, but I'm interested in what's between the ears in health.'

'What do you mean?'

'Well, take yourself, for example.' Evie looked squarely at Emily. 'From your injuries I can tell a lot about you emotionally and how you think.'

'Yeah, right,' said Emily, laughing. 'I thought – shit, here comes a tree!'

Evie ignored her jibe and continued talking in her calm, gentle voice. 'The fact you have broken ribs tells me you're having deep trouble being the woman you think you should be in your relationship with a man. You sold out your true self. It tells me you're rebelling against authority in some way. And the fact you had an accident tells me you not only want to rebel against this authority, but you have lost your voice from it. No doubt, from your injuries, you're finding it hard to breathe, which tells me that you are fearful, not able to take in life fully. It tells me you sometimes feel that you don't even have the right to take up space and exist in this world.'

'Crap,' said Sam, who was leaning on the verandah post, rolling a cigarette. 'You don't know our Emily then.'

'Fine if you think it's crap, Sam,' Evie said. She turned her clear gaze on him. 'A person takes on addictive habits when he is trying to run from himself. I'm sure you have that feeling of "what's the use?" in life. I know you feel guilt, futility and inadequacy.'

'Doesn't everyone?' Sam said defensively.

'Drug addiction and alcoholism,' Evie continued, 'are forms of self-rejection from someone who can't see the light of God within them.'

Sam's eyes were blazing. 'So you're calling me a drug addict now? And an alcoholic? How do you know?'

Evie looked heavenward. 'I'm guided by intuitive energies from Source.'

'See! She *is* a God-bothering nutter.' Sam shot a glance at Emily, then looked back at Evie. 'What right do you have to come here and judge us?'

'I'm here because I was called here. And I don't judge.'

'Ooh! Called here, were you? Direct line to God, eh? He got you on the 1800 Source hotline, did he?'

'No. It was Penny, actually. She knew your family needed more than just medical healing. I know she feels terrible guilt, but that's her journey.'

Emily froze at the mention of Penny's name. She felt Evie's steady gaze on her, and somehow felt calmer.

'I've been out to enough remote bush-nursing stations to know that the displacement from the land will affect your spirit. You see, the body and its health reflects your thoughts and emotions and these mountains are your heart-place. The medicos may dismiss it as hippy shit but the more science and spiritualism become aligned, the better people will heal.'

'And what about yourself?' Sam said, resting a foot up behind him on the verandah post. 'Do you have any pearls of wisdom on yourself?'

Evie smiled. 'Are you asking to avoid reflecting on your own self? Is that why you haven't yet given up your addictions?'

Sam let out a strangled cry of frustration, grabbed up his tobacco and matches and stormed off towards the stables.

'He's still using, isn't he?' Emily said, watching him go.

'I think so.'

'He said he gave me everything he had. I burnt it in the campfire, but he must have more somewhere. He's not normally so hostile.'

'Do you want me to look?'

'He'll be angry,' Emily said sadly.

'It has to be done.'

'I know.'

'Leave it with me.'

Evie went inside, leaving Emily to meditate on what she'd just said about herself and Sam. This woman, a complete stranger, had perfectly summed up their lives. Each painful breath Emily took reminded her of her battles with Clancy over the past six years, and her family's struggle with bureaucracy.

Evie came back out, a plastic packet in her hand. 'That should be the last of it.'

'Thank you,' Emily said.

They sat in silence for a time, the buzz of march flies disturbing the dogs now and then.

'Evie?'

'Mmm?'

'Why is it that people reckon mountain grass-fed cattle farts and global warming are intricately connected, when there are massive cities and factories that keep pumping out stuff and most people don't even question it? Some days it's all too big and upsetting to digest.'

'My dear girl,' Evie said, 'you can't alter what people think, do, say or how they act. It's how *you* respond to situations that counts. Not how you react, but how you respond. Worrying is a complete waste of energy. You need to work out your own true path and not worry about others. How are you going to respond?'

'Respond to what?'

'The situation you're in.'

'Like losing the cattle runs?' Emily paused, thinking. 'The Mountain Cattlemen's Association's organising a protest ride in Melbourne in three weeks' time.'

'And is that the answer?'

Emily shrugged. 'I doubt it. But we have to make people aware!'

'Sometimes the more we protest, the more we're *anti* something, the more fuel we add to that fire. We perpetuate the negative situation. Better to be *pro*-something. It creates a better flow of energy.'

Emily sat in stunned silence staring out to the trees. Evie was right. The more they railed against the government, the bigger the battle they seemed to face. The more they went head-to-head against the scientists, environmentalists and bureaucrats, the less ground they seemed to gain. Emily suddenly thought of Ratgirl in the ambulance and her fury over the bilby. Suddenly, horrifyingly, she realised she was no different to that strange angry girl dressed in a costume (except Ratgirl had the gorgeous boyfriend). They were both protesting against something, and making the problem even bigger. She thought of all the money that had been spent by both sides of the alpine grazing debate on campaigning, protesting, advertising and spin. It was money, time and energy that could've been spent on the land itself. It was such a backwards way of doing it and it meant that the one thing that mattered, the land, was lost in it all.

She frowned and turned to Evie. 'So you mean I should be pro-environment and pro-grazing? Is that what you're saying?'

'Firstly, ban the word "should" from your vocabulary. That word is a waste, a noose!' Evie reached out and touched Emily's hand. 'You can be anything you like, dear, but you'll create more change being pro-something, coming up with answers and solutions, creating flow, instead of hitting one energy against another.'

'Ahh!' said Emily. 'But how do I do that?'

'Wait one sec.'

Evie disappeared into the house again. Rousie stood, stretched and settled back on his haunches. He sat his head in Emily's lap, nosing Jesus Christ out of the way, and sighed deeply as if to say, bear with her. Bear with this strange old woman. Have patience.

Evie returned with an armful of books.

'The best way to make a difference and to heal yourself and the people around you is to control the thoughts in your mind. I've brought some reading for you.'

She unloaded the books onto Emily's lap.

Beyond the Brink, *The Future Eaters*, *Ask & it is Given*, and the odd one out – a government publication with a dry, lengthy title.

'What's this one?'

'It's a study on how the Tasmanian National Parks organisation use cattle and the cattlemen's expertise to periodically graze wilderness areas there. It's particularly interesting as it shows people working together, not against each other, to manage the land,' Evie said, tapping the cover. 'It shows that, perhaps, in a controlled way, the cattle do belong here on this mountainside, and that local people are worth listening to.'

'But I thought you were against the cattlemen?'

'I'm not against anything, my dear.'

Evie stroked Emily's head and the energy from her hand sent warmth flowing through Emily's scalp and body.

'I simply believe in balance. Now, you need to get on with your healing and then you can go on that ride in Melbourne. Your people need someone like you, to give them a new direction.'

'What do you mean like me?'

'You don't see it, my dear, but you radiate light.'

'Light?'

'Yes. As does your youngest.'

'Meg?'

'Yes.' Evie gently placed on Emily's lap the old photo album that usually lived in the lounge room, with photos haphazardly added to it over the years, particularly on wild days when it was too rough to ride out on the plains. 'Take a closer look. Children are purer. They haven't had time to disbelieve.'

Evie left Emily alone to flip through the album. With astonishment Emily began to see the way the camera picked up a shining white glow around Meg's form. Either the crown of her head was lit as if by a halo, or the outline of her body shone with silver light. In some photos the light was subtle, in others it was clear and strong. One taken at the Mt Ewan spring captured Meg looking deep into the camera lens. She seemed one with the spring that gushed out of ancient rock to sustain the gentle fronds of deep green ferns. Meg crouched beside the silver bubbling water and beside her, caught in mid-flight, was a winged insect. Of course, Emily knew it was a dragonfly. But the way Meg's eyes shone as the flying creature hovered near her made them seem somehow connected, like earth sprites or fairies.

'No,' Emily said, shaking her senses back in place.

She snapped the book shut. Where was all this taking her? Before the accident, she'd been a simple mother of two children. Now, more and more, she was finding she didn't know herself at all.

Fifteen

Luke wound the Datsun up to its full speed of ninety kilometres along the four-lane freeway. He was given angry toots and the bird by other frustrated drivers, which made him even more furious than he already was. The fights with Cassy were intensifying. Just as he had vowed to break up with her, she had gone and injured her foot. He felt bad about leaving her to hobble about the house fending for herself, so for the past few weeks he had stayed. But it had been an intense and fiery time of tears, tantrums and yelling matches. This latest fight had been over the cattlemen. Luke knew Cassy had deliberately picked it because he was packing to move to Dargo.

He glanced into the rear-vision mirror, fleetingly meeting his own eyes. Luke knew he wasn't a bad person, but this last fight with Cassy had revealed his uglier side. The more he fought with her, the less guilty he had to feel about leaving. He remembered how she had hobbled into the kitchen on crutches and slapped a newspaper onto the kitchen table.

'It's placard-painting time,' she'd said.

'Now?' Luke had looked up from the stack of papers and books he was putting in a box. 'Cass,' he said wearily, 'you know I'm leaving next week. I've got other stuff to do.'

She ignored him, jabbing a finger at the newspaper. 'Says here there's a protest ride in the city next week. Thousands of those bloody redneck cattlemen, hundreds of 'em riding horses. Can you imagine the stress those animals will be under? Bastards!'

She pointed at the small map in the paper.

'They start at the MCG, then down Wellington Parade to Flinders Street Station, then up Swanston and onto Bourke Street to Parliament House.'

'Really?' Luke said. He wondered whether that pretty girl from the hospital would be there. 'Sounds great. I'd love to go. I love horses.'

'I've got to let Indigo and the guys at PETA know. We've got to move fast.' Cassandra stopped suddenly and gave Luke a strange look. 'What did you just say? *You love horses*? You never told me that. I thought you loved cars.'

'What? I don't even like cars.'

'But you're always tinkering with the bloody Datto.'

'That's because it's always breaking down.' He picked up one of the magazines he was packing and pushed it in front of her.

'*Horse Deals*? You read *Horse Deals*! What for?'

Luke shook his head, knowing that in the two intense years they'd been together, Cassy hadn't taken a scrap of notice of what he liked and didn't like. It was all about what she liked. Life in the city with Cassy was so in-your-face, with no stillness, he'd somehow been able to stop feeling altogether.

As he looked at the cover of *Horse Deals*, the thought of sitting on a beautiful, perfectly educated stockhorse in the mountains gave Luke hope.

'Have you ever had a working dog lean on your leg and look up at you?'

'What?' said Cassy.

'Do you know what that feels like?'

'A dog on your leg?'

'No! Not a dog on your leg. That look a working dog gives you. The warmth and love in his eyes.'

'What are you on about?'

'Or the way a horse will bend his body round for you simply by touching him lightly on the flank.'

'*What*?'

Luke snatched the magazine back.

'You'll never understand. You're too in your own head to even notice!' Luke had raised his voice. He could feel himself shaking. It shocked him, just how much rumbled below the surface in him. A kind of fury, and a deep, deep sadness that he had lost any connection to the life he loved. No soil, save for the box of seeded parsley on the back windowsill. No animals, save for greasy-looking starlings and hungry little sparrows that flitted about the back step.

'In my own head? I'm doing this for the good of the world. I'm going to that cattlemen's rally for the sake of the environment.

What are you going for? To look at horses! You're going to be a park ranger up there in less than a fortnight and here you are backing them?' Fury blazed in Cassy's eyes. 'I can't believe your hypocrisy!'

'Me, a hypocrite! *You* protest about everything outside of this place,' Luke was shouting. 'But what about making a difference here? What about a community garden? Or a backyard battery-hen rehab project? Or teaching city kids about food and the land and the cycles of life and death? Why don't you do something good for a change, instead of crapping on other people? Actually *produce* something yourself.'

'I can't believe you. If you've got all the answers, Einstein, why haven't *you* done anything like that? I'm the one doing the good. I'm the one making the difference. Lately, you just sit around, not talking. You don't smile. You don't even care!'

'Because I've been dead, Cassy! Dead! For the past two years!'

'What do you mean dead?'

'I don't know,' Luke said, nearing tears, running his hands through his dark curls. Emotion blurred his vision. He sat in stony silence, trying to make sense of the newspaper text in front of him. Anything to keep a lid on the emotions he now felt.

Quotes flashed up at him from the page. They were the sentiments of rural people on their knees. '*Enough's enough*', one quote read. '*Tired of being treated like second-class citizens*', said another. '*The state government think rural people don't count*'; '*A risk there will be no Australian farmers in the future*'. The words began to swim on the page again. Luke had heard these sentiments all his life. It just depressed and confused him even more. Cassy, shocked to see him break down, placed a hand on his shoulder.

Furious, Luke shook off her touch with a bear-like roar. He flung the box he was packing to the floor and stood so suddenly the chair fell backwards with a crash.

From the hallway Karla called out, 'Are you two having wild sex on the kitchen table again? Please move my assignment off the table if you are!'

Luke grabbed his keys. He knew the way he felt wasn't all Cassy's fault. But he also knew he needed to get out of this crazy, faltering relationship.

'I'm going out.'

'What do you mean *out*?'

'*Out* out,' Luke said, slamming the front door so hard the picture of Krishna came crashing down in the hallway.

And that is how he'd come to be on the freeway in his little buzzing Datsun with nowhere to go. He wanted desperately to go back to the house where he was raised, where his mother had cooked the vegies she had so carefully grown, where he was free to go yabbying, chop down a sapling looking for bait, or simply wander in the culverts beside the empty roadside. All that space and stillness.

But he knew he was remembering the place with the rosiness of distance and time. The reality of that life on the wheat farm was a different story. His father was worn down and crumpled by stress, his weathered face creased with lines. His mother, drab in her work clothes, with very little reason to smile. The day the footy coach came crying on the doorstep to tell them the team had folded. The way his mother had fought alongside the other people in the town to keep the hospital open. Then they had closed the school, and allowed city-folk to sink their money into managed investment schemes so farms were bought and ripped up for trees.

They, thought Luke. Who where 'they'? All these people driving past him in their comfy clean cars to their offices? He was about to become part of the massive 'they'. He was about to join the big bureaucratic giant that managed the forests, the schools, the roads, the hospitals. He felt daunted and dwarfed. How could he fit in, with a man like Kelvin Grimsley as his boss? But at least he'd be living in the heart of the mountains. Maybe near that girl he'd met. She seemed the type who wasn't sucked into all the city guff spewed forth each day from billboards, radio stations, newspapers, televisions, shop windows and the painted sides of buses. She seemed natural, like the land itself. Grounded.

'Bugger this,' he thought. He pulled over into a side lane and dialled the number of the woman he'd spoken to in VPP Human Resources. When he at last had her on the line, he asked if he could meet the outgoing Dargo ranger today, if not tomorrow.

'I'm not sure we can accommodate your request at such short notice, Mr Bradshaw. It's really not my department. Your orientation with the outgoing ranger is scheduled for next week.'

'That's okay,' he said wearily. 'I'll just drive out there myself and take a look at the town.'

Luke steered out into the traffic, his mouth set in a determined line.

'Dargo or bust!' he yelled, banging the steering wheel and suddenly feeling much, much better.

Sixteen

The main street of Dargo was wide and lined with large walnut trees that dappled shade across the road. Luke was instantly taken with the town. A blonde girl with a big bum walking along the roadside caught his eye. She was hard to miss in her hot-pink top and torn denim shorts, and was walking a Pomeranian with an arse that looked much like its head.

Another woman, wearing a fluoro vest, was on a roadside slasher, cutting the long grass beneath the shady trees, while an elderly man sat in a verandah chair and waved lazily as Luke drove past.

After that, the street lay empty. The houses dozed in the afternoon summer sun, protected by their leafy gardens and the tall trees that grew in the fertile river-flat soils.

Luke caught glimpses of the bush-covered hills beyond the town, too many to count, wave after wave of steep pitched rises tapering upwards towards the mountains. He smiled, feeling hopeful that, soon, this place would be his home, and the people in it his friends. And he would come to know this country.

Within moments he was in the heart of Dargo. One store and, opposite, one pub. He pulled up beside a phone booth and took in the sight of the humble township. The store had a grey corrugated-iron roof with the words 'Dargo Store' stencilled in large white lettering in the same font he used to stencil in black ink on his dad's wool bales.

The pub had a rusty red roof with 'Dargo Hotel' painted in the same glowing white text and the thick timber upright beams and slab-cut weatherboards spoke of bushmen and their skills. Luke looked again to the store.

In the deep shade of the verandah, a bench seat hosted two elderly men, who were sitting, smoking, and not saying much of anything to each other. To the right of the store, a shadecloth was set up over a lawn with white plastic tables and chairs for the tourists and their need for cappuccinos and lattes.

Luke felt like a coffee now, then berated himself for becoming such a city boy. He should be heading to the pub for a beer and parking the Datsun there. It would look small and wimpy next to the row of dusty four-wheel drives and utes, though. They had all manner of blokey items on their trays, including tatty-eared working dogs, fuel drums, welders and chainsaw boxes. Luke thought he'd head into the store first for something to eat, and to find out where the Parks station was.

The old men on the bench nodded g'day and watched with mild curiosity as Luke passed. The screen door shut behind him, enclosing him in the cool, dark interior. The ceiling fans whopped overhead and as his eyes adjusted from the bright sunshine outside he saw the place was a hive of activity.

A lean woman sorted letters behind a postal desk, while a young girl in a singlet top and shorts stacked vegetables from a box into tall glass-faced fridges. From a noisy kitchen another woman thumped the basket of the deep fryer and drained a batch of chips. As Luke stepped towards the counter a juvenile wombat trundled out and began to chew on his bootlaces.

'Hello,' Luke said, a smile on his face as he stooped to scratch behind the animal's ears.

The counter was crowded with stubby holders, postcards, lollies and community fundraiser chocolates, and the shelves were crammed with camping and fishing gear.

'Are you right?' asked the girl in the singlet, pushing her glasses back up her nose and tossing a cabbage up and down in her slender tanned hands.

'Just looking for the moment, thanks,' Luke said shyly.

'Fine, take your time,' she said, then stepped forward and berated the wombat, scooping it up. 'Rack off, Sophie. You're supposed to be in bed.' She bundled it into a bag behind the counter. 'Sorry 'bout that. She's a real tart. She likes the boys.'

The girl looked him up and down, then went back to her fridge-stocking. Luke felt the scrutiny from the locals, like he'd stumbled into a frontier town. He remembered what Kelvin Grimsley had said about the hostility here. He wondered if it might be better not to mention he was the new ranger.

He was relieved to spot a bookstand featuring self-published titles on local history. Perfect, he thought. He could read up about the place before he started the job. He picked up a book with a black and white photo of an olden-day whiskered miner on it and flicked through it. One passage caught his eye and he began reading.

'Time and time again, Emily shines out in the Flanaghan story as far more than just tough. A tireless worker, astute businesswoman, dedicated mother and steadfast no-nonsense friend.' No-nonsense, Luke thought to himself. He liked the idea of that, and, so far, he really liked the look of Dargo too. There were no monster shopping malls with giant super stores, no dozen-bay carwashes, no vast entertainment complexes for children and no glossed-over reality.

He shifted the weight of his feet and read on.

'Early in 1878 Jeremiah Flanaghan borrowed some horses and took his wife, Emily, his children and all his worldly possessions into the mountains. Emily rode a saddle mare and carried her fourth child, a nine-month-old baby. Her husband fitted an armchair on each side of the second horse for the older children to ride in. Blankets, rugs and so on were stuffed in around the children and they were strapped to the chairs so they would not fall out.

'The decision to pin all their hopes on this rather risky-sounding venture and shift the young family and all its possessions to a remote spur in the very heart of the snow country could not have been an easy one to make. But both Jeremiah and Emily were courageous and ambitious enough to give it a try, in the hope that it would somehow lead them into opportunities later on, that other less adventurous types would miss out on.'

Luke glanced up from the book. Adventure. That's definitely what had been missing in his life. Perhaps here he would find his way.

'Emily!' came a voice from the doorway. 'Emily!'

Luke looked up to see a good-looking bloke calling back through the flydoor. He seemed kind of familiar, but Luke just couldn't place him.

'D'ya want a pie?'

A voice from outside called, 'Yeah! Thanks!'

'Shut the bloody door, Flanno. You're letting the flies in,' said the girl in the singlet.

'Sorry, Kate. Bossy bag.'

'I'll give you one in the bag,' she said, setting aside her vegie-packing. 'What can I get you?'

'Just Dad's fortnightly order on the tab,' he said, handing over a list, 'and two pies.'

'Sauce?'

'Yep. Thanks.'

When the screen door opened again and a young woman walked in, Luke didn't recognise her at first. She wore thread-bare, faded green work trousers. They were several sizes too big, rolled up at the legs and hitched over her waist with some old braces. Under the braces she wore a blue-checked flannelette shirt, one sleeve ripped off at the shoulder, the other tattered. There was a rolled towel under one shoulder of the braces, obviously to stop it rubbing on an injury that was taped heavily. Her look was topped off with an old, oil-stained Caterpillar cap. She looked like a hillbilly, straight out of *Deliverance* country, but under the hat, he recognised the sweet face of the girl from the hospital. Luke stifled a smirk, barely believing his luck. Here she was! Right here!

As she swiped the grubby cap from her head he was struck again by the prettiness of her face. Despite her clothing, she was stunning. From behind the shelves, he had time to study her better than sitting beside her at the hospital.

As he did, Kate set down the pies on the counter and let out a long, slow wolf-whistle.

'My, don't you look gorgeous, Emily?'

'Yeah,' Emily said, 'bloody bewdiful, eh? Trust Auntie Flo to deliver my horse, my saddle, my boots, my undie collection and my stockwhip up top, but no other clothes! I considered one of Gran's frocks, but florals ain't my bag.'

'I heard you'd done a runner from the hospital. Apart from the clothes, you're looking better than I imagined,' Kate said. 'Let me deck you out in a new flannie and trousers.'

'Thanks, Kate, but I'll find something at Dad's later.'

Luke sucked in a breath before he stepped out from behind the shelves.

'Geez!' shrieked Kate. 'I clean forgot you were there! You scared the crap out of me!'

'Sorry.' He looked at Emily. 'Hello again.'

'*You!*' said Emily, her eyes widening as she saw the gorgeous guy from the hospital standing in front of her. Those dark curls, the worn green T-shirt and the jeans that hugged his fit body.

'Yes, me!'

Emily smiled as she spoke. 'What are you doing here?'

Luke wasn't ready to tell her he was going to be working for Parks. He realised he still had the book in his hands. 'Um . . . shopping for books?'

Emily recognised he was holding her family history.

'It's a good story, that one,' she said, eyes twinkling.

'An introduction any time now would be nice,' said Sam, leaning on the shop counter.

Luke and Emily looked at each other and burst out laughing.

'I'd like to introduce him to you but I don't know who he is.'

Sam and Kate frowned.

'I see,' said Sam.

'I don't,' said Kate.

Emily held her hand out towards Sam. 'We met once at the hospital. This is my brother, Sam Flanaghan, and this is Kate.'

'Sam Flanaghan?' Luke said. 'As in the singer? I *knew* I knew you. '

Sam flashed a courteous smile. He was used to being recognised.

'Nice to meet you both. And you?' Luke said to Emily.

'Emily Flanaghan.' She held out her hand and he shook it, Emily revelling in his touch.

'I'm Luke. Luke Bradshaw.'

'A pleasure to meet you properly this time, Luke.'

'A pleasure it is.' They held each other's hands for a fraction longer than normal and held each other's gaze, too, until Sam cleared his throat.

'Time to get on.'

'Yes, see you round,' said Emily, suddenly letting go of his hand, blushing and almost bumbling out of the store remembering what she must look like.

Luke was left watching her through the dark gauze of the flyscreen.

'Made up your mind?' Kate asked pointedly.

Yes,' Luke said, 'as a matter of fact I have.'

'Well, good for you.'

'Pie, please, with sauce, and this book.'

'Reading up on Emily's family history, I see?'

'What?'

'The book. It's all about Sam and Emily's family.'

'Great,' said Luke.

'Can I help you with anything else today?'

Luke paused. He wanted to ask who Emily's man was. If she had children, she had to have a partner or a husband, didn't she? Luke's heart sank at the thought.

'Um. Yes. Can you tell me where the VPP office is?' Luke could see Kate was curious as to why he was asking.

'Down the street on the right. Opposite the school. You taking over from old Darcy?'

'I suppose so.'

'That surprises me they've sent someone new. There's been talk that the VPP'll run this side of the mountain out of Heyfield, a hundred clicks thataway as the crow flies,' Kate said, pointing towards the back of the store. 'But you can ask old Darcy about that. Doesn't agree with what they're doing down there in the city. Kicking the cows off and that. I reckon that's why he's getting out now.'

'Darcy?'

'Yeah, Robert Crosswell. We call him Darcy. He can tell you all about it, but if you're looking for him, you won't find him around here today.'

'Where is he then?'

Kate flicked her head in the direction of Heyfield.

'He'll be in a meeting. Always in meetings over there. But you can still check out the ranger's office. It'll be unlocked.'

'It will?'

'Sure.'

'Thanks,' Luke said. He picked up his pie and sauntered out of the store, wondering how the people in Melbourne's VPP could think this place was hostile. They all seemed so nice and friendly.

Seventeen

Emily sat in Sam's ute outside the pub, perving on Luke as he ate his pie in the shade of the shop verandah across the road. She was just wondering what he was doing in town, when Bridie arrived towing an overweight, panting Pomeranian.

'Emily! Thank God you're alive!'

'Hey,' Emily said, getting out of the ute and hugging her friend. Suddenly Emily was transported back to the Cattlemen's and the night before the race. It was as if meeting Bridie that night had somehow opened her up to this path of change, this life without Clancy. Just being near her had given Emily the courage to really believe she could leave him, and she was grateful to her for that. She was overjoyed to see her now in Dargo.

'I heard you'd taken off from the hospital,' Bridie said. She looked at Emily sympathetically. 'And I heard you've left Clancy.'

'Yep.'

'You doing okay?'

Emily nodded.

'Good for you. Where are the girls?'

'Dad took 'em to the beach for a treat, and to get away from all the bloody protest ride organising just for one day. It's been pretty insane.'

'Didn't you wanna go with them?'

'Me? Nah. Not the beach. Don't feel like I want to go anywhere just yet.'

'That's understandable. You'd look shocking in a pair of swimmers with all that gravel rash. But how are you, really?' Bridie asked.

Before Emily could answer Bridie waved her silver-ringed fingers in the air and said, 'No, don't answer that. You look like shit so I don't have to ask!'

'You're the second person to tell me I look like shit. No wonder I haven't ventured into town till now! All I'm getting is insults,' Emily said, smiling.

'Listen, if you're going to look like shit, I'm the *best* person to bump into. Hey, what are you doing now?'

Emily shrugged. 'Kate's just getting our grocery order ready, Sam's getting a carton and then we were heading back up.'

'Right, that's it. You've got an hour or so to spare. You're coming to my place. Here, hold this.' She picked up the fluffy dog and shoved it at Emily. 'Get in. I'll drive,' said Bridie, clearly impressed with Sam's sporty V8.

'But Sam?'

'What about me?'

The girls spun about to see Sam with a beer carton under his arm making his way to them.

'Sam bloody Flanaghan!'

Sam tilted his head to one side taking in the blonde curvy girl, his face blank.

'It's pudden guts,' Bridie said. 'Remember? Dargo Primary.'

Still Sam looked blank.

'She's changed, hasn't she?' Emily said.

'Yeah. Whoever *she* is.'

'*She* is Bridie McFarlane!' Bridie said, doing a twirl and curtsy, pushing out her large, denim-clad bottom.

'Hooly dooly, *Bridie*! You're, you're . . .' Sam was stuttering, hypnotised by her generous breasts that rose up out of her singlet top. He set down the carton, '. . . you're bloody eye-poppingly, amazingly *gorgeous*!'

'Well, that's a bit strong, but I have shaken my pudden-guts image and grown up.'

'And out,' Sam said, quickly adding, 'in *all the right places*!'

'And you haven't changed,' Bridie said. 'Still a pretty boy tryin' to get the world's attention.'

'But not the only pretty boy in town today,' Emily said. 'Check out the fella over at the store, Bridie.'

Bridie glanced at Luke, who was now getting into his little car. He smiled and waved.

Bridie gave a low whistle. 'Cute as! Well, you've got a bit of competition in town for a change,' Bridie said, tapping Sam on his chest. 'Who is that honey-babe?'

'Some city-boy blow-in,' Sam said.

'Just like you, hey?' teased Bridie. 'What's his name?'

'Luke Bradshaw.'

Before Emily could stop her, Bridie was bellowing out, 'Hey, Luke!' Luke wound his window down. 'Feel like having a beer with this fella here?' Bridie pointed to Sam.

Luke shrugged, got out of his car and began to walk over to the pub, a big grin on his face.

'What are you doing?' hissed Emily.

'Shhh,' said Bridie, winking. 'Tactics.' She beamed at Luke and said loudly, 'Sam here needs some company for an hour or so. Are you up for a beer while I take his sister to my place to get her minge waxed?'

Emily turned bright red and stifled a mortified scream. Luke laughed. 'Yeah. Sure.'

Bridie held her charming smile and directed it towards Sam. 'Mind if I borrow your ute?'

'No worries,' Sam said, while Emily looked amazed. He never let *her* drive his ute. 'Have fun.' He and Luke turned and made their way inside the old crooked door of the Dargo Hotel.

Emily slapped her friend on the shoulder.

'How could you! I can't believe you said that about my minge in front of him. My God, Bridie. What were you thinking?'

'It's my trade. I can't help it. Might as well be upfront with people.'

'Well, let me tell you about being upfront. You aren't going anywhere near my front bum with hot wax!'

'Oh, get in,' said Bridie.

Emily stood her ground.

'*Get in*!'

Bridie drove about two hundred metres down the road, bunny-hopping Sam's ute all the way, and turned the engine off outside an old miner's cottage. A new sign was screwed to the white picket fence: *Beauty in the Bush*.

Bridie smiled as she watched Emily read the sign.

'Get it?'

'Get what?'

'Beauty in the Bush,' she said, then burst out laughing. 'It gets me every time! Beauty in the bush,' she said again, indicating the bush-covered hills surrounding Dargo, 'and beauty in the *bush*,' this time pointing to her crotch.

'Oh my God!' said Emily, getting it at last. 'That's a classic!'

'Yeah. The fellas at the pub think it's a scream. And it sounds better than Beauty in the *Country*!'

Again they laughed hard, before subsiding to silence.

'It's great to see you again,' Emily said sincerely.

'And you too. It's so good you've moved back up.' They paused, both thinking of Clancy.

'You know Clancy's seeing Penny from the hospital,' Emily said.

Bridie bit her lip and nodded. 'He's been here drunk every weekend. Comes up from Brigalow, Friday through Sunday. Word's out Road Transport are after him most Monday mornings cos he's so topped up with booze he shouldn't be drivin'' the truck. We don't know if he's here for Penny, or if he's hoping to catch you.'

'So he knows the girls and I are up on the plains?'

'Not for sure, but I reckon he thinks you're most likely there.'

'Do you think I should see him? Talk to him?'

Bridie turned to face her. 'Dunno. Probably. But maybe not just yet. You need to get strong, girl, inside and out, before you take that man on. He is bad news with a capital B.'

'I know. It's just, I don't know . . . life hasn't turned out how I thought it would,' she said quietly. 'The whole thing sucks.'

'Hey,' said Bridie, 'I know, Em. But I'm here to help you. We can help each other. My life didn't turn out the way I thought it would either. But this is our chance to make it better. C'mon inside. Bring Muff with you.'

'Muff?'

'Yeah. My dog.'

'You called your dog *Muff*?'

'Yeah. She reminds me of one of those old-fashioned things ladies warmed their hands in. You know, those rolls of fur. Look at her, she looks just like a muff.'

'You wax bikini lines and you called your dog *Muff*?'

'I know. Priceless, isn't it? The boys think that's a scream too.'

'I bet they do.'

'I never told them I've got a cat, though. I'd never hear the end of the pussy jokes!'

'Well? What's the cat's name?'

Bridie shook her head and raised a hand up to her mouth to stifle a giggle. She muttered the name into her hand, but Emily couldn't hear it. She was already laughing from Bridie's infectious wheezing laughter.

'What?'

'Beaver. Okay? The cat's called *Beaver*.'

'Beaver!' screamed Emily and both girls dissolved into fits of laughter. 'You, dear Bridie, are the queen of fur!'

'Well, what are you waiting fur! Let's get you up on the slab!'

For all her gaudy dress sense and brassy blonde locks, Bridie had done up the cottage beautifully. Emily felt soothed standing in the whitewashed salon with the soft towels, dim lights and scent of roses, but her reflection in the full-length mirror made her heart sink.

'Oh, my God. That's not me,' she said, turning sideways to check out her backside. 'I can't believe I was talking to that hot bloke looking like this.'

'I know. You have kinda got that quarter-horse look going on, what with your hogged mane and that rounded arse. Those pants really don't do much for you.'

'Oh, geez, Bridie. I don't reckon you can do much for me either. Let's just forget the whole thing.'

'Go on with you! I can work miracles. I'm a professional.' Bridie wove her fingers together and cracked them. 'Now, I don't play Enya, or Nora Jones. Can't stand the woeful moaners. I will however do Dolly P. And at a stretch I'll play The Corrs.'

'Got any Sunny Cowgirls?'

'Do rabbits like to fornicate? Course I have. Now get your gear off,' she said, handing Emily a robe. 'We'll have you Princess Mary'd in no time, darls.'

As Bridie left the room, Emily stripped down to her underwear. She looked again in the mirror and rolled her eyes. Her undies were white full briefs that rose up over her tummy and sat low on her thighs. Printed in black lettering across the front was *Why, hello mummy*!

'You complete dag,' she said to herself before pulling them off and clambering up onto the table and covering herself quickly with a towel.

Emily let out a scream as pain ripped along her skin.

'Geez, Louise!'

'Get over it, wuss,' laughed Bridie. She set aside the small white strip of cloth and dipped the waxing knife into the pot, then expertly ran the metal blade across Emily's shin. 'Wait till I do your bikini line!'

'I told you, you are not going anywhere near my bikini line, you sadistic bitch! I don't mind mine looking like Muff.'

'You've been married too long. That thing has to come off! Besides, what's worse? Collecting a tree at full pelt on a horse or having a Brazilian?'

'I dunno. I've never had a Brazilian. What exactly is it?'

'You don't know? Where have you been?' Bridie asked incredulously.

'Dargo, Brigalow. Certainly not Brazil.'

Bridie gestured with the wax knife. 'Where do I begin? Have you ever been to Tasmania?'

'Nup.'

'But you know what the map of Tassie looks like?'

'Yep.'

'Well, after Mum and Dad moved us there for the logging, I got very familiar with the map of Tassie. Are you picturing a map of Tasmania?'

'Yep,' said Emily, 'I'm picturing it.'

'I clearfell the bits down the east coast and west coast,' she said, demonstrating with the knife on her own clothed crutch, 'and I do a strip across the top from Burnie to Launceston, but I stop halfway at the midlands about Campbell Town and I certainly don't wax any further south than Oatlands. And I don't go anywhere deep south, near Geeveston. Got it? All clear?'

Emily frowned.

'Well, if you want it *all clear*,' Bridie said, patting Emily's arm, 'that's called a Chihuahua. But I wouldn't recommend it. The regrowth is shocking, so I'd sooner selectively log with a Brazilian.'

'Oh, my God. You can't half tell you're a logger's daughter. You really are tragic.'

'Thanks. Once the painful bit's all over, I'll give you a facial and you can really chill out.'

*

Later, lying back with cool cotton-balls resting on her eyelids, Emily felt her body relaxing. The tension she held there began to let go and she felt overwhelming gratitude again for her friend. She had never experienced anything like what Bridie had done for her.

Scalp massage, face massage, neck and shoulders. Thanks to Bridie she now had a chance to heal on the outside, and thanks to Evie she was healing on the inside.

For the past few weeks on the high plains Evie had nourished Emily's body with good food and fed her mind with good books. Emily had read and read, absorbing as much as she could: novels about young girls finding themselves and realising their dreams, magazines on permaculture, information on grasses and how they had evolved with grazing as a tool for their survival. Emily's mind was opening up like a flower and her body was healing. Evie had explained to Emily that neardeath experiences could do that to a person.

'It's normal,' she assured, 'to come out of these things with an altered state of awareness of your world. There are lots of cases of people, like you, who nearly died and who returned with a fresh appreciation of life. They often end up having deep humanitarian and ecological concerns. Your fate always has been and always will be interdependent with the fate of the world.'

Sometimes, listening to Evie was like listening to some wise ancient prophet, then she'd swear, or burp, or curse Jesus Christ, and she seemed so normal. She held Emily in a state of intrigue and Sam in a state of annoyance. The one thing that irritated Sam more than Evie was her feisty little Jack Russell. Sam would lift his lip and growl at it as it walked past, and it would lift its lip at him and growl in return. But, deep down, there was a level of humour in the constant stirring from Sam of Evie and her dog. Slowly, Emily recognised that Sam was learning too, even though he didn't know it.

She saw, also, that the girls were learning intensely with Evie. She took them down to her mountain cottage and they played in her garden, learning about the plants and the way the draw of the moon pulled the roots earthward and the leaves skyward, depending on its wax or wane. At night, she taught them the patterns in the stars. Emily herself knew many plants, but Evie knew more. She knew their scientific names and their Aboriginal names, and she knew whether they were good tucker plants or good medicine. Although unfamiliar with horses, Evie went regularly to the stable to dress Snowgum's injuries with herbal compounds and manuka honey. Snowgum was still unrideable as her wounds lay right where the girth would cinch tight, but Tilly and Meg took her out each day so she could pick at the fresh mountain meadows. One day Emily had found Meg standing with her eyes shut, her hands hovering above Snowgum's wounds.

'What are you doing, Meggy?'

'Reiki,' the four-year-old had answered matter-of-factly. 'Universal healing. Evie showed me how.'

'Meg tried to do it to me, Mum,' Tilly said, 'when I fell out of the tree. But it still hurt.'

Emily had laughed at her girls and the change in them. In their past life, with Clancy, they had been shut down, trying to keep out of the way when their father was in one of his unpredictable rages. Now they were out every day with their ponies, grooming and saddling them up themselves, or spending hours just sitting astride them bareback and talking as the ponies grazed. Even Emily had ventured out on one of Flo's old hacks one day, and the sheer dreaminess of riding the plains with the cool mountain air on her face had made her feel almost whole again.

With her legs waxed, tingling with ti-tree oil and her face glowing from Bridie's facial, Emily sat up smiling.

'Thanks so much! I feel like a new woman.'

'Oh, I'm not done with you yet. There's hair and make-up to come. But you'll have to come into the kitchen for that. Then I'll dig out some of my skinny clothes for you and then we're going to the pub.'

'Oh, no, we're not.'

'Oh. Yes. We. Are. C'mon, I've got my hairdressing certificate – or at least half of it. I dropped out but I should remember enough.' She steered Emily into the kitchen.

'But what if Clancy's —'

'He won't be there on a Thursday. He never comes up on a Thursday. Look, pub it is. I'll call now and let Sam know we'll be there soon and to line up the beers for us.'

With that, she was gone to rummage around the bathroom for some scissors and a towel. As she heard her talking brightly to her cat, Beaver, Emily decided Bridie was the best, bossiest, funniest friend she'd ever known.

Eighteen

Luke Bradshaw tucked into a thick rump steak. As he chewed on the tender, locally grown grass-fed beef, he thought of Cassandra. She'd be spitting chips if she saw him eating beef, and that somehow made the steak taste even better.

Beef was buggering the world, she'd told him once, horrified that his family had at one stage run cattle. She'd given him her spiel about everyone becoming a vegan to save the world as they stood outside a giant Direct Factory Outlet. Then she'd dragged him inside to buy new runners, made in some sweatshop in China. She was so full of it.

But then Luke started to feel guilty. Cassy had propped him up and kept him at his studies in that big strange city. He did owe her. Perhaps he should call her? It had been pretty childish and mean to just walk out on her like that. He decided he'd phone – after he finished his steak.

'You thinking about your girl again?' Sam said, setting yet another beer on the table and sitting down to join him. 'I can tell by the frown.'

Luke shook his head. 'She's not my girl anymore. I'm cutting all ties. Moving out here a free man.'

Sam sipped on his beer. 'You might think that, but women, they think different. From what you've told me, she sounds like the sort of ex who'd boil your bunny in a stove-top pot.'

Luke grinned. 'Yeah, maybe. What about you? Got a girlfriend?'

Sam shook his head. 'In my game there are girls everywhere, but they want you for all the wrong reasons. They're lusting after the fella on the stage – not me. So I'm only going to let them down in the long run. I've been the sort to have a girl in every port. But even that gets wearing after a time.' Sam shrugged. '*C'est la vie*. That's why I'm enjoying being back here so much. There's no women to get distracted by.'

'Good,' said Luke. 'Sounds like a top place.' He swigged on his beer, feeding the bravado behind his words. 'Women are the last thing I need right now. Just give me a block of land and a couple of horses, plus a river to fish in and I'll be sweet.'

'Just between you and me,' Sam said, leaning closer, 'back there in the store, if I read the body language right, you've already got a thing going for my sister.'

Luke held up both his hands in protest.

'Whoa there,' he said, shaking his head. 'I don't do sisters.'

'Yeah, sure you don't,' said Sam with a wink. Luke grinned, knowing Sam wasn't far off the money.

'She's married, though, isn't she?'

'Not anymore she isn't. But luckily for you, I know she won't be interested in you now.'

'Oh?' said Luke.

'She won't go for a *ranger*, mate. It's like dating the enemy round here. Once she finds out you're one of them, she'll soon lose that spark. Your mob wouldn't like it and our mob wouldn't either.'

Luke nodded, taking in Sam's words. He was shocked at the disappointment he felt in learning he didn't stand a chance with Emily. After all, he'd known the girl for all of five minutes in two brief meetings. But something drew him to her so deeply he just couldn't pin down the rush of his confused feelings. He decided to shrug the whole thing off.

'*C'est la vie*,' he said, echoing Sam. 'I don't really go for girls in dungers anyway.' They both laughed.

Just then the pub door swung open on the other side of the lounge and Bridie came in.

'Announcing,' she said in a booming voice, 'Miss Emily!'

She reached outside the door and dragged in Emily. Luke's jaw dropped. Emily had been transformed from a grubby girl in oversized farmer's clothes to the most stunning woman he'd ever seen. Her dark hair was cut sharply and had that sexy just-romped-in-the-bed look. Her large dark eyes shone and her full red lips looked innocent yet tempting all at once. She was wearing a tight-fitting red top that showed the curve of her breasts and her slender waist. That was all he could see from where he sat in the lounge. She was divine. She was heavenly. He wanted to scoop her up in his arms and kiss her.

But something kept him glued to his seat. A shyness, a self-doubt, and the thought of Cassandra in the back of his mind. He swivelled around, shoved in the last mouthful of steak and kept his head down.

'What were you were saying about girls in dungers?' Sam said, nudging Luke and getting up to go over to the girls.

At the bar Sam slung his arm around his sister's shoulders and looked at Bridie. 'You're a genius. Not even the best make-up artists on my music videos could pull off a stunt like that!'

For a moment Emily looked crestfallen, her self-image still bruised from life with Clancy.

'You know that's very rude,' Bridie said, folding her arms across her chest.

'I didn't mean it like that!'

'I can see you haven't improved much since school.'

'Well, I can see you have,' Sam said, eyeing her tight black top appreciatively. 'You look fantastic too!'

Bridie turned to Emily. 'He's no better than your ex-husband. You poor thing, you've had a lousy selection of males to share your life with. Your father excluded, of course.'

'Oi! That's a bit harsh,' Sam said. 'I just meant Emily looks great.'

'Mr Vanity,' Bridie said, turning her back on him.

'Miss Self-righteous,' Sam said huffily.

'Come on, you two, be nice. Let's just have a drink. Three beers please, Donna,' Emily said.

'No, make that four,' said Bridie. 'Luke, you are joining us, aren't you? Or are you going to sit over there looking like a goldfish and staring at Emily all night?' She winked at him. 'Emily's child-free tonight. The girls are staying at Rod's so you best make the most of the local talent. It's pretty thin on the ground round here.'

Luke looked uncomfortable, but he stood and came over to them.

Emily smiled when she saw Luke lob onto a bar stool beside her, his cute grin complete with dimple lighting up his face.

'Welcome to Dargo,' she said, turning towards him and raising her glass.

'Why, thank you,' he said, and the four of them clunked glasses.

It wasn't long until they had the pub rocking. Emily was swinging round on the tiny dance floor near the eight-ball table, her head tossed back, looking up at the hundreds of stubby holders from all over the countryside stapled to the pub's high old walls. She was laughing while Luke swept her about to 'Thank God I'm a Country Boy', taking care of her injuries with his gentle touch.

Even the fact that Luke came from the city didn't bother her at this moment, though she'd never, ever been attracted to a townie before. All she knew was that she hadn't felt this alive for years. In the days before her accident, and before Evie's coaching, she would've reacted badly to discovering that Luke was the new VPP ranger. She was a cattleman's daughter. The Parks people were, collectively, the enemy. She could tell Sam was amazed by her reaction when she heard about Luke's job. She had thrown her hand carelessly in the air and said, 'That's life!' Then, cheekily, she'd asked, 'Are you coming to our rally in Melbourne next week?'

Luke had smiled. 'I just might do that. It sounds like it'll be big.'

'Be sure to wear your new Parkies uniform,' teased Sam.

'No way. It might get torn off me by your mob.'

'Now that'd be a sight to see,' Bridie said lasciviously.

Sam cast her a jealous look. 'Don't be sexist.'

'Pot calling the kettle black,' said Bridie and she poked her tongue out at him.

Emily watched the way Luke, a virtual stranger, seemed so at ease amongst them. She thought they were lucky Luke was moving into Dargo. He seemed polite and kind and very smart. Unlike some of the other arrogant young guns who had come to the area to work with Darcy the veteran ranger, Luke appeared keen to learn from the locals. Everyone in town respected Darcy, who had been born and bred in Dargo. But he was one of a dying breed of rangers, those who actually came from the land. The locals were suspicious of newcomers, particularly university graduates. The young guns had what they thought was knowledge of the land in their heads, but they did not yet know the land in their hearts and their hands. This new ranger seemed different somehow. When the song ended and they sat back at the table, Emily decided to test the water.

'I've been reading something you might be interested in,' she said.

'Yeah? What's that?' Luke asked, leaning closer.

'A friend of mine gave me a government land management

plan from Tassie that really makes sense. Our own mountains here could be managed like it.'

'Oh, come on!' Sam said. 'Don't talk shop with the poor bugger now, Emily. Leave that bloody subject alone. He's just rocked into town on a social visit. He's not even in the job yet.'

'No,' Luke said, not taking his gaze from her. 'It's all right, I'm interested to hear. Really.'

Emily cast Sam a sarcastic look. 'In Tassie, they classify the land as having different uses and that influences how it's managed. They set up committees made up of local groups, from Aborigines, to cattlemen, to conservationists, to fishermen, to four-wheel drivers and foresters. And the government employees facilitate and guide from the sidelines.'

'Yeah? Well, that sounds like it makes much more sense to me than the "shut down the grassroots bases and run it from the city" approach,' Luke said.

'Exactly!' Emily said, her eyes brightening.

'That's the major flaw in the system,' Luke said. 'The people in the offices dishing out the funding and making the decisions are in Melbourne. They aren't the ones riding through the land swathed with blackberries every day. It's so easy to get out of touch being based in Melbourne. Believe me, I know!'

'Yes!' said Emily.

'Oh, come on, you two,' Sam said. 'This will go on all night. Just don't get her started on the government policy to put out every natural fire started by lightning. She's just like Pa, endlessly predicting a holocaust of fire. Can we *please* just get on with pubbing?'

'But, Sam, this is so exciting,' Emily said. 'Having someone like Luke in Dargo could mean the start of Parks and the cattlemen working together!' Emily's eyes met Luke's and she could feel his excitement too.

'No offence, Luke, but if it didn't work with Darcy, it won't work with anyone,' Sam said.

'But Luke is the start of a new breed,' Emily argued. 'He's got the letters after his name and the bureaucrats love that!'

Suddenly the familiar beat of Sam's number-one hit was blasting from the jukebox.

They turned to see Bridie dancing and grinning at them.

'You little fox. Turn that effing song off!' Sam was off his stool and running to flick the switch on the wall. The song died suddenly.

In the silence that followed Bridie said crossly, 'Why'd you do that? I'd just put six bucks' worth of songs into that.'

'Donna will give you a refund.'

'But I wanted to hear that song!'

'Well, I didn't.'

'Well, I did!'

'Well, I don't! End of story.'

Bridie and Sam were facing each other, frustration and annoyance on their faces.

'Party pooper,' she said.

'Shit stirrer,' he said.

Moments later, the jukebox was firing again, minus Sam's song in the playlist, and Sam and Bridie were dancing together like a pair of courting birds, laughing, smiling, mucking about.

Emily shook her head at the sight of them. What a confusing pair, one minute having a stoush, next minute best buddies. She and Luke, on the other hand, seemed to click effortlessly on every level. She felt like she'd known him for years.

At the end of the song, Emily reluctantly let go of Luke's hands and excused herself, suddenly feeling giddy. She wasn't used to drinking. But on her way to the toilets she found it hard to wipe the smile from her face. The loos were right round the back of the old pub so Emily made her way along the side verandah, past the piles of empty silver beer kegs that gleamed in Dargo's solitary streetlight.

As she washed her hands she checked herself out in the mirror, still startled by her new look. She couldn't wait for her hair to grow long again, but she was amazed at the difference Bridie's styling had made. And while Emily didn't normally like make-up, she did like how Bridie had highlighted the fullness of her lips and brought out the sparkle in her big eyes. For the first time ever, Emily glimpsed the depth of her own beauty.

She leaned towards the mirror and tried to look into the core of herself. Where had she gone when her body had lain so still on that rocky bank? What had her eyes within really seen?

She had a flash, a quick vision of a sawn-slab hotel with a sagging bark roof and sawdust floor. Of drunken miners, Tipperary men, the shysters of the town, giggling as they shaved a horse's mane and tail. She saw the handsome young minister of her dream asking for his horse to be saddled. Then a glimmer of the priest being shunted forward on the pub verandah to receive his horse. The men were drunkenly lurching and laughing as they backed the horse up to him and presented the shaved horse with the bridle hung on its backside on what was left of its tail.

Rough men rebelling against any kind of authority. So much like Uncle Bob. God and grog. This place was founded on it. Emily's reflection focused again on the here and now and she breathed in suddenly. She shook her head. Evie spoke of energies and had given her books to read on time theories. Could all this goldmining palaver still be going on here, in some other dimension? And the Aborigines, were they still here too, gathering moths up on the plains when the seasons were right?

Emily was shocked at her thoughts. She was a simple mountain cattleman's daughter, who liked to drove cattle, ride educated horses, drink at the pub and eat a counter meal occasionally. She didn't ask questions about life, death, the universe and everything. Suddenly she burst out laughing. It was no use fighting it. Since the accident, she was irrevocably changed – and she liked it. She was learning so she could teach her girls to have a mind as open as the universe and a core of integrity as strong as the pull of gravity. Like Evie. And Bridie was teaching her she deserved the joys of life and she deserved beauty along with it.

Emily strode back into the pub and took Luke's hand, leading him onto the dancefloor with a confidence she'd never felt before. Her eyes shone. She felt truly beautiful.

That was until she noticed an eighteen-wheeler, lit up like a neon sign, rolling into town. As the truck pulled up outside the pub and the air brakes hissed like snakes, Emily froze. It was Clancy.

Respond, Emily said to herself. Don't react. Clancy stood on the road with his legs wide apart and his arms curved out from his body like a gunslinging outlaw from the Wild West. His red truck, like a giant armoured steed, loomed behind him. He watched her through the window.

Emily turned her back and kept dancing. This was her life now. He was father to their children and she would help him honour that role, but from now on she was free to do what she liked. Right now she was simply dancing with her brother and her friends. There was nothing wrong with that, was there? That old doubt niggled. The fear slipped into her being again.

When she turned around, Clancy was in the pub.

'Good to see you, Em,' he said. 'You look great. Too good really, considering.'

They could all tell he'd been drinking. Emily knew he must be in a bad way, driving a truck with any alcohol in his system meant instant disqualification of his licence. He must be ripped.

'What do you want, Clancy?'

'I can talk to you, can't I? You're still my wife.'

'No, I'm not. I think you know it.'

He flicked his head in Luke's direction. 'So this is your *new* fella, is it?'

'Clancy,' cautioned Emily, as if trying to calm a savage dog, 'he's not my fella.'

Clancy looked at Luke through narrow eyes.

'Have you fucked her yet?'

Luke, shocked, pulled a face. 'Mate, no! I've only just —'

'Don't you *mate*, me!' Clancy lurched forward to Emily and shoved her violently against the wall. 'Slut!' The pain left Emily momentarily stunned.

Bridie moved straight to Emily, dragging her away, while Luke and Sam pounced on Clancy from behind. Maddened by rum and misery, Clancy's big limbs flailed the air. He broke free of Sam and swung about. Blindly, his fist connected with Luke's face. A crack of pain and the scent of warm blood trickling from his nose stopped Luke in his tracks until he realised Clancy was coming at him again.

'Get off him!' roared Sam. Donna was there now, barking orders for them to stop, and three logging men, who'd been propping up the bar all night, rushed over, pulling Clancy away and out to the car park.

Emily went straight to Luke, offering him serviettes to stem the bleeding while apologising over and over.

'I'm fine,' said Luke, not looking her in the eye. 'Just leave it. Okay? I'm fine.'

'I'm really sorry,' Emily said again. Luke turned away.

Sam put a hand on Luke's shoulder. 'You right, mate?'

Luke nodded. Breathing heavily, swiping blood from his nose, he got up. 'I'll catch you later, okay?'

'Can I —' began Emily.

'No!' Luke almost shouted and then he made his way out a side door to the cabin he had hired for the night. As he groggily crossed the grass in the beer garden, he felt the anger towards them simmering. He'd walked from his own horrible domestic dispute into another much uglier one. Sure, Emily seemed like a nice girl, a gorgeous one in fact, but maybe she and her mates, especially her bloke, were too rough for him. He remembered again Kelvin's warning about getting too close to the locals. Now he understood. Locals equalled trouble. From now on it would be best if he kept his distance.

Emily stood in the pub, torn, hardly able to believe such a great night had gone so horribly wrong. Should she go after Luke? She barely knew him. And he'd seemed so angry. Not that she could blame him. She felt her own anger towards Clancy rise in her.

'Stuff this!' she said, shoving aside a chair and rushing to the door.

'Where are you going?' Bridie asked but Emily stormed out without replying. She was on a mission. She marched across the road to where some of the blokes were counselling Clancy. They were trying to figure out the easiest way of getting him and his truck back home to Brigalow without him raising hell again. He was slumped down on the step of his truck, his head in his hands. The alcohol that had fuelled his rage was now drowning his system into docility.

Emily stood in front of Clancy, taking in how pathetic he looked. Because they had children together, she knew their bond was lifelong, no matter how much he'd hurt her. But she would no longer tolerate him treating her this way. Respond, she told herself. Don't react.

She put her hands on her hips and her eyes bored into him, forcing him to eventually look up at her.

'Clancy, I know you're hurting, too. But don't you ever, *ever* turn up drunk again and treat me and my friends that way! For the sake of the girls and the sake of yourself, you'd better clean up your act.'

Emily's voice was strong, but calm. She channelled the energy of the stars above her and she radiated a power she had never known before. Then she turned and walked away, her head held high, her breath coming steadily.

Nineteen

'Geez!' said Flo. 'Everyone's geed up at the 'G today!'

From the Flanaghans' horse truck, Emily looked at the amazing scene unfolding before them. The parkland surrounding the giant sports stadium that was the Melbourne Cricket Ground was filled with four-wheel drives, horsefloats, trucks, goosenecks and campers, and tethered to every tree or vehicle was a horse. Over five hundred riders had come to protest the grazing-ban legislation to be voted on in the coming weeks by the Victorian Government.

But it wasn't just mountain cattlemen who would converge on the steps of Parliament House. Other country organisations had jumped on board too, all wanting to voice their dissatisfaction about city-centric government policy. Hundreds upon hundreds of people would be marching on foot, following the cattlemen's horses through the city streets to the state parliament building.

'Sam will be glad to be missing this,' Emily said to Flo as

she helped Meg and Tilly onto their ponies. 'It's going to be bigger than *Ben Hur*! No doubt they would've asked him to sing and he doesn't need the pressure right now.'

'He was wise to stop home,' Flo said. 'He's doing such a good job there, staying off that gunk he was on.'

Next to her, Rod's two-way radio crackled to life, announcing it was time to ride.

'You right to go?' Rod said, holding onto Meg's lead rope and looking down at Emily from where he sat high on his big gelding, Redgum.

'Almost,' Emily said, shoving a spiral-bound government document into her saddlebag.

'What's that you got there?' Flo asked.

'Oh, just a little something I plan to hand-deliver to the boys and girls in parliament.' Emily smiled. 'It's the Tassie legislation I was telling you about.'

'Oh yeah?' said Flo. 'The one that has scientists saying controlled grazing is good for the land?'

'That's the one. The Tassie government actually *invites* cattlemen to graze cattle in parts of the Cradle Mountain conservation area. If I can just get someone to look at it here. You never know, the buggers could actually end up *asking* us to graze our stock in the mountains to help manage them, not ban us from them!'

'Well, good on you, girl,' Flo said, settling her toey chestnut. 'We gotta try everything. If today doesn't sway a few minds, we could lose the whole bloody lot!'

'How do you expect to hand that document over?' Rod

asked. 'You know security will be tight and the organisers are pretty strict on everyone behaving their best.'

'I'll think of something, Dad,' Emily said. 'Trust me.'

Out of the crowd of horses came a booming voice.

'Let's show the bastards!' Internally Rod, Flo and Emily groaned. It was Uncle Bob. Evie's words echoed in Emily's head like a mantra.

'It's no use being self-righteous. Humility is the key. Don't take the high ground. Take the positive, proactive ground. Sow seeds of thought in people's minds that work in the land's favour. This "us and them" mentality won't get you, or the land, anywhere.'

Bob sat heavily on his bay gelding, his big beer belly pushing out over the front of the stock-saddle. His nose was redder than ever. He fell in line next to Emily and Tilly.

'Geez, woman, what have you done to yourself?' he said, peering at Flo. 'You're not wearing make-up, are you? And you've dyed your hair?'

Flo pulled her hat up slightly and fluttered her eyelashes.

'Brow shape and eyelash tint. Beauty in the Bush, my darlink.' She blew Bob a kiss.

'Be buggered. You trollop.'

'She looks great, Uncle Bob, don't you reckon?' Emily said.

'Scrubbed up better than I've seen her in a long time.'

Flo leant forward and pulled her top lip down. 'Bridie even did ol' Flo's mo!'

They all laughed, Emily relishing the fact the family was all together, even though she knew Bob would get under everyone's skin, as he always did. Like an army, they fell in step and joined the other riders who held Australian flags and placards, while others pulled their hats down low and rolled smokes in the light rain.

Emily led Meg on Blossom, who was shampooed to a dazzling white, while Tilly sat well in the seat of a lively Jemma, keeping her cool. The weeks of riding alone up on the plains had brought a whole new level to the girls' confidence and Emily was so proud to have her little ones there beside her. Ahead of them a large green-and-gold banner read 'Mountain Cattlemen Care for the High Country'.

The sound of the horses' hooves fell like heavy rain as both shod and unshod hooves clopped against bitumen. Following the throng was a trailer with men and women armed with shovels. When a horse lifted its tail and spilled out a pile of dung, it was flung by the 'poo crew' into the heap on the trailer. A sign read '*Mobile Parliament – Crap Fed in and Bad Decisions Made*'.

A call came from behind her.

'Hey, Emily!' shouted Baz Webberly.

'G'day, Baz!' she said, her face lighting up at the sight of him. 'Thanks for bringing Snowgum home for me. Flo told me what a trouper you were.'

Baz nodded in Flo's direction.

'She's the trouper. Flo kept her going. Bugger me, it's great to see you here, ain't it, Flo?'

Flo carried her head high, agreeing with a gentle smile.

'Yep, they tell me I was dead,' Emily said. 'But I'm resurrected again. This is the second coming.'

'Oooh! I never say no to a second coming!' old Baz wheezed. 'Your Auntie Flo knows that's right, eh? Hey, Flo!'

'Bugger off, Baz,' said Flo, clearly loving his attention.

Now the puzzle had come together, Emily thought. That explained why Flo was paying so much attention to how she looked. Flo and Baz were keen on each other!

Emily smiled. Another good thing had come of her accident. She looked behind her. The street, lined with elms, their leaves turning from summer green to yellow, framed the crowd of horses and their riders as far as she could see. Horses of all colours, their coats wet from the rain, ears pricked, heads tossing against the bit or cast low, ears forward in curiosity as they all rode quietly forward.

She laughed and pointed out to Rod a joker on a horse who had painted on its flank, 'jobless horse'.

'Makes you wonder what our horses will do if the bans come in,' Rod said.

'We'll have to sell most of them, won't we, Dad?'

Rod shrugged. 'No point keeping 'em if you're not working them. Things change. Very few people nowadays have seen a truly work-fit horse or dog. Or for that matter, work-fit people. I think we've been left behind!'

Emily nodded in agreement, thinking of the high plains and the old chaff house, the shingles a little worse for wear. The handle, hard to turn now, would've crushed many a tonne of grain for the horses and the house cows, the pigs and the goats. Back then it was a matter of survival.

She looked up at the ornate facade of Flinders Street Station and across the road to modern Federation Square. The city was so vastly different from the quiet, unpretentious natural world on the high plains. But as she passed the boozers at Young and Jackson she realised that maybe they were all one and the same. Here, just like in Dargo, were honest, hard-working folk still holding fast to that laconic Australian humour that was drowning under the weight of bureaucracy and political correctness. Emily gave the fellas at the pub a smile. One wolf-whistled back and she blushed.

On their way up Swanston Street they passed a row of police horses groomed to show condition. Their polished and gleaming gear was a contrast to the cattlemen's horses with bridles plaited from hayband and scuffed and worn stock-saddles. As they rode past a coffee shop, Bob called out, 'Can someone get us five hundred coffees? To go!'

Then a woman on the footpath looked skyward and yelled out, 'Sorry about the rain!' Riders within earshot all turned to look. Didn't she know that her water supply came from the farming lands surrounding Melbourne and that water levels had been critically low for months?

A good-hearted old rider called to her, 'Don't you go apologising for rain now, pet. We love it and so might you!'

As they waited the idle traffic lights chimed to each other across the street, alternating their call like bellbirds in a shady summertime grove. What a strange place this inner city was, Emily thought, devoid of nature, save for pigeons and sparrows. She wondered how Sam endured it, but then she heard Evie's words, 'Each to their own.'

As they converged on Parliament House, politicians in dark suits and their staff began to emerge on the steps to watch the spectacle of two thousand protesters and hundreds upon hundreds of Akubra hats and horses.

One by one, each cattleman speaker got to the podium. Some in tears as they talked of losing their heritage and access to the land. Others had fight in their words and finger-pointed to biased government scientific studies.

Emily sat silently on Snowgum, her head bowed, her hat pulled low. She listened with fresh ears this time. She heard the passion in the cattlemen's plea, but very few of them gave the reassurances the city people needed – that cattle in most cases benefited the environment. It was as basic as that. Emily knew that not all alpine areas were suited to grazing. She knew that in the old days, when the environment didn't rate as highly, the mountains were grazed bare by stray cattle, horses, goats and all manner of domestic animals turned loose when the mines shut down.

How could she show these people that, in her country, there was such a light stocking of animals on the sturdy sub-alpine soils that grazing was a help not a hindrance to the landscape's health? But she had no scientific backing to prove it. Emily began to feel the familiar emotion of desperation creeping in. What could she do? How could she get the truth through to the people who made the decisions without them seeing the land for themselves?

Suddenly she remembered the legislation she had in her saddlebag, written in government lingo. She dragged out the document from her saddlebag, found a pencil in her stockmen's notebook and scrawled on the top, '*Mr Premier, PLEASE, read this*.' She gazed up to the mighty steps of Parliament House. She felt a rush of blood.

'You right to stay here?' she said to Tilly and Meg, who nodded.

Emily kicked Snowgum to a canter, wove around the barricades, and set the mare sailing over the temporary fence that separated the riders from the parliament. Security ran towards her as she urged Snowgum up the slippery steps.

'Excuse me, Miss. You can't come up here,' one man said, stepping forward to grab at Snowgum's reins.

'Yes, I know. I'm sorry, but this is for the premier.' Emily held out the document. She was just metres from him. She looked up, locking her dark eyes onto his. She cast the premier a broad smile.

'G'day!' she called out. He nodded and returned a smile to the pretty young girl who rode so well. The premier stepped forward and took the document.

'I'll make sure I read it.'

'Thank you,' she said and turned Snowgum to ride back down the steps. As she did a massive cheer went up, before a cluster of cameras and policemen engulfed her and Snowgum. The mare danced on her hooves as the crowd jostled around her.

'What was it you delivered to the premier?' one journalist called out.

'Is it true you're the cattleman's daughter who fell from her horse earlier this year?' asked another.

'What's the message you gave the premier?'

Emily looked at the media scrum and took a deep breath.

'I gave him the way forward for sensible land management of the Alpine areas – unlike these blanket bans,' she said.

The journalist fired more questions at her, but now a policeman was standing beside her, looking frighteningly serious.

'You'll have to come with me, Miss,' he said.

Even as she was being led away for a stern dressing-down by the Victoria Police, Emily was happy. She knew that she had sown a seed, just like Evie had said, and could not one seed grow?

Twenty

The new Dargo VPP ranger put his hands on his hips and surveyed his riverside bush block just outside Dargo.

'Paradise,' Luke Bradshaw said to himself. Luke had bought the block on the spur of the moment earlier in the week, with the money his father had given him after the farm was sold. Until now, he'd no urge to spend it. But now Luke had a place of his own, it was like a weight had been lifted from him. He wondered how Cassy was getting on in Melbourne. Without the phone connected yet and his mobile out of range, there was no way Cassy could reach him. Perhaps he should give her a quick call from the Dargo pay phone. It was only fair. The last time he'd seen her she'd become increasingly hysterical over their separation.

He scanned the river that wound in an 'S' shape for the length of the block, and pushed Cassy from his mind. He wanted to savour his twenty acres that ran up a steep hillside to a dam. His eyes settled on the shabby little cottage facing north-west towards the river.

'Lick of paint,' Luke said to himself optimistically. He'd paid bugger all for it. The land itself, despite the thick weeds, was brilliant; fertile riverside soil on the flats rising up to steep paddocks and bush-covered hills. Beside the house was a shed and, behind that, a good set of redgum horse-and-cattle yards from the days when the property was much bigger.

Parked in the shed was a secondhand WB Holden ute. Luke knew he'd be supplied with a work vehicle, but after the confines of Melbourne and Cassy, freedom was high on Luke's list of priorities and simply owning a ute made him feel free. He'd always wanted a WB. Like the house, the ute needed work, but also like the house, it had so much character.

Luke's final splurge was buying two of the best-bred Australian stockhorses he could find in *Horse Deals*. He'd trialled them both on his way to Dargo, after packing up and leaving Melbourne. Like the house, Luke had bought the horses on the spot. He thought he'd ride one and breed from the other, depending on which one he bonded with best.

The owner had trucked them up the very next day, throwing in a third horse for only a couple of hundred dollars extra, because he could no longer afford to keep them.

The bonus gelding had fantastic stockhorse breeding but was a green-broke baby with no experience. Luke didn't need three horses, and certainly not a youngster. But there was something in the eyes of that young chestnut that attracted him. He could always sell it on. So now he had two chestnut mares with pretty white markings on their legs and faces and the matching three-year-old in his yards.

Today he'd have to fix some of the fences and get the water-lines sorted before he could let the horses out into the paddock, but he was looking forward to watching them discover their new home.

The first night in the cottage he'd barely slept at all as he lay on his back in his swag taking in the sag of the ceiling and the lean of the doorframe. All things he could fix eventually, or paint over, or tear out. It would take many hours of work, but for the first time in years Luke felt excited, like his life had some momentum and purpose.

In the past few days he'd spent some time with the outgoing ranger, Darcy. Luke came to see the rotund man with few words as a knowledgeable bushman but one who had become jaded with the hierarchy over the years and was now on the lazy side, comfortable in a government job. He'd shown Luke all over the mountainside, going over the day-to-day tasks like which rubbish bins to empty in the parks, where the huts were, which boomgates needed shutting when snow fell.

Luke sighed. He started work officially next week but he didn't want to think of that now. He had two beautiful new horses to get to know and his very own horse arena, set up by the previous owner. With a spring in his step, he set off to the stables to get his new saddle, reminding himself of his vow not to think of the one thing weighing down his mind. Emily. He wasn't going to walk into a complicated situation like that – a mother of two little kids with a psycho ex-husband. Him a ranger in a tiny town and she a soon-to-be evicted cattleman, if the Bill went through. But, no matter how hard he tried, Luke's thoughts returned again and again to Emily.

That same Saturday morning, Emily was standing at the bar of the Dargo Hotel while Donna waited, not so patiently, for her to make up her mind.

'Bottle of Bundy? No! Carton of beer? No! Bottle of vodka? No! Oh, hell, I don't know what he likes,' said Emily.

Emily had been back from the protest ride in Melbourne for a week now, but the guilt she felt about Luke getting clobbered by Clancy had trailed her all the way from Dargo to Melbourne and back up to the high plains.

When she heard Luke had bought a house and some land, she was utterly surprised. No other young ranger who'd been stationed with Darcy had ever shown any interest in staying on. They were only doing time to earn points so they could get a job closer to Melbourne. Dargo was a place to bolt from when the weekend rolled round.

So Luke's purchase was the talk of the town. Still, Emily thought, it gave her a good excuse to visit him so she could give him a housewarming present and an apology.

Earlier that morning, on her way down from the plains, she had dropped the girls into Evie's with the float in tow to deliver for Flo's weekend campdraft.

Emily was looking forward to a day just to herself. As much as she adored her girls, it was also a treat to have some time out. She had set out down the mountain in a buoyant mood, but at the thought of coming face to face with Luke again, her palms grew sweaty and her heart beat faster. Was she nervous because she thought he didn't like her anymore – or scared because she thought he *did* like her? As she stood at the bar, Emily realised she knew nothing about him. What did he like to drink? She did know he drank beer.

'Make it a carton.'

'Stubbies or cans?' asked Donna.

'Er? Um?' Donna rolled her eyes. 'Cans? No! Stubbies? No! Oh! *Stubbies*.'

'Stubbies,' said Donna. 'Light or full strength? Draught or Bitter? VB or Cascade? Crown or Blonde?'

Emily squirmed with uncertainty until she saw the teasing look on Donna's face.

'Beer, Donna. *Just bloody beer*!'

Donna heaved a carton up onto the bar. Emily frowned. It wasn't the most glamorous apology gift.

'Nah. Sorry, Donna. Not a carton. Make it a bottle of Bundy.'

Donna gave a loud sigh and narrowed her eyes. 'He must be *some* fella.'

Emily sat the Bundy bottle on the passenger seat of the farm ute and drove towards the old river road. It'd been years since she'd been out past the big bend and she barely remembered the little house tucked away in the bush. When she saw the For Sale sign with the sold sticker on it, she realised the drive got very steep. She should've thought earlier to ditch the float. Not knowing if there was any place to turn around, she pulled over onto a flat patch of paddock inside the gate and set out to walk the last little way, glad she'd chosen Bundy and not a heavy carton. She called Rousie to her heels and strode up the steep hill, her body protesting at the sudden burst of exercise after her long recuperation.

At the top of the rise she saw, nestled in a pretty spot, the rust-blotched tin roof of the house with smoke drifting lazily from the chimney. Dargo was full of these discoveries. Each river bend or hill revealed another patch where some old-timer had died along with their small farming dreams, leaving a meagre mark in the form of a cottage, a shed or two and some yards. These dilapidated dwellings were gradually getting bought up by city folk for their bush hideaways. It had begun to give Dargo a transient, seasonal feel, but the tourists also brought jobs, drinkers, spenders and a bit of interest to the town.

The future for Dargo now lay not in cattle or timber or gold but in tourism. But judging from the weeds, absentee city own-ers spelled trouble for the land in some cases. The place was a fire hazard. Emily hoped Luke would get the place straight before the next summer fire season.

There was a patch of yellowbox on a levelled knoll just above the house and Emily caught a glimmer of movement there. As she neared she could see it was a rider on a horse in an arena.

A young chestnut gelding with a wide blaze and white stockings was drifting around the sandy spot on the knoll in a collected canter. Emily quietly moved closer, and leaned back on a tree to watch.

What she saw took her breath away. The rider, Luke, sat deep in the saddle, moving as one with the horse. The gelding's effortless movement told Emily Luke had gentle and skilful hands. He wore a wide-brimmed hat pulled down low and a blue singlet that showed off his muscular arms. His broad shoulders looked as if they would swing an axe well, Emily thought, and his denim jeans, Wranglers, accentuated his long, strong legs. His boots, held heel down in perfect cowboy rider position, were scuffed and old.

Luke turned the gelding in a dreamy figure-of-eight then dropped his weight back in the saddle so the young horse stopped in an almost flawless halt. Then Luke stroked the horse. The way he smoothed his palm over the gelding's glossy neck made Emily melt. She tried to keep her eyes on the horse, taking in its conformation and style, but she couldn't stop staring at Luke. He was pure magic on a horse. She felt like a perve, watching him from the trees, and wondered whether she should walk back now and get the float. But what if he saw her leaving? She decided she would call out to him, so as not to startle his young mount.

'Hello!' She began to walk over to him, Rousie close at her heels.

Luke was shocked to see Emily there. It was like he'd conjured her up with his thoughts. He rode towards her, his face in shadow under his hat, the gelding's ears pricked and eyes bright at the approach of the stranger.

Emily glanced down at the ground over which she walked, so that when she looked up again, Luke was right beside her.

'A vision splendid,' she said, looking at the glossy chestnut horse, but thinking of Luke.

'He's for sale.'

'He is? But I didn't know you . . .' Emily's voice trailed away.

'You didn't know what?'

'I didn't know you could *ride*. City boys don't ride like that.'

'That's a bit discriminatory.'

Emily gently stroked the gelding's neck, thinking of Evie and her advice on not judging others.

'Yeah, it is a bit. I'm sorry. I've been really condescending, haven't I? It shouldn't matter that you come from the city.'

'Not anymore. Besides, I was only ever a city boy temporarily. I was a Wimmera wheatbelt boy before that.'

'Wimmera!' Emily thought of the wide expanse of flat farming country, so different to her own farmland. She could picture his dark good looks and lean body in that dry, sun-drenched landscape. So he *was* a country boy! Something inside Emily lit up. It was like finding out he wasn't gay. Suddenly Luke was so much more appealing to her, a real possibility. She shook her head and cringed.

'That's *two* apologies I owe you. One for taking you for a city boy and being rude about it, and the other for Clancy's behaviour. Are you okay?'

Luke raised his hand to his face, touching a small scar on his nose.

'Fine now.'

Emily held up the Bundy.

'A housewarming gift and a bottle of sorries. *And* I brought you a copy of that Tassie legislation I was telling you about and another on an enquiry into the '03 fires.'

Luke smiled. 'Cheers! I love my Bundy. And thanks for the info. I'll be sure to read it.'

Emily turned her attention back to the young horse. 'You've obviously ridden a bit?'

'I used to get about on horses round the sheep, preferred it to bikes. The farm's all trees now, though, worse luck. Dad sold it.'

Emily felt the stab of regret. When a country boy said those three words, 'Dad sold it,' he would be dying inside.

No wonder Luke had seemed so lost in the city with his Ratgirl girlfriend.

'I'm sorry,' she said.

Luke shrugged. 'My brother wanted the money, and Dad wanted out.'

Emily looked up to him sitting astride the beautiful horse. She felt breathless and restless and suddenly very shy.

She'd come straight from the high plains, rough and ready in her old jeans and a long sleeved T-shirt. She ran her fingers through her hair, wishing she'd thought to call into Bridie's first. Then a vision of Clancy flashed in her mind. She was a separated single mother of two. What gorgeous guy would want a girl with that kind of baggage? Emily's thoughts ran on out of control as she realised she was developing one major crush on the new park ranger.

'Feel like a ride?' Luke asked, smiling at her.

'What?' she said, suddenly shaken out of her tailspin. 'You? I mean, me?'

'The horse, I mean.'

Emily loved the graceful way Luke slid from the horse and landed close beside her. He was much taller than her, his shoulders so broad and inviting she wanted to reach out and touch him. She bit her lip and handed him the bottle of Bundy and documents, thinking of the gesture as another seed sown. Then she took the reins from him and swung up into the saddle.

'So he's for sale, you say? What's his background? How much do you want for him?'

Luke tipped his head back and laughed at Emily's rapid-fire questions. Emily took in his melting smile and his mocha-coloured skin and unshaven jawline. She wanted to lean over and kiss him there and then. Instead she squeezed the horse into a walk, circling Luke as he explained how the gelding had been thrown in with the other two mares. Emily could feel the gelding was well educated and nice and forward but needed many more hours to get him beyond the green stage. She urged him on to a trot.

'He had a bit of buck this morning, so watch him,' Luke said. 'Nothing mean. Just trying to take the pressure off himself.'

'If I do buy him, droving will do him good,' she called to Luke. 'It's the best way to educate young horses.' Then she stopped, realising that if the Bill went through there would be no more droving next year. She decided to steer the conversation away from droving. 'What's his name?'

'I've been calling him Bonus because he was a bonus but it's for you to choose.'

'He sure is a looker. But a new boy in my life is the last thing

I need right now,' Emily said, then blushed, realising how her words must have sounded. Luke just smiled.

'You can take him on trial, if you like,' he said.

Emily's eyes widened. 'I can?'

'Sure. Take him for, say, three weeks, then let me know.'

Emily thought for a while, her fingers twirling the gelding's long chestnut mane.

'I don't really need a new horse and I don't know if I can afford one either. If the grazing bans go through, we'll be selling all but a few of ours.'

She saw the muscle in Luke's jaw clench. He didn't say anything, just nodded. She wondered if he'd taken her comment as a dig. She squeezed the gelding into a canter, pleased with the way he collected himself up.

Luke watched Emily's strong tanned hands on the reins and the way she sat as if glued in the saddle, at one with the horse. He could see the muscles move in her legs beneath her tight jeans and he enjoyed the way she talked softly to the horse. But something about Emily made him prickle. He wondered what her crazy ex-husband might say about the horse? Would he cop another on the nose because of it? Trouble, Luke thought. He'd better keep his distance. But still his heart skipped as Emily pulled the horse up just short of him and beamed at him.

'Oh, hang it,' she said. 'You only live once. I've got the float with me. Can I take him now? Just on trial. We've got mustering and droving coming up. At least I can get him started.'

'Yeah, sure. Take him now,' said Luke. 'Great.' But the open friendly tone had gone from his voice.

Emily dismounted, wondering if it was the second mention of droving that had done it, or if Luke was keeping his distance because of his job. She knew he'd have been instructed by his bosses to give the cattlemen a wide berth. She held the gelding while Luke unsaddled him.

'Come inside for a drink if you like, and I'll grab your number. You'll have to excuse the mess.'

Just as they were about to yard the gelding they heard a car approaching. They turned to see a shiny new green bubble car hurtling over the rise. It skidded to a halt outside the house in a cloud of dust, the driver clearly not used to gravel. Cassandra got out, casting Emily stinging looks. Emily's heart sank like a stone in a river.

'Well, hello, Luke,' Cassy said coldly.

'Hi,' Luke said. There was an awkward silence.

'If you don't mind,' Emily said, too loudly, 'I'd better get on and leave you two to it. I'll just lead him down to the float. Thanks. I'll be in touch.'

She shot a glance at Ratgirl, taking in her strange clothes, and said a quick goodbye to them both. Then she walked away, leading the gelding as fast as she could.

All the way back to the float, Emily swore to herself over and over. How stupid was she? As if Luke would have the hots for her. Her husband had punched him, she was a cattleman's daughter and he was a ranger. And, she said to herself, even worse, he still has a bloody girlfriend!

*

'What are you doing here?' Luke said the moment Emily was out of earshot.

Cassy delivered her most sultry look. 'I miss you. Plus you'd forgotten some stuff and I thought I'd run it out to you. But obviously you're not missing me. You're clearly not lonely at all out here.'

Luke shook his head. 'You shouldn't have come, Cass.'

'I can see that!'

'It's not what you think. She's interested in the horse.'

Cassy huffed. 'Right . . . At least show me where you're living.'

'Ta-daaa!' Luke sang, sweeping an arm in the direction of the cottage. 'There, you've seen it. Happy?'

Cassy looked mournfully at him.

'Luke, don't act like that.'

'Like what?'

'Like you hate me.'

'I don't hate you, Cassy, I just don't know what you're doing here. It's over.'

Tears welled in Cassy's eyes. 'But we had a life together.'

'Had is right,' Luke said. 'Past tense, Cassy. We went through all this before I left.'

'I know,' she said, head hanging. 'At least show me inside. I'm busting for the loo.'

'Loo's not inside. It's round the back. A long drop.'

'Serious?'

'A room with a view. Just watch out for the wombat hole.'

'Yikes! How can you live like that?'

'C'mon, Cassy, you're the one who was always talking about composting toilets and sustainable waste systems and getting back to nature.'

Cassy cast him a sullen look and stomped off around the side of the house in her Doc Martens. She looked so out of place here, Luke thought. Sure, they'd been bushwalking together a few times, but it was always with a bunch of her enviro-mad friends. They were people who celebrated the environment, spoke frequently of protecting it, but only ventured into the bush periodically to 'commune' with nature as if a dose of camping would make them somehow more pure or whole again for the next round of city living.

In the house he briskly showed her the rooms.

'Bedroom, kitchen, lounge, porch. There. Tour all finished.'

'Luke. Please. I've come all this way.' She stepped towards him as they stood in the bedroom doorway, the bed unmade before them. She reached out, ran her hand along his stomach and hooked a finger into the top of his belt. 'Just one for the road, before I go?'

'No!' Luke's eyes flashed as he pushed her hand from him. He could see tears resurface in Cassy's eyes. What had happened to that feisty girl he'd first met, he wondered? Out here, Cassy seemed bland and almost stupid. He found he couldn't stop himself comparing her to Emily.

'Cassy, I'm sorry. I really am.' He took her by both hands, and stooped to look into her eyes. 'But we're not going to be together again.'

'Ever?'

'Ever.'

She began to cry.

'You'll be fine. You will be.'

Cassy nodded, smearing tears across her face. She sucked in a breath, looked up at him and jutted out her chin as if trying to regain her strength.

'C'mon,' Luke said. 'I'll take you to the pub for lunch. Before you drive home.'

Cassy nodded sadly and forced a small smile.

'Hey, do you want to ride the horses down to town?' Luke asked.

Cassy shook her head. 'No way! Horses terrify me.'

And at that point, Luke knew there was no turning back.

Twenty-one

At the pub, Cassy frowned at the blackboard, then looked despairingly at the menu in her hand.

'Do you have any vegan dishes?' Cassy asked Donna, who was standing, hip jutting out, tapping a pen on her teeth while she waited.

'We have vegetarian meals,' Donna said, holding the order pad close to her chest. Luke shifted uncomfortably while Cassy sighed.

'Do the vegie burgers have eggs in them?' Cassy asked.

'I'm not sure. I can read the packet for you.'

'Are they cooked on the same grill as the meat?'

'We can use a frypan if you like,' Donna said, trying to keep her voice light. She was used to the city customers who came in droves during holiday periods and demanded so much more than the locals. It was part of her job to accommodate them, so she shifted her weight to the other hip and cemented a smile on her face.

Cassy looked up. 'I suppose I'll just have to have a garden salad. No dressing. And a small bowl of fries *if* they're cooked in clean vegie oil.'

'Fries?' Donna said. 'We can do a you a batch of chips, in fresh oil, if you like.'

'*Yes*,' said Cassy rudely, '*I would like*.'

Donna thanked them as she gathered up the menus, her smile fading the moment she turned her back.

'Cassy,' hissed Luke, 'this isn't Melbourne.'

'I know,' she said. 'Oh, how I bloody well *know*. Why anyone would want to live here is beyond me.'

Luke glanced around at Donna, who he could see was talking to the cook behind the big bain-marie. Cassy followed his gaze.

'Stop being embarrassed, Luke. It's my right to be a vegan. I don't see what the fuss is about. Don't they know it's wrong to eat animals anyway?'

'Cassy,' he said tiredly, 'you only say that because you've never been hungry in your entire life. You're surrounded by good food and can eat what you want, when you want. Don't you see, yours is such a privileged view? If your family was starving in some third-world country, you'd be grateful to be eating at all. Especially meat – rat, or guinea pig, or dog, you'd be eating all of it, even the entrails, just so you and your family could survive.'

'Luke, stop! Yuck!'

Luke looked levelly at her. 'I respect your choice, but please don't dump on the barmaid here because she doesn't share your world views. They mean well. They are nice people.'

Cassy's eyes flickered. 'Yes, I can see you think they're nice.' Her gaze bore into him and Luke felt the Cassy of old stick like hooks in his skin. 'These people not only grow beef, they do it on pristine wilderness. It's criminal. Farming livestock ought to be stopped! Those poor cows.'

'Then what would happen to the cows if everyone stopped eating meat, Cassy? Have you thought of that? All the breeding animals would be put down because the farmers can't afford to run them on the land for nothing. So the animals you're trying to protect would end up dead anyway. It's the way the world works. Besides, the way they raise cattle here is far more environmentally friendly than all those beasts fed on corn in feedlots in the US. Get some perspective.'

'*Me* get some perspective? If you had any perspective you wouldn't have bought a property in a place you don't even know! I can tell you're trying to pick a fight, Luke, so let's just change the subject.'

'Fine,' he said, clasping his fingers together. 'I hope you enjoy your meal.'

'Yes, Luke. I'm sure I'll enjoy my meal. Our *last* meal together,' she added bitterly.

They were sitting in broody silence when the door of the lounge opened and a big bloke in an oilskin, beanie, grimy jeans and boots walked in. Donna, coming from the kitchen, smiled at him.

'In for lunch again today, Bob?'

The big man peeled off his coat, revealing a burgeoning blue singlet with white text on it: *Dargo River Inn, Liquor up the*

Front, Poker in the Rear. Grey hairs curled over the neckline. He sat at a table and took off his beanie, revealing messy long grey hair with a bald patch on top.

'Bob's regular, please,' Donna yelled towards the kitchen. 'Salad or veg with your steak today, Bob?'

'Just chips, thanks, sweetheart.' He pushed a twenty-dollar note towards her, and she set off to the bar to pull him a beer.

Luke saw Cassy looking distastefully at Bob's singlet. Then he saw Bob look sideways at Cassandra. He visibly flinched at the sight of her spiky hair and facial piercings.

'Geez,' Bob said, 'you fair dinkum gave me a fright, girl. It is *girl*, isn't it?' he asked, looking Cassy up and down, taking in her black, androgynous clothes and chunky kick-your-head-in boots. Cassy narrowed her eyes just as Donna set down Bob's beer.

'This is our new park ranger, Luke Bradshaw,' Donna said, 'and his lovely lady-friend.'

'Ahhh,' said Bob.

'This is Bob Flanaghan,' Donna said. Bob made no attempt to shake Luke's hand. Instead he skolled his beer, never once taking his eyes from Luke.

Flanaghan, thought Luke. One of Emily's cattlemen clan. Trouble, too, from the look of him.

Bob set down his empty beer glass. 'So you're the new bloke here to fence us out of the cattle runs if the bans are passed, are ya?' Luke was about to answer when Bob turned to Cassy. 'Be careful hanging out with your parkie boyfriend, love. You'll be in trouble if you get tangled up in one of his electric fences with all that metal in ya. You'll get a *zap*!'

He laughed as he gestured towards Cassy's piercings in her brow, ears, nose, mouth and tongue. Cassy scowled at him.

'I'm sorry, darlin', but it looks like you ran fair through a fence and you've still got barbs and bits of star pickets in ya.' He leaned forward so he could see past Cassy to Luke. 'How do you kiss her with all that metal in her face?'

'I don't have to listen to this,' Cassy said.

'He's only having a joke, Cass,' Luke said, looking up at Bob. 'We're just here for a quiet lunch, mate.'

'Lunch, eh? Then a bit of fishing after, maybe. Looks like she's already fallen in the tackle box!'

Bob began to wheeze with laughter as Donna stepped forward with a fresh beer.

'Bob, leave the young lovebirds alone.' She turned to Luke and Cassy. 'I think our Bob has had a few before coming in,' she said as by way of apology.

'They ought to lighten up,' Bob said. 'And one way of lightening up would be to take all that metal out of your face. You got shares in BHP Steel or something?'

'Bob, settle,' said Donna before she breezed off to the kitchen again.

Cassy stared at Bob, fury written on her face.

'How can you stand it here in this redneck town?' she asked Luke.

'They don't ever stand it for long,' Bob said, swigging again on his beer. 'Got no bloody clue, you bloody city slickers. You think you're doin' a good job, do you, eh? You wait till that ban comes through. One spring it'll take, one good spring with no grazing and we'll have a fire through that so-called park of yours and it'll all be buggered. You bloody greenies have no idea. You'll wreck the lot of it.'

'And you're not wrecking it now with your shitting, farting cattle?' Cassy said. Luke shot her a look to silence her, but she kept on. 'When they do pass that legislation and you're banned from the mountains, thousands of people will be celebrating, you hear me?'

Bob's face began to redden. His eyes flared intense blue. 'You bloody stupid greenies have got it all wrong! You think kicking farmers off the land and planting trees is a good thing for the environment – now we got trees all over the countryside! I'd like to see you find ways of eating the bastards. You townie mongrels take your long showers, shop every day and live in them big houses, then blame *us* for buggering the environment. Well, you can eat the crap from China for all I care. Just stop kicking us farmers in the guts!' Luke remembered Darcy caution him about Bob Flanaghan. He could see Bob reach boiling point. He was beyond reason.

Lunch or no lunch, it was time to leave. Luke stood up.

'Where ya going, Mr new parkie boy?' Bob slurred.

'No point talking while you're full of piss and bad manners, Mr Flanaghan,' Luke said. 'You come and see me another day and we can talk.'

'Huh!' snorted Bob. 'Talk! That's all you bloody government bastards do is talk! Well, we'll give you an induction to your job you'll never forget, kiddo. We'll see you in the Wonnangatta next week.'

Luke tilted his head quizzically. The Wonnangatta?

Bob rambled on. 'The cattlemen are taking a mob into that park to show what a shithouse job you're doing with the land. And the media will be there to record what a mess you bloody VPP people have made of it. Once that gets out, there's no way known they'll kick the cattle off. Youse bastards are stuffed.'

Luke knew the VPP's Wonnangatta National Park was in an area even more remote than the Flanaghans' grazing runs. It was the most isolated cattle station in Victoria, and in its heyday had been a thousand acres of beautiful natural pasture, bushland and river flats, nestled in a valley over two thousand feet above sea level.

To evict cattle from the area, the government had bought the property at great expense about twenty years ago. But the logistics and cost of a bureaucracy managing land that vast and remote was a nightmare. Luke had never been in the Wonnangatta but his ears pricked up at Bob's news that the cattlemen were planning to take cattle in illegally as a media stunt. Emily might have the face of an angel, but her uncle had the face of an arsehole. Luke Bradshaw had no problems going straight out to the phone box across the road from the pub to ring Kelvin Grimsley's mobile.

Cassy sat on the back tailgate of Luke's ute swinging her legs as Luke made the call. She looked like a hyena that had dined well that day, such was her joy in seeing Luke dob in the cattlemen's plans to his boss.

Luke was surprised to hear Grimsley answer his phone on a Saturday and even more surprised to find he already knew about the cattlemen's plan to take cattle into the Wonnangatta. The Mountain Cattlemen's Association of Victoria had emailed the VPP.

'They think they're being courteous and playing fair by telling us,' Kelvin said over the phone. 'But they don't know the number of headaches they give us. They acknowledge it's an illegal action but still they do it! They have no idea of the paperwork and cost it generates. It's taxpayer money they're wasting!' Kelvin's card in his hand, Luke ran his index finger over the embossed VPP logo.

'Can I do something to help?' he asked.

'I'll have your Heyfield supervisor call you first thing Monday.' Kelvin began to outline the plans they'd put in place. 'Darren is drafting a Coordinated Incident Plan and formulating a Risk Management Assessment of the potential situation in regard to the proposed protest. Then he's compiling a rostered crew of staff both in the Heyfield offices and on the ground and he's going to liaise with the DLSC&EL Corporate Communications Unit at every stage and formulate a Media Unit outlet. I'll have him draw me up a flow chart of the Departmental Responsibilities for each unit during the protest. That way we can notify staff right from the top, starting with the Deputy Land Stewardship and Biodiversity officer down to the Forest and Biodiversity Utilisation Unit. But as you're just a ranger on the ground, you don't need to worry about any of that, Luke. You're not yet adequately trained. Darren at Heyfield can guide you.'

'So he'll phone me Monday?' said Luke, his head swimming from all the government lingo.

212

In Melbourne Kelvin Grimsley tapped his teeth with his finger as he thought. He wondered where he should roster Luke onto the Protest Response Strike Team. But the boy had such limited training it could be a risk. He was yet to complete his 4WD training unit, his unit one fire combat block or his minimal environmental impact camp-out instruction. At the interview he had seemed like a bright young man, but it would be risky to take someone so inexperienced out into a volatile situation. Kelvin cursed the cattlemen again for the trouble they caused and for the disruption to his weekend.

He recalled that Luke had been a farm boy and Kelvin felt a glimmer of disappointment over this fact. Agriculture was such a simplistic pursuit, and country people were often dimwitted and narrow-minded, he found. Still, Kelvin rationalised, at least the boy had a university degree.

'Yes, Luke, Darren will set up a conference call first thing Monday morning. Nine o'clock.'

Luke thanked Kelvin and hung up. Nine o'clock was first thing? Luke laughed to himself remembering his life on the farm. Nine o'clock was time to come in for a cup of tea after two hours of work.

'Well? How did you go?' Cassy asked. 'You didn't say much this end.'

Luke shrugged.

'Got anything to eat at home?' Cassy said.

'Hadn't you better be getting back to Melbourne?' Luke said. He could tell Cassy was winding herself up for another predatory pounce. He had to get her out of here.

'Luke, I'm starving. I need food!'

Back in his house, he opened the cupboard.

'Baked beans. Or tinned baby corn spears.'

Cassy rolled her eyes and reached for the baked beans.

Luke didn't feel like talking to Cassy so he picked up the documents Emily had left him. He sat down heavily in the chair.

'What are you reading?'

'Nothing,' he said. Cassy turned her back.

The first document was Tasmanian. He frowned, wondering how that was relevant to the mountains he was about to caretake. He flipped to the next. It was a submission to the Victorian Government after fires in the area in 2003. Emily had marked a page with a sticky note and highlighted the text in green. The extract had been written by descendants of the original cattlemen. They talked about the cattlemen in the thirties who would throw out a match every couple of hundred metres along the ridge lines ahead of the snow season, so that fire in the area would not be a problem come summer.

Luke looked up to see Cassy stirring the saucepan on the stove top. Her face was set. He could tell from her expression she was gearing herself up to drive away after this last pathetic meal. He felt sorry for her, but he could no longer offer her comfort. He went back to his reading, thinking of Emily and her pigheaded relative, Bob. Was it simple truth that the once open, rolling grassland in the area had been taken over by scrub since grazing and burning controls by government?

How could these stubborn, proud, uneducated people be

making claims like this? During his degree Luke had studied CSIRO findings that proved livestock grazing in alpine environments was not, in his lecturer's words, 'an effective fire mitigation tool'.

He wondered now who had run the studies and where the truth lay. Luke could understand the cattlemen's frustration with the whole process, but wondered why Bob had to be so aggressive. He threw the paperwork on the table. It was all too confusing, and at the heart of his confusion was Emily.

Cassy set down two plates of baked beans.

'Our last supper,' she said and then began to cry.

Luke shut his eyes. He just wanted her gone from his life. And now with the clash of information swirling in his head, he wanted the whole cattlemen debate, even Emily along with it, gone too.

Twenty-two

Emily shifted in the saddle as the young gelding plunged through the dogwood scrub towards the Wonnangatta National Park. The bush around her smelled sweet from the overnight shower. Thirty other riders were following her, their horses pausing to step over high logs or weave around trees. Rousie had his tongue fully out, front paws up on a log, ears pricked as he watched the small mob of Hereford cows ahead lumber steadily down the slope.

There were no roads into the Wonnangatta National Park, just hair-raising tracks that four-wheel drive enthusiasts tackled in the summer holiday season. Before the ride, Emily knew there'd be screamingly steep mountainsides to slide down into the station and over a dozen deeply gouged river crossings to forge.

Snowgum's injuries still made her unrideable for such a long, tough trek. Emily had wondered if her own body would take the rough riding, and if she'd be able to handle Luke's young horse, who was still green at moving through and around trees.

But once sitting in her old stock saddle on the beautiful young chestnut, Emily felt as if she'd truly come back to life.

The plan by the Mountain Cattlemen's Association was to take three groups of cattle – ten in each herd, from three different mountain regions across Victoria – into Wonnangatta as a media stunt with a message they hoped would reach the minds of the men and women in the Victorian Parliament.

'What's the worst that will happen to us by going in there?' Emily asked her father.

Rod shrugged. 'We could be fined a thousand dollars a head but I doubt there'll be arrests. The police and Parkies know it'd be public-relations suicide.'

Hang the fines, Emily thought. The land mattered more. Before taking on the last steep ride into the valley the group stopped to take photos of the Hereford cattle rubbing their sweaty ears on the treated pine posts of a Parks sign that read: *Welcome to Wonnangatta National Park – No firearms, no domestic animals permitted.*

'The cattle can't read,' Emily joked and they all laughed, but she could feel the group's nervousness. The men and women astride their horses weren't law-breakers, or troublemakers. They were just passionate about the land.

Emily had thought guiltily of Luke as she watched the cattle lumber forward into the designated Parks zone.

Flo reined her horse to the left to hasten the mob as they slowly pushed through the overgrowth.

'I remember when there were bridle trails all over these hills,' said Flo.

'All gone now,' Rod answered, as he slid down an embankment on his horse, twisting out of the way of a branch. He turned in his saddle so Emily could hear. 'You were just a little tacker when I last came in here on the drive to take the cattle out. Just shows you how quickly the scrub gets overgrown.'

'And there hasn't been a fire in here for decades, by the looks,' Emily said, touching one of the clean, upright trunks of the eucalypts with her fingertips as she rode past.

Rod twisted his mouth to one side.

'Makes me nervous just bringing people in here. If I were Parks, I wouldn't let the public near the place. Alight, it'd be a deathtrap.'

Emily pulled her horse to a halt at the top of a rise and looked down across the massive valley that ran as far as the eye could see.

The river flats were yellow with Saint John's Wort weeds. The dirty-blond swathe of tall, rank grasses, which whispered in the wind inviting fire, were only interrupted by large darker-leafed domes of blackberry bushes dotting the plain. In places, particularly near the winding creek bends, the blackberries had joined in clumps, some as high as a house.

Her father pulled his horse up next to hers and followed her gaze.

'*That* is a National Park?' Emily said amazed. 'We're going to be hard-pressed to drove the cattle through that. The weeds are as high as the cows' horns!'

Emily could see the Parks contractors had slashed a small area of grass around the site of the homestead and camp

218

grounds. They must've made the cumbersome journey over the tracks with a ride-on lawnmower tied to the back of their ute. What an absurd thing to do when there were thousands of acres of overgrown valley flats. Getting a tractor in would be a nightmare, but if cattle weren't used to control the overgrowth, tractors and chemical sprays were the only options.

Emily looked at the site of the homestead that had been built by the pioneering family who farmed the area over one hundred years ago. The house was all but rubble now, burnt down by vandals over the years. Now composting toilets and neat Parks signage dotted the small area for the comfort of holiday makers. Tents sprung up in summer for idle days at a place where men had once toiled and tilled and women had birthed and raised children in the hard slog of life that comes from isolation.

Emily felt like crying. This once-beautiful property was going to ruin. The massive overgrowth was testimony that government money and a handful of staff couldn't manage land properly alone. Couldn't everyone see, simply by looking at this land, that this country needed the help of the cattlemen and their grazing animals to manage it? The vista that spread out before Emily confirmed all she had heard about the 'lock it up and leave it' approach of public-land management.

'Dad,' Emily said, 'doesn't anyone *care*? Are they that heartless?'

Rod shook his head. 'I don't think it's about lack of care. You know some of the Parkies are really good fellas. Take that Luke. I reckon he's all right. But I think they're all constrained from the top down. Both money and mindset.'

Emily felt a buzz run through her, hearing her dad say Luke's name.

Rod talked on. 'The Parks boys on the ground are already stretched. They're relying on funding to trickle out from Melbourne for sprays, staff and equipment. While they wait the weeds are taking hold. Darcy said the last straw for him was when the funding policy changed. Because some clown in Melbourne deemed there wasn't enough money to do anything about the huge blackberry problem, they made another weed a "higher priority". Darcy couldn't believe it.'

Emily wondered how Luke would fare in the midst of such a system. Would he be absorbed into the culture of the giant organisation and swamped, like her dad said, by the mindset? She knew he'd be pressured by locals to do more burning off, but fires were also controlled by the heavy weight of bureaucracy.

When the winds and the temperature were perfect, the opportunity for a safe, cool burn was often lost because of the official process required. To start any burn-off Luke would need the go-ahead from Melbourne. It was so costly once they got dozers, fire trucks and men on the ground, plus helicopters on standby, that only a small portion of burns ever took place.

Gone were the days when men like her grandfather would expertly feel the air temperature on their skin, the breeze on their face and cast an eye around the bush to see if the time was right. Then her pa, riding along on his horse, would puff on his pipe and drop a match here and there and let the slow trickle of flames do their work. In her grandfather's day, one person was able to effectively manage thousands of acres of healthy bushland, rejuvenating it the way nature intended. Gently, with expertise and care, like the Aborigines had done. Now in the hands of a giant bureaucracy, burning-off cost millions and its effectiveness was disputed and doubted by academic 'experts'.

Emily realised how close they were to being locked out of their own high-country station. Seeing Wonnangatta filled her with despair.

'So, is this what our land on the high plains will look like?' she asked her father, her voice cracking with emotion.

Rod reached out and gently pulled the rein of his daughter's horse. The gelding took a step nearer him and Rod laid a hand on Emily's knee.

'C'mon, Em,' he said gently. 'They'll have to see sense. This place proves what we've been saying to the bureaucrats, politicians, scientists and public all along. How can they not see grazing helps manage land like this?'

'But what if they don't see, Dad? What then?'

Emily mirrored her father's sad expression. All his life he had lived with the discrimination that came from being a Flanaghan, a cattleman. It hurt to see his daughter go through the same distress.

'It's okay, Em. You just pull your hat down tight and keep on riding. That's all we can do.'

'But why are they so quick to condemn us, Dad? Like we're just a bunch of uncaring old ratbags and rednecks raping and pillaging the mountain country? Seems they're quite happy to have hydro schemes, ski villages, logging and tourism all over the mountains, but they're making our grazing cattle a crime. The government gives its blessing to bulldozers and chainsaws up here, but not our cattle.'

'It's just how it is, Em. You can't let it get to you. It'll consume your life.'

'Like it has yours?' Emily's eyes sparked, challenging her dad, who she knew had all but given up. Resigned to his fate, she could tell he was just going through the motions on this protest ride. His heart was no longer in it.

'C'mon. We've got to keep moving,' Rod said, pressing his horse away with his heels.

As they rode closer to the valley floor and the cattle eagerly made their way to the flatter, grassy creek flats, Emily looked back to where they had come from. The track had the steep pitch of a church spire. Some riders were leading their horses down, half sliding and hanging onto the branches of trees. There were calls of excitement and laughter in the air, knowing they were almost safely down. Clipped to Rod's belt the two-way radio crackled to life.

'This is the Mansfield mob. We've sighted you Gippslanders. Can you see us?'

Far off to the north, against the backdrop of a giant mountain, were the tiny specks of cattle and riders.

'Welcome to *Weed-angatta*, Mansfield mob,' Rod said. The riders let out whoops and cheers. To their left on the steep bank came another call. There, the Licola riders were picking their way down the hill on a treacherous zigzag track, letting their cattle find their own way down.

'*Weed-angatta*, here we come too!' the Licola group called on the radio.

As the sound of the helicopters throbbed overhead a crowd was gathering near the ruined homestead on the valley's floor. Four-wheel drives appeared from the hills. Campers, too, made their way over and gathered, all looking skyward as the helicopters descended.

As the choppers landed, they stirred the air and whipped the heads of grasses back and forth in a manic dance like eddies in a flooding river. The crowd of bushmen, campers and cattlemen watched the media crew tiptoe their way through the grass. Women in office clothing and dainty shoes, men in white shirts with ties. The crew, wearing standard arty black, lugged camera tripods, boom microphones and heavy shoulder-bags. The media pack looked so at odds with the landscape that some people laughed.

As the crew set up their gear, each party of drovers was given the cue to move the herds forward. As the three small herds came together the cows were too weary and hungry to bother much with pecking orders. They all grouped as one and began to graze as the horsemen ringed round them. Rod rode forward carrying a microphone and the Australian flag upon his tall chestnut horse.

With the cameras rolling Rod delivered his heartfelt speech. Emily wondered just how many passionate words had been spoken or written over the years, with no changes to the outcome. She fingered her leather reins as she listened to her father's words.

'Mr and Mrs Average have it so good that they don't worry much about tomorrow. Well, I think Mr and Mrs Average need to take heed of what's going on. The approach that we can turn on the telly for our entertainment, drive to the supermarket for our sustenance, keep up the consumer spending, use fossil fuel as if it were there forever, needs to be addressed.

'Up until now the public conscience has wanted someone else to do something. They say the government should do something. This has resulted in government policies that are conceived to placate the voter. Kicking a few cows off the high country fits comfortably into this approach for many politicians. But we say an uneducated majority of voters has no right to allow the "lock-it-up and let it burn" approach to public land management. This approach will result in massive flora and fauna decimation with the hottest holocaust of bushfires to come – and with certainty, they will come.'

Emily shivered. She had seen her fair share of firefighting in her young life, though never anything too serious. But as the years rolled past and the bush around them never saw the gentle lick of a cool-flame burn, she wondered when that mighty fire would arrive. Now it was autumn, they had most likely survived another year, but all the bushmen knew this was a disaster waiting to happen.

Redgum shifted his back leg and rested a hoof, and Rod paused again until his horse stilled.

'How is it that early mountain cattlemen families survived

fires when the only fire control they had was a hessian bag, a bough off a tree and a box of matches? The Aborigines before them had even fewer control measures. They knew how to use fire at the correct time. They did not put out all the natural fires until the fuel build up was so massive. Now look about you! Look at this mess. All the Elvis helicopters available, the thousands of well-trained firefighters with millions of dollars worth of state-of-the-art firefighting gear, cannot be effective here once this gets underway.'

Emily felt her eyes sting with tears. She had witnessed her own country going that way with cool-burn bans and now, having seen Wonnangatta, she could foresee the Flanaghan station in the same state – a riot of weeds and fallen-down fencing with just the rutted wheel marks of four-wheel drives through the guts of the country. She backed her horse up and rode away, keen to simply be on her own for a time, overwhelmed by how hopeless she felt. She thought of her girls at Evie's house and wished she could hold them close now for comfort.

A woman reporter with a notebook and shiny patent-leather shoes stepped in front of her, wary of her horse.

'Having a good day?' she asked. Emily looked down, noting that her face, although pretty, was covered heavily in make-up and there were sweatstains on her white blouse. Her streaked blonde hair looked windswept and no longer chic.

'It's not exactly a picnic, but it's close enough,' Emily said, trying to be cheerful.

The reporter looked about. 'This place is beautiful, isn't it? Look at the flowers and all that grass.'

'Beautiful?' Emily wondered aloud. This setting? Yes, the setting was beautiful, but the management of the land was shocking. Appalling. Heartbreaking even. Didn't this woman see it too?

Emily looked at the woman's smiling, squinting face and realised she didn't see it. She just saw trees, grass and space. It looked *pretty* to her. Emily suddenly realised that people with no knowledge of the land *couldn't* see – not even when it was staring them right in the face.

They saw green so they thought there was no drought. They saw grass and flowers but they did not see weeds. They saw creeks and steep hills but they did not see erosion and dull life-less water. They saw cattle in amongst high-country flowers and thought it was bad. They didn't realise that over thousands of years the grass had evolved for grazing, offering up the sweet-est bits in their leaves so they were mown by the animals to exactly the right length.

They didn't realise the cattle were time-controlled and lightly stocked on the area so the plains had months and months to rejuvenate. Emily saw for the first time that they didn't know what they were looking at and they even didn't know what they didn't know!

'Want to have a ride?' Emily said. The reporter hesitated. 'He's very quiet.'

Emily was off, out of the saddle, grabbing the reporter's bag. Offering her up the stirrup. 'On the count of three,' she said, bunking her up before she had the chance to say no. Then she led the woman across into the deep grasses.

'See this grass here?' Emily said, running the palms of her hands over the tops of the seed heads. It was well over waist-high. 'This will all fall over and rot. It's all one species. All the native grasses have been buried alive underneath. They don't stand a chance if this other stuff isn't kept in check. That's what grazing does. And see this yellow stuff? Pretty though it is, it's a weed. Saint John's Wort. Toxic and highly vigorous. No native orchid stands a chance when this stuff's about. And you know blackberries, don't you? Just look at that creek over there. That dark vegetation, all blackberries. You can't even get to the creek.'

The woman began to nod.

'Yes, I see.' She looked across the valley. 'It's everywhere! This grass, those weeds, the blackberries . . .'

'Not so beautiful really,' Emily said.

'Well, no. Not when you point it out like that,' the journalist said. 'Now I see what you mean.'

Good, thought Emily. Another seed sown.

Twenty-three

Luke sat uncomfortably in the back seat of the Parks four-wheel drive next to Kelvin Grimsley. While Luke's Heyfield supervisor, Darren, tackled the last steep pinch on the track into the Wonnangatta Valley, his workmate, Cory, continued to play with the satellite navigation equipment in the front passenger seat. Through the canopy of leaves, on the saddle of a giant hill, they had seen the TV news helicopters arriving.

'We'll wait until the television crews have left,' Kelvin said. 'The less potential for confrontation with the cattlemen, the less airtime the story will get.'

Luke knew the government's media department had given Kelvin a clear brief should they get caught by any reporters or journalists. He had watched Kelvin rehearsing his statement over and over on the trip into the Wonnangatta. He didn't seem to be taking in the bush around him at all.

For Luke the trip had been amazing. The river crossings they drove through had been gouged deeply by four-wheel drives over time, but the beauty of the ribbon-like river winding its way through the valley was staggering.

Now up on the crests of hills and with only a few short steep kilometres into the Wonnangatta, Luke felt his excitement rising. He was getting paid to do this! His first days on the job had been like one big adventure. The only downside was that he would no doubt run into Emily and her family. He didn't want to see her in this context but what was he to do? He had a job now. He had a house in the township. He was aware how clouded things were between Parks and the cattlemen and he knew now it was best to leave things well alone with a cattleman's daughter. But still he longed to see her. Just one glimpse.

'There they go now,' said Darren, pointing to the helicopters lifting up from the valley floor. 'Leaving just in time to meet their broadcast deadlines. Looks like you won't get your mug on telly after all, Kelvin.' Darren glanced at Kelvin in the rear-vision mirror, smiling. Luke could tell Kelvin was disappointed.

'There'll probably be newspaper journalists travelling with the cattlemen,' Kelvin said. 'But only I'm to give the statement, okay?'

'Right you are,' said Darren, winking at Cory.

Kelvin checked his watch.

'With the choppers gone, now's the time to find the cattlemen's camp and get a count on the cattle.' He swung about to see if the police four-wheel drive was close behind them. 'Thank God we've got the Bairnsdale boys to back us up if things turn nasty.'

Nasty? Luke wondered. He had seen the worst of the

cattlemen, Bob Flanaghan. Angry and rude though he was, Luke didn't think Bob would be violent. Still, Kelvin had been at this job for decades. Perhaps he had seen nasty.

As they drove into the Wonnangatta, Luke was shocked to see the level of flammable vegetation that covered thousands of acres. He'd heard the Parks boys recounting their journey in bringing a slasher over the goat tracks and for an instant he wondered why they hadn't burned or grazed the area. It would be much cheaper and faster. He saw the weeds and alarm bells began to ring in his head. The place was a shambles.

As they lumped their way over the valley, they saw smoke drifting up lazily from an afternoon campfire. Heading towards it, they found the bulk of the cattlemen camped over by a river bend on a large bare area of ground.

'No sign of the cattle,' Kelvin said, scanning the scene. 'Looks as if they want to play funny buggers with us and they've hidden them.'

There was no sign of Emily either, thought Luke, as he surveyed the campers and scanned the horses for a sight of his young gelding.

'Stick around while the cattlemen are interviewed by the police, then you'll have to go and look for the cattle. If we can't locate them, we can't fine them.' Kelvin sighed and shook his head, his bearded jaw clenching. 'Ignorant mongrels. Now remember, boys, be professional at all times. Say as little as possible to them.'

Luke noticed that the cattlemen barely glanced up from what they were doing. Some men boiled billies, others sat around the fire drinking tea or beer. Some of the women, hot from a day in the saddle, were towel drying their river-wet hair after a swim. They didn't look like a bunch of protesters. More like people comfortable with each other, and the land.

Rod Flanaghan stepped forward. 'Afternoon, gentlemen.'

A young policeman tipped back his hat and nodded, while the older rotund sergeant with a clipboard returned Rod's greeting. Luke stood in his khaki cluster of colleagues and listened.

'We have reason to believe you have cattle on a designated VPP area,' the sergeant said. 'This is an illegal offence and such an action would constitute a fine of $1000 per head for the owner.'

'You have to find the cattle before you can fine us,' Bob said. Rod cast him a glance to silence him.

'Don't play smart with me,' said the sergeant. 'We know there are cattle here. Who owns the cattle and how many are there?'

'If there are cattle, they'd be owned by each and every person here. And if you want to find out how many, I suggest you count them yourself,' said the Cattlemen's Association president, who stood next to Rod.

'How many cattle are here?' the sergeant asked again, while Kelvin Grimsley gave an audible huff of disgust.

'I think you'll find the ear mark is different on each hypothetical beast and if you want the owners of the hypothetical cattle, you'll have to take the names and addresses of everyone at this camp,' the president said.

The policeman nodded and handed his clipboard to the president.

'I want all the names and addresses listed. If cattle *are* found in the park, each person will be charged accordingly.'

'Certainly, sir,' said the president.

In silence, each man, woman and child wrote their name willingly on the paper. The Parks men looked on. Luke could feel their nerves settling now they could see the group weren't interested in conflict.

Luke wondered how many dollars and man-hours had been spent on trying to calm this storm in a teacup? Wouldn't government money and energy have been better spent on the land itself?

Hidden in the trees, Emily and Rousie kept watch on the cattle. Next to her Bonus was dozing, his head dropped, lip hanging, back foot hooked upright, Emily holding onto his reins while she listened out for vehicles or voices. Not far away, Flo was keeping watch, gazing out over the ti-tree to the river flats below.

The plan was to keep the cattle out of the rangers' sight until morning. On dark, they'd find a flat spot and run some solar-electric tape round the cattle to keep them contained overnight, but for the time being they'd keep them on the move. Tomorrow, at dawn, they would drive the cattle up the steep bridle track to the east of the valley and onto the edge of the Park to a logging road, where portable yards and a semitrailer would be waiting to cart the cattle back to their respective owners.

'Rawhide one, are you on channel?' came a familiar voice.

Sam? Sam! Emily couldn't believe it. He'd been adamant that he was staying home. She was thrilled to hear his voice. Finally he was stepping back into their cattlemen's world. At last she was getting her funny old brother back.

'Copy. This is Rawhide one. Is that Cowpoke two?'

'Yes! This is Cowpoke two. Papa Bull has given me your location and me and Curvy Cow are bringing you some sustenance.' Before his voice was cut off on the radio Emily overheard a slapping sound and an 'Ouch!' from Sam.

She knew Papa Bull was Rod, but who was *Curvy Cow*? What was Sam on about?

Within a few minutes Emily heard Sam's ridiculous bird call from the hillside above.

'Ki-ki-ki-ki-kick-off-the-cows! Kick-off-the-cows! Ki! Ki! Kiiiii!'

Emily repeated the call, laughing. Up until now, she had felt tense, worried that she might be the one caught red-handed with the cattle, even though feisty Flo was there to dress down the authorities if need be. But now it was beginning to feel like fun.

Emily squealed when she saw Sam coming towards her with Bridie in tow, her face lighting up at the sight of her friend. 'Curvy Cow! What are you doing here?'

'We're the inside intelligence,' Bridie said. 'Dargo was all but dead after you guys rode out of town. So Sam and I raided the black and brown in the make-up box and went commando, black beanies and all. We staked out VPP headquarters and found out what they were up to. We couldn't leave you down here like sitting ducks.'

Sam and Bridie high-fived, their eyes shining.

'But you two hate each other.'

'Internal feuding ceases when external foe approach,' Sam said.

'Yeah, whatever,' said Bridie. 'He still annoys the crap out of me.'

'You love me,' Sam said, digging a finger in her ribs.

'Piss off!' she said. 'Don't touch the fat.'

'She loves me,' he said again to Emily just as Bridie gave him a good shove, sending him sprawling down the hill.

Sam stood up and brushed himself off.

'The police are listening in on the radio so we're to use it only for emergencies. They've taken everyone's names and it's yet to be seen if they'll collectively arrest us or just fine us. The police and Parkies are now out looking for the cattle. Both went to the north and south ends of the valley, not in this direction. One of them even got bogged in a creek crossing and the Mansfield mob had to winch 'em out! It was a classic.'

'Yeah?' said Emily, hoping like crazy it wasn't Luke who had bogged the vehicle but thinking he was too farm-boy for that.

As Sam talked, Bridie unpacked a thermos and some food from a backpack. Emily let out a low whistle and Flo, who had failed as a sentry, shook herself awake, clearly surprised to see Sam and Bridie. She began to make her way over.

'Is new ranger boy there?' Emily asked casually.

Sam shrugged. 'Couldn't tell you. Bridie and I kept the

vehicle in the trees on the south side and walked our way up the creek. I haven't laid eyes on them. Just seen their vehicles. Why does it matter?'

'Oh,' Emily said, squinting, 'it just feels a bit rich. You know, taking the fella's horse on trial, then using it to bring cattle through his National Park his first week on the job.'

'He'll get over it,' Bridie said.

'I s'pose he will,' Emily said.

Once they'd eaten and tossed the scraps to Rousie and Useless, Sam stood and stretched.

'Okay, Rawhide one, we'll go back to base camp. Are you right here for another hour? Then we'll send up a relief party.'

'Can Curvy Cow stay with me?'

'Why not? We'll send Hilarious Heifer back to Papa Bull and she can have more of a nanna nap in her swag.'

'Who are you calling Hilarious Heifer?' Flo said gruffly, but with a twinkle in her blue eyes.

And with that, Flo, Useless and Sam walked away up the steep bush-covered hill. The cattle were beginning to stir, wanting to browse the bush around them.

'We'd best mount up and keep them together,' Emily said. She helped Bridie onto Flo's horse, and went to block the lead cows, which were starting to take the herd towards the long grasses of the river flats.

Bridie tilted her head. 'Is that a vehicle I can hear?'

Emily paused, her ears straining for sound. Yes! She could hear an engine far off in the trees below. Then she caught glimpses of a ute winding its way towards them.

'Let's push 'em up higher.'

Emily sent Rousie scooting around the herd and began forcing the cattle directly uphill.

Ten minutes later, Emily paused for a breather, the cattle, too, stopping on a ledge on the hillside. One cow bellowed.

'Shush!' Emily said. She called to Bridie, 'I think we've lost them.'

Then, to her horror, she looked up and saw Luke standing above her on the mountainside. He had his hands on his hips and was decked out in the khaki of his Parks uniform. He wore shorts and sturdy walking boots and Emily noted his legs were muscular and tanned. His arms were strong and delicious in his short-sleeved shirt. For days she'd wanted to see him. For days she'd longed to know if the spark she felt for him was reciprocated. But now, at this very moment, he was the *last* person she wanted to see. He had caught them red-handed with the cattle.

Emily urged the gelding up the steep pinch towards Luke. As she neared, she could see Luke's chest rising and falling and the sweat on his brow from his fast walk up the hillside in their pursuit. Emily couldn't help thinking he looked so gorgeous in his uniform.

She, too, was sheened in sweat, her checked shirt tied about her waist, the straps of her red gingham bra showing on each sun-tanned shoulder under her red Bonds singlet. As she slid from her horse to stand before him, their eyes locked together. Emily waited for his anger.

Instead, in an instant, Luke bent towards her, kissing her.

She tasted the sweet salt on his lips and savoured his strong body pressed against hers. At last, she thought! She cupped his face in her hands and closed her eyes, not wanting this dream to stop. Her hands slid down his neck and broad, hot shoulders, then the curve of his long, strong back. His hands glided deliciously over her body as he kissed her again and again. She pulled back from him for a moment and they looked deep into each other's eyes. Both laughed at the ridiculousness of the situation, and kissed again, only this time it was softer, more tender.

'Um, excuse me,' came a small voice. Bridie was sitting on Flo's horse down the slope with the cattle staring up at them, 'can you arrest me like that too?'

They laughed and then Emily and Luke were kissing again.

'I'll just be here,' Bridie called. 'Don't mind me. I'll keep an eye on the cattle. But I must say, that is one thorough frisk job you're doing, Mr Ranger!'

Smiling, Luke took the reins from Emily and hitched the gelding to a fallen log. Then he took Emily's hand and led her gently to the base of a giant granddaddy tree. Its great grey base was ringed with soft green moss sending a delicious pungent scent into the still hot air. Her back, as she leant on the solid trunk, felt cool, while Luke's body pressed against her felt hot. She closed her eyes as they kissed and ran her hands under his ranger's shirt and felt the smooth warm skin beneath, the trail of hair that led down his belly, the firmness of his horseman's waist.

'What are we doing?' Luke breathed.

'I don't know,' Emily said, stunned by the intensity of their passion.

'They'll be up here soon. The other rangers.' He kissed her again. 'I'll find you,' he said breathlessly. 'Tonight. I'll find you.'

Luke pressed his lips to hers a final time and then was gone, loping down the mountain. Leaping logs, swinging round tree trunks, looking in every way like he belonged here in the bush.

Emily stood at the top of the hill watching him go. Bridie, below, glanced up at her.

'What was *that*?' she said. 'Tarzan?'

'I don't know, but I ain't no Jane.'

'Was it bush tucker man?'

'I don't know.'

'Was it the croc hunter?'

'I don't know! All I *do* know is that was out of this world and weird – and wonderful.'

Twenty-four

Still breathless from Luke's kisses, Emily stood beside her horse as the police took their names and details. A group of cattlemen gathered. It all seemed so serious and stupid, Emily thought. She bit her lip to stop a smile.

She glanced over at the rangers. They were scribbling notes on the incident and talking with each other, all except for Luke. He was leaning on a tree, head bowed, arms and ankles crossed. He was looking down at the ground, but she could feel his presence like a burning white heat. When he glanced up and caught her eye, Emily's heart skipped a beat. She was utterly hooked on him. For a fleeting moment his face conveyed his secret attraction to Emily. But he looked to the ground again, trying to settle his face into a mask of passivity.

Emily felt a twinge of annoyance. Had he said something about the Park, she wondered? Surely he could see with his farmboy eyes that fining the cattlemen would be a bureaucratic joke. It should be the government being fined, Emily thought.

From beneath her hat she'd looked down to the scuffed toes of her boots as if she were the criminal. Now she felt the earth pulse. The life of the soil. This was what was driving her. This land. She decided to do as Evie had suggested and hold true to her promise to protect it.

She raised her head to gaze, not defiantly, but gently at the policeman with her large dark eyes. She summoned the energy of the earth that thrummed beneath her and, just as Evie had taught her and the girls, imagined a powerful beam of light pouring into her from the heavens, streaming right to the core of her being. Suddenly she felt strong and powerful in the calmest, most gentle way. It was like those moments when she had hovered over the treetops in that strange but surprisingly normal-feeling limbo between physical life and spiritual eternity.

'It's simple science,' Evie had once said. 'We are all simply energy, and our thoughts and emotions control the vibrations of our energy. It's just we have forgotten this fact.'

The policeman faltered as he read Emily her rights. In his job, he had developed a steely facade, but Emily, like a tiny flower pushing through concrete, had made it through his armour. He stopped speaking, shut his clipboard, and steered her away from the group.

'Look,' he whispered, leaning in close, 'we're just doing our jobs. And they're just doing their jobs.' He indicated the Parks rangers with a flick of his head. 'There's no way known the government would be stupid enough to proceed with charges against you. It would be a media circus and politically disastrous. So don't worry, okay? This is just for show. Just procedure. You'll be fine.'

Emily nodded. 'Thank you.'

The policeman shrugged. 'I know you're good people.' He cleared his throat. 'I know you're doing this for love, not trouble. I just have to do my job, that's all.'

Emily watched as the men climbed into their vehicles. Luke glanced up briefly and gave her an uncertain smile. From beneath the brim of her hat she had half smiled back, hoping no one else had seen. For a moment she felt as if she was Juliet, and Luke her Romeo. Then she told herself to get a grip. Starting something with that man was like playing with fire.

As the sun sank beneath the giant mountain and illuminated the hills, the cattlemen's campfire was cranked up so that flames danced wildly and sparks flew. Beers were cracked and platters of biscuits and cheese passed about. On another more sedate fire, bush stew was cooking in a giant black pot, and there was damper wrapped in shiny foil in the ashes.

Emily swigged on a stubby, laughing at the cattlemen's tall tales. There was an element of bravado about the people around the fire, but Emily felt sadness in each of them that they had been driven to such measures. None of them was a law breaker by nature.

The sound of laughter and squealing came from the nearby riverbank, and from a small track in the trees Bridie and Sam emerged in the half-dark. They were dripping wet and chasing each other. They made their way to the campfire and Bridie crouched down beside Emily, breathless. Her eyes were shining and her hair, normally styled and straightened to within an inch of its life, tumbled down in long blonde ringlets. She wore wet boardshorts and a bright-pink singlet, with an aqua bikini top underneath, curvaceous and gorgeous in the heat of the evening. She leaned closer and whispered to Emily, 'Sam just tried to kiss me! Down at the river.'

'And?'

'I told him he couldn't.'

'Why?'

'Because I'd just eaten tuna and spring onions.'

Emily laughed. 'Why would you go and do a thing like that?'

'Because I'm trying to lose weight and the chops have been really fatty.'

'No,' Emily whispered back. 'I mean, why didn't you let him kiss you?'

Bridie looked down at her body. 'Because, look at me. He's come from that rock-star world of glamour girls who are stick thin and gorgeous.' She grabbed a handful of flesh on her hip. 'As if he'd really be serious about a fatty-boombah like me.'

Emily reached for her hand. 'Oh, Bridie. You're gorgeous. Men love curves. You've been reading too many magazines. There's no way those skinny girls can come near you once you unleash that wit of yours – not to mention those boobs. Any man would be hooked. Even country music stars.'

'Yeah? You think so? You think I should kiss him?'

Emily grinned. 'Well, maybe after you've cleaned your teeth.'

In that moment, Sam ambled into the firelight holding his guitar.

'Who wants to hear a tune?'

The campers cheered, Emily the loudest. It had been years since the cattlemen had been treated to Sam's singing in this informal way. He'd been too busy with the bigtime. But now here he was, Rod Flanaghan's son, home from Nashville with a dinner-plate belt buckle and fancy guitar, ready to play again. Her brother *was back*.

Emily shifted up on the log as her father came over to the campfire and sat next to her, pride and love for his son on his face. Emily knew all their family love and the teachings of Evie had helped Sam in some way, but Emily could now see a new energy in him – he was falling in love. Sam strummed a few powerful notes and began to tune his Maton with a couple of twanging plucks of the strings. Then his fingertips hit the worn wooden face of the guitar and drummed a lively lead-in beat.

'A one, two, a one two three four . . .'

And he was away, Sam Flanaghan singing again. It was a new song, a song Emily had never heard before, but she was pretty sure she knew where Sam had discovered his muse.

'Peachy bottom! Honeyed hair! You get about like you just don't care,' he sang. 'When I see you sittin' over there, you make me wanna be your chair! Ouch, I love it when you treat me mean. Hottest lovin' mama come and sit on me!'

The campers let out a 'woo-hoo' at his funny but funky song, spurring Sam onto another verse. Emily laughed while others clapped and danced, some joining Sam in singing the chorus, Bridie with a smile like the sun.

They grooved for two hours, Sam fronting a solo concert in the middle of nowhere. He made their eyes shine in the firelight and their hearts sing. Emily knew the joy and togetherness they felt that night was founded on generations of such nights shared beneath the stars. Friendship, food, music, bawdy jokes, a campfire and a love of the land, these were the constants, no matter what the day, the year, the era. Eventually the tired campers took themselves off to bed, covered in dust, spilled beer, tomato sauce and rum, but all with the warmth of community in their hearts. Emily was the last to kick the straying, smoking logs into the fire. Reluctantly she took herself off to her swag, the longing for Luke heavy on her mind.

As Emily lay in the tent, she could hear the crack and tick of the bush about her. Her sunburnt shoulders were radiating gentle heat and she could feel her body sweating beneath her singlet and cotton boxers. She sighed. It had been such a big day, but her mind kept going back to that meeting, those kisses on the hillside with Luke. It just didn't make sense. His words ran round and round in her head: 'I'll find you.'

As if, she thought, rolling over angrily. He'd be tucked up in a rangers camp somewhere with his boss sleeping just metres away. She shut her eyes and counted, but still sleep wouldn't come. Instead of tossing and turning, she dragged her swag out and pulled on her boots. She needed to cool off by the river and have some space to think. Rousie stirred at the entrance of the tent, stretched and made a comical noise.

'Shush you,' Emily said.

Outside, the night was exceptionally still and there was a sliver of moon in the sky. There was just enough light for Emily to see the lumps of swags scattered about in the campground. Some slept in tents, others on the ground. No need to be huddled near the fire on a night like this. A little way off she could make out the paler-coloured horses as they dozed on nightlines amidst the trees. She could see Bonus's gleaming white socks.

She and Rousie made their way downstream to a grassy spot that jutted out in the river bend – perfect for a cool sleep beside the water. She thought the mozzies might bother her but was beyond caring. She lay for a time, looking up at the gap in the gums to the stars beyond.

The river tinkled quietly over rocks in a soothing sound. Emily called Rousie to her side and pulled the tarp over her head. For a short time she lay in the silence. Then she heard Rousie's low growl, and a sharp bark. Flipping the swag open, she propped herself on her elbows and looked around, holding tight to Rousie's collar as he barked. In the shadows stood a man.

'Emily?'

'Luke!' she said, happiness flooding through her. 'How did you find me?'

'I said I would.'

He stepped out of the shadows and came to kneel before her. But his handsome face was set like stone.

She frowned, her body suddenly tense. 'What's wrong?'

He paused. A deep frown slashed between his brows.

'I came to tell you the Bill's been voted through parliament. You've been banned from your cattle runs.'

Emily felt the impact of the news like a blow. An awful silence followed. Luke desperately tried to fill in the gaps.

'They got word through on the sat-phone tonight. Emily, I'm sorry. I'm *so* sorry.'

Around her the night-bush murmured and beside her the river tumbled by. Far from here, in the plush carpeted rooms of Parliament House, a group of men and women in suits had just altered Emily Flanaghan's life, and reset her daughters' futures forever, with one stroke of a pen.

Were they really losing their cattle runs? Emily's eyes closed. After all that had happened. After finally coming home to the mountains. Her whole body shook as Luke drew her into his arms. Stroking her hair, he held her close as her tears soaked into his blue singlet. She could smell him, all clean from a river swim. Then he was kissing her tears away, and despite her grief, desire flowed through her and she began to kiss him back. She sought comfort in the warmth of Luke's kiss, the wetness of his mouth. She wanted to forget everything: the bans, the loss of her land, the empty, uncertain future. She just wanted to lose herself in him, there beside the river. They began to peel away each other's clothing and she felt the warm night air on her naked breasts.

She moaned when his bare chest pressed against hers and she began to cry again. He made a gentle sound to soothe her, then lifted her chin and kissed her softly, until the passion was rekindled. They began to kiss harder. Her breath in flutters,

Emily slid her fingers to Luke's belt buckle, undoing it, then releasing the button of his jeans. All the while they kissed and kissed as the river slid by.

Luke kicked off his jeans and pulled Emily's shorts down over her strong, firm legs. They lay naked, pressed together, hands roving all over each other's bodies. Desire coming as quickened breath. Luke gently pushed Emily's hair from her face as he kissed her on her forehead, behind her ears, over her shoulders and her breasts. He pulled her beneath him and looked deep into her eyes, hesitating.

'Don't stop,' Emily pleaded.

As he pushed into her, Emily cast her head back, wanting this, wanting him more than anything.

He moaned as he felt her warmth and murmured, 'You're so beautiful, Emily.'

Emily ran her hands along Luke's back and reached for his firm backside. She pulled him into her, deeper and then deeper still, breathing in the smell of him, pressing her face into the soft hollow of his neck. She was carried on the crest of a wave of desire as they moved as one, faster and faster, and she clenched her teeth as she felt herself coming, stifling her scream. What they were doing felt illicit, like an affair. A betrayal to her clan. Luke, too, held his cry inwards as he came. They were each fraternising with the enemy. It was exciting. It was scary. It was confusing. But, Emily thought, as Luke gently kissed her gently over her face, it was also beautiful.

She didn't want to think of what lay ahead. She just wanted to preserve this moment for all time. She lay in Luke's arms, not speaking, gazing deep into his eyes in the faint moonlight as his fingertips drifted over her skin. Eventually, still wrapped tight in each other's arms, they fell asleep.

In the depth of darkness just before the dawn, the sound of screaming woke them. It wasn't a human scream but something more guttural, like a terrified horse. Luke and Emily sat bolt upright. There was no sign of Rousie. Emily panicked. She couldn't breathe, the terror keeping air from her lungs. It was as if her ribs had been crushed all over again. Upstream they could hear the deafening sound of horses thundering along the river stones at full gallop. The crack of hooves on rock was unmistakable.

'The horses!' Emily said. 'Something must've spooked them.'

The horrible scream came again, like a stallion roaring for his mares. A wind came howling towards them downstream along the tunnel of the riverbed, creating an awful moaning sound, like a man gone mad. The gust hit them with a cold fury and whipped the trees about, so that bark and grey fingerbone limbs were flung around them. Emily and Luke grabbed for their clothes, the sound of the horses' hooves bearing down on them getting louder and louder. If they didn't move fast, they would be trampled. They dressed as quickly as they could, scrambling up the bank and sprinting towards the campsite to wake the others.

But when they emerged from the thickets, trembling and gasping for air, they were met by stillness and silence. They looked about. No one stirred. The air was calm. The horses all dozed peacefully on the nightlines.

From the heart of the camp, Rousie came towards them, cowering as he walked, his tail jammed between his legs. He whined and whimpered and pressed his wet nose into Emily's palm, as if to apologise for leaving her side.

'What *was* that?' Luke asked in a whisper.

'I don't know. I mean, it was horses. Obviously. Galloping in the riverbed.'

'Are these all your horses?' he said, pointing to the cattlemen's mounts. Emily nodded. 'Surely they'd be going nuts by now. They must've been able to hear or smell the other horses.'

A little way off they could make out the white faces of the cattle, all camped quietly behind the tape of a white electric fence, many of them lying down and chewing cud.

'Were they brumbies, do you think?' Luke asked.

Emily shook her head.

'There aren't any brumbies in this area. Maybe over Mansfield way, but none here – certainly not a whole mob like that.' She reached out for Luke's hand. 'Luke, I'm scared.'

He pulled her to him and she pressed her face against his warm body.

'I know. It's pretty freaky.'

He began to stroke her hair. It gave her a little comfort, the memory of their lovemaking coming to her again. He pulled back from her.

'I'm so sorry, I'm going to have to go now. It's nearly dawn.'

'Yes,' Emily said, suddenly remembering their situation.

He reached down to kiss her quickly on the lips.

'I'll see you again?'

It was a question more than a statement and it sowed a tiny seed of doubt in Emily's heart. Then he was gone, jogging along the grassy flat towards the rangers' campsite at the homestead.

Emily sat in her tent, her knees hugged to her chest, feeling the swell of mixed emotion in her. Fear, passion, devastation. She waited for daylight, knowing she would have to deliver the news that parliament had voted to ban alpine grazing. She curled up in a ball, dragging a jumper over her shoulders, and began to doze.

Before long she was woken by noises outside the tent. Bacon and eggs sizzled, billies boiled, tea stewed and the clank and clatter of tent poles rang out as the campers packed up in the blue morning light. It was time to get droving and as saddle bags were stuffed with food, water bottles filled and buckets carried from the creek to the horses for a drink, Emily took comfort from the normality of the scene. She went to bash on the flimsy walls of Bridie's tent, pitched nearby.

'What?' came a deep voice within.

'Sam? What are you doing in there?'

'Got lost, didn't I,' he said.

'Only packed one tent,' came Bridie's voice.

'Bridie,' Emily said, 'get your bodacious arse out here! I *really* need to talk to you.'

'Okay,' said Bridie, 'I'm busting for a bush wee anyway.'

'Oh, noiyce,' said Sam. 'She's all class this bush chook.'

Emily heard a whack and then an 'ouch' from Sam.

'Don't smack me.'

'That's not what you said last night,' Bridie said.

'Oh *please*,' said Emily. 'This is serious.'

Bridie, dishevelled but glowing, finally emerged from the tent wearing a red satin nightie with black lace trim lining her over-ripe bosom.

'You brought *that* camping?' Emily said, momentarily distracted from the news she was about to tell.

Bridie looked down at herself. 'Worked, though, didn't it?'

The girls drew each other into a quick hug and laughed. Then concern flashed on Emily's face.

'What's wrong?' Bridie asked, pulling back.

Emily could barely say the words. Sam poked his head out of the tent, looking up at his sister.

'Luke came to find me last night,' she began, 'to tell me parliament's passed the Bill. It's now legislation that we can't graze cattle up on our runs.'

Sam disappeared into the tent and quickly dragged on his clothes. 'Well, they've finally gone and done it. After all these years.'

'I know. Can you believe it?' Emily said. 'All that time and effort, and for what?'

'Does Dad know?' Sam said. Emily shook her head, looking skyward. 'How do I explain how I found out? That I've been over in the Parkies' camp being sociable?'

Bridie shrugged. 'It doesn't matter it came from Luke.'

'Oh, I think now it might,' Emily said.

'I'll tell him,' Sam said. 'I'll go now. You girls get packed up. We've got to be out of here in an hour.'

Bridie and Emily set out towards the place where Emily and Luke had slept. The sun had still not risen far enough above the hill to touch the riverbank. Emily shivered as they walked through the trees.

'Last night . . .' she began. 'There's something else I have to tell you about.'

Bridie turned to look at her.

'Something really weird happened.' Emily told the story of the sound of galloping horses and the deafening roar and the wild wind. Bridie was about to make a joke, but when she saw Emily's frightened face and heard the way her voice trembled, she drew Emily into a hug.

'Some really weird things have been happening to me since my accident, Bridie. I've been seeing stuff. And hearing stuff. And my head, it's as if I don't think the same as I used to.'

'What kind of stuff do you see and hear?'

'You know. Things from the past. Weird things like the horses. But also people.'

'You mean, like, "I see dead people"?' Bridie whispered, taking off the line from the movie *The Sixth Sense*.

'Yeah. Kind of.'

'Oh, well,' said Bridie with false bravado, 'that's normal after such a big trauma. You know, your near-death thingy. You just need a bit of time.'

'I think I'm going mad.'

At that point they walked out through the ti-trees and there, lying open on the grass, was Emily's swag. She walked into the cold river water and waded upstream. There was no sign of hoof prints. No sign of limbs being torn down by the violent wind. She waded back downstream and looked at Bridie with a questioning expression.

'You must've just dreamed it, Em,' Bridie said gently.

'But,' Emily said frantically, 'Luke was here too. He heard it too!'

Bridie shivered. 'C'mon, darls. Let's have a quick wash and get back to the others. I'll fix you up so you'll look real flash on that beautiful horse of yours today. Despite what those city dickheads have done, today can be a celebration, the end of a beautiful era. Don't let them ruin your day or your life. See it as a positive. It's almost a relief that it's over. No more fighting. No more protests.'

As Emily dunked herself into the fresh, freezing water, she gasped. But her goosebumps weren't just from cold, they were also from fear. She wanted to feel exhilarated about being with Luke. But it was all so clouded now. Their new love had been overshadowed by their terrifying night, and the cold hard fact that she was now an evicted cattleman's daughter, and he, a park ranger. Emily splashed ice-cold river water over her face again and again, and tried, as best she could, to wash the memory of Luke and the night away.

PART THREE

Twenty-five

Gradually the days grew shorter on the Dargo High Plains and there came a chill in the evening air. Winter was approaching and it was time to move the cattle from the alpine runs and down to the lower slopes of the mountains. This time the job was weighted with sadness for Emily and her family, because it would be the last of their mustering and droving trips.

Emily stood up in the stirrups, dropping Snowgum's reins. 'Saaaaalt!' she called across the empty plain. 'Saaaalt!'

Sam repeated the cry from his bay brumby. Their voices reached out over the snowgrass clearing and through the twisted white branches of the trees. Flo and Rod joined in the cattlemen's cry.

Away in the bush, the cattle turned their heads and flicked their ears in the direction of the sound. As the calls came again, cows lowed gently to calves and tossed their heads as an indication to move, some mothers bunting their large babies impatiently. As the cries of 'salt' continued, the Herefords began to move faster through the bush, reaching a jog, crashing through the ti-tree and ducking under low-slung snowgum branches.

On the salting plain, Emily heard them coming. It was always so rewarding to see the healthy, round-bellied cows emerge from the snowgums.

On the grass at the cattle camp there were bare patches where the Flanaghans had laid salt piles in the summer season and the cattle had persistently licked at the salt until it was all gone. The soil up top was salt-deficient, so to keep the stock in good health and to make them quiet and obedient to their calls, salting was a regular practice for the cattlemen.

Emily normally loved salting in rain, hail or shine. But today she was wracked with sadness. This would be the last time they mustered this run, the last time the call of salt would ring out across the high plains. This land was now a 'park'.

She felt the presence of her forebears. They would've seen the same sights, conducted the same process, with gear not much different from her own, the salt wrapped in hessian sacks, rolled and tied to the front of the saddle.

Emily dismounted and began to unhitch the sack. The sack was heavy and damp from the early morning mist and her ribs twinged as she heaved it onto the ground. As she bent to tug at the hayband knot, water on the brim of her hat tipped out suddenly onto the ground. The weather had been coming in all morning. Alongside her father, she walked around the plain, tipping out little hillocks of the coarse salt.

The cattle were coming fast out of the bush, their calves gallivanting in little skips and letting out snorts of excitement.

They carried their tails up and skitted about in babyish fun.

As they reached the invisible bubble that was their flight zone, the cattle stopped abruptly, skidding to a halt and bumping into each other, to sniff at the air. Then the boldest, a big deep-red cow, thrust her head down and ambled forward, bursting the bubble, closing the flight zone in around the riders. She extended her tongue out to the salt, then shoved her nose right in so that white granules stuck to her moist pink nostrils. Other cows came forward too, tossing their heads at Rousie, who lay panting not far off, the lure of the salt too great for the cattle to be much bothered by a dog.

Emily retied the bag and flipped it back over the saddle, while Flo counted the cows.

'Fifty-six. That's less than a third of 'em,' she said.

'Let's shut the gate on these and go see if we can find the rest down at Shepherd's Hut,' Rod said.

Emily legged Snowgum about and rode on beside her family, pulling her collar up and her hat down to the weather coming in from the east.

Since Wonnangatta, Luke had called her father's house several times, leaving messages. At first Emily had toyed with the idea of meeting him, but as the letters from the bureaucrats came in, notifying the Flanaghans of the revocation of their grazing licences, Emily felt that old anger simmering, even for Luke. After all, he was a VPP man. He was part of their eviction. He couldn't be a part of her clan. He may have made love to her by that river like he meant it, but hadn't he stood aside, mute, right when Emily needed him?

Flo came to ride beside her.

'You know we'll be out of range for the next two days once we get over this ridge. You'd better call the girls.'

Emily smiled at the thought of Tilly and Meg tucked up warm beside Evie's woodstove, happy in her calm aura and kind ways. Emily pulled out her phone from her oilskin pocket just as Flo added, 'And you'd better give that Luke a ring, too. Put the poor bastard out of his misery.'

Emily flashed a glance at Flo. Emily had left a cheque for the gelding for Luke at the store with a short note that gave him nothing at all. No clues to their future.

'You can catch us up,' Flo said, urging her horse away. 'Do the right thing, Emily,' she called.

Emily suddenly remembered what Evie had told her when she returned from the Wonnangatta, still stewing over her treatment there. Evie had said mildly, 'Carrying around the energy created by an argument with someone is like carrying around a great big bloody anvil in your pocket. It simply won't serve you. You're best to clean up the messes you make and get rid of those anvils!'

But as the winter approached, Emily still felt an anvil there. It was like she was dragging the idea of Luke with her everywhere she went, even though he was the last person on this earth she wanted to love. He was a ranger, sent to evict her from her runs. She had better end it. Flo was right. She had to call Luke, finish things properly before they'd even begun. No more carting anvils about. Not Luke's. Not Clancy's either.

She didn't have Luke's number in her phone, so with her

icy fingers she dialled a connection company and asked for the VPP's Dargo office. As she sat astride Snowgum in the misty rain, it took her a while to realise she'd been put through to head office in Melbourne. She sat listening to a slick advertising recording being played over and over on the other end of the VPP phone.

By the time Emily had been waiting fifteen minutes, she was seeing red. She knew she'd have to canter Snowgum hard down the steep and slippery track to catch her family, though she didn't want to push the mare. But she hung on the line, knowing she had to clear things with Luke. She listened to the over-cheerful advertisement selling passes to the 'great outdoors' as if the bush was just another commodity, like a six-burner gas barbecue or a new PlayStation.

'But I don't want to find out about kayaking or rock climbing or bloody fishing,' she muttered. 'I just want to talk to a human!'

Emily pictured herself carrying the heavy anvil with her. The vision stopped her from pressing the off button on her phone. Finally the crisp professional voice of a VPP staff member came on the line.

'Um,' Emily began uncertainly, 'I was after Luke Bradshaw at the Dargo branch.'

'I'm afraid I don't have that number. I only have the Heyfield headquarters. You'll have to call them out there,' the woman said from Melbourne.

Just the way she said 'out there' stirred Emily's blood. Surely, given the woman worked in an organisation whose job was to care for the land, she should not think of Dargo and Heyfield as 'out there', but as the very reason for her job.

'Perhaps you have his mobile number on a staff list?' Emily suggested.

'I'm sorry,' the woman said, not as an apology, but as a barrier. 'Under the Privacy Act we cannot disclose the mobile numbers of employees.'

Emily wasn't used to such officialese. She clenched her teeth. How could Luke have sold his soul to an organisation like this?

'Never mind. Thank you for your help,' Emily said. She tried to tell herself the woman was only doing her job.

Emily sat contemplating calling the branch at Heyfield, but she didn't want to leave a message. It would have to wait until after droving. Instead, she dialled Evie's house to tell the girls she missed them, and she'd see them in a couple of days for droving. She hung up and rode on.

On the lee side of the mountain the rain had stopped, but when gusts of wind shook the trees, big fat droplets spilled from their leaves onto Emily and Snowgum as they passed underneath. The horses' hoof marks ahead of her had cut grooves into the muddied track. Emily had to ride quickly to catch up but she also wanted to savour the landscape. Once the cattle were mustered, there would be no reason to ride this way again.

She squeezed Snowgum into a canter and called Rousie along with a whistle. He leapt over logs, ears pricked, and fell in behind Snowgum's hocks on the track to Shepherd's Hut.

Emily reined her horse from the four-wheel drive track onto a shortcut, a narrow footpath only the cattlemen, the cattle and the wombats knew. She rode past trees that had been blazed by men a hundred years before. Despite its remoteness, this place had once been alive with the sounds of people and their toil. They had laid whole hillsides bare with their mining and dug channels for miles to bring water to the crush. They had cut trees to stumps on the tops of hills to build shelters and yards and rough bush furniture. Many starved and perished when the mist or snow bamboozled them, but a few wily pioneers made it rich from the gold they found in the alluvial creekbeds and in the bellies of hillsides.

In those earlier days, the sound of axes had rung out across the still bush. Bullock drays, anchored steady by sawn logs, gingerly scuffed their way down precipitous slopes with heavy loads of mining equipment. The creekbeds and the hillsides had been alive with men. Some went mad with isolation, some with fleas and flies. Others, like the Flanaghans, had stayed and thrived. Now, though, this land was called a 'Park', to be locked up and preserved as pristine wilderness rather than used.

What did those shiny-bottomed city bureaucrats know of this land? No Parks ranger had ever been on this track, Emily thought angrily. She knew it would only be a few seasons before tracks like these became impassable. Without regular traffic and a day out with the chainsaw clearing the way now and then, the secret places, like the fairy dens near hidden springs, would no longer be found. They wouldn't even survive. The gentle filtered sunlight would be blocked by the overgrowth of robust grasses and weeds. The mid-story dogwoods and wattles would grow and smother the open grassy areas. And as more and more snowgum bows fell from the weight of snow on Park land, and the bans on gathering firewood and burning were enforced, the land would become choked with fallen limbs. That limbs dropped in winter was the natural way, but the government policy to put out the fires from electrical storms wasn't natural.

Every year, as Rod, Emily and Flo travelled down with heavy backpacks to spray weeds, they commented on the fire policy, and all of them predicted an inferno, if not this coming summer, then the next. They could plainly see the disaster looming. A fire hotter than nature intended. A fire that would utterly destroy, not one that would breathe new life to the seeds of gums, so that the land grew fresh from saplings and wildflowers.

Emily shut her eyes momentarily as she rode, feeling Snowgum's steady rock beneath her. She'd read the accusations in the papers that it was the cattlemen and their cattle who had brought the weeds here, and who perpetuated them. It was so easy to point the finger and accuse with such ignorance. She reached out and pushed away against the firm trunk of a tree so she did not collect her knee on it. The tree felt cool and strong. She sensed the energy at its heart and in her mind she said farewell to it. Those men in the city were locking her out from all this.

Then, like a ray of sunshine through the tree canopy, she remembered Evie's words.

'If you focus on the bad things in your life, you'll get more of the bad. You reap what you sow in your thoughts and actions.'

Emily suddenly realised she was being negative again. Her whole family was. Maybe they had spent so long focusing on the bad, on the bureaucrats, they had in some way created this situation themselves? Maybe it was time to start thinking differently.

As Emily and her silver-grey mare slipped down a steep bank, the vegetation began to alter beautifully from snowgums to groves of woolly butts. Soon they were trotting across a green meadow towards a small hut. The hut, named Shepherd's, had been built by her great-great-grandfather and was now shared by rangers, shooters, bikers and four-wheel drivers. This time of year there was nobody about, and there wouldn't be until summer came again.

She could see smoke curling up from a campfire and her family sitting on sawn-off stumps watching the flames. The time to start the change was now, Emily resolved as she rode towards them.

'What took you? Sam's eaten your share of the jam sand-wiches,' said Rod.

'You bugger!'

Sam grinned at her.

'How'd you get on with your phone calls?' Flo asked.

'The girls are great. Happy as Larry.'

'And?'

Emily shook her head. 'And nothing. Couldn't get through to Dargo VPP.'

'Ahh,' was all Flo said.

As Emily dumped her saddlebag down she said, 'You know, I've been thinking —'

'Thought I could smell rubber burning,' Sam said.

She gave him a shove so he almost fell off his log, then sat down next to him. Rod handed her a pannikin of tea and she wrapped her hands around it and blew at the steam.

'We're all moping around as if this is the last drove ever,' said Emily. 'I say, let's choose to enjoy this trip and not see it as an ending. Let's see it as a beginning.'

'What are you talking about?' Flo said.

'Never say never.'

'Isn't it never say die?' said Sam.

'Whatever!' Emily said, laughing. 'But maybe, just maybe, if we all start to think positively, act positively, and begin to live like we know that they'll ask the cattle back here to help manage the runs, it might just happen.'

'You reckon?' Rod said, shaking his head.

'I know it sounds like it's done and dusted,' Emily said, leaning forward, 'but once the grazing stops and the snowgrass and scrub get away, eventually there'll be a fire here too hot for the land to handle, then the soil erosion will come, then the river pollution, then the weeds will run rife. Now, I know none of us *wants* that to happen to our land, but we all know that a huge fire is on the cards. How can a Parkie on a budget look after all this? One day, they'll have to ask us back to help.'

'Ha!' said Flo. 'In your dreams.'

'They'll even pay us for it.'

'You reckon?' Flo added sceptically.

'Yes! If we start putting out positive energy, thoughts, words, actions, it'll come back that way. We reap what we sow.'

'She's got in your head,' Sam said.

'Who?'

'Those words you're saying. They're not yours, they're Evie's. She's talked you into thinking you can do anything. Be anyone. But look at you. Look at us. We've lost.'

'No, we haven't,' Emily said, turning to him. 'Do we look like people who have lost? We've got our health, each other, our animals. We might not have *all* our land but we still have some, and isn't this the best life in the world? We can still continue to have it this way.'

'There's just one thing you're forgetting, Emily,' Rod said. 'Income. Now the bans are in, you know as well as I do that we'll have to sell two-thirds of this herd. How can we all survive financially on that?'

She tossed more sticks on the fire. 'There's still Bob's land. He might somehow help us?'

'And pigs might fly,' muttered Flo.

'And there's Sam. If you get out there again with your music, you'll have the media at your fingertips. We could use that as a positive way forward. Not pushing an anti-government line, but a pro-environment one.'

Sam frowned. 'I know what you're saying but isn't it too late? They've kicked the cattle off.'

Emily knew Sam didn't want to cloud his music, his one joy, with all the negativity that had come with being a cattleman, but surely, if they took it from a new angle, and gave the public their side of the story in music, things might turn around.

'I'm not saying continue on with the same old fight. I'm saying continue on, but this time light the way for people.'

'Praise the Lord, hallelujah!' Sam said in a Nashville accent. 'You ought to go on one of them big American happy-clappy religious TV shows. You'd be rolling in greenbacks the way you're talking!'

'Sam,' said Rod, toning him down, 'Emily's right. It's all about finding the positive spin, and I guess when you're in the middle of something you tend to lose sight of the good stuff. I was like that for a long time after your mother died.'

Sam and Emily looked at their father's lined face in shock. He *never* talked about their mother. They sat in silence. He went on.

'Then I started to see the blessings she'd left behind. In you.' His blue eyes fell on Emily and then on Sam.

'It was actually at this hut, the first time you'd both come mustering on an overnighter. Remember? Your first night out here?'

Emily and Sam nodded. How could they forget? They'd ridden their ponies for hours on end, too excited to complain of cramps, rubbed calves from the stirrup leathers or freezing hands. Exhilarated to know they would be sleeping in a hut tucked away in the hollow of a massive mountain. Emily tried to recall how old she had been. Sam was at least five so she must have been almost seven. Her father had been swamped by a black cloud of grief before that time, until something in his mind lifted and cleared, like fog on a moonlit night.

'It was that night,' he said, 'around this campfire, with you sleeping in your little bed rolls and your ponies tethered to that very same tree over there, that I realised Susie was still here with us. I realised it was up to me to see the good, not the bad. That's when I knew I could keep going, no matter what.'

He tossed the remains of his tea into the fire. The family sat in silence, save for the hiss of the tea fizzing on the hot stones of the campfire.

Emily flung off her hat and moved over to hug her father. Flo smeared a tear over her cheek and patted Rod on his leg.

'Geez,' she said. 'Will you look at us? Talk about *Days of Our Lives* on the Dargo High Plains.'

Emily laughed, feeling the moment slide into history. But it lingered with them all. It was an ending, but it was also a new beginning.

Twenty-six

Two days later on top of the Dargo High Plains, in the blue hue of pre-dawn, Emily dropped the rails of the old chock and log yard to let the cattle out. They were beginning the last drove on the steep winding road that fell southward to Dargo. Rousie at the lead steadied the cattle as they made a rush for the long roadside grasses. They knew it was home time and were keen to begin their walk to the warmer climes on the lowlands. They set off at a cracking pace and Rousie, along with Sam on his brumby, worked hard to hold them up and get their heads down to settle them.

There were three hundred head of cattle, with a further two hundred and fifty of Bob's to collect from a holding yard on a lower ridgeline of the cattle run. Flo had the cattle in hand for Bob, who had rung to say he wouldn't be there for the muster, nor the drove. The family had taken the news with a collective roll of the eyes. It was typical Bob.

Once the herd was settled, Rod called out from his horse,

'Sam and Flo, you take the front. Em and I will take the back.'

'As long as we can swap,' Sam said. 'Flo will want to yak all the time and I need to compose a few songs.'

'You're here for droving not composing,' Flo said.

'And you're here for droving not yakking,' Sam said.

'You cheeky little sod!'

'We're all supposed to be in Emily's positive happy-land. Remember?' Sam teased.

The family tactic of thinking positive had started out as a joke but it had kept them buoyant during the muster as they'd gathered and yarded the cattle across the mountainside.

'Fine,' said Flo crossly.

'Fine,' said Sam, but each had a smirk on their face as they rode away to the lead of the mob. Useless watched his mistress go, then snuck into the back of the horsefloat near the yards, in the hope of snoozing there for the day. Soon, though, Flo's deep voice bellowed out, '*Useless*!'

'Wish them luck,' Emily said with a grin to her father.

'Same every time, isn't it? Sam and Flo pretending to fight, but loving every minute of each other.'

But it wasn't going to be the same any more, for any of them, Emily thought again with a jolt. Rod and Flo still owned one hundred acres of private land surrounding the homestead on the plains, but the loss of the government licence spelt the end of their cattle enterprise up here. A small number of cows could be trucked up next summer, but it really wasn't a viable proposition.

Bob, as the owner of three hundred acres of private alpine land, was the only family member who could still make a living from the plains. Despite her efforts to keep her thoughts positive, Emily still found it a crime that Bob should be left with land, when he didn't look after it. Yet her father and aunt, who managed land with respect and love, had been evicted.

Emily looked at the red hindquarters of the healthy cows and their calves as they moved along the gravel road, the tops of their tails sporting little fat rolls from spending months on the lush summer alpine pastures. Emily loved following a herd, getting to know each and every beast at the tail end. The one that would turn and argue with a dog, the old girl that would try to sneak off in the bush for a pick of green, the slow ones, the lazy ones, the stroppy ones who bunted others. They were all individuals and she loved each one of them. Collectively, cattle were peaceful, obliging and curious creatures.

Now most of them would have to be sold. The sorrow rose in her again when she thought of the letter Rod and Flo had received from the government, declaring they were entitled to compensation. They just didn't get it! No amount of money could compensate for the loss of their cows.

These cows were special, for they held the memory of droving days past. They weren't so much 'trained' for the road, but instead had shared the journey with the humans and the dogs over the years. Their memory of each curve, each climb, where to rest and where to drink would be lost too.

With her emotions swinging again from joy to despair, Emily was suddenly grateful her dad was here to ride with her on this last stretch, along with Sam and Flo, and soon her daughters on their ponies. Her family steadied her, made her feel calm within the storm of her life. Her family and Evie.

She knew Evie would be at the high-plains house packing the back-up vehicle for the day, while the girls got an extra sleep-in. There was no sense in getting them up at the crack of dawn on the first day of the week-long drove. Evie, with the girls, would act as a pilot vehicle, bringing the riders drinks and ferrying them to pick-up utes at the end of the day and helping to set up camp.

'You happy riding up the back with me?' Rod asked Emily now. She nodded. She wanted the distraction of the cows and her dad's conversation, rather than the isolated job of riding in the lead where she knew she would mull over the situation with Luke. She also didn't want to think anymore about the cattle bans. All those anvils she was carrying. It was a wonder Snowgum wasn't buckling at the knees from the weight.

Droving was a lengthy, slow business. It sounded romantic, but the reality was droving could be a challenge mentally when the weather was rough. Emily had endured days where the cows began tonguing from heat or were frisky from cold, or they battled howling winds so wild it was hard to keep them mobbed. This morning, though, the weather was mild and the cows content to walk along.

She dismounted and led Snowgum for a time, checking her wounds, worried the mare would not be up for the entire trip. There were spare horses, but Emily liked to travel the road with old Snowgum. She was an easy-natured creature who enjoyed the work, flicking her ears forward, looking about the bush, occasionally hunting in Emily's pockets for an apple. Other horses on droving days were not so obliging, wearing sour faces the whole way with ears pulled back, or baring their big, horsey teeth to bite at the rumps of slow-moving cows. Other horses jig-jogged or pulled when they were fresh. But Snowgum was made for the road.

Hours later, as the sun was getting low, the Flanaghan drovers made it to the Twelve-Mile yards, a cattle camp used for generations by the family. Sam, riding ahead, had already dropped the rails and the lead cows walked straight in.

With the sun gone, Emily's fingers felt like ice. Evie had already lit the fire outside the hut and Emily was looking forward to spreading her hands out before the dancing flames. She knew Tilly and Meg would be camping in the old hut with her tonight and she smiled happily at the thought.

As she unhitched Snowgum's girth she felt the mare flinch. Emily swore under her breath when she ducked her head to look at the old wounds from the race-day fall. The slight press of her fingertips made the mare stomp her foot and flick her tail, her ears pinned back in an uncharacteristic expression. Emily could see the proud flesh opening up again and bright blood freshly weeping from the wound.

'Flo,' she called out, 'come here.'

She indicated the mare's wound and Flo shook her head.

'Well, that's buggered that. Still, it was worth a try. I'll get Evie to run me back up to the plains and fetch me float and grab another from the mob. I'll see if I can radio her now and get her to bring some of her goop to put on Snow's wound.'

'I knew I shouldn't have tested her. I should've left her longer to heal.'

'Nah, she loves it, don't ya, girl?' Flo said, giving Snowgum a good scratch on the neck. 'Tell you what. I'll get your new gelding, if you like. Good chance to give him some work. We've got to put a positive spin on it, remember?'

Emily smiled sadly. She no longer wanted the gelding because he was a constant reminder of Luke, but she knew this was a good chance to train him as they went. Flo took Snowgum's reins from Emily. 'I'll see her right. You go get yourself warm.'

At dawn the next morning, Bonus stood as Emily dragged the girth tight. She lobbed into the saddle and soon they were tailing the mob, her belly full of Evie's hot breakfast and rich coffee.

'You travelling okay?' Emily asked her girls as she looked down from her new eager horse to Tilly and Meg, who were riding by her side on Jemma and Blossom.

Tilly beamed at her mum. 'Are you serious? *Yeah*!'

As the girls chatted happily to each other, Emily tipped her head back and let the swaying movement of the horse relax her. She gazed skyward to the azure blue that shone through the canopy of gumleaves. It was a glorious, gentle autumn day. Perfect for droving. Then she flopped forward, pressing her cheek to the gelding's neck. While she missed Snowgum's predictable calmness, Bonus was taking to the life of a drover's horse with ease.

By one o'clock, the cattle had reached Evie's house. Sam and Flo herded them into one of Evie's house paddocks for the time being, while Emily helped the girls hitch their ponies to a nearby shady tree. They were expecting Evie to come out and join them, but to their surprise it was Bob who appeared from the house and scuttled down a side path.

'What's he doing here? The sly old dog,' said Flo to Rod, then she called after him, 'You here to do your share of the work, eh, Bob?'

He didn't look up. As he rounded the side gate, he nearly ran smack into Emily, who was stooping to fill a bucket of water for the horses from the corrugated-iron tank.

'Bob!' Emily looked at his face and was shocked to see the strain on it. He'd been crying, the tears still fresh, his brow knitted in a frown, his mouth slanted sideways. Emily was stunned to see he was in agony. Emotional agony. He said nothing, brushed past her, fired up the engine of his ute and was gone.

'What's with him?' Flo said, arriving on the ground with a thud as she slid from her horse.

'I really don't know,' Emily said, still stunned from seeing her rough, tough uncle crying like a baby.

From over the stone wall Evie popped up her head, her white hair almost glowing in the sun.

'Come in! All the two-legged ones, mind. Not the four.'

Jesus suddenly went nuts, barking and leaping up and down behind the wall.

'*Jesus Christ*!' they chorused.

As she walked towards Evie, Emily asked, 'What was *Bob* doing here?'

'You and he, aren't . . . ?' Flo wiggled her eyebrows up and down. 'I mean, you're not . . . ?'

'*No*,' said Evie, eyes twinkling, 'we're not. Of course we're not. He came to me for a healing.'

'A what-ing?' asked Flo.

'A healing,' Evie repeated mildly. She turned and began to walk away, calling over her shoulder, 'Everyone needs one at some point.' Then she tactfully changed the subject. 'I like your horse, Emily. He's very handsome. Thought of a name for him yet?'

Emily jogged to catch up with Evie, shaking her head. 'Luke called him Bonus, but all I can think of is Trouble.'

'Trouble? That's not something you want to focus on or attract.'

'I know, but it's a name that keeps coming back to me. I just don't know what's coming. What my life's going to be like from now. I don't even need a new horse. Not now all this has happened.' She waved her arm about to encompass the cattle in the bush yards.

Evie looked at Emily with gentle green eyes.

'He's no trouble. He's a stud muffin.'

'Well, I can't exactly call him that.'

'A hunka-spunka? Hot stuff? Like his previous owner, eh?'

'Evie!'

'C'mon,' Evie said, linking her arm with Emily as Jesus danced about their feet. 'You're all invited for a quick bite.'

'Oh, Evie, don't worry,' Emily said. 'We've got tucker left over from yesterday. That'll do us for the rest of the day.'

'No, you're all my guests, please,' Evie said. 'Sam,' she called out from the garden. 'Lunch inside for you all.'

'We'll be along soon,' called Sam from where he stood with Rod, making hasty repairs to one of his stirrup leathers.

Evie walked Emily along the path where wild hollyhocks and lupins flowered colourfully amid Evie's new plants. The girls ran on ahead, happy to have arrived at what had become their second home.

Emily kicked off her boots, stepped into the cool stone cottage and walked along the hallway to the back of the house where Evie had built a sunny kitchen.

Evie lifted a quiche from the oven and set it beside a fresh and colourful array of dishes: salads and homemade pasta in a free-range egg mayonnaise, steamed new potatoes garnished with mint and drizzled with pale butter made from Evie's milking cow. Crisp lettuce, snow peas, carrots and cucumber set out on a platter. It looked so inviting.

'Yum! What a feast,' Emily said.

'If you're going to do great things with your life, Emily, you'll need your body to support you. Fuel it with the good things.'

'What great things am I going to do? What now? After the cattle are taken down to the lowlands and sold, what then? Dad's already worrying about how we're going to manage.'

Evie just smiled up at her as she sliced the quiche.

'You will know your path,' she said calmly.

Emily had become used to the way Evie spoke. At first it

had unsettled her, then amused her, but now she knew there was truth in all Evie said.

With the special meals Evie had cooked up at the high plains station, Emily had been amazed by how the weight had fallen from her body. At Brigalow they had lived near a corner store, where ice-creams and chips and lollies were always a temptation. Eating Evie's meals, she and Sam had felt their bodies detoxing of sugars and preservatives and the junk food they'd slowly become accustomed to.

Their tastebuds had adjusted quickly to the simple yet delicious food Evie set before them. Even the girls seemed to shine with more energy. Each day, Emily had seen her own dark hair growing longer and more glossy, the scars on her body smoothing over, her breath coming more easily, her bones meshing, her energy restored.

Sam came into the kitchen, followed by Rod and Flo.

'What a spread!' said Flo. 'This is the best droving fare we've ever enjoyed.' She gathered up a plate and passed it to Rod.

'Thank you, Evie,' Rod said, 'for *everything*.' There was weight in his words. He wasn't just thanking Evie for the lunch, but also for her care and love of his daughter and granddaughters.

Emily looked around the clean, tiny kitchen. There were herbs hanging from rafters and tomatoes growing on the windowsills. On the bench was a big bowl of fresh apples, a jug of homemade lemonade and a special plate of honeyed natural sweets for the girls. From the old wooden chairs to the kitchen table, the whole house had the same serene energy that radiated from Evie.

As Emily bit into the nutritious food, she could taste Evie's love. For the first time, Emily felt as if she had a mother caring for them. How ironic was it that someone like Evie had at last come into their lives, on the last drove?

With the meal over, Rod, Sam and Flo stood and thanked Evie, giving her warm hugs, Rod's embrace lingering longest of all. The girls, eager to get back on their ponies, danced down the hallway and banged their way through the screen door. On the way down the path, Jesus had a go at Flo's leg, his teeth meshing with the cloth of her jeans. She responded with a high kick that sent the little dog sailing into a snapdragon patch. He rolled over, wagged his tail and jumped up onto the stone wall to bark at her with a dog's grin ear to ear, as if it were a game. Flo passed him, muttering profanities.

Inside the cottage, Emily started gathering up crockery and stacking it neatly in the sink.

'You're a good girl, Emily, but I'll do that. You go on with your family. Enjoy the rest of the day.'

'Part of me doesn't ever want this day to end. Part of me knows that once these days are over, this is it.'

'Are you thinking in negatives again?'

'Oh, Evie! I just can't seem to stop my thoughts running away with themselves.' Such was the challenge of a soon-to-be jobless drover, Emily thought, with miles of dusty road ahead and endless space for thoughts to run riot.

'You need time, my darling.'

'Time? Time for what?'

'To truly heal. You can see Snowgum's still not wholly

healed. Well, neither are you, my dear.'

'So what should I do?'

'Go where your heart and soul calls.'

'You mean up top?' Evie nodded. 'For the winter?'

Emily had seen photos of the old-timers in their snow shoes, as if they had tennis racquets strapped to their feet, outside the high-plains homestead. Looking at the pictures, she had shivered to see they were wearing not much other than waistcoats and jackets, or the women in long thick skirts, but their smiles radiated a warmth all of their own.

Emily imagined being there with her daughters, skiing or riding in the snow down to Evie's little cottage.

'It's doable and it would do you good.'

Emily sat, contemplating winter on the plains. It would be tough, but no tougher than living in the tiny town of Dargo and wondering each and every day if she might bump into Luke, or even Clancy, who she knew was still seeing Penny there. Evie sat down and pulled Emily down to sit next to her.

'There's something else on your mind, isn't there?'

Emily nodded.

'A man? Two men? The old and the new?'

Emily nodded again.

'Until you truly love yourself it isn't wise to try to love another. Heal first, darling, then love.'

'I know,' Emily said. 'Deep down, I know.' She looked into Evie's eyes and felt such utter trust that she was suddenly blurting out the story of being down by the Wonnangatta River with Luke and the terrifying sound of the horses.

'What does it all mean, Evie?' The fear was back in Emily's voice.

Evie smiled. 'It means you both have a gift. That your union created an energetic freedom for the earth. Horses mean freedom.'

Emily frowned, confused. 'But the energy felt dark.'

'You know there was a murder in the Wonnangatta and the station manager was chased to his death on horseback?'

Emily did know of the folklore of the place, but had not connected the two incidents. She shivered.

'You and Luke share a special power. United, it's a strong light energy that draws out the dark and dissipates it.'

'So we should be together?'

Evie shook her head. 'Not if there's no anchor of self-love on which to tie your passion for him. Time, Emily, is what you need. You and Luke are for another time.'

From the hallway came a shout from Sam. 'Time to go, gasbagging girls!'

Evie gave Emily a quick hug and then Emily was gone, jogging along the hall, feeling altogether sad that she and Luke were not to be. Not this time.

Twenty-seven

On the very last day of the drove, it poured. Instead of cursing the weather, Emily viewed the low grey skies and the heavy silver streaks of rain as a gift. A good autumn break would set them up well for winter on the lowlands. But just one good season on their former mountain runs would be enough to fuel fierce fires next summer, given the right conditions. Without the cattle keeping the grasses in check, the annuals would soon seed, go rank and lodge flat on the ground from the wind, stifling the soil and growth of other less vigorous native grasses below. For the umpteenth time, Emily tried to shove the negative thoughts about the fate of her mountain landscape from her mind.

With just a few steep bends to go, Emily was riding alone at the back of the herd with no one to distract her. Think positive, she told herself.

The cattle were travelling well. Her father was riding slowly ahead on the gentle curve of the road. He was close enough to steady the lead cattle and far enough on to warn oncoming traffic to slow down. It was nice that it was just the two of them today. Emily could savour these last hours of droving in solitude. Just her and her dad and the bliss of rain.

Sam, who could only ever tolerate droving in short bursts, had absconded a couple of days before to see Bridie, restless to get the songs he'd thought of on the road down on paper. Evie was minding the girls at Tranquillity and cooking up an end-of-droving feast for them all. Emily knew by this afternoon she and Rod would have the herd tramping into the township of Dargo and into a paddock there. Then a big dinner by the fire.

Rivers of rain fell from the brim of her hat and cascaded down the back of her oilskin. She wore waterproof trousers, but beneath her wet-weather gear she was damp right through, her clothes steamy against her skin. But at least her body and limbs were warm. At one point the rain was so heavy some of the cows stopped, pinned their ears back and turned about, looking at her as if to say, 'Are you mad? How can you make us walk in this?' She answered their query with a loud crack of her stockwhip. The leaders jolted, mooed, then turned to walk forward once more.

So loud was the rain, Emily didn't hear the vehicle approaching from behind until it was almost upon her. The gelding danced a sideways step at the sudden sight of the white four-wheel drive, but she soon had him steadied.

Emily drew in a breath. There in the rain shone the bright VPP logo on the door of the four-wheel drive. The lairy green paint was at odds with the muted sodden bush surrounding them. She steered the horse around to the driver's side. Luke wound down his window, frowning at the rain that dashed inside.

'Hi,' he said. 'Wet enough out there?'

Emily looked at his handsome face. He'd cut his hair short, which gave him an almost military look in his khaki uniform. Gorgeous though he was, when Emily saw him sitting there in that flash four-wheel drive, with all the bells and whistles, all she felt was sadness and resentment. How could she ever love her way around the fact he worked for an organisation that had just unhinged her life?

So far, not one man had been brave enough to speak to the Flanaghans about the bans directly. Instead, their life as they'd known it had been brought to a halt by letters sent from Melbourne on weighty, expensive paper. The responsibility was never delegated to just one man. It was dished out by men who could stand behind another, then another.

'Have you come out to make sure we've got all the cattle off the mountains?' Emily said coldly. She saw the look of shock on Luke's face before he covered his response with a smile.

'No, I trust you. I was just out doing the flood monitoring. Might have to close the Lower Dargo Road if this rain keeps on.' He looked skyward, then glanced back at the horse. 'How's he going?'

'Good,' said Emily, not giving Luke anything, but feeling guilty, knowing the horse was far from good. He was brilliant, and she should tell him so.

'Thought of another name for him yet?'

Emily squirmed. 'Not really. Not officially. Evie nicknamed him Hot Stuff.'

'Hot Stuff, eh?' Luke gave her a wink. 'Like Salsa. Bit like how you danced in the pub that night.'

Oh, God, Emily thought. He's flirting with me. Part of her was delighted. Part of her devastated. How could he flirt when here she was taking cattle down the road for the very last time? Didn't he get it?

'I think I'll just stick with Bonus,' she responded dully.

Luke picked up on her continuing coldness, realising he wasn't going to warm her, realising the gap between them was too huge. He fell silent for a time, the rain drumming on the roof of the vehicle, the gelding shifting his feet, ears back, rain trickling down his already soaked rump, not happy to be standing in the rain.

Emily whistled Rousie and growled at him to stop hassling the cows, who were now also standing, resting, steam rising from their backs.

'I tried to call you,' Luke said softly.

'I know.'

'Should I try again?' he asked hopefully.

Emily shook her head and rain spilled off her hat. 'No. Don't.'

'Okay,' said Luke. 'It's your call.' He started the vehicle so that the gelding jumped a little. Luke looked out through the fogged-up windscreen waiting for Emily to speak. She didn't. She sat staring ahead at the big herd of beautiful cows they would be forced to sell.

'Well, I'll leave you to it, then,' he said. His voice was cold now too. There was hurt in it. He drove round the cattle, tooted

286

the horn at Rod, who was waiting at the top of the hill for Emily and the herd to keep coming, and then was gone from sight.

'C'mon, Mr Bonus-Salsa,' Emily said to the disgruntled gelding, 'move your hot arse. We got cows to yard and boys to forget. We're almost home.'

On the river-flat road into Dargo the rain eased and a cold wind was racing through the grasses. The early autumn leaves of the giant walnut and elm trees that flanked the main street were falling like silver confetti. The iridescent leaves stuck to the dark wet road so the cattle looked as if they were walking over a pathway of shining coins.

As Emily and Rod drove the cattle through Dargo and past the pub, some locals came out to the verandah, beers in hand, toasting the cattlemen's last drove.

Across the road at the general store, Emily paused for a tourist, who was hellbent on taking a thousand photos. As she smiled for the man, Emily felt the sadness at knowing she and her family were no longer living history, but dead history. What they were doing on this day was now a thing of the past, to be captured on some bloke's digital camera and shown to people who didn't really understand. The last drove in Dargo.

She neck-reined her horse about and hunted the cheeky, curious cows in the mob away from the store's gardens and outdoor coffee tables. In the town's heart, the cattle were perky, knowing they were close to home. They trotted for a few hundred metres before Emily and Rod guided the leaders into an open gateway that lay between an old miner's cottage and the river. It was one of the Flanaghans' paddocks that was flush with fresh grass.

The cows instantly had their heads down, grabbing up great mouthfuls of feed. Emily sat listening to the rhythmic sound of the cattle eating as they tore at the sweet grasses that had been rested over the summer months. She observed their glossy coats and knew they would make top dollars in the sale yards in such condition, but she had no desire to see them go. It broke her heart to know that these quiet beasts, bred selectively over generations in the mountains, would now go elsewhere. Perhaps to slaughter, perhaps to another farm where they weren't treated kindly and with respect. She shook the thoughts from her head and chose to think instead about the night ahead with her family. Emily manoeuvred the gelding around the gate and swung it shut, marking the end of an era.

Twenty-eight

Passing by the dining-room window of the Flanaghans' family homestead, Emily looked in and smiled. There were Tilly and Meg, bright-faced, helping Evie carry dishes for tonight's feast over to the old redgum table. The table was decked out with fine old crockery and silverware, and at the centre sat a candelabra ablaze with white tapering candles. Emily recalled her grandfather had won the candelabra with a Hereford bull at the 1955 Bairnsdale show. The light from the flames cast an angelic hue on the girls' faces.

At the old sideboard, Rod was pouring port into delicate crystal glasses, also trophies won by long-gone livestock at a long-gone agricultural show. Emily hadn't seen some of these old things in years. They had mostly been shoved to the back of the sideboard cupboard, but Evie had declared tonight was special.

So things had been dusted off, polished up and were now being used and enjoyed. Even the big old dining room, normally shut off from the rest of the house and used as a storage place, had been cleaned out and restored to its former beauty. The open fire burned brightly, illuminating the beautiful big painting above it of a cattleman's hut, and there were fresh flowers in the vase on the sideboard. Evie had brought the house alive.

Emily, hungry now and keen to get her jobs done so she could join the others inside, walked over to the feed shed and scooped dog pellets into a bucket as the kelpies danced in their pens. Flo's cat, Muscles, wove in and out of her legs, miaowing up at her.

Above her, the stars were bright in the crisp night air. She felt tired from droving, but exhilarated that her body had coped so well. It was her mind that had not. Not since seeing Luke today on the road.

In the near-darkness, Emily rattled out biscuits into the dogs' bowls, talking to each dog but making a particular fuss of Rousie, as she always did. Then she made her way to the shed, swung her leg over the four-wheeler bike and revved it into life, Muscles leaping onto her lap for his moggy joyride. Zooming away down the road, she travelled the two kilometres to Bob's house.

There were no lights on. Flo had said he'd shot through again, though no one knew where to. When Bob left, they always took it upon themselves to check his animals. He'd been known to leave horses in yards for days without food or water so that they had chewed the top rails down to thin splintery sticks. Once, he'd left his dog, DD, on the chain for so long in the summer that the animal nearly perished from thirst. Emily hated going to Bob's house. It was snaky and spidery and a constant reminder to her of the loss of her grandparents, who had kept the garden as a child's paradise.

She remembered the pond with golden fish swimming lazily in the sparkling water and the stepping stones leading to a soft, ferny fairy glen. There were flowers and windchimes and special places to sit. But since Bob had lived there, he ran the crossbred killers in the yard and the garden was all but gone now. The place had a depressing feel to it.

Tonight, as she approached the house, she frowned. DD wasn't bouncing madly up and down on the end of his chain. Emily shone the headlights over to the empty kennel. Tied to the upright starpicket on which the dog was normally tethered was a piece of cardboard torn from a beer carton. On it, in Bob's scratchy hand in permanent marker: *Thank you, Emily, but have sent DD on holiday.*

Emily sucked in a breath. Surely he didn't mean he'd shot the dear old dog? Mad though it was, it was a character and so much a part of the place.

She frowned and made her way to Bob's henhouse. Again, a ripped-up beer box.

Gave all the girls away to Donna. Emily took in the dark interior of the empty chook shed. She marched over to the paddock where Bob kept his riding mare. Normally Emily would throw her a bucket of chaff when Bob wasn't about as he kept the mare in a sparse and weedy paddock and she often looked ribby, her coat dull. Another piece of cardboard was inside the feedbucket that hung from the fence. *Gave the mare to Kate.*

What was going on? Emily ran over to Bob's house and a sensor light flicked on. She saw that the back lawn was mown short, and all the rubbish on the verandah had been taken away. The curtains were drawn. The place looked completely deserted but, more surprisingly, it also looked *clean* and *tidy*.

Emily jumped back on the bike, waited for Muscles to join her and then sped along the drive to the homestead. Just as she was heading inside the house she saw headlights. Sam's sporty ute drew up, and he and Bridie tumbled out, laughing.

'Hi, drover!' Bridie said, looking stunning in a red top with funky black jeans. Sam, all in Johnny Cash black, gave Emily a quick hug.

'I can see you've made an effort,' Sam teased as he took in Emily's old farm clothes.

'What do we do with her?' said Bridie, her blonde hair swept up Jane-Mansfield style in a thick red ribbon.

'What's wrong with this?' Emily said, looking down at her chunky woollen work jumper.

'We are going to pick out something for you to wear. You're not coming to our special dinner like that!'

'What a bossy pair you make,' Emily said, as they rambled along the big hallway into the heart of the house.

Once they were all gathered at the dining table, Emily, now wearing a pretty checked cowgirl shirt, couldn't hold back her news any longer and blurted out, 'I think Bob's in trouble. I'm really worried about him.'

Everyone turned to look at her.

'We've been worrying about Bob for years,' said Flo dryly.

'But this time it's different. There's no sign of any of his animals and he's left all these strange notes and the place is *tidy*. I mean *really tidy*.' Emily twisted her hands in her lap. 'You don't think he's done himself in?'

'No, of course he hasn't,' Evie soothed. 'Bob's been coming to me for healing.'

'Geez!' said Flo, recalling Bob at Evie's house. 'The only healer Bob would've ever heard of is a blue heeler, not a spiritual healer. Evie, how did you get the man to come to you?'

'I didn't. He came to me after the bans.'

'Yeah? Why?' Sam asked.

'I can't tell you why,' Evie said, 'but I can tell you he's okay. He's not going to do anything silly . . . well, I can't guarantee that, but you know what I mean. He's not going to do himself in.'

'Phew,' said Emily.

'Let's drink a toast to Bob then, wherever the flock he may be,' Flo said, the pre-dinner port already warming her up. And they raised their glasses.

'To Bob!' they toasted. 'Wherever the flock he may be!'

Emily sat watching her family eat in the flickering light of the candles and the open fire dancing across the old walls. Evie's roast beef and vegetables kept them all so busy that for a time the conversation was slowed to a series of 'Mmms' and 'Oohs' and 'More please!' But as they finished their dinner Evie sat at the end of the table looking at them all. 'What now?'

'Dessert?' said Tilly hopefully.

'Yes, darling, but first I'd like to hear from each of you. What now for your lives? Rod, how about you go first?'

Rod set down his glass and cleared his throat. He laced his fingers together before him and thought for a time.

'Firstly, we'll sort out the cattle. Keep a third of the best and sell the rest of them. Then, I don't know. I thought I could go fencing and slashing. There are plenty of hobby blocks round here that need a handyman and the Melbournites who own them aren't short of a penny. It'd tide us over financially until we find something else. Might even be a nice little business.'

Emily could hear her father talking himself into this new life. She felt a prick of sadness, but she was also proud that he was open to trying new ventures after a lifetime of being a cattleman.

'Flo?' Evie said.

'Mmm, well . . .' began Flo, 'I've had a proposition from Baz.'

'Not another one!' said Sam cheekily.

'Not that sort of proposition. Well, yeah I've had plenty of *those* sorts of propositions from Baz. But he's goin' into livestock cartage and wants me to run a truck this side of the mountains for him.'

'Flo's going truckin'!' said Bridie delightedly. 'Can I be your stylist? You've got to look good. You'll get more clients that way. I'm thinking translucent tops, tight jeans, sexy boots. But still classy, kind of like Nicole Kidman in the *Australia* movie. Oh, Flo, your business could boom.'

'Look out! We'll have a heap of understocked properties

round here 'cause all the blokes will be selling their animals in the hope they get lucky with the truckie,' Emily said.

'That sounds great!' Evie said. 'Now, Sam? You?'

'Well,' he began, his eyes shining as he gathered up Bridie's hand, 'I'll have to answer Bridie's part for this too, because . . .' They looked at each other joyfully. 'We're moving to the New South Wales north coast – the hub of country music! She's helped me write enough songs for a new album and we want to record them. We've booked a house and a studio for the winter there. Once I've done some demos, Ike's going to look about for a really good contract. We've written some great stuff.'

'All written lying down, I presume,' Emily joked and Sam kicked her under the table hard on the shin. The pain in her leg wasn't enough to stop her happiness at hearing Sam's news. But as all eyes fell upon her, she felt the pressure.

'Your turn, Emily,' Evie said.

'I . . . I . . .' she stammered, 'I don't really know.'

'C'mon, Emily,' said Sam.

'Well, I'm thinking of heading up to the plains for the winter. Just the girls and me.'

'Yay!' chorused the girls.

'We can live in the snow!' Meg said.

'And build igloos!' said Tilly.

Rod looked concerned. 'Are you sure? It'll be tougher than you think.'

'I know. But Evie'll be down the way. We can ride or ski to her. We're only likely to be snowed in for three weeks max. It's not like a Flanaghan hasn't lived that way before.'

'Are you sure you want the girls in such isolation?'

'Yes! I'm sure. I need the isolation. I'm not like you all. I haven't got a clue what I'm going to do next. I had my heart set on being a cattleman and I need that time to figure out what to do.'

They all sat contemplating Emily's suggestion. They knew she was still healing emotionally. Still healing from her broken marriage and the loss of her dreams. None of them, save for Evie and Bridie, knew the full extent of her confusion over Luke, though, and the part that he played in her wanting to bunker down in the snow.

'Then it's settled,' Rod said at last. 'Emily, off you go into self-imposed exile with your girls. But please, please, remember you can always come back here before the spring, if it gets too much.'

'I'll be fine, Dad. I'm sure.'

Twenty-nine

One week later, on her first night on the plains away from her family, Emily couldn't believe the depth of her loneliness. In the darkness, she led Bonus and Snowgum from the float to the stable. She could feel the wind bite her lips, so cold she had to pull the neck of her jumper up over her mouth. With just the low gleam from her head torch lighting the way, she put the horses in a stall and returned to get the girls' ponies, who shared the third bay of the float. Her breath hazed before her in a chilly mist.

Her fingers were numb with cold as she fumbled around in the dark for the heavy horse rugs. She shook the imagined spiders from them and took them to the stable to heave on the horses' backs. Each snorted contentedly and got down to the business of chewing their chaff. As Emily shut the stable door, she caught a flash of another woman's hand on the latch. She felt the energy of the touch.

'Emily,' she said aloud. She could feel her presence there in the darkness of the big old sheds. Fear zinged through her. Wind railed, far up in the treetops, but down here on the ground, it was dead still, giving the bush an eerie feel. Frogs croaked down by the well and the click of branches in the trees was all about her.

A sudden loud tap of a branch startled Emily and she whirled about as if there was something there in the darkness. A wild dog? A hunter? A ghost? The night of the phantom horses in the Wonnangatta still haunted her. She felt panic rise in her chest.

Control your thoughts, she told herself. Her great-great-grandmother had spent many nights in charge alone with her eleven children while her husband went off in search of gold in those cold, lean years. How brave and tough she must've been to have created a welcoming home on top of an isolated and sometimes hostile mountain.

Looking into the blackness of the bush, Emily realised that, with time, she would no longer flinch at the eerie sounds of the night. It would become part of her. But right now she felt daunted. She had the sudden urge to rush inside and huddle close to Meg and Tilly.

She summoned her courage and forced a smile to her face. She had wanted this, ever since the accident. She was here at last. Blissfully alone, with the energies of her forebears floating all about in this precious, most beautiful place. The wind whipped up again and Emily heard a snowgum limb crack and fall. She pulled her hat down low, tilted her head to the wind and made her way back over to the house.

The warmth from the kitchen didn't extend to the bedrooms,

so when she checked the girls they were still covered by old featherdown quilts, and their beanies were jammed on their heads. In the candlelight, the gentle fog of their breath came steadily, in and out, in the icy air. Emily agonised again about her decision to bring them here, to a place so cold and remote. Was she doing the right thing? Could she and the girls remain here the whole winter? This first night she doubted it, but then she thought of Evie and the comfort of knowing she was nearby on the mountain.

On their arrival, late in the dark, they found that Evie had left the fire smouldering, a giant new candle alight, freshly baked bread on the table and a pot of wallaby stew made tastier with bacon warming on the stove. Evie had also stocked the big old meat safe with spuds, onions, carrots, swedes, flour, rice, apples and pasta and filled the cupboards with tins. Emily had also brought food, so she knew that if they were snowed in, there'd be plenty of rations. Evie had left a note: *Time heals and so do good thoughts. Enjoy!*

Emily sent Evie a silent thank you in the night for her care. Now she fell heavily into bed and eventually drifted into a fitful sleep, wakened throughout the night by the ghoulish wind moaning about the homestead.

'What have I done?' she said aloud in the darkness in the dead of night, feeling utterly lost.

In the morning, Emily woke to complete silence, the wind blown out and gone. She lifted the blinds and gasped at the fairytale landscape before her. The world was white with snow, soft and peaceful. She leapt out of bed. Her clothes felt damp, even icy, when she pulled them on. She hurried to cajole the woodstove alight and set Meg and Tilly's clothes out to warm.

When she went to the toilet, she realised the pipes would be frozen and the water had been drained from the cistern. Flo had warned her she'd have to bucket water from the well to flush the toilet, and to keep it empty so the porcelain didn't freeze and crack. The seat was so cold it burned the backs of her legs like a freezebrand. Her feet and nose stung from cold. When she went to make tea in the icy kitchen, she realised there was no running water. She'd have to scoop up buckets of snow for the stovetop. Emily laughed, realising she had a lot to learn.

Heading outside with a collection of saucepans, she enjoyed the crunch of snow underfoot. She shooed Rousie away from where she gathered the snow. It seemed to fall deepest on the eastern side of the woodshed, but all about her was a snow-laden landscape. The calls of crows and currawongs sounded out from the snowgums. Rousie barked at the excitement of this cold, strange, white world and his bark echoed through the bush.

When she went back inside, the kitchen felt cheerier, the fire now lively and spilling warmth into the room. She heard Tilly and Meg talking in their beds. Emily rushed into their darkened room and whipped up the blind.

'*Look! Snow!*'

The girls shrieked and jumped up to dress. Outside, they ran about and tossed snowballs in the air, which Rousie leapt and snapped at with a Tassie-devil clack of teeth. They built snow-men, using sticks for arms, gumleaves for smiles and gumnuts for eyes. Soon, though, Emily cajoled them into leaving the snow-family. There was work to do. In the stables she handed a hay fork to Tilly and pushed a wheelbarrow into the stall. Emily let both horses and ponies out into the day yard. The horses slung their heads down low and snorted at the snow. Bonus pawed the ground, then trotted around the powdered paddock. Emily took in how the drifts settled on the poa grasses and the horizontal limbs of the trees. The world was soft and crisp. It was paradise. But so, so cold!

By the time Emily had fully unpacked the ute, the sun was arcing up over the tree-line and the gum boughs were pelting down sludges of ice whenever the wind blew, making a sound like hail.

The roofs of the homestead and stables, glaringly white, were now beginning to reveal the grey of the corrugated iron beneath as the snow melted, pouring down from the roof and spilling onto the ground. Small holes had been punched in the tin to allow water into the guttering beneath it, but most of the melt fell like rain from the tin. As the sun warmed the paddocks, the grass began to reappear and the world turned from black and white to full colour again.

They traipsed inside, Emily stripping the wet clothes from the girls. They shivered, their feet and fingers red raw from the cold, stinging. Meg cried and Tilly whinged, but Emily soon had them huddled by the fire, dressed in fresh dry clothes and content. She set the mountain of wet clothing to hang beside the fire, then cooked a bacon and egg brunch to warm them. As the girls ate, Emily sat with a cuppa and began to make a list.

Over several generations, the place had begun to look tired. For the past twenty years, the family's energies had been focused on attending a constant round of meetings in towns and in Melbourne with an ever-changing roster of sometimes insipid, sometimes hostile government workers, all in order to keep their grazing runs.

The Flanaghans had never been landed gentry. Their enterprise had been built on brothers and sisters, mothers and fathers all working together as one unit. There may have been hired help now and then, but most of the work they did themselves. One legacy of the constant battle with bureaucracy was that time was always in short supply. The high-plains base had suffered. Jobs started were rarely finished.

Emily saw these next months as her chance to put things right. She was the custodian of this place now. The woman in her dreams had shown her that. All the huts and dwellings, crafted by hand by her forebears, would slump into the soil if she didn't look after them. She would still care for this place, even if she didn't have cattle. The government be damned!

She picked up a pen and began to write a list.

Fix Block Paddock fence
Rebuild Lanky's corner strainer
Clad northern stable wall
Nail loose tin on woodshed
Re-swing door in stable . . .

And so it began. A blueprint for the winter days ahead. The

jobs would be crammed in around the labour required to run the home. There was still mothering to be done, Tilly's home-school lessons, the cooking, cleaning, firewood to be fetched and animals to be tended to.

Many of her domestic duties were not so different to those she'd had in suburban Brigalow. But up here, the work took on a whole new meaning. It was linked to women of the past, who had raised children here. She sensed them around her now. She felt their grief at losing children to horse accidents and illness. She felt their pride as they watched their children thrive and grow into fit and competent adults. She felt their mixed emotions when their children moved away to have families of their own.

All that was in front of her with her own girls. Always, in the Flanaghan brood, there'd been one or two children who loved the place so much they put their roots down here, despite the harshness of the climate and the landscape. Emily knew, now, she was one of them. The one who simply had to remain in this wild beauty. She couldn't tell yet, but Meg or Tilly might have it in them, too. This self-imposed exile, she reasoned, could just be the making of them.

Or the breaking of them. As the days wore on, cabin fever set in. Emily was tested to the limits by her girls. They were good kids, but their endless banter began to get on her nerves in the tiny rooms. She found herself saying over and over, 'Not so *loud*!'

There was no sending the girls off to their bedrooms to play.

It was just too cold. So they all squashed into the kitchen and annoyed each other.

Meg was at first fascinated by the candles on the table and was always blowing at them, making the flames flicker and waver. Tilly's irritating habit was to pick at the wax, sometimes spilling it hot onto the table surface.

'Ow, ow, ow,' she'd say, flicking her hands. Emily would clench a scream inside herself, trying as best she could to humour them to bed early, rather than hunt them, just to give herself some space.

When they did at last fall asleep, Emily would sit down to a book, only to find dissatisfaction brewing in her again. She glanced up to the gas mantel above her that constantly hissed like a pot simmering on a stove. Reading beneath that noisy, dim light was not as pleasurable as reading in a quiet, warm, modern, brightly lit home. She told herself not to be so fussy.

She had many, many more luxuries than the Emily long before her, who had lived in a two-roomed hut on the King's Spur. It made Emily realise how spoiled she had been in the suburbs, with food at the store and light and heat at the flick of a switch and running water at the turn of a tap.

She struggled with the ever-present dull smell of smoke. It was in her hair, on her clothes, in the house. The fires in the kitchen woodstove and the dining room had to be kept going at all times or the house became an iceblock. Socked feet still froze on the cold linoleum, so they had to wear slippers always, and some nights Emily sat on the couch in the dining room in two jackets, dozing off from exhaustion but unwilling to move away from the fire.

She dressed and undressed as quickly as possible, and never was it warm enough to lie naked between the sheets. In that big, icy cold bed, she longed for another body to warm her. To have Luke beside her, naked. Instead, she was covered neck-to-toe in thermal underwear, pyjamas, socks and even a beanie. There was no shower and the cold bathroom only had a bath, the water heated in a small wood furnace. Baths were now once a week, so Emily only vaguely knew she was getting fitter and leaner from the constant work of carting wood from the shed and water from the well. In bed now she ran her hands under her clothing, feeling her belly firmer, her waist more slender.

'*Ahh, ah ah, thinking about you naked*,' she sang in her best Sunny Cowgirls voice. She had another flashback of Luke and her at the river. All the quashed desires that lingered deep within her came rushing to the surface. A longing came over her so powerfully she thought she would suffocate if she couldn't touch him again. She could visualise Luke here in this very bed, lying with her, both of them naked. She exhaled and ran her hands gently over her skin beneath her pyjamas, giving herself goosebumps, feeling pleasure rise.

She began to sing again. '. . . *and I'm sweating from head to toe just from dreaming 'bout that shirt of yours on my bedroom floor. Undressing you with my eyes – tell me, baby, do you read the signs. Oh-oh-oh, thinking about you naked.*'

Emily recalled the sensation of Luke's body under her finger-tips. The way she'd slipped her hand down his belly and been delighted by the firmness of him there. How she longed to experience the weight of him pressed against her, the skin on their bodies touching, feeling the electricity between them. Their breath coming fast from passion. It had been so different with Clancy. Luke's lovemaking was generous, his moves so in line with the needs of a woman.

'*Oh and here you come, stirring naughty thoughts around this head of mine. Leave me breathless, restless, you do. Oh honey if you only knew. Oh, oh, thinking about you naked . . .*' she sang.

Then Emily sighed. She grabbed a pillow and shoved it over her head. She had to stop thinking like this!

She exhaled and forced herself to picture Bert Newton. Or Dame Edna. She began to sing a medley of Rolf Harris songs. Anything to shake Luke from her mind. But there he was again, in her mind's eye, lying on a mossy riverbank, kissing her. Naked. His buttocks moving rhythmically under her hands as he pushed into her.

'Arrgh!' she cried out in frustration. She began to recite nursery rhymes, and an hour after she'd gone to bed, she finally found sleep.

Deep in the night, the curtains stirred, but no window was open and there was no breeze outside. Emily was not awake to see, but as something gentle drifted by, only Rousie lifted his head from where he lay by the fire and flopped his tail down once in a lazy wag.

Thirty

After weeks of living in snow, the horses and ponies now picked their way through the rocky, icy-white landscape with sure-footed certainty. Emily, Tilly and Meg rode out most days on adventures across the mountains. On this day, the fog had lifted early, leaving them with relatively warm, settled weather.

Emily was keen to teach the kids all she knew of the mountains and today she had a hunch the roads from Dargo would be closed after such a heavy overnight fall. Today she knew she wouldn't be caught by the rangers taking Rousie onto Park land. They were on their way to the Long Spur, where Emily would show the girls one of the conservation reserves their great-grandparents had established.

As they trotted over the snowplains, it was a joy for Emily to see Meg and Tilly's faces bright with exhilaration. The little ponies looked comical, like Thelwell cartoons, leaping the tufts of grasses and dodging rocks, while her girls stuck to their backs with ease. There had been a couple of spills in the early days, but the soft cover of snow over spongy snowgrass had broken any falls, so that now, young though they were, Tilly and Meg were confident and happy to ride for hours at a time.

In the natural snowgrass clearings, they paused to look to the high mountain tops, watching clouds race towards them in great tumbling walls that would eventually obliterate the views. Some days were perfectly still, others perfectly wild, an icy wind whipping the horses' tails in a frenzy, wrenching hats from their heads. Most days were a mix of both heaven and hell, the weather forever changing and changing fast.

They rode with scarves about their faces to stop the icy sting of the freezing air entering their lungs. Emily carried a backpack of food and, tied to her saddle and to Bonus's pack saddle, were her cattleman tools.

Emily was training the young gelding as a packhorse. He might as well be versatile. She had strapped her grandfather's old saddle-packs to him, weighted evenly either side. Inside them she stored a chainsaw – not so big as to be a real nuisance but large enough to slice through the limbs of trees that had fallen across the fencelines. She also stored loops of high-tensile wire, some fencing pliers, staples, a hammer, a hatchet, a small shovel and some strainers. Bonus was a steady-minded horse and had taken to his job well, trailing Snowgum happily on the end of a lead rope. If the gear caught on a tree, he wouldn't spook. He'd plant his feet and wait patiently for Emily to come and unhitch him. Despite him being a constant reminder of Luke, Emily was beginning to love the horse as they journeyed together on the snow-topped mountains.

Some of the fencelines Emily checked as she rode were those that separated the Flanaghans' own small acreage of private land, but most of the fences ran between paddocks that were now classed on a map as national park. A large portion of the land had never been fenced so there was some work to be done if Emily and her family were to continue to run a small token herd up on the home paddocks and state forest areas of the now diminished and divided station.

When they reached the Long Spur track, Emily saw that snow had settled quite deeply. She pointed out the Mount Hotham and Dinner Plain ski-fields on the ridgeline opposite to the girls. Tiny black dots of skiers, like ants, weaving this way and that down the mountainside, surfing the white snow drifts. At the end of their skiing day, the holiday makers would head to the showers, the bars, the restaurants and the bands, or even flick on the TV or surf the internet for entertainment.

Emily found it amazing to think she could see such sophisticated 'civilisation' from where she stood. The stillness here was in stark contrast to the busy, self-obsessed and distracting buzz of the ski-fields.

Here she sat on her horse with her daughters in land that was still beautiful after one hundred and fifty years of controlled cattle grazing. This spur was one of her favourite places and a particularly lovely lunch stop when mustering, apart from the grating view of the ever-expanding ski villages and communication and electricity towers opposite.

The Long Spur ran alongside a stunning cliff that dropped into a massive valley of bush below called Devil's Hollow. Emily sat trying to get her head around the fact that her family and their stock were banned from here. How could that be, when on the opposite mountain thousands of skiers were welcome to run riot over the landscape?

Emily had nothing against the skiers, but she did feel enraged by the developers who profited from the landscape in such a way. As she watched the swarms of people skiing over the mountainside and the sunlight reflecting off the ski villas that poured sewerage out into septics that seeped down the mountainside, the government decision to ban the cattlemen, while encouraging the developers, sat heavily with her.

What the skiers never saw was the massive scarring their winter follies left behind. They were never up here in the summer to see the way the land was compacted so that the vegetation struggled to grow. Even when the snow melted and the soil was watered back to life and warmed by the sun, vegetation that should have been shooting to green remained brown and undernourished.

She could see the scars of roads, and runways of an airport, and soon a pipeline for a sewage-treatment plant and dams for more water supplies would mar the mountain. She could see the sharp angles of roofs of private villas huddled round cul-de-sacs like transported suburbs. She turned her horse away.

'C'mon, girls, let's go light a fire and have a hot drink. We're almost there.'

Despite a new VPP sign declaring everything was now banned from the land, including domestic animals, firearms and fires, they continued on towards a brand-new bright yellow

boomgate. It hurt Emily to see it there. It was a lairy pronounce-
ment that this land was now managed from afar, in Melbourne,
and she and her children and her animals were no longer welcome here. She set Snowgum at a canter and, leading Bonus,
jumped over the low rail. The girls' ponies, small enough to
squeeze around the strainer post and a boulder, followed their
mother, Meg's knee catching on the post.

'Why'd they put that there?' Meg said in annoyance.

'Because a man in Melbourne said they had to,' Emily
answered.

They rode on a way down the eastern ridge until the snow
got so deep they opted to turn back towards her grandparents'
reserve. Emily had wanted to see the plain where she and Sam
had last salted cattle but she decided it best to keep closer to
the ridgetop. The weather could close in at any moment.

On the ride back up to the boomgate Emily ducked off the
track. There she pointed out a sign her dad had made.

'It says, Flanaghan Reserve Number Five,' Emily explained.

'What's a reverse?' Tilly said.

'A *reserve*,' Emily corrected. 'It's an area of land protected
from people and some animals, to help keep it healthy. This
one is a sensitive spring that we don't want four-wheel drives
or cattle or people in.'

'Why is it a five?' asked Meg.

'Because it's the fifth reserve your great-grandparents set up.
They made ten reserves all up over this mountain.'

Emily's grandparents had opted to enclose special areas of
the mountains nearly sixty years earlier, long before the term

'conservation' was thought of in government departments. In some places the fences had also kept the four-wheel drive enthusiasts at bay, who seemed to like to carve their vehicles through boggy patches, steep slopes prone to erosion and river crossings just for fun. While the cattle might never return to this ridgeline, the four-wheel drives that came in their hundreds from the city and surrounding regions were still permitted into the Park in summer time. Preservation of the economy at all costs, thought Emily wryly of the government rules that encouraged spending.

As they rode towards the reserve, Emily was disappointed to see a tree had recently fallen, knocking a fence post sideways. The reserve's fence wire lay slack, flung back against the earth. Emily drew her horses up.

'Shall we fix it for old Pa and Ma?'

Tilly and Meg nodded.

'It shouldn't take long,' Emily said, glancing up to the sky, knowing the rough weather would eventually come.

The girls dismounted and tethered their ponies as she lit them a small fire and put the billy on it, scooping up clean snow and placing it inside the tin. She set out cups and filled each with a spoonful or three of Milo and a dash of sugar.

With the girls settled and drinking happily, Emily examined the damage done by the fallen tree. Soon the sound of her chainsaw cut through the air, shattering the peace of the mountainside as she severed the twisted old snowgum from the fence. As it cracked and splintered away and she kicked it with her boot, she saw that the old post her grandfather would've dug into the ground was shattered.

'Bugger,' she said. A new one was needed. The job would take a little longer. Still, Tilly and Meg were warm by the fire and it was a while before dark. They had a good two hours' ride back to the house, but the horses were fit now and well used to the cold, as were the girls. She also knew there was a hut just half an hour's ride down the eastern slope should they really get stuck.

Emily cast her eye about. No suitable trees on the former cattlemen's side of the Park. One was too twisted. One would split at the knot. The others were too small or too big. She took an axe and the chainsaw and soon found her tree. It was close handy, the perfect diameter. She set about to fell the tree.

Rousie pinned his ears down as the chainsaw droned away. The noise was enough to mask the sound of an approaching vehicle which had pulled up at the boomgate. A man got out to unlock it.

By the time the tree fell with a loud crash that echoed out across the massive valley below, the ranger's vehicle, with chains on the wheels, had rolled to a stop not far from the campfire. As Emily cut the chainsaw engine she heard the sound of doors slamming. She looked up, startled.

She breathed in sharply when she saw it was Luke and felt excitement and horror buzz through her. Then she noticed the older VPP man, the red-haired one, who'd been at the Wonnangatta, with a very serious look on his face. She was about to call out a greeting but she saw how Luke avoided her eye, busily pulling on his coat, a hat, and gloves, grabbing a notebook from his pocket.

Together the men made their way towards her, following the snow tracks made by the horses. They looked so official and serious, marching through the trees.

'What do you think you're doing?' asked the older man.

Emily was about to begin explanations and excuses when she felt the earth pulse beneath her boots and a warmth radiate through her body with a fiery strength. She thought of Evie, and her great-grandmothers, Emily Flanaghan and Joan Flanaghan. She held her head high and in a strong but friendly voice said, 'What am I doing? Why, I'm introducing myself to you in the polite, old fashioned way, as bushmen always do,' Emily held out her hand. 'Emily Flanaghan, very pleased to meet you, Mr . . . ?'

The man looked down at her hand as if it stank of dead fish.

Luke intercepted. 'Emily, this is Mr Kelvin Grimsley, acting region manager for the VPP.'

Luke couldn't believe his luck and his misfortune combined. It was wonderful to see Emily again, looking so beautiful and strong. She was decked out in an oilskin. Under her hat, her face shone from good health, her lips pink and kissable in the cold.

Her daughters reflected their mother's self-contained competency as they sat on logs by the fire, but they were looking at him and Kelvin with wide possum eyes, clearly scared their mother was in trouble. Luke saw the gelding he had sold her was laden with packs, work fit but well fed, standing calmly hitched to a tree.

But how awful to find Emily on Park land with a freshly

fallen tree at her feet and his boss from Melbourne by his side. Luke swallowed nervously. He could tell it was going to get ugly.

When they'd first spotted the little girls sitting beside the campfire, Kelvin had spat out his horror to Luke.

'Fancy bringing children out under such dangerous conditions! She must be *mad*. And to cut down a tree on Park land! That just confirms everything I know about the cattlemen. I even think it's the same woman who hid the cattle from us in the Wonnangatta. A typical Flanaghan. Trouble!'

Now Kelvin stood in front of Emily, casting daggers with his gaze. 'You do know it's an offence to fell trees in a national park?'

Luke had sympathised with Emily, but some of the stories Kelvin had told him about the cattlemen's antics, and the scientific data on grazing he'd given Luke to read, had almost convinced Luke their eviction was just a necessary change. But now, seeing Emily in this world, Luke just knew she and her girls belonged here.

He looked at his boss and the word 'wanker' came to mind. Luke had spent the day with Kelvin Grimsley at a VPP luncheon-conference on the Hotham snowfields. Although the High Plains Road over to Dargo was closed due to snow, Kelvin had insisted he travel over it with Luke as part of Luke's four-wheel-drive training component. Kelvin was proud to announce that, as VPP-registered staff, they were permitted access to the snowfall areas of the Dargo High Plains in a time of closure.

Luke knew Kelvin's role as acting region manager was coming to an end soon and he was making the most of it. Kelvin had talked several times about the benefits of having a vehicle and time to travel about away from his Melbourne desk. He'd also been crowing about the trip to Wonnangatta, the fine process still underway, and about the new legislation and plans for the Park.

Because Kelvin had appointed Luke, he'd taken him under his wing. Luke endured Kelvin's condescending mentoring with good humour, in the same way he'd endured Cassy's bossings. He reasoned it was only for a couple of days and soon Kelvin would return to Melbourne, slipping back down the ladder. Luke would then be left in peace in his new job, which so far seemed to involve a lot of driving to the Heyfield office and not so much work out in the bush.

He'd met some nice VPP colleagues at the conference, confirming there were some really bright people in the organisation, people around his age, who were fun and enthusiastic about their work. They'd all filled their bellies with food and enjoyed a couple of glasses of wine before Kelvin announced it was time for them to leave. The road back towards Dargo was reasonable until they reached Mount Freezeout, where snow had begun to thicken, and the tyres started spinning, even in the four-wheel drive. Kelvin was clearly excited to get the new chains out from his off-road kit.

'We'll be late getting home tonight,' he said to Luke. 'But don't worry. You'll be paid overtime.'

Luke cast Kelvin a glance. It had never crossed his mind he should be paid extra for being late. On the farm, they worked until dark or beyond until the job was done, and there was no talk of overtime. At the VPP, everyone reminded him to work exactly seven hours and thirty-six minutes a day. Apparently the extra six minutes earned him a RDO every fortnight. But Luke couldn't understand the prompt laying down of tools once the clock ticked over, even if the job was an hour shy of getting done. There'd been no rostered days off on the land.

As they inched their way over Lanky's Plain, where the snow lay thickest, Luke had pointed out the smoke curling up from the trees into the clear winter-blue sky.

Now, Kelvin continued to stare coldly at Emily and she returned his stare, not with contempt but with pride.

'Isn't it obvious what I'm doing?' she said, gesturing to the broken fence. 'I cut a tree down because I needed a new post. For the reserve.'

'I'll say again, it's an offence to cut down a tree from a national park,' Kelvin said.

Emily looked at him incredulously and then to Luke for help, but his eyes, she thought, regarded her with impartiality.

'I'm hardly likely to duck down to Bunnings to get a post, am I?' she said. 'Not when there's a perfect one just there in the bush!'

'You are not responsible for fencing in this area,' said Kelvin.

Emily looked again at Luke but his eyes would not meet hers. Was he just going to stand there and say nothing?

'Excuse me,' she said, the anger creeping into her voice, 'but I *am* responsible for this fence. My grandparents put in that reserve to protect the spring in that thicket there. I figure it's my responsibility to preserve my family's work and to protect the spring.'

'Your family no longer has any claim over this land,' Kelvin said with satisfaction. He'd had years of battling these cattlemen from his offices. To now be out in the field with one and experiencing their arrogance again was enough to make his blood boil.

'I don't want *claim* over this land,' Emily shot back. 'I just want to *care* for it.'

'Care for it by cutting down trees?' Kelvin said. 'You cattlemen only *pretend* to be environmentalists. If you really cared for the high country, you'd take your kids, your horses and your cattle and you'd get off this mountain!'

Emily's mouth dropped open.

'You arsehole,' she said, the words escaping before she could stuff them back in. She saw his jaw clench and a flash of hatred on his face.

Kelvin steered Luke away from her, talking quietly. Luke nodded, frowning, and wrote something down in a notebook.

They came back.

'If you continue to abuse me, this will become a matter for the police,' Kelvin said. 'Plus, you have endangered the lives of your children by bringing them into such remote and rugged conditions when the Park is closed. It begs the question whether you are fit to be mothering these children at all.'

Emily was speechless with rage. Didn't this man know that the Flanaghans had taken their children all over this mountain for generations? Didn't he know that some of the boys were packing horses in the snow to help get mail and supplies through to hungry miners from as young as nine years of age?

How dare he insinuate that she was risking her children! She knew they were safe. She had plans and provisions for every scenario. She had her animals with her too, and they had the best bushman skills of all. Rousie and her horses would guide her home no matter what. She stood with fury lighting the ends of every nerve so that her clenched fists quivered like live fish on hooks.

Kelvin stepped back. 'Now, my colleague, Mr Bradshaw, will inform you of the Park breaches you face.'

And Luke, ashen-faced, began to read from his notebook. She looked at the face she once thought was beautiful and the lips she had kissed and dreamed of kissing again, as he read in a monotone voice.

'Dogs are prohibited on Park land. You will be fined for breaching this regulation under Park policy. You will incur a fine for riding horses on Park land without an out-of-season permit. You are in serious breach of Park policy in the felling of a tree. That too will incur a fine. You are in breach of Park safety venturing into an area that is closed to the public. The presence of children here is also a serious act of negligence and the police and family services will be informed of this. The lighting of fires in a non-designated campfire area is also a breach of Park policy. The total of these infringements will amount to $2,312, pending a hearing.' He then began to read her her rights.

Emily listened, her mouth open. She couldn't believe what

she was hearing from Luke's lips. When he had finished, he tried to maintain his steely look, but Emily was sure she could see shame on his face. He wouldn't look her in the eye. She felt the fury rise within her. An icy breeze whirled snow about and brought with it a white mist that blanketed everything about them. Emily stood with the anger and distress swirling in her.

'How can you do this? How can you be like this?' she said softly, the question more to Luke than Kelvin. She was devastated. She was only trying to do the right thing by the land, by the people who had cared for the land before her. She paid her taxes. She respected others. And she truly did care for the land. How could Kelvin Grimsley say that cattlemen weren't environmentalists, when most of her family had lived as environmentalists long before it became trendy to do so? Yet here she was being treated like a criminal in her own sacred place. And here was Luke, siding with Kelvin and kicking her when she was lower than low. For weeks she'd heard nothing from Clancy – as if his girls didn't exist. His lack of support for Emily still stung her. Now here was Luke treating her the same way. Did the fact they had been lovers count for nothing? She called out to Meg and Tilly. 'C'mon, girls. Let's leave these gentlemen to their *Park*.'

'You'll be hearing from us, Ms Flanaghan,' Kelvin Grimsley said.

As the weather worsened, he retreated to the warmth of the four-wheel-drive cab and waited for Luke to join him. But Luke remained out in the freezing snowfall, wanting to help Emily pack away her gear on the horse they held in common.

But the immense pressure of feeling his superior's eyes watching his every move held him back. Yet the image he saw over and over in his head was the devastation on Emily's face. He was furious with himself for being so weak. He could see both sides now: Kelvin doing a job he truly believed in, whether it was wrong or right; and Emily, evicted from a place that was in her heart. He'd seen her as the girl who'd be the answer to his drifting. He thought they had the land in common, the horses in common and, when they'd made love that night at Wonnangatta, their souls in common too, but now he wondered if he'd burned a bridge forever.

Sadly, he watched as Emily's girls efficiently put out their fire, packed the billy and pannikins onto their saddlebags and swung up onto their ponies. Emily quickly stashed her tools into Bonus's packs and expertly hitched the packs tight again. He could tell by the way she jerked the straps that she was furious. Then she lobbed up onto Snowgum. She grabbed up her reins and rode right past Luke, nearly knocking him over. She set her eyes on the man in the vehicle and he stared back at her with contempt.

Luke couldn't help it. He called out after her, 'It's a near white-out. Will you be right to find your own way back?'

'More right than you'll be,' Emily said bitterly, knowing she should guide them back to the main road in this weather but too angry to offer. And she kicked Snowgum into a canter and popped her and Bonus over the boomgate. Her girls, in a rush of bravado, followed their mother at the jump, the littlest pony just clipping the yellow boom with the tip of her nearside rear hoof. Then they jogged away as fast as they could in the snow, keen to leave the strict and scary men behind. As they veered left off the track into the snowgums, Emily fought back tears. But she had little time to let the emotions get the better of her. It *was* a total white-out. They couldn't see more than a metre in front of their horses. Stuff them, she thought. Emily tugged her hat down low and flipped her collar up. She smiled. She knew if she simply gave Snowgum her head, the old mare would guide them all safely home on the winding bridle tracks.

Thirty-one

When they at last reached the homestead, they were surprised to see Evie's little four-wheel-drive Suzuki parked in the shed, the chains on the wheels still crusted with snow.

'Evie!' Meg shrieked.

'You go on inside and get warm,' Emily said. 'I'll fix the ponies.'

'Thanks, Mum,' said Tilly, her eyes aglow at the thought of their very special visitor. Then the girls were running inside to the warmth of Evie.

When Emily came in she found Evie dishing up steaming soup to Meg and Tilly. They were already scoffing chunks of fresh bread coated thickly with dobs of Evie's homemade butter.

'What are you doing here? The snow! I thought you'd come up after it melted.'

'I didn't know we were going to have such a season! Plus, driving in snow is easy-peasy compared to driving in bulldust in the desert,' Evie said with a wink.

As Evie sat Emily down in front of a steaming plate of delicious chicken and vegetable soup, Emily realised she knew almost nothing of Evie's past. She knew she was a nurse, she knew she had worked in Aboriginal communities in the desert, but she didn't know where she came from, about her family, if she had children.

Emily was about to ask when Evie said, 'You look like you've had a tough day.' Emily felt a wave of despair as she recalled Luke's strained face and cold voice. She bit her lip and looked to her lap. Evie patted Emily's hand. 'One moment.'

Evie pulled out a platter of chocolates from the meat safe and passed them to Tilly.

'There you are, my darlings. You go sit by the fire and enjoy these. We'll bring you a hot chocolate in just a moment.'

'Thanks!'

The girls gone, Evie drew up a chair next to Emily and sat facing her.

'Tell me,' she said, her green eyes blazing.

Emily felt so confused. She felt beaten and broken. She told Evie about Kelvin Grimsley, who had acted so superior, who had come onto her family's sacred place and made her feel like nothing, like she was an outsider in her own heartland.

'To top it all, Luke was there,' Emily said, 'and he did *nothing* to help me. Instead he threw the book at me! They're going to fine me and inform some other department I'm not a fit mother!'

'Shush, shush,' Evie said, drawing Emily into her arms. 'What a load of rot. You're a fine mother and a fine bushman. Luke knows that. He was just protecting himself.'

'But worrying about a *job* ahead of what is morally right, I thought he was so much better than that.'

'Oh, I think you'll find he is. But perhaps Luke was protecting himself from something else.' Emily looked confused. Evie lifted her eyebrows. 'My dear, can't you see? He was protecting himself from you.'

'From me?'

'Yes. He's in love with you.'

The words seemed to hang in the air around Emily. She frowned. 'But —'

'There are no buts. He has a soul connection to you that runs so deeply it frightens him. And the time isn't yet right in this lifetime for you to join him.'

Emily almost rolled her eyes but something stopped her. She could see such conviction in Evie that she began to allow her words to sink in. Evie never tried to *prove* her theories to her and Sam. She just spoke as if things simply *were* as she said they were.

'We all have a body, right? And inside that body is a soul that, when we die, leaves this planet for the non-physical realm. Sometimes those souls come back into other bodies. That's why sometimes when you meet someone it feels like you've known them for an age. You get that feeling because you *have* known them for an age! Sometimes thousands of years over many lifetimes. Sometimes there are advanced souls in the non-physical world that guide you in the physical world. That's how it is for all of us. The more you're tuned in to it, the more you'll see it.'

Emily shook her head. Until Evie, until her accident, she'd never contemplated stuff like this. Some days she was up for Evie's strange notions. But tonight she was tired. Her face felt raw from the day in the bitter cold. She felt deeply hurt by the encounter with Kelvin Grimsley, and by Luke's silence. A log in the kitchen woodstove moved, making her jump.

'My God,' said Evie. 'You're a mess, girl! C'mon, I'll make you a hot chocolate as well,' she said, getting up from the table. 'I think I better slip some of your Aunt Flo's harder stuff into it too. Now get up off your backside and onto that couch in the dining room to snuggle with your girls. I'll bring it in.'

'Thank you. Thank you so much, Evie,' Emily said wearily.

Emily dozed off. She dreamed of cattle in the snow, plunging deeply through drifts, Tilly and Meg following them on ponies. Emily was screaming at them all to stop, but no sound would come from her mouth. The snowy landscape was silent, despite her internal screams. She watched in horror as the girls, their ponies and the cattle all tumbled over the cliff, bodies thudding violently on rocks as they fell. On the mountain opposite, the skiers watched and toasted the sight with shining glass flutes of bubbling champagne.

She woke suddenly to the shrill ring of the phone, gasping. Evie must've put the girls to bed as they were no longer with her on the couch. She grappled on the mantelpiece for matches and lit a lantern. In the armchair beside her Evie was stirring awake.

'Who could that be?' she said sleepily.

Emily hurried to the phone.

'Emily?' There was a delay as the radio phone beamed its signal to the satellite tower and back.

'Dad?'

'Just had a call from Parks. Any sign of two rangers up your way? It seems they're missing. Were due back this afternoon in Dargo but there was no show.'

She asked her father the time.

'It's after midnight.'

'Yeah, I've seen 'em,' she said.

'Where?'

'Out on the Long Spur.'

'When?'

'Dad,' she broke down, her voice cracking, 'it was awful. They tried to ping me on all fronts – when all the girls and I were doing was fixing a bloody fence at Ma and Pa's reserve at the spring. They reckon they'll fine me or take me to court. And they said they'll get the family services in – that I'm not a fit mother. Just for, for . . . I dunno what! So I left 'em. Out there on the Long Spur at some new boomgate in a white-out.'

'Oh, Emily,' her father said.

'I thought they'd be right! They're supposed to be rangers. They weren't far off the track.'

'That young bloke is brand new and wouldn't have been up there more than once or twice, and you know it. And the other fella, well, he's from Melbourne. Plus you know it's a black spot for radio reception that side of the range.'

'The trees were blazed – I even did a couple of fresh marks myself on my way through.'

'They wouldn't know to look for the blazes.'

'I know,' she said quietly, guilty that she hadn't guided the men out to the main road where modern snow markers of orange plastic flagged the worst of the snow-covered road. 'I was so mad, Dad. I'm sorry.'

'I'll have to tell the authorities. If they're really lost, there could be all kinds of enquiries and you could find yourself more than fined!'

'Dad, I'm sorry. I'll set out at dawn and see if I can find them.'

'Don't rush out in the morning. The weather's not meant to lift until mid-morning anyway. I'll call you. Chances are they'll send a chopper across from Hotham at first light.'

'A chopper! Are you serious? They've only been gone one night. They'll be okay if they stay with the vehicle and I know at least one of them has the sense to do that,' Emily said, thinking of Luke.

She shook her head. She was so confused by Luke's behaviour. He was a farm boy, but he'd been touched by a government culture that seemed to skew real life. She thought of him reading out from the infringement book, his voice monotone and devoid of emotion. Was a job so important that he couldn't speak up for her?

When Emily put down the phone, Evie was standing behind her, her hair sticking up on one side from sleeping in the chair.

'You must be like a sapling,' Evie said.

'A sapling?'

'Yes, not a rigid tree trunk. Saplings bend with the winds of trouble. They bounce back quickly when times are still. But trees that are inflexible in the wind simply get blown over. Try not to resist what life throws at you, Emily. You must be flexible and bend with it. Be in the flow. And remember, never shrink to be a tussock.'

'A tussock?' Emily said, leaning forward and hoping for more pearls of wisdom. 'Why not a tussock?'

Evie looked her in the eye and Emily saw a twinkle. 'Because dogs and wombats crap on tussocks.'

Evie began to laugh, and so too did Emily.

They both made their way back to the dining room where they stoked up the fire and resettled themselves under blankets on the couches. There was no way Emily could sleep now, knowing Luke was still out there, probably with the vehicle running for warmth, shut in the four-wheel drive with only his boss for company. But, Emily thought angrily, he deserved it.

The next day, despite what Rod had said, Emily set out early with the wind whipping coldly about her. Evie stayed behind with the girls, who for the first time were not begging to come out for another ride. Even though the weather was rough, Emily knew their reluctance was mostly because they didn't want to go near the grumpy man again. Meg had mentioned him several times last night, saying in Evie's words that he had an angry energy.

Emily didn't want to go near Kelvin again either, but as she rode Bonus towards the Long Spur, she knew she was doing this for Luke.

Suddenly, the clouds parted and sunshine poured down upon the snow. She thought about Evie's view that Luke loved her. If he did, surely he would've stuck up for her. With the warmth of the morning sun on her face, Emily realised now that she couldn't help but love Luke too. No matter what he'd done. She also heard Evie's words again, that the time for them was not right. She thought of Evie's talk on souls last night and 'other lives', past and future. If she and Luke couldn't be together in this lifetime, Emily decided now she would look for Luke first in her next life.

She felt comforted by that thought and urged Bonus on faster. He was breathing heavily, as the effort of walking through deep snow was great, but he was also fit and lean and completely bonded to Emily. Even though she was riding out to find two lost men and the situation could be serious, Emily felt a lightness. She was enjoying the solitude, the first time in weeks she'd had time off from being a mum, just her and Bonus. Her one link with Luke. What a gift he was.

As she rode, she recalled a story about her grandfather's bushman's knack for finding people who had become lost on the vast ridges of the high plains. On one occasion he'd ridden right up to a large log in a gully where he figured the bushwalker may have wandered, hopelessly lost. Sure enough the walker was there, lying asleep on the lee side of the log, cold, but none the worse for wear. The walker was woken by the deep voice of Emily's grandfather saying, 'So, do you want to be found today, boy?' It seemed only fitting that here again, Emily was looking out for stranded people on the mountain. Ironically, they were VPP employees in the year of the bans.

On the last zigzag pinch onto the track, Emily pulled her horse up short in the cover of the trees. There they were, and with them a further three vehicles that had clearly travelled from Mt Hotham. There were rangers everywhere, laughing and chatting. There in the huddle were Luke and his boss. Relieved for him, Emily watched for a while.

She was about to swing her horse around when Luke looked up as if he'd sensed her there. She saw his expression change when he saw her sitting astride the big young chestnut amidst the snow and the twisted limbs of the trees.

He smiled at her. The most gentle, beautiful smile. He slowly shook his head and mouthed 'sorry' to her. Emily didn't return his smile. He's not for me in this lifetime, she told herself, and she suddenly felt a powerful freedom.

She was beholden to no man, Emily realised. And she was no longer only a cattleman's daughter, but a cattleman in her own right. She was a strong woman who could survive on her own in a rich, wonderful life. Like a sapling she would bend to any troubles that came her way.

'Goodbye,' she whispered. 'See you in another life.'

She turned and urged her horse on, sliding, laughing and tumbling down the track, enjoying the bright clear warmth of the sun and keen to be home again with her girls and Evie.

Thirty-two

Weeks later, Emily was surprised to see a solitary yellow daffodil blooming beneath a sprinkling of snow beside the stable. Spring had arrived on the mountains, and this one special winter with her daughters was coming to an end.

After that first bloom, spring began to reveal itself all around them. She pointed out to Meg and Tilly the shoots of Granny Bonnets emerging from the icy soil. Above them, bright green, red and blue parrots skittered overhead, flirting in their own private mating ritual. Mother Nature was nudging Emily to accept that her self-imposed isolation was over. It was time to pack up and go back to the lowlands, time to make a new life.

As she carried bags out to the ute, Emily held within her a sense of accomplishment – she had not merely endured the winter here, but thrived in it. She had ticked off many of the jobs on her list and also added more, knowing she was free to come and go from here as she pleased. It was her home. She was no longer answerable to any man. She felt altogether changed and altered.

She now had a lean, fit body, and her mind was sharp too. The only thing worrying her was how she was going to earn an income. She had no formal qualifications for anything. But she pushed the worries away and focused on the positives.

Tilly and Meg had also thrived in this wilderness and as she watched them now, dragging their backpacks onto the verandah, she saw they were very different children to the meek little ones she'd mothered in the suburban house in Brigalow. She realised how withdrawn the girls had been there, hunkering down in front of the television if Clancy was in a rage. But now, they no longer asked after their father, and seemed so alive and engaged with the world around them, that they offered to help with everything and asked questions all the time.

There was no need to pack everything up. The horses would stay in the vast home paddock and the food could remain in the pantry as Emily knew they'd be back soon. She now planned to live between the two houses – her father's on the lowlands and here.

She was heading down now to enrol the girls at the school for next year, then would travel back up for the summer holidays. Perhaps she could get a job in the pub or the store so she could pay the bills that would no doubt soon follow now they were heading back to the modern world.

As they reached the foothills of the mountains, the rivers were fresh from snowmelt, the water rushing and burbling over rocks. On the road into Dargo, the giant walnut trees, once winter skeletons, were beginning to shoot huge green shady leaves. The gums frothed with flowers.

Emily drove past the church and the school. She held her breath when she passed the ranger's office, both wanting and not wanting to see Luke. But his vehicle was not there, and Emily laughed at herself for the mixture of relief and disappointment that swirled in her.

The Tranquillity driveway was flanked prettily with walnut trees and elms in true Dargo fashion. Emily drove past Bob's house, surprised to see DD back on the chain bouncing up and down. For the first time the dog's coat was glossy and he was actually fat.

Bob's lawn was mown, not grazed. And the daffodils in the garden beds that had survived from her grandparents' days had been joined by other bright spring blooms that had obviously been *planted*. Emily frowned. Had someone else moved into Bob's?

Emily had barely switched off the vehicle before Meg and Tilly were out, bounding up the verandah steps. They ran into the house calling out, 'Grandpa, Grandpa!'

There was no one about. The house was silent, the kitchen empty. They came banging out of the big wooden screen door their faces subdued.

'No one's home.'

Emily frowned again. She'd rung to say they would be home around lunchtime.

'They're probably out working,' she said. 'We'll see them later. Come on. Help Mum with the bags.'

The girls, a little grumpy now, lugged bags into the homestead. As they walked along the hallway they heard a noise.

A snickering.

'Shush,' Emily said to the girls. 'Did you hear that?'

Meg and Tilly's eyes lit up. 'They're playing tricks!'

They all dashed to the one closed door of the house, the dining room. Swinging it open, they were met with a chorus of voices shouting, 'Surprise!'

The Flanaghan family stood around the table, which was laden with Evie's lunchtime feast. Emily was amazed to see Sam there with his arm around Bridie. Sam's cheeky handsome face glowed with good health and Bridie beamed a welcoming smile at Emily. Evie stood beside Rod, who radiated love and pride for his daughter and granddaughters. Next to him stood Flo, who towered over Baz, her arm slung about his shoulders. And beside them, to Emily's astonishment, stood Bob.

Bob had lost weight, shaved his head, and had a fresh tattoo of a flaming comet on his forearm. He was wearing tight black jeans with a silver studded belt and a black T-shirt with Keith Urban's funky country rock designs on it. He even had an earring!

Emily, tears brimming, rushed to hug each and every one of them as they told her how fit and strong she looked and how beautiful the girls were. They began to trip over their words and their conversations ran this way and that as Emily tried to find out all their news.

'Sam's album will be out next year,' Bridie said. 'Ike reckons Compass really like the demos we recorded and they'll sign him!'

'And Bridie's going to get paid as my PA and wardrobe assistant,' Sam said, clutching her hand, clearly proud of her.

'Stylist,' Bridie corrected.

'*Stylist*. That's it! I couldn't do it without you, babe.'

'And we couldn't do it without Bob,' Bridie added, casting Bob a wink.

'We needed cash fast to help pay for the rental house and the studio, so Bridie coaxed me into a couple of pub gigs,' Sam explained. 'Before long we had bookings every week, not just weekends either. I started to feel a bit, you know, over it. With that pressure back on I was about to turn it all down and give it all away again, when Bob walked into our lives.'

'Bob was touring up the coast,' Bridie said, 'weren't you, Bob?'

Bob nodded. 'I blew a fuse in me head around the time of the grazing bans. Thought, I can't do it anymore.' He shivered at the memory, but his eyes lifted and settled on Evie. She smiled at him.

'Luckily Evie suggested I go walkabout for a bit. To find what really floated my boat. I was just about to give up when I bumped into Sam and Bridie in a pub in Coolum.'

'Man, did we do some drinking that night!' Sam said. 'And some D&Ming. We sorted out all the crap between us.'

'In the finish,' Bridie said, 'Bob came on board as Sam's band manager and roadie. He's the one who rounded up the best musos to play with Sam on his pub gigs, and he's the one who's organised all the gigs. It frees Sam up and takes the pressure off me.'

'He's a natural,' Sam said. 'One of the best I've worked with and he's still a new kid to the muso game!'

Bob grinned. 'You can't help be good at doing something you love!' His round red face softened for a moment and he looked earnestly at Emily. 'I've worked out I hated being a cattle farmer. Hated it with a passion but felt obligated to do it. And that's why I'm crap at it. I'm so sorry I've wasted so much of my life, and wasted so much of your time, before I figured that out.' Emily was about to soothe things, but Bob held up his hand to silence her.

'I've been an arse. But with things taking off with Sam in the next twelve months, we know the three of us are going places. United States or bust.'

'And this time we're doing it drug and dickhead-free,' added Sam.

Emily smiled at Sam.

'There's more, though, isn't there, Bob?' Bridie prompted.

'You bet,' he said, turning back to Emily. 'You're good at what you do because you love it too. I can see you're a bloody good mum and a bloody good cattleman. That's why I'm leasing you my land up on the plains and down here on the lowlands. If you'd like.'

Emily's mouth fell open.

'You don't have to say yes right away,' Bob said. 'You do your sums, work out if you can make a go of it. The lease payments won't be huge, because one day I'll be leavin' the lot to you and your girls anyway.' Bob shrugged. 'Because you're the one the land deserves the most. That's why old Hughie upstairs spared your life after that horse accident. Least that's what I reckon.'

A smile lit Emily's face. Bob was giving her a go on the land.

She loved the way he'd put it too; that the land deserved her. Not the other way round, that she deserved the land. It didn't work that way in her mind. The land did deserve someone who not only loved it, but could read its messages, understand it and above all respect the balance needed in its management.

'Thank you, Bob,' Emily said, tilting her glass towards him in a toast. 'Thank you so very bloody *much*!'

Emily beamed. Her dream was alive again. The life of a cattleman now stretched out before her, like a road suddenly cleared. She glanced over to her father and smiled at him. He was never one for noise or fuss, but Emily could see the happiness he felt.

She looked at Evie and she, too, had a calm expression of satisfaction on her face, as if she had orchestrated the whole thing. Then, suddenly, Emily realised that in many ways Evie *had* made all these miracles happen.

'A toast,' Emily said. 'To us! The Flanaghans – that includes you too, Evie.' And they all chorused Emily and drank.

When the meal was done and the table cleared, Rod delivered a pile of mail to Emily's lap.

'Welcome back to the real world,' he said.

'Gee, thanks, Dad,' Emily said dryly as she flicked through the envelopes until one caught her attention. The black lettering read *Family Services Dept*. Her heart leapt. She tore the envelope open anxiously and began to read.

She sat for a time in silence as the rest of the family buzzed about the kitchen, washing up, stacking plates. Skylarking. It took them a while to notice Emily's silence.

'What is it?' Bridie asked.

'They want to investigate me as a mother,' Emily said. 'They say I've put the girls in danger and I have to go into Sale for an interview.'

'Are you serious?' Bridie said. Flo grabbed the letter. Evie read it over Flo's shoulder.

'That's a shocker,' Flo said. 'You couldn't get a better mother than Emily. How could they? Bastards!'

'It's understandable,' Evie soothed. 'Anyone who doesn't fit with convention is a threat to bureaucracy. Emily doesn't fit into a neat little box. This is just the government men throwing their weight around, trying to justify their pay packets. It's a storm in a teacup. Once the girls settle into school next year at Dargo, they'll pipe down.'

'But that's not the point! Those mountains are our way of life. How can they condemn her for that?' Flo said.

'They'll let it go. It's just a power play by the man who saw her on the mountains. It's a rap over the knuckles because they're jealous of Emily's freedom and oneness with the land.'

There was that word again, Emily thought angrily. *They*. She knew they lived in a lucky land, but the era of the public servant was upon them and to Emily it felt stifling after being away from it for months on the high plains. Here was another letter in her hand in cold bureau-speak, threatening her very existence again.

'Well, I've had it with the "*them*". I'm going to find out just who started this and who "they" are.' She thought of storming into Luke's office over it, but she knew it was the men in Melbourne pulling all the strings.

Evie shook her head. 'Let it lie, Emily. Let them dig their own graves. You don't need to jump in and finish the hole for them. Fight this with positivity.'

Emily nodded, but Evie's coaching gave her little comfort. If she lost her girls, her life wouldn't be worth living. Could the government do that? Take her daughters from her?

Deep in the night Meg came in and quietly curled up with Emily in the bed.

'Go to sleep,' Meg said, resting a hand on Emily's forehead.

How did Meg know she'd been lying awake in the darkened room for hours now?

'Okay, darling,' Emily said, pulling Meg to her. 'I will.'

'Sweet Mummy,' Meg said sleepily. 'The granny will be happy about Uncle Bob's land.'

Emily opened her eyes. 'What granny?'

'The granny that helps you.'

'You mean Evie?' She felt Meg shake her head.

'The granny that follows you in the snow. The one that watches you when you split the wood.'

'What granny?' Emily said.

'You know,' Meg said. 'You know, Mummy.'

Thirty-three

'Take it steady,' Flo said as she hauled herself up next to Emily in the truck. 'You gotta glide the gear knob gently into place, as if you were holding your fella's precious one-eyed trouser snake. No grating gears. Okay?'

'*Okay*!' Emily rolled her eyes and looked at Flo's squint of concern in the early morning light. She flicked the gear stick into neutral.

'You gotta go easy on the clutch, too. Double clutch in the bends.' Emily looked at Flo, beginning to regret asking to borrow Baz's stock truck and trailer to take cattle up to the high plains. Flo was acting like a mother hen with their precious new red DAF.

'I've got my licence. I know how to drive it! Stop panicking.'

'It's not an *it*!' Flo said. 'This big revvin' baby is my Hugh Jackman.' She patted the truck. 'Aren't ya, gorgeous? Huge Jack-man!'

'If you're so worried, you drive it, I mean *him*, and take the cattle to the plains for me!'

Flo shook her head. 'No, you go on alone. I trust you.' She carefully shut the truck door and Emily wound the window down and looked over to her father's house.

'Tilly! Meg! You coming or what? Hurry. We've got a big day ahead,' bellowed Emily from the cab. The girls slammed through the screen door, their packs in their hands and smiles on their faces as Flo helped them up into the DAF.

'Don't you go spilling food in Auntie Flo's cab, you hear! Or put grubby fingers on the windows.'

'Flo!' barked Emily.

'All right.' Flo threw her hands up in the air. 'I know you'll look after it.'

As Emily pulled onto the Tranquillity driveway she deliberately bunny-hopped the truck for a few metres, watching the horrified look on Flo's face. Then she let rip with two good blasts of the air horn and stuck her middle finger up at Flo before rolling the rig away down the drive.

Since she'd taken over the lease of Bob's land, Emily hadn't stopped working. She had set out to restore not only his land, but also her father's tired old Dargo house.

Any spare time she had she spent scraping flaky paint from the walls and puttying, sanding and painting. On the plains she began fencing, and on the lowlands ripping trenches for poly-pipe in a new watering system that would keep the cattle out of the river that ran through Bob's Dargo property. At night she tallied cattle sums, trying to work out how much she could make to spend on the land and during sleepless hours she tried figuring out drought strategies. In between it all, she was forever busy with the girls. She no longer cast her mind to Clancy. She'd heard he was living in Bairnsdale with Penny, and it was Penny who was urging him to get in touch with the girls – but so far he hadn't called. Word was out he was a changed man. Perhaps he needed a bossy nurse to make a fuss of him, Emily concluded. Instead of worrying about bumping into Clancy around Dargo, Emily now worried about running into Luke and went to all kinds of measures to avoid him. So far, so good. She'd seen neither man. It suited her that way.

As she rolled along in the truck, the girls singing to an Adam Brand CD, Emily's mind was miles away. In a good year she could still run three hundred head on the lowlands. But that was in a good year. Since the rain in autumn and only a few inches in spring, no more had fallen and the landscape around Dargo was barren, with dams in some paddocks running dry. It wasn't even December yet, and already they had endured some hellishly hot, windy days.

In a year like this she could run, at a stretch, two hundred head of cows on the lowlands, but she needed to help Bob's land on the plains recover. She planned to stock it lightly in the first two years of summer with just a hundred and fifty cows. She didn't want to stretch her lower country, so she opted to sell fifty head. The cows were in good nick and the extra money would go towards fencing up on Bob's. Now was her chance to make amends to the run up there. To set it right.

Instead of droving, Emily had chosen to truck the one hundred and fifty cattle up in several trips, so small were the numbers now due to the bans. While she was sorry they weren't droving, Emily reasoned she could use her days more efficiently this year, fencing cattle out of areas that needed rehabilitation. Emily told herself they could always return to droving once the seasons were more generous and Bob's land was in better shape.

She looked out at the garden that would swelter once the sun was up. Yesterday the girls had been playing in a pitiful few inches of water in an inflatable pool beneath a weeping willow. There wasn't enough water in the tanks, nor the river, to warrant the sprinkler being on much at all, but the garden from the road looked like an oasis of green in a frazzled landscape. At least the prospect of an intense fire season had allowed them to justify running the taps a little around the house for the girls to play with. That small buffer of green could be a saviour should fire come this summer. She revved the truck up a gear and rattled on to pick the cattle up from the yards.

Luke Bradshaw frowned when he saw the giant dusty red truck with stock trailer pulled over in the middle of seemingly nowhere. He stopped the VPP vehicle behind the truck and looked about, sniffing the pungent waft of cow dung coming from the empty truck. He heard a dog bark to the west of the road and saw someone over by a stream. He started striding over the tussocky plain towards them. Soon Emily's black and tan kelpie was bounding over to greet him, a big kelpie-grin on his face and his tail wagging frantically.

Luke saw Emily standing beside the stream. She looked gorgeous in her grubby jeans, a thick leather work belt and a tight blue singlet that showed her curves. Her brown shoulders, wet from the river, glistened in the warm afternoon sun. An Akubra hat shaded her pretty face. Luke knew she would be nervous she'd been 'sprung' with a dog in the national park. Her goldy-haired girls looked up from their panning and he could read the fear on their faces that their mother was about to get in trouble again.

Luke wasn't going to play by his ranger rules today.

'Hi!' he said, as best he could to convey a friendly casual air. 'Struck gold yet?' He stooped and ran his hands over Rousie's ears.

Emily tilted her head and answered cautiously, 'Nope. Not yet.'

'How have you been?' he asked gently, with an uncertain smile.

'Fine.'

'Em, I'm sorry. Okay? About last winter. *Really* sorry.'

Luke stood before her, apology written on his face in a frown. He was gorgeous in his shorts, his fit, strong legs a deep brown, his lace-up boots looking worn and rugged. She looked into his dark eyes and saw the kindness in them.

'I've left it too long, I know, but I . . .' His voice faded.

Emily stepped back. 'I don't think you've ever met my girls properly,' she said, changing the subject quickly as she digested Luke's apology. She watched as he crouched down to Meg and Tilly.

'My name's Luke. What are your names?'

The girls looked at him, but remained silent.

'Luke's a friend of Mummy's,' Emily said. 'Say hello!' Tilly and Meg blinked at the man before them. He seemed nice now, but after their day in the snow with the cross old ranger, they were wary.

'This is my youngest, Meg, and this is Matilda, but we call her Tilly,' Emily said, speaking for them, her tone a little forced.

'Hi, Meg and Tilly!' He moved over to the stream. 'You going to show me how to pan for gold?'

Emily ushered them over to the stream and reluctantly they set about dipping their pans into the water. But soon they were laughing, splashing and chatting with Luke. Emily joined in cautiously, but part of her was still hurt by his presence there in his uniform on what had once been Flanaghan land. She knew Evie would say 'forgive and forget'. Perhaps she should put that day in the snow behind her and allow herself to feel joy he was here, being so kind. She was grateful he hadn't mentioned the fact she had a dog and a stock truck in 'the Park'. He seemed to understand now. Standing near him by the stream Emily felt her heart flutter again. She had quashed her feelings for him long enough.

The sun was dipping down beneath the treeline and the cold came in quickly.

'Well, it looks as if we won't find gold today,' Luke said, winking at Emily but talking to the girls. 'It's time for me to go. We'd all better go.'

'Can we go panning with Luke again tomorrow?' Meg asked

Emily, grabbing hold of her mother's hand with wet, cold fingers, her eyes bright.

'Luke has to work. And you're going to Evie's for a visit, while Mummy goes fencing. Maybe another day.'

'Oh!' Meg said, stamping her foot. 'Mummy! You must let this nice Luke into our life. He's one for keeps, like you said about the hairy guinea pig when we got him!' She frowned up at Emily and Emily, shocked, frowned back at her daughter.

'Back to the truck, *now*!'

Meg and Tilly stomped off, while Luke, grinning, stacked up the pans and passed them to Emily. Their hands touched momentarily. Emily felt the zing. He caught her eye.

'It's Saturday tomorrow,' he said. 'I'm not working.'

'Well, I am,' Emily said.

'What are you doing?' Luke said cheerfully. 'Maybe I can help?'

Emily couldn't believe it. Here he was part of the group that had taken this land from them and he was offering to help! But Meg's words stuck in her head. Let him in, Emily, she thought.

'I'm riding out round Bob's run to check the fences and do a few patch-up jobs.'

'You got a spare horse? I could come with you and learn a bit about the place.'

Emily looked at him, amazed that he would want to. Hesitatingly she nodded.

'Yeah? You could ride your gelding, if you like. He's coming along really well.'

'I would like,' Luke said. 'I'd like that a lot! I'll see you first thing, then.'

And before Emily could change her mind, or warn him away, Luke was gone, jogging over the snowgrass plains towards the truck. There he cheerfully helped the girls into the cab and waved to Emily as he got into his vehicle and revved away.

'He's really nice, he is,' said Meg, when Emily clambered into the driver's seat.

'Shut it, Meg,' Emily snapped.

'But he *is* really nice,' Tilly added.

'You shush too,' Emily said, her nerves dancing.

'Why is Mummy so cross about Luke?' Tilly said, rolling her eyes and folding her arms across her body.

'Because she likes him but she thinks she's not allowed to because he's a ranger,' Meg said wisely. 'And she's worried about giving us a new daddy – when we still have an old daddy.'

'All right, you two! Yes, I like Luke. Okay, I really like him and your old daddy will *always* be your daddy. You don't just swap daddies. But can you please stop talking now?'

'You really, *really* like him?' Meg said.

'For a boy, he's really nice,' Tilly said again.

'Yes,' Meg said. 'For a boy. He'd make a nice other Daddy.'

'Will you two just be quiet?' Emily said, lamenting that she hadn't said no to Luke. She was nervous, like it was a first date. She began to run through what daggy work clothes she'd packed. Then she realised the only clean pair of undies she had with her were the bright-green ones with the white lettering that read *Plough my patch* with an arrow to the crutch. Too late to rinse her most normal pair, which had a puppy on them with *Bury your bone here*. They would never be dry in time. The green ones it would have to be!

'Oh, *God*,' Emily groaned, wondering why she was thinking of Luke and her undies at the same time.

'It's okay,' Meg said. 'God knows, Mummy. He knows everything.'

Thirty-four

Outside the pub, Cassy Jacobson swung the wheel of her new little green Jazz. She was furious. She'd driven all this way only to find Luke wasn't home. Now she was searching the town for the ranger's office.

Her eyes narrowed at the giant four-wheel drives that lined the pub. She let out a huff when she read the stickers on the back: *Fertilise the Bush – Doze in a Greenie*. They were also plastered with chainsaw stickers. She couldn't believe Luke had chosen to live in this bloody town. She couldn't believe he was still dicking about in that dump of a house by the mosquito-infested river.

Cassy dragged off her hat, which looked like a crocheted green teacosy, and ran her silver-ringed fingers through her spiked-up hair.

The store was closed and no one was in sight along the street. If she wanted to find Luke's again by nightfall, she'd have to go in the pub. But she just couldn't. Those rednecks would probably eat her alive. Carnivores, she thought. She looked up the quiet street. This place really was too much.

A few hundred metres up from the pub Cassy saw a sign that swung on a wooden pole. She started the engine of her little green car and drove closer. Squinting, she saw that it read *Beauty in the Bush.*

She parked outside the tiny cottage and went through the picket gate, knocking on the squat white door.

Evie answered. She calmly viewed the girl wearing what looked like the Aboriginal flag fashioned into a caftan and boots that could crush a cat's skull.

'Hello,' said Evie. 'If you're after Bridie, she's taken the girls to the river fishing.'

Cassy looked at the woman with the strange green eyes. She was wearing very daggy clothes and had her long grey hair in braids.

'No. I just want directions to the ranger's office.'

'Oh,' said Evie, 'come in then.' She opened the door wide and stepped back against the wall.

'I don't need to come in for directions, do I?' said Cassy almost rudely.

'No, but I do need to sit. My leg is giving me hell,' lied Evie.

Before she knew it, Cassy was perched on a white couch with a huge fluffy ginger cat on her lap and a cup of camomile tea in her hands.

She was fuming. She just wanted to find Luke, but this old woman seemed like one of those desperate, lonely kinds. She probably shared the cat's food out of the tin and wore the same undies for a week. Cassy decided she'd endure her for just ten minutes.

'You're lonely,' said Evie.

Cassy's eyes widened. '*Me*? Lonely? No!'

'Then why travel so many hours to see a person who's no longer your boyfriend?'

Cassy stiffened. Bloody small towns. Everyone knew everything about each other.

'That's none of your business.' She set down the cup and pushed the cat off her knee. 'Now, if you'll just give me directions, I'll be going.'

Evie looked levelly at her. 'My name's Evie. Would you like me to do a healing for you? No charge.'

Cassy shook her head but Evie stretched her hand out to her. The moment Evie's palm came to rest on Cassy's bare forearm, Cassy felt a tingle race along her skin and in an instant she was crying. Crying like a baby. She let Evie gently put her arm around her shoulders and guide her back to the couch. She offered her a tissue and sat while Cassy blubbered.

Years of hurt came rising up from within. Her father leaving her, the strong disapproving tones of her mother who had tried to buy her love every step of her life, the way the negatives of the world had weighed upon her since she was a little girl. She realised it had been the purity of Luke's spirit and his unhurried ways that had captured her. She now saw he didn't love her. But, more importantly, she realised she didn't love him. She just loved the idea that she was cared for by him. That simple fact had made her feel less intense, not so anguished. Not so . . . so . . . her hateful, hopeless self. Twisting the tissue, Cassy watched as Evie shut her eyes. The old lady's eyelids began to flicker and she inhaled deeply through her nose.

'God says you are loved.' This statement prompted a whole torrent of further crying from Cassy. 'He also says to get a sense of humour.'

Cassy looked at Evie, wanting to slap her, but there was something about her that made Cassy realise she was for real. She was connected to something. Though what that was, Cassy couldn't say. She certainly didn't believe in God. Cassy looked up at the white pressed-tin ceilings of the old cottage. She was beginning to get the creeps.

'There is nothing to fear,' Evie said in a voice that sounded strangely altered.

She was silent for a time and Cassy wondered if she had finished what she had called the 'healing'. But then Evie spoke again.

'God is showing me injured wildlife. Burnt wildlife. You are there. In the centre of them all, caring for them.'

'Wildlife?' Cassy queried. She'd never had much to do with wildlife, really, except for dressing up as them for the protests.

'God said your path is with the animals.'

'The animals? But what about Luke?'

She watched Evie's eyes roam from side to side behind her eyelids as if scanning something.

'God says I am not a clairvoyant and if you want one, go

read *Cleo*.' Then Evie burst out laughing, her eyes still closed. 'Oh, he's a funny bugger this God.'

Cassy stood. 'You're taking the piss out of me. This is all crap. I can't believe you sucked me in.'

But Evie didn't respond. She sat with her eyes still shut. 'God says remember your sense of humour. He says you will do good in the world, but this town is not your place. Luke has a soul-connection to another.'

Cassy again felt the emotion rise and tears well. The woman was right. What the hell was she doing here? She'd been hanging on to Luke for months now, and he'd been trying so gently to let her down, to lose her. She shut her eyes. When she opened them Evie's intense green eyes were on her.

'Okay?' she asked gently. Cassy nodded. Evie gave her a glass of water and then, without a word, ushered Cassy from the cottage.

'Travel safely,' Evie said.

On impulse, Cassy gave her a quick hug and thanked her. Then she got in her car and drove away from Dargo, feeling all of a sudden enlivened and empowered. She had asked for directions, and Evie had certainly given her that! Wildlife. She would work with injured wildlife and she would start this summer during fire season. She squealed with excitement and turned her CD of world music up full-pelt.

Thirty-five

As Emily pulled on her clothes that morning she berated herself for having worried what undies she was going to wear. As if Luke Bradshaw would even get a look in! She wasn't going to show him, even if he was interested.

Outside, the sun was gently hitting the eastern walls and roof, so the high-plains homestead was alive with creaks. It was going to be a warm day. Emily could hear the girls waking, stirring, talking to each other, slowly remembering that today was the day they were going to Evie's, who was taking them into Dargo to do the shopping. Before the excitement led the girls out of bed, Emily made her way along the hall to the bathroom to clean her teeth. Fresh breath in case he kisses me, she thought, before shoving the thought away.

In the gloom of the bathroom, Emily stared at her reflection in the mirror. Her eyes, big and wide and dark, her glossy black hair, now longer, framing her face. Her skin was clear and smooth. Perhaps Luke could like her, she wondered? As she bent to reach for her toothbrush she caught sight in the mirror of a woman standing behind her. A flash of white nightgown, a sweet smile, long, dark-grey hair hanging soft around the woman's face. Emily spun around, knocking over the cup of brushes and toothpaste with a clatter.

There was no one there.

'Okay, Emily,' she said, calming herself. 'It's just normal nowadays. Get used to it. Eh, Granny Emily? I know you're there. But what is it you've come to remind me? Is this the work I'm supposed to do? Playing tour guide to a VPP ranger?'

Sleepily, Tilly pushed open the bathroom door. 'Who are you talking to, Mum?'

Emily blinked her way into the here and now.

'The granny, silly,' Meg said as she bumbled her way past Tilly and picked up the toothbrushes from the floor. 'You know. The one that watches over Mum. She's happy about the nice man, Luke. She wants them to work together.'

'Oh, Meg,' Emily said. 'What are you on about?'

'You know, Mummy.'

Emily crouched and hugged her. 'You just know stuff, don't you, my little one?'

Meg shrugged and began squirting Shrek toothpaste out of the tube.

'Hey! Not so much,' Emily said.

As Emily sat with the girls eating breakfast she shut her eyes and pictured how things could be. She and Luke working together, deciding which part of the Parks needed grazing and which should be left for another year. Which areas needed cool burning and problem areas that required weed control. Could life really be like that, she wondered? Perhaps old Emily was telling her that. Maybe these mountains were their work together, her and Luke? Fantasy land, she eventually told herself.

After dropping Tilly and Meg at Evie's, Emily was again inside checking her face in the mirror when Rousie barked to tell her someone was approaching. Emily watched Luke drive up in his old WB, thumping along the rutted track. She was relieved to see he was out of his uniform. When he got out and stood before her in his Wrangler jeans, boots and a woollen work jumper, Emily felt weak at the knees.

'Morning,' he said, reaching for his wide-brimmed cowboy hat and jamming it on his head.

'Good morning,' Emily said nervously. 'Like a cuppa before we go?'

Luke shook his head.

'Nah, let's get cracking.' He rubbed his hands together. 'Can't wait.'

'I was hoping you'd say that,' Emily said. 'I'm not one to sit about. Follow me.'

'With pleasure,' Luke replied with a broad smile and Emily could hear the flirtation in his voice. This could work, she told herself excitedly. She led him over to the stables, her heart racing.

Inside the old stables, Emily watched as he ran his beautiful hands over the old upright posts that met with sturdy bearers beneath a lofty shingled rooftop, which had been covered over on the outside by roofing iron to preserve it.

'This building is *amazing*. Look at the timber work!'

Emily glanced up as she gathered the bridles from carved wooden pegs.

'I know. They were pretty handy in those days.'

'Pretty handy nowadays too, from what I can tell,' Luke said, catching her eye and hoping she'd catch his compliment as well.

'Grandad built these stables, and out here . . .' she said, stepping through a side door, 'is where Granny used to keep her goats.' She pointed to the solid post-and-rail fence that cornered off a high-plains meadow. 'That old stone wall was part of the piggery. And this head bale here is where Grandad used to milk the cow when he was a little tacker.'

They rested their elbows on the yard rails, looking through them to the view of Flanaghan Station with its old shingle roof outbuildings and the homestead at its heart.

'This place is awesome!' Luke said.

'It's pretty special, yeah. You're the first government bloke that's been on the place in decades, you know. It's not that we don't ask you blokes here, it's just none of them seem to want to come and see for themselves. It's like they're not interested in the history of the place. I think it's easier for 'em if they pretend all this isn't here.'

She turned to look at him, the morning sun falling on her smile. 'It's good to have a government bloke come in and see first hand what heritage the bans are killing.'

'Emily,' Luke said, turning to look into her eyes, 'I'm not a government bloke and I'm not out to kill anyone's heritage. As long as you're here, no one can take this place from you.' He frowned. '*Government bloke*. Ouch. That hurts.'

'But you are a government bloke. You work for VPP.'

'It's a job, Emily. A ticket out of the city for me. It isn't who I am. I was chucked off my land too, remember? The government caused that too. All those tax rules that let outsiders buy in for so-called carbon credit tree farming. It's as ludicrous as what they've done to your family. The only difference is my dad gave up. Yours hasn't.'

Emily smiled at him, suddenly seeing his point.

'Sorry,' she said. 'You're right. We're in the same boat. I won't call you that anymore.'

'Good. I'm glad.'

There was a moment when Emily thought he might lean over and kiss her. She wanted him to, but Luke drew away.

'Now, let's go catch these horses. I can't wait to see more of this place!'

As Luke threw the heavy stock-saddle up onto the gelding's back and reached under for the girth, he watched Emily as much as he could without being obvious. He was intrigued by her. She was so self-contained. Tough, even. Not angry and hostile like Cassy, but resilient, like the landscape about her. He saw how she saddled her grey mare, the way it was second nature to her, her movements swift and confident. She talked as she tacked up, explaining how she'd liked the name Salsa that he'd mentioned on the road back in autumn but she'd settled on Bonus instead. Her chatting was fuelled by nervousness, Luke could tell. He couldn't take his eyes from her pretty face and her competent hands that were as strong as a man's yet still beautiful. She was being very formal, almost old-fashioned, with him. It was as if their encounter at Wonnangatta had pushed her further away, rather than brought her closer to him. He had to find a way to relax her somehow, to find an unguarded version of Emily within. As she bent to clean Snowgum's hooves with a hoof pick, Luke caught a glimpse of bright green underpants lairing out from the top of her jeans.

'Whoa! Interesting colour choice,' he said, grinning.

Emily set Snowgum's hoof down, looking at him, frowning. 'What?'

'Your undies.'

'Oh, God!' Emily flushed red as she tugged up her jeans. 'Sorry. They're foul.'

'Don't be sorry. I love green. It makes me think of grass.'

'You don't want to know about my undies, honestly. It's a long story.'

'Well, I like long stories and we've got all day,' said Luke, grinning as he led Bonus from the stable. Emily was still rolling her eyes with embarrassment and smiling when she swung up onto Snowgum.

Seeing Emily astride a horse, looking so much a part of the country, Luke could barely keep track of her words as she explained where they were headed. All he caught was something about Bob's runs and the western side of the road. He nodded, dumbstruck, wondering how he could get closer to this girl. He was besotted. But the VPP thing still seemed to sit between them like a great silent shadow.

'You right to trot for a bit?' Emily asked and she was off before he could answer, sitting easily in the saddle, the stocky mare rolling along the track, curving in and out of snowgums. The gelding beneath him was moving well. She'd done a good job on him. Bonus was responsive yet steady and he moved over the rocky, twisting track with ease and confidence. Emily must be some horsewoman! More admiration rose up in Luke for the extraordinary girl riding in front of him.

On the way, Emily pointed out trees with stories to them, plants he hadn't heard of, and access to tracks that had never been marked on a map, nor ever would be. She told him of old-timers who had huts out here and of the best places to tickle a trout or look for gold. They rode up gentle hillsides and slid down steep tracks, Emily knowing where each fence curved away.

Every place she took him was breathtakingly beautiful. As they journeyed further into the heart of the high plains, Luke felt Emily opening up to him. She was forgetting his ranger status and talking to him now as a friend again. She spoke of Bob's inability to farm, the way he'd done wrong by the land. She spoke of her plans to rehabilitate the damage he had done. As she talked, Luke's admiration for Emily began to inflate like a balloon. His feelings for her swelled so that as the morning moved on, it felt like desire for her might burst him apart.

*

By the time the sun was high and hot, Emily led Luke to a mountain brook shaded by a dappling of snowgums. The water ran across a grassy plain and then bubbled and splashed down over a small waterfall. Emily hitched Snowgum's reins to a sapling and unbuckled her saddlebags from the mare.

She'd packed a very special smoko. Normally she'd just shove in an apple and a bottle of water, but today, knowing Luke would be along, she'd rummaged around for as many snacks as she could find. She clambered down a small embankment and settled herself on a mossy bank beside the deep pool. Luke followed and settled next to her, watching as she took a thermos from the saddlebag and offered him a cup of tea or coffee.

'This is a flash smoko spot *and* I get a choice of what to drink,' Luke said with a smile.

'You could have Milo too, but there's only one sachet so you'll have to share it with me.'

'I don't mind sharing with you,' he said invitingly.

Emily lifted her head and looked into Luke's eyes. It was a moment when she knew she could've leaned over and kissed him. But she wanted to savour this. To test him a little. She quickly poured him a drink and passed it to him.

'Thanks.' Emily could feel his frustration, the desire still leashed. Now she could tell he wanted her. Now she knew she wanted him. It was time to have some fun. To let Luke in.

She kicked off her boots, pulled off her socks and stood suddenly, unbuckling her jeans and whipping them down to her ankles.

'What are you doing?' Luke said, looking up with a mix of delight and confusion on his face at the sight of her tanned bare legs.

'It's tickling time.'

'Tickling time? I didn't know you were into fetishes,' he said with a grin.

'The trout,' Emily said, pulling her shirt down over her loud green underpants.

'Isn't that illegal?' Luke stood and took his boots and jeans off too. 'It's out of season. You'll need a fishing licence and you're not using the right equipment. You're just heading for trouble, young lady.'

'You'll have to arrest me,' Emily said, wading into the stream.

'Only if I can frisk you again first.'

It sparked a memory of Wonnangatta, and their first kiss, in both of them. She smiled at Luke as he followed her to the mountain stream. Emily bent down, placing her hands deep under the water. Her fingertips felt about on the unseen rocks below the surface until she found what she was searching for. Expertly she soon had a trout gathered up in her hands. As she lifted it in the air its silver, spotted body glistened in the sunlight.

'Got him!' Luke said, smiling at her.

'Got her, you mean.'

'What are you going to do now? Eat her?'

Emily shook her head. 'Nah. Set her free.' Emily gently placed the trout back down into the darkness of the rocky ledge. 'Put her back where she belongs.'

'She's like you,' said Luke, turning to face Emily as they stood thigh-deep in the cold mountain stream. 'You belong here.' He took her hands and held them both, then leaned towards her and gently, cautiously, pressed a soft kiss to her lips. His mouth hovered near hers, waiting for her to return the kiss.

Emily answered by moving close, pressing her body to his, kissing him deeply. The relief of touching him again was phenomenal. Arcs of electricity sparked between them as they ran their hands over each other. Breathless, Emily led Luke back up onto the mossy bank.

They lay next to each other, the earthy smell of life rising up around them. Luke drank her in with his hands and mouth. He pulled her shirt from her and her singlet and expertly unclipped her bra. Then with sunshine on her skin, he kissed her neck, her breasts, moving his mouth down over her stomach.

'Mmm. Plough my patch, eh?' he said from where he lay, running a finger along the elastic of her undies playfully.

'I thought, you being a wheatbelt boy, that'd crank your tractor.'

'You did, did you?'

Emily bit her bottom lip and nodded.

'I'm not into ploughing. It's not so good for the soil over the long term,' Luke said, slowly, tantalisingly easing her underpants down over her curvaceous, firm hips. 'I prefer direct drilling.'

'Direct drilling, eh? I don't mind a bit of direct drilling myself,' Emily said, running her fingers through his hair and looking skyward to the blue.

'Do you now?' continued Luke as he began to draw her

knickers down. 'I find direct drilling is gentler, slower, and lasts much, much longer.' As he slowly delivered each word he punctuated it with a kiss to her thighs, her belly and then beyond. Emily arched with pleasure at his deft, practised touch. Never had she felt a man perform so expertly with such assurance. The quickness of his fingers, the dance of his tongue on her, the confidence in his moves. He sent her heavenward on a wave of pleasure to the very last gasp.

He came to lie on top of her, and continued kissing her. Emily, a dreamy smile on her face, ran her fingernails gently up and over his back beneath his T-shirt. She nuzzled in his neck and pulled him down onto her. She wanted him close, inside her. She dragged his T-shirt over his head and the press of their naked torsos, skin on skin, sent them on a new surge of desire. Luke pushed into her and together they bucked against each other, the pungent smell of the mossy bank releasing perfumes into the ether.

They were lost now. In each other. In the landscape. They rolled over so that Emily sat astride Luke. He was the one lying back now. She was the rider. Luke, deep within her, Emily moved as if at a gallop. Luke, teeth gritted, eyes half-closed, grabbed at her beautiful hips and urged her onwards. As they both came in waves he reached up to her breasts and cupped them, then Emily fell forward, her hair brushing his face as they breathed and kissed and kissed and breathed.

'I'll always remember this special place,' Luke whispered.

'If you think this place is special, wait till I show you Mayford one day.'

*

It was getting late by the time Luke and Emily made it back to the homestead. Their faces were flushed from the heat of the day, their races over plains, the laughter that had spilled up constantly from them as they bantered, flirted and joked.

She left Luke to rub down the horses in the stables and ran inside to ring Evie to apologise for being late in collecting Tilly and Meg. When she picked up the phone there was a message waiting for her, and Evie's kindly voice came over the line.

'No need to get the girls,' she said. 'They begged me to stay for a sleepover at Auntie Bridie's. We'll see you back on the plains at my house tomorrow afternoon. No hurry, my darling girl. You enjoy the solitude.'

The solitude, Emily thought, smiling. She wondered if Luke would stay.

That night, Luke and Emily moved about the kitchen as if they had belonged in each other's company for an age. There were no inhibitions anymore. No off-limit topics. Emily spoke of the effects of the bans, and Luke of the adjustments he'd had to make within the job. He sketched out his family situation. And he spoke of Cassy. Emily told him about Clancy.

They kissed in front of the open fire in the lounge room and made love there again. Snuggled up naked beneath a blanket, they lay in front of the fire, Emily flicking through the old photo albums and telling stories of life on the high plains. At one point, Emily stopped mid-sentence to find Luke gazing at her, gently brushing the hair from her face.

'You are so beautiful.'

'And so are you,' she said.

They kissed again and then, holding hands, walked down the hallway to the bedroom. She pulled him down onto the cattleman's bed, where they loved and tasted each other again and again throughout the night.

The next day they rode out together again. A ride out on a mountain ridge. Making love in a cattleman's hut. A picnic by a stream. Then, as the sun sank beneath the line of the snowgums, Luke gathered Emily up in a hug and gave her one long kiss goodbye.

Watching him drive away down the mountainside, Emily felt like he was crossing back over that divide, the one that would see him back in his Parks uniform and on the job on Monday morning, while she returned to her life as a mother and a cattleman, set apart on the mountainside.

Thirty-six

For the following week, Emily wasn't sure if she was lethargic from the unseasonal heat or from love. Her thoughts constantly ran to Luke and her body felt listless and languid. The mere recollection of their lovemaking caused her to flop down on the nearest chair or log and sigh. Never had she been so physically and mentally affected by a man. She wondered how on earth she'd cope with her girls' energy and the work she had in front of her, wanting instead to just wallow in the blissful memory of Luke.

She'd only talked to him once since their weekend together. He'd phoned to say he'd been called into Heyfield for a week of fire training. His conversation was brief and to the point, he was in a rush, but Emily could hear the excitement in his voice. As she set down the phone she knew the feelings were mutual.

Now, though, as she thought of Luke, she wondered where he'd be. Today was going to be bad for fire. She could tell by the way the summer storms rolled past the homestead, cracking fiercely with thunder, then sparking with lightning across the purple mountaintops. No rain followed to quench the storms and dowse the lightning. Instead the wind was warm and gusty and already the day was taking on an eerie hazy feel. The bush was limp after days and days of heat. Luke would have to bypass fire training on a day like today, Emily thought, and would be in for the real thing – on a fire crew.

With the dry electrical storms and the air heavy with heat, there would be no more time to dwell on Luke. Emily called Tilly and Meg over from where they played on a gum-bough swing near the house.

'There's going to be fires about,' she said, trying to keep her voice light. 'So I'm going to send you down the mountain to Evie while I get the cattle closer to the yards. Grandad Rod and Auntie Flo will pick you up.'

The girls nodded solemnly. They knew not to argue with their mother when it came to talk of fire. All their relatives were part of the volunteer fire crew and they had heard the serious grown-up talk about fires their whole lives.

Here at the high-plains homestead, the ute had the firefighting unit on it with the boxy water tank, as it did every summer. The girls had been helping their mother rake leaves and clear tree branches and bark away from the house for weeks. They'd even been allowed to tether their ponies to the verandah posts, to keep the grass extra short round the house.

Over the winter, Emily had done a good job of reducing the fuel load around the homestead as she burnt many of the loose sticks and bark in the house fire. But snowgums were messy trees, and seemed to toss an endless scattering of bark and branches down come summer and spring, so that the work renewed itself each day.

'Your great-grandparents always said, "Firefighting is done in the spring and autumn months",' she told the girls. 'No use doing it in the summer. It's too late then.'

She looked out across the treeline to the mountain. It would be too late for most of the government country. She thought with frustration of the constant pleading by the local fire crews to get the all-clear from the Melbourne authorities for fuel-reduction burns in the autumn. But they were either out of money in the budget or the ideal weather conditions for burn-offs had passed by the time they were organised in the head offices. The people living in the mountains did the best they could on their own country, but lived nervously, knowing that the fuel loads on the government-run lands and investment-scheme plantations around them were dangerously high.

Now Emily could see from the weather she'd have to put their own family fire plan into place, hoping she'd done enough to protect the homestead. But she felt that sinking feeling again when she considered that none of the run country's new spring growth had been kept in check by grazing this year since the government cattle bans.

Hundreds of acres of spring snowgrasses would now be tinder dry. The weeds too, once kept down by the cattle, would also be shoulder high and whispering their dry stalks and seed heads together, calling forth a fire. It was country that couldn't handle hot fires. She worried for it. But for now she must worry first about her girls and getting them out to Evie's and then to the lowlands at Dargo. She went inside to phone her dad at Tranquillity.

'I don't like the look of it,' Rod said, gazing out from the homestead towards the ridges of the Dargo High Plains. There, great leaping forks radiated down from the heavens and clouds tumbled blackly to the north. Behind him, the screen door banged as another gust channelled cool air into the hot belly of the house.

'I'm taking Meg and Tilly to Evie's now,' Emily said. 'Could one of you pick them up and run them down to Bridie and Sam in Dargo? And can Flo bring the stock truck and trailer up for the cattle while I go muster the cows?' She swallowed nervously, knowing there was so much work to do. 'We'd better get everything out of here, Dad, before we get called away to another fire. It's not looking good.'

'They've already issued a high alert and we're all on standby here. The forecasters got it so wrong, *so wrong*,' Rod said.

From the weather patterns, Emily and Rod knew they'd be busy in the coming days as volunteer firefighters. It was a frustrating job as it often took them away from their own land and families, but if they could make sure their cattle were in Dargo along with the girls, they would at least be freer to fight fires in other regions.

All the locals knew that if fires threatened, the government would spend millions and call in the army for heavy equipment and manpower to protect assets like the city's water catchment, the ski fields, roads, and power and communication infrastructure. They'd ship in crews from interstate and overseas, setting up entire tent cities. Hotshots from the USA, men from Canada, teams from New Zealand. Fire was big business if it affected big business. But if it was just wilderness that was under threat, or a few private houses, like their own homestead on the plains, the firefighting was mostly left up to the locals.

Emily could hear lightning cracks over the line.

'I'd better go, Dad. See you soon.'

'You take care, you hear?'

Rod Flanaghan put down the receiver and jumped as thunder suddenly boomed, loud as a cannon, above the house. He stepped onto the verandah to watch the rain arrive, slowly at first in giant lazy drops that landed, splat, on the green garden outside. Then it began to teem down, steam rising up from the hides of the bulls that stood in the house paddock, listless and uncomfortable in the summer heat.

Then, as quickly as it had come, the storm passed. The cold air pockets moved on and the wind again felt like a fan heater on high. Rod looked up and saw what he had expected. Thin coils of smoke were drifting up in the mountains already as the fires from the lightning took hold.

He shook his head, fear settling in the pit of his stomach. Everyone round here knew the government land had a fuel load on it so high that an inferno was on its way. Rod tried to count the decades since the area had been burned.

He cursed the department policy to put out every lightning strike, instead of allowing some naturally lit fires in the cooler months to trickle along harmlessly and burn away the vegetation that created such a volatile environment come the summertime. His daughter was up in that.

As he ran outside to find Flo and get the stock truck and trailer on the road, all he could think of were the stories his father had told him of the '39 fires, when eighty or so people died. His father had told him how the stables on the high plains had almost burned, a dog escaping when the rope he was tied with smouldered right through. Three times the family had managed to save the homestead and yards. But in that '39 fire seven hundred Flanaghan cattle had perished, the fat in them sizzling to white ash.

Rod had fought many fires, although never a giant monster like the one of '39. But today he knew something massive was on its way. In their inability to truly see and read this land, whitefellas had been laying the trail for this fire for decades. And now, Rod Flanaghan shuddered, they would all have to pay.

Thirty-seven

It felt like an age to Emily as they wound down the mountain bends to Evie's cottage. There was so much to do in such a short time, and as the day got hotter, the winds stronger and the haze thicker, Emily felt fear driving her forward, faster and faster. On the radio the callers' fire reports were becoming increasingly urgent.

She was relieved when she at last saw Evie, waving from behind the stone wall of her lush garden. There was less haze on this northern side of the mountain and, with the shady greenery, the place seemed unlikely ever to burn. Emily tooted the horn and watched as Jesus Christ went nuts, barking and chasing his tail in manic circles. Leaving the ute to idle, Emily leapt out, helping the girls with their bags.

Meg and Tilly hugged Evie, and Emily gave her a quick kiss on the cheek.

'Thanks so much for minding them.'

'My pleasure, my dear. They'll be safe here for the time being.'

'Dad should be about three hours getting the cattle, then he or Flo will collect them. I'll be along after with the horses.'

'Right you are.'

'Are you going to come down with us when we leave? I don't reckon it's a day to be staying behind up here,' Emily said, looking to the smoke haze now spreading out over the landscape to the west.

'Try moving me,' Evie said.

'But —'

'I'm fine, love,' she said. 'I've done all I can to prepare.'

'We'll check you on the way down,' Emily said. 'If the fire's heading our way, I'll chuck you in the stock truck with the other stubborn cows and *make* you come, if I have to.'

Normally Evie would've laughed along with Emily at this point, but she seemed distant, almost dreamy.

'You sure you're okay?' Emily asked again.

Evie nodded and her smile returned. 'I'm fine, really I am. You just go, and know your girls are safe with me.'

'Thanks,' said Emily, giving Evie a hug. 'I'd better run. Got cows to get in.'

'You'll need to run with that at your back,' she said, looking up towards the smoke, 'but God will carry you along the way.' Evie raised a hand to Emily's cheek. For the first time Emily noticed a tremor in Evie's touch. 'Goodbye, dear.'

'See you soon!'

Emily gathered both her girls to her and kissed them.

'You help Evie out, okay? Grandad will be along soon. And I won't be far behind with the horses in the float.'

As Emily climbed into the ute she smiled to see Evie's arms around Meg and Tilly's shoulders as if she was draping her wings over them. She truly was an angel. On impulse Emily wound the window down and yelled, 'I love you, Evie!'

Frail on the wind, came Evie's reply, 'And I love you, my girl.' Then she was gone, out of sight, as Emily roared the ute away around the bend.

Emily rushed inside the homestead and gathered up the boxes of precious things they had already packed during long hot nights that week. She took down the old family photographs that had been on the walls for years and wrapped them in a blanket, the face of old Emily staring up at her from one picture with her lively dark eyes.

'I know,' Emily said to the photograph. 'I know you're watching me and I'll be careful.'

Emily had been through the fire drill several times before during scorching summers like this one. She knew the procedure and moved like clockwork. She and Sam had done it many times as kids. All the Flanaghans were fire-aware. Ever since the early nineteen hundreds, when the government had restricted the family from burning, they had tried to come up with other ways to protect themselves should a fire break out.

After the fierce '39 fires, the Flanaghans had built a fire bunker near the homestead. It was still there and the family checked and restocked it every year. Emily's grandfather had called it their 'life insurance policy' and Emily knew it was one of several bunkers he'd built on the mountain, such was his conviction that a raging hot fire would one day come.

Emily glanced at her watch as she loaded the boxes and some old handmade furniture onto the ute and drove it quickly to the bunker.

Inside in the gloom she shone the torch about. It was damp and cool in there. Rousie flopped down on the dirt floor as if to say, this is the place to stay. She set the boxes down and whistled Rousie out, sealing the bunker up behind them. As she did, she imagined what it would be like to actually use it one day. She and Sam had only ever gone in there to tell ghost stories and scare themselves witless when they were kids. She shivered at the thought of being in there while a fire raced overhead.

At the homestead, she disconnected the gas and dragged the canisters away from the buildings. She checked a small pump at the water tank and hooked it to a hose that ran up onto the roof.

After climbing a ladder, she quickly plugged the gutters with rags, her boots screeching on the tin. She checked that the line leading to the roof sprinklers was still nailed securely to the roof.

From the peak of the homestead, she looked around at the beautiful high plains trees and the home meadows, grazed short over the summer by the horses. The snowgums were listless from heat, stirred occasionally by erratic blasts of hot wind. She loved this place and would hate to see it burn, but it wasn't the first time the Flanaghans had faced the destruction of fire and Emily knew it was all part of choosing to build a house in such a place.

Suddenly the wind dropped. Emily stood for a moment on the roof, staring up at the sun, which was now a sinister orange ball in the sky. As she did, she was sure she could hear the faint sound of a woman calling out. Old Emily? She shook her head. It was nothing, she told herself, nothing but the wind. She had to hurry. She climbed down the ladder.

In the shed she dragged out several big old dusty signs that were hand-painted in Flo's sloping text. Emily propped one up next to the pump. The sign read: *Hi CFA, If you make it this far, please start this pump*. Then she set the other white signs along the drive. They had thick black arrows painted on them and they pointed to the water tank and pump. It was the family's 'Plan B' and they hoped one day in a fire, it might work.

Back in the house Emily skolled a big glass of water, threw on a long-sleeved woollen shirt and ran to hitch the float onto the ute.

She paused, sticking her head inside the ute cab to listen to the radio as people keeping watch in the fire towers reported the locations of towering columns of smoke. It seemed the winds were fanning the fires away from them. Relieved, she continued on.

She jogged to the horse paddock to catch Snowgum. Bonus followed them into the yard, where she put the pack frame on him and strapped heavy water backpacks onto him. Ready to ride, she whistled Rousie to her as she swung up onto Snowgum. At the house the ponies whickered to them from the ends of their tethers and trotted in half-moons as they passed.

As she rode out towards the snowgrass plains, she could smell the smoke. Although it was barely past midday, the day was growing dark. She swallowed down her nerves and got on with the job of finding her cattle out on the runs.

On the Block Paddock, where the cattle had last been moved, Emily checked the two knapsacks hitched to either side of Bonus's pack frame. The gelding took the weight well. He'd done plenty of packing over the winter, but his ears flicked nervously as he listened to the slosh of water following him with every step. At a trot, the sensation of the water moving its weight independently unsettled him. He shifted sideways and tossed his head.

Emily tried to soothe him, but when he continued carrying on, she said sternly, 'If you don't like it, mate, you'll just have to lump it. This is an emergency!' She tugged on his lead rope a little. He seemed to take in her gruff tone and sharp check as a message, and knuckled down to his job.

After trotting north for about half an hour, Emily found the cattle hiding in the shade of a thicket of snowgums, on the fringe of an open plain. The cows cast their ears forward at the sight of the rider and some ambled out curiously, sniffing the air, made nervous by the smoke. Emily sent Rousie out around them and followed his cast in a canter, leaping ditches and logs.

On the end of the lead, Bonus put in a couple of bucks as they travelled, not liking the weight and feel of the knapsacks, but after another growl from Emily, he settled again. Thankfully the straps on his pack had held. She knew they could waste no time. Emily soon had the cows and calves mobbed, but a quick head count told her it wasn't the full one hundred and fifty. Emily grimaced.

'Twenty-five short,' she said. The open plain gave her a view to the east where the sky was clear, but to the west there was a wall of smoke. Heartened that the breeze had dropped, Emily decided to take the cattle she had back to the yards. Some was better than none and she might have time to search for more. The truck would still be half an hour away and the wind was fanning the fires away to the south-west in the direction of Wonnangatta.

At the yards, Emily bustled the cattle into the pen nearest the loading ramp. Around her, the day had turned to dusk and the wind was gusting every which way. Every now and then a blackened leaf spiralled down and landed on the ground, like confetti from hell. One leaf, alight, or an ember would spark a fire.

She remounted Snowgum. If she could just take one last look for the rest of the cattle, she reasoned, just one gallop across the plain, she might find the remaining cows and calves.

She had heard horror stories about how cattle fat burns hotter than trees, so that firefighters had discovered eerie white shadows cast on the ground, caused by the radiant heat of a burning beast. She just couldn't leave her cattle to die like that. The sooner she found the cattle, the sooner she could get out of here. And then she'd be back in Dargo with her girls, shouting them a lemonade at the pub after this fiery day was done.

She swung Snowgum about, Bonus following at a canter, and rode away from the yards.

'Find 'em, boy,' she said to Rousie and he bounded on ahead, his nose to the wind, his eyes keen, despite the ever-thickening haze of smoke.

Thirty-eight

At the yards, Rod and Flo peered through the thick fog of smoke to find most of the cattle in the pen. There was no sign of Emily. To their horror they saw flames sparked by embers beyond the treeline beginning to chew up the grassy plain. They knew Emily would be searching for the remainder of the herd. Rod's eyes watered from the smoke.

Surely he couldn't have lost her again, he thought in anguish.

'Emily!' he screamed to the empty bushland. Flo, her face set, got on with the business of loading cattle onto the double-decker truck and trailer.

'Where *is* she?' Rod said as Flo swung the inner door of the truck shut.

Flo looked out towards the blinding smoke-filled plain. 'I dunno.'

Rod was furious. How could she do this? How could she leave him and her girls? How could they endure losing her again?

As time passed and they loaded as many of the herd as they could onto the truck, then the trailer, in a scramble, Flo began to see the mad roll of her brother's panic-filled eyes. He looked about desperately, calling out Emily's name over and over, climbing high onto the top rails of the cattle yards, bellowing until his throat ripped with pain. He had no means to look for his daughter. He had no way of finding her. He knew he should never have let her muster the cattle alone, but he had so wanted her to be able to step out from his shadow. He'd wanted her to see she was so much more than just a cattleman's daughter. Rod cursed himself. Flo came over and tugged on his arm.

'Rod!' she screamed above the roar of the manic wind. 'We have to get out of here!'

'No, I won't leave her!'

'We have to get the girls out. We have to leave. *Now*!'

As Rod saw his sister's terrified face, he began to pray. Over and over he prayed, the same way he had last summer as he sat outside the operating theatre of a Melbourne hospital, praying for the life of his daughter.

'Rod,' Flo said again, 'she knows the country. She knows to go to Mayford. She'll be fine once she gets down off the King's Spur. It's our Emily. She'll survive. It's her girls we have to worry about now.'

Rod nodded. Numb and mute, he clambered up into the truck while Flo let the remainder of the herd that wouldn't fit on the truck out into the biggest, barest yard, in the hope they would survive. As Flo drove on towards Dargo at a madman's pace to beat the fire front, she radioed through that Emily Flanaghan was missing. Her words jabbed urgently into the radio and each one pierced Rod like a knife.

Shaking, Flo turned to Rod. He was hunkered down in his seat. We *can't* lose Emily, she thought. Not again! She began to feel the panic rise. Then Flo shook some sense back into herself. She had to comfort Rod.

'Emily's savvy. She'll be right. I know she will. Any minute now and she'll come riding through the trees on her fat horse and her gangly goofy dog and we'll be on the whisky in the Dargo River Inn. After you've given her a proper flogging and then one from me to follow for scaring the crap out of us. Again!'

Glancing up from the steep winding mountain road, Flo was crushed to see her brother crying as his eyes searched the smoke-filled landscape in hopeless desperation. Flo jammed the gearstick into second as she took on the first of many bends down the mountainside, praying that Emily would find her way. Praying the fire wouldn't beat them to the girls at Evie's house.

Emily at last spotted a red hide in the trees in the distance. The cows were in the far-flung corner of the paddock. Emily swore. She'd already put far too much distance between her and the yards for her liking. The smell of smoke was now definitely a taste and even Snowgum was getting twitchy, throwing her head and jiggling her bit between her opened mouth. Her mood was infectious, and Bonus was sweating from nerves as well as the oppressive heat. But Emily couldn't leave the cattle. She urged her horses on.

The cows and calves were stirry in the hot gusty wind, with the haze of smoke all around them and the sky so dark. It took Emily and Rousie a while to mob them.

So focused was she on the cows that it was a shock to glance up and see the tumble of smoke moving towards her. Emily realised the wind had swung.

The flames on the horizon came fast, gobbling up kangaroo and poa grasses in an instant, gnawing on the bleached skeletons of snow-fallen trees. In the distance, the fire was exploding, fizzing and whining like fireworks as it ignited the oil from green gum leaves. It consumed everything in its path. The fifty-degree temperatures created thermal eddies in the air, and burning bark and embers were twisted upwards in the sky.

Fire was now spotting all over the plains. The weather had turned and fire had come from out of the skies. Emily knew there was no way she could now drive the cattle into the wind that way, towards the yards.

She had to think quickly. A voice came into her head. *Breathe slowly, regain your calm*. Instantly, Emily thought of the gully to the north-east, which would take her to the King's Spur and then on down to the Little Dargo to Mayford.

She knew fires burned more slowly downhill and the wind, if she was lucky, would push the main front beyond it. Mayford, she thought suddenly. It was the valley she'd seen in her dream at the time of her accident. The place where old Emily's hut had stood before it was consumed by fire years before. Mayford, she thought again, where her grandfather's fire bunker was and the big deep pond in the meandering river that was spring-fed and always full. She knew there was an island in that deep pond. She and Sam had swum to it as children. Mayford. Mayford. Mayford. It became like a mantra. If she and the cattle could get there, she knew they would survive.

Thirty-nine

On the Little Dargo River, as Luke set down his back-burning drip torch and reached into his vehicle for a bottle of water, he froze. A woman was on the radio repeating over and over that Emily Flanaghan was missing on the Dargo High Plains. Her voice was full of fear. Although the words were barely audible above the noise of two dozers, which were putting breaks in to protect Dargo, Luke was certain of what he heard.

He didn't pause to tell his fellow VPP crew members where he was going. He jumped in the VPP vehicle and swung it about, driving straight for the High Plains Road through Dargo.

At the base of the mountain road a police car was parked with lights flashing, their reflection bouncing eerily off the smoke haze. The policeman was setting out signs saying the road was closed. A volunteer fire crew member was helping him.

'Sorry, mate,' the cop said. 'It's no go. Not even for rangers. The mountains are alight. It's deadly up there.'

Luke got out of the vehicle.

'But there's a girl missing. Emily Flanaghan. We gotta get up there,' Luke said urgently.

'I know, mate,' said the firefighter. 'We gotta get to a lot of places, we gotta get to a lot of people, but the clowns in Melbourne say we gotta stay here and protect Dargo. A whole town is more important than one person.'

'But Emily's missing and her family needs help!'

'The Melburnites ain't going to pull a unit out, not when there's a whole township in the firing line. I'm sorry, but there's nothing we can do right now.'

Luke looked at the well-meaning fireman. He knew this kind of dilemma happened to them each year with the hierarchical nature of the firefighting organisation. They knew the lie of the land, how the fires would run, how the weather changed, but the shots were called by people further up the ladder. Luke could tell this firey was jaded and worn out. Of course he cared for the Flanaghans but he'd seen it all before.

'I'm going up,' Luke said.

'No, you can't —' the policeman began as a big red stock truck came roaring into sight on the other side of the road block. They heard the driver change the gears down as it slowed and at last hissed to a halt. The pungent smell of cow manure greeted them as the cattle bellowed on the back of the truck.

Luke recognised Emily's father and aunt as they got out of the cab. Then felt a pang of sorrow when he saw the distressed faces of Emily's girls staring out at him from the windows of the truck.

'You've got to help us!' Rod said, running over, his arms outstretched. 'My Emily's out there! Please!'

The policemen stepped forward, a frown on his face.

'I'm sorry, sir.'

Rod turned to Luke and Luke flinched at the utter fear in the cattleman's blue eyes.

'Luke,' he said, grabbing hold of his upper arms and clutching them so his skin bruised, 'she's still out there! We've got to send a crew up.'

Luke looked across to the firefighter, who shrugged.

Flo stepped forward to put a calming hand on her brother. 'Rod, please. They're not going to send a crew into that and you know it.'

'Just give me a truck and I'll go myself!'

'Rod,' Flo said, 'you know they can't. If she makes it to Mayford, she'll be fine.'

'Mayford,' Luke repeated, looking at Emily's girls, and then he was running, leaping into the VPP vehicle. Before they could stop him, Luke was gone, revving up over the bank beside the road, spinning dust up with the wheels.

Up on the high plains Luke struggled to find the homestead gateway, so thick was the smoke. When he realised he'd overshot it, he reversed back. Perhaps she was there? He bumped along the driveway and got out. It was almost dark around the house. He called out, 'Emily!'

No answer. The girls' ponies trotted about urgently on the

ends of their ropes. Luke frowned. Emily would've come back to get them. She mustn't be here.

Then he saw the signs. The arrows. He ran in the direction they pointed, hoping he'd find Emily, but instead he discovered Flo's instructions on starting the pump. He flicked the switch and ripped on the cord. The motor shuddered to life and Luke watched as water from the tank spurted up through the hose and out through the sprinklers on the rooftop. Silver jets spouted up and over the building, filling the gutters, dowsing the house in a cooling skin of water. The ponies, soothed by spray that fell as mist upon their sweaty coats, settled a little. Luke threw them each a biscuit of hay and left the pump running, knowing the big tanks would run like that for a good few hours. He got back into his vehicle, now thinking only of Emily. Mayford, he thought. He had to find her on the Mayford track.

Back on the road, Luke flicked the headlights. They shone on a warped, eerie world of dull, dirty brown. Adrenaline coursed through him. He was shocked at how quickly the fires had been and gone in places. Trees were still burning high up in the trunks, the understorey of the bushland black and smoking. He had to veer around fallen logs that smoked and sizzled. Near the creek where he and the girls had panned for gold he had to chainsaw through a still smoking fallen tree so his vehicle could pass.

Dead birds littered the road along with smouldering wallabies and possums. Some, still alive, hulked their bodies along painfully. Their suffering was so tangible Luke felt the hurried knock of his heart, and sweat pouring from his body. The smoke made it hard to breathe, but so, too, did his fear.

There were patches of unburned bush. A fireball could swing with the wind and travel back to devour him in those patches of dry deadwood and grasses. He was still so new to this country and realised he had been stupid to come – but how could he leave Emily alone up here?

Through the smoke he saw the VPP sign to the Mayford track. He swerved the vehicle as best he could with the water load on and lumped his way over the ridged track. So stuffy was the air in the cab, he pulled his T-shirt from beneath his overalls up over his nose and mouth. He squinted along the track, beginning to lose hope of ever finding her.

Luke travelled slowly in this way for nearly forty minutes, the panic in him rising. At last in the gloom he saw a smattering of cow dung. It was a clue that raised such hope and relief in him he almost cried. He knew she would be there with the cows. The dung was fresh and the country that he travelled through was Park land. But what if it was just a stray cow that had pushed through the fence?

As he began to cave in to doubt, suddenly there she was in a clearing. Emily Flanaghan. She was standing beside a new fence that until a moment ago had divided the Park from her family's cattle run. The gleaming wires were flung back against the grass. Six strands of silver, like broken guitar strings. Behind her stood her mare, dancing nervously from where she was tied, flicking her charcoal tail against her flanks of snowdrift white, and next to her, Bonus, laden with knapsacks, moving about but obviously lame in the offside rear leg.

To the right, a mob of glossy, white-faced cows and calves

spotted him and lowed, as if pleading for help. He looked again to Emily, who was smiling at him in amazement. Luke jumped out of the Cruiser, his strong legs propelling him quickly over the tussocky plain between them. Crying with relief, she ran to him. Together they embraced. Kissing each other, tasting the sweat, the tears and the soot.

'Luke! You can't be here!' Emily held his face and gazed deep into his eyes. She was so relieved and yet so horrified to see him here in the mountains that were engulfed in flames. It felt so wonderful to hold him, but it came with the horrific realisation that it was not just her life at risk now, but also his.

'We've gotta get out of here!' she said.

'I know! Come on,' he said, taking her hand, starting to lead her towards the Parks vehicle. She pulled her hand away.

'But, Luke, I'm not leaving my girls,' she said, gesturing towards her cattle. 'And I'm not leaving Snowgum or Bonus.'

'Are you crazy?' he said. 'Emily! You've cut the fence. Let them go. They'll find a way out on the tracks.'

She shook her head.

'Not through that mess they won't,' she said and he knew instantly what she meant. He looked with shame at the long rank grasses and weeds that had grown up on the Parks side of the fence since winter.

'Emily, I can't let you —'

'Can't let me what, Luke? Damage Parks property? Take cattle onto a restricted area?'

'No. I can't let you go.'

'Well, nor can I! You have to come with me,' she said.

'You're crazy to go that way. I reckon we've got half an hour before the hottest fire from hell hits. I'm telling you, if you go that way, via the road and the ridge, you're fried!'

'But where is there to go from here?' He looked about at the wall of trees and grasses.

'A special place,' she said.

'Emily,' he cautioned.

'Luke, you've got to trust me. If you go in the vehicle via the road, you're dead.'

She jogged over to Bonus and took one of the water packs off him.

'Here, spray this over me.'

Luke pumped the spray unit and together they showered each other with water, wetting their clothing. They sprayed the horses too and gave Rousie a quick drink out of Emily's hat. Then Emily gathered up Snowgum's reins and lobbed up onto the grey. The mare swished her tail and bowed her head, keen to move on, away from the onslaught of the furnace-like wind. Emily grabbed Bonus's lead rope and let rip a piercing whistle to her kelpie.

'Bonus is lame. You'll have to dink with me.' She held out her hand to Luke. He looked from her to the vehicle that had the fire unit on it.

'Safer to go this way,' she said looking into his warm, dark-chocolate eyes. She saw beyond the fear that shone in them. In his eyes was love. Pure love. He took her hand and electricity pulsed through in their touch. He swung up behind her.

Her quick-footed dog was soon round the cows and calves.

Small blackened twigs were falling all around them now. Ash drifted down, sticking to their wet skin. Then a furious wind hit them full force at their backs. It whipped Luke's hat from his head, and flung it away into a patch of thick young dogwoods. The cattle were panting as they crashed through the bush, hot tongues hanging out so far they looked like a butcher's shop display. The heat, the stress and the smell of the fire caused them to roll their eyes in panic.

Fireballs ignited and exploded on the tinder-dry ground. Where the grasses were grazed on the cattlemen's side, the flames only trickled along, but on the Parks side they leapt and noisily licked at seed heads whipping wildly in the wind, then jumped from the mid-story dogwoods and began to climb the trunks of the trees, their burning bark falling like liquid flames.

'Hang on,' Emily said over her shoulder as she urged Snowgum down the mountainside. She had unclipped the lead on the gelding who was now following, his nose pressed near the tail of the mare.

Luke tightened his arms around Emily, feeling comfort from being so near to her, but the fear still pulsed through them all; horse, humans, dog and beast. Emily steered the mare from the road to an unseen bridle path. Visibility was very poor and Luke was amazed Emily knew where to turn. He sent up a silent prayer for forgiveness that he had doubted this girl and her connection with the land. She was an amazing rider, a true bushwoman, and he felt her strong body flexing to the jolts as the horse moved over the rough terrain.

He berated himself for listening to the VPP stories about

the cattlemen. This girl, for one, was incredible. He listened to her talk to Snowgum as they dropped down through the scrub on a southerly slope, the mare responding to her calm, gentle voice.

Externally Emily seemed in control, but internally, adrenaline coursed through her body. Her eyes stung, her chest burned, both she and Luke were coughing in dry, rasping gasps, the pain in their lungs intense. Snowgum was breathless too, her sides heaved against their legs and blood was coming from her nostrils. Ahead of them in a dark haze, the cattle half-slid down the slope, Rousie hunting the ones that tried to veer off in a different direction. He was overheating too, and Emily was terrified he'd cramp and she'd have to carry him.

She spoke encouraging words to the dog and was relieved to see him respond with a small flicker of his tail. She was relying heavily on Rousie to get the cattle down. He'd turn to look back at her every now and then, as if to tell her this was madness. She urged him on. She knew that it was madness, that she shouldn't have gone back to search for the cattle. But there was no turning back from this now.

Suddenly the mare slipped and lurched sideways, righting herself just as quickly. Luke clung with his legs and held onto Emily's slim waist, only just staying on. To the left, a large limb cracked, loud as a shotgun, and banged to the ground. The mare shied violently but again the riders stuck.

The trees whirled madly about and more ash showered down. Embers stung their skin like wasps. They could hear a roaring behind them. Fire or wind, they weren't sure, but there was no looking back. The mare called out in a shudder-ing whinny, her black eyes rimmed white with fear. A choking dryness to the smoke-filled air starved them of breath and their eyes stung and watered.

Ahead of them, the cows were trotting and half sliding down the track, bumbling through bushes. The froth about their mouths trailed down to the dry ground. The day was becoming as black as midnight, Emily relying on her animals' intuition to guide her down the mountainside.

At last the vegetation began to thicken and change. The greenness brought on by damper soil emerged around them. The slope levelled off and soon they were pushing their way though thick ti-tree. Here, the world felt slightly cooler and the air clearer. They ducked their heads to avoid the scratching fingers of the ti-tree.

With relief, they emerged on the other side into a clearing. Emily pulled up her horse and watched as the cows and calves splashed into the shallows of the river. They began to draw water in great, lengthy draughts. Rousie lay in the shallows, panting and lapping at the water. Emily flicked her leg forward over her horse's neck and slid to the ground, letting Snowgum drink. Luke looked down at her.

'Thank you,' he said.

'Oh, we're not out of it yet,' she said. 'We could still boil alive in these shallows. We have to take the cattle up further. There's a big rock island there. We'll have to swim them. If Rousie can hold them on there, they might just make it if the fire jumps the river.'

'And us?' he said. 'Do we get in the river?'

Emily shook her head. 'I have a better plan. C'mon. There's no time. You'll have to walk upstream. I'm going to need my horse for this.'

And she was riding again, splashing into the shallow, fast-running river, swinging her stockwhip about her head, letting fly with a loud crack.

'Get up, girls!' she called and soon the cows and calves were stumbling upstream. It seemed to take so long. The air was easier to breathe near the dampness of the river, but it was dark as night in the gully, and fear still drove them on.

Emily was transported back to the night at Wonnangatta and the terror she and Luke had felt when they'd heard the ghost horses galloping past. Now she realised it had been some kind of warning. A future projection of what had been coming in their lives.

She urged the cattle on, and most of them now plunged into the wide, deeper pool. Rousie was swimming too, barking in the water as best he could at the stragglers. At last the final cow and calf heaved themselves up onto the island the river held at its heart. A giant old willow had taken root there many years before, offering a green canopy of shelter, but the cows still bustled and called out beneath the terrifying blacked-out sun.

The heat was intense. Emily and Luke turned towards a thundering roar high above them on the mountaintop, interspersed with explosive cracks as tree trunks succumbed to the inferno raging on the ridge above them. They stood transfixed as spot fires began to ignite all about them and the oxygen was stolen from the air. The mare threw her head and clashed her hooves on the river stones as the fire hunted wallabies, possums, lizards, snakes and other bush creatures to the riverbank. More fearful of fire than humans, a wallaby darted right under Snowgum's belly, its breath quick with panic and its docile brown eyes alert with terror. Bonus stuck close to the mare, too fearful to trot away.

'C'mon,' Emily shouted at Luke as she hitched Snowgum's reins and Bonus's lead to the willow tree. She undid the knapsack from the saddle pack, slinging it on the riverbank with a heavy thud. 'You have to get wet,' she told Luke.

She led him into the shallows and as she took his hand, he felt his own hands shaking uncontrollably. He was almost blind from the smoke.

'After this we're going into a fire bunker, okay?'

'Yep,' Luke croaked, amazed that there was a fire bunker here in this remote river-bend. He wanted to ask her about it. But no sound came. He could barely speak, barely swallow. Emily pulled him towards her.

Frighteningly warm water rose up over his clothing and, close to blind in the smoke and the darkness, he began to panic. But then he felt Emily's quiet, steady hands on either side of his face as she gently dragged him under water. He felt like he was in the presence of an angel. As the fire front hit the ridge directly above them and began to race downhill towards them, its terrifying roar was muffled as they both plunged underwater.

In the mountain stream, Emily pressed a last kiss to Luke's blistered lips before they surfaced to burning bark and leaves hitting the water with a fizz. Smoke curled over rock and ripples. Luke gulped at the thick, poisoned air and found himself coughing uncontrollably as they stumbled blindly from the river, Emily grabbing up the water pack.

All the while he felt Emily's hand leading him. Choking in the smoke, they half crawled up an embankment, the soil hot under their palms, the screech of green gumleaves burning above their heads. He heard Emily grunting with effort as she tore away old grasses, rocks and tin. Then she ushered him into the dark quiet space of a fire bunker, which had once been a Flanaghan goldmine.

It smelt of cold earth, of worms, of death and decay. But it was cool and the air, though musty, was easier to breathe.

Luke couldn't speak. All he could do was lie on the cool, hard earth trying to drag tiny breaths into his bleeding lungs. His body was stinging in agony where embers had burned him like cigarettes.

'Here,' Emily said. 'Drink.' She placed the nozzle of the back pack into his hands and he felt a trickle of water pass over his lips, but he could not swallow.

'The horses,' she said. 'I'm going to hobble them in the river. I'll be back.'

Luke tried to lift his head to protest but he felt a giddy rush and simply had to lie in the darkness.

'Emily,' he whispered, knowing she would be back soon in his arms. 'Emily Flanaghan.' Then he passed out.

Forty

A sudden noise in the pitch-black bunker jolted Luke awake. His head throbbed with pain. His mouth was so dry and his tongue so swollen he could barely swallow. He reached blindly for the nozzle of the spray pack, his hands grappling helplessly in the darkness. He knew from the silence that the fire had passed, but how long had they lain here?

'Emily?' he croaked, conjuring her face in his mind, reaching out to the darkness to hold her. 'Are you okay?' A joy came to him, knowing they had survived and they would be together. 'You are the most beautiful cattleman I've ever met.'

She didn't answer. Maybe she hadn't heard him? He heard the tin being tugged open at the door. A strange, gentle light touched his eyelids.

'Emily? Emily?' Luke stretched his blistered and blackened fingers and felt around on the bare earth for her, then he reached out towards the light.

'It's all right,' came a man's voice. 'We've got you, buddy.'

Luke felt a hand on his shoulder. 'Can you see?'

He shook his head. 'Emily? Where is she? Emily!'

He began to scramble about on all fours, terror wrenching his heart, his mind crazy with questions.

'Mate, there's no one else in here. You are one lucky bastard, though.'

'But . . . Emily?'

'I'm sorry, mate,' the rescue worker said as he shone the torch around the cavernous den. He could see an old mine shaft, boarded up long ago. 'There's no one else here.'

Through searing pain, Luke tried to open his eyes. With blurred vision, he could only just make out the fluoro overalls and hard hats of the SES men who crouched down next to him. Outside the bunker, the blackened world looked as if an atomic bomb had hit. A crash of a falling tree prompted the sudden burst of rising embers from the charred landscape. The pain was too great. Luke had to shut his eyes again.

'C'mon, we've got to get you out of here. It's dangerous for us all.'

'But Emily? Emily?' Luke yelled, until his voice again gave way to just a croak. 'The cattle!'

'Cattle?' the rescue worker said, barely able to make sense of Luke's speech.

As the men radioed out that their three-day search was over – the ranger had been found and needed medical help – Luke became angry. They must've been flown in from another region, with no idea Emily might be in the area, let alone that she was missing. How could the rescue be so uncoordinated, Luke wondered? They'd been instructed to find the government employee but not the cattleman.

'But, Emily. The cattle,' he tried again. It hurt to talk, but a fury was rising in him.

'There's no cattle here, mate. This is Park land now. The cattlemen were kicked off it. This must've been a cattleman's mine and fire bunker. How the hell did you find it? We only found *you* because your vehicle's burnt to a crisp up top and the track and ventilation shaft that sticks up outta the ground stands out like dog's balls now it's all burnt.'

Luke sat up, ready to roar, but no sound came. He was giddy.

'Settle, mate. You're in shock. Calm yourself. The medicos will be here with something good for you in just a little while.'

What the worker didn't want to tell Luke was that there was no sign of the cattleman's daughter. He didn't like to say that the fire that had just destroyed a million acres of Park land was so hot, no man could discern if the fine white ash now blowing in the wind was that of cow, horse or human. White dust, like the powder of angels' wings, taking flight over vast areas of charred mountain wilderness.

On the chopper ride out, Luke pressed his fingertips at the cool cotton pads that covered his eyes. He felt the pain of trying to shed tears from eyes that had none. As they flew over the black-faced mountainside, he didn't see the big metal VPP sign hanging twisted and blackened. He didn't see the burnt matchstick trees, seared from top to bottom.

Lingering flames still burned on the breeze-side of the tree trunks and in the guts of hollow stumps. But Luke didn't see them. He didn't see the way the fire had crawled to a stop within metres of the Flanaghan homestead, as if God had had some hand in this giant unreasonable plan. He didn't see the rubble of the old hotel, which had been Evie's leafy green haven. She too was gone. To ash and dust? No one knew. The only colour in the garden now was the striped tape of the coroner's investigators.

What Luke *did* see in his mind's eye was the bravest, most beautiful girl he'd ever known. A girl on a ghost-grey horse, standing in a thicket of snowgums. The land was written on her palms and fingertips and, he knew now, the land had been written in her heart.

As the chopper landed on the Dargo oval in a cloud of dust and ash, Luke heard the paramedics groan at the sight of the media hovering nearby.

'They all want the scoop on the ranger who went to rescue the cattleman's daughter. I'm sorry, mate,' said the pilot.

Through his puffy eyes Luke could make out the cluster of journalists and a sombre group of people watching in silence as they wheeled him into a waiting ambulance to take him to the bush hospital. He knew that if they'd found him and Emily alive, there'd be whoops of joy. But his homecoming was so weighted down by the tragedy of losing Emily he wished he'd been taken by the fire too.

They settled him into a hospital bed in a room that faced

the main street. Through the curtains he could see the nurses shooing away the pack of reporters, who hung about like hyenas on the scavenge.

He looked up at the ceiling while a nurse checked his vital signs. He recoiled from the woman's cool touch on his stinging skin. The only human touch he wanted was Emily's. He thought of their night in the Dargo homestead, by the fire, when Emily had told him about her mother dying in this very hospital. And now Emily was gone too. Seeing his distress, the nurse fussed over him with extra gentle care.

The sun had faded to just a small patch at the foot of Luke's hospital bed when Flo led Rod into the ward. The old cattleman was bent over and almost shuffled. It was a shock to see this tall proud father so broken by grief.

Behind them, Bridie and Sam ushered Tilly and Meg into the room. Luke could see they'd all been crying. Emily's wild-haired, smiley children were now pale-faced and silent. Their eyes were full of fear and confusion. They were lost without their cheerful, busy mother. Luke's breath caught in his throat at the sight of them.

Rod came over to him and drew Luke up in a hug. The two men held each other, both unafraid to cry for Emily. Their bodies shook. The hearts of those who watched twisted in agony.

There was a whole life ahead of them, without Emily.

Rod pulled back.

'Thank you,' he said, 'for going to look for my daughter.'

Luke, his face contorted, shook his head violently.

'It was my fault. I should've made her stay. But I . . .'

Rod put a hand on his arm, and Luke could feel he carried the same strong energy within him that Emily had.

'You can't make Emily do anything she doesn't want to do.'

Luke smiled, comforted by Rod talking about her in the present tense.

Once they saw Luke's smile, the girls clambered up on Luke's bed, holding him tightly.

'Don't go, Luke,' Tilly said.

'No, don't go. Mummy thinks you're really, really nice,' Meg said. 'She wants you to stay with us.'

And at that point Luke's heart broke for Emily Flanaghan's daughters.

Forty-one

The next morning, when Donna from the pub began to scream, Kate downed what she was doing in the general store and ran out to see what was wrong. The old men on the bench seat muttered that Donna had clean gone off her rocker. They watched her standing with her hands held up to her face, frozen in the middle of the main street, gazing towards the river and yelling, 'Oh my God!' over and over.

Donna's cries rang out, the sound making it to the Beauty in the Bush cottage along the way. There, Rod, Flo, Bob, Bridie and Sam were quietly going about the strained business of organising memorial services for Emily and Evie, while Meg and Tilly sat numbly watching *Play School*.

For the past few days Bob and Sam had been trying to contact Evie's family, but it was as if she had no past, no contacts. They could find no traces of her previous life. Nor could the media, who were hounding them, looking for something more on the old lady who'd died in the fires. It was as if Evie had blown in from nowhere. And since no body had been found in the debris of her house, it was as if she'd just blown right out again.

With all the leads on the stories of the two missing fire victims going cold, the city journalists were packing their gear into the boots of their cars at the motel when they heard Donna's screams.

As the Flanaghan family ran down the main street to Donna, they followed her gaze across the river to the winding Lower Dargo Road. They couldn't believe their eyes.

There, at the bridge, rode Emily, swinging her stockwhip over her head. The crack rang out as the lead cow gingerly walked onto the wooden bridge. In front of Emily, twenty-five footsore, scorched and blistered cows and calves took their agonising last steps homeward.

Emily was crying through her swollen, stinging eyes as she made her way towards the crossroads at the pub and the store. Her clothes were singed rags, her eyelashes burnt and gone, her lips blistered, her Akubra hat, once cream, was now mottled black with holes where embers had smoked. Snowgum, head down but ears cast forward, let out an exhausted whicker, her lips blistered red and weeping. Emily sat bareback on the mare leading a hollow-gutted Bonus, his pack saddle hanging over his back as he limped along.

Tilly and Meg sprinted towards her. Rod, Flo, Bob, Bridie and Sam all followed, calling out with joy and disbelief. They ran right through the herd towards Emily, dispersing the cows. Relieved to no longer be driven, the beasts began to browse the rich green grass of the Dargo Hotel beer garden. Rousie, foot-sore, flopped down in a patch of long green grass, his job done.

A frenzy erupted around Emily. She was covered with burns, bruises, scrapes, blisters, sunburn and cuts, but she felt no pain as she swept her precious girls into her arms. She held them to her and felt their tears of relief and joy on her face.

Tilly and Meg breathed in the smell of their mother. She smelt scary and wonderful all at once. She smelt of fear and fire and long days and nights in the bush. She smelt of dogs and horses and cattle. But she also smelt of home and of love.

Then Rod was hugging her, Flo and Bob too, and Sam and Bridie, with beaming faces of joy. As they all clustered around her, firing questions, they didn't notice Meg slip away. Nobody saw how the little girl ran towards the bush hospital as fast as her legs would carry her.

Luke was up from his hospital bed. He was dressed. He was leaving, going back to his bush block to begin a life without Emily. He could barely imagine how he was going to do it. As he pulled on his boots he looked up, surprised to see Meg standing in the doorway, framed in golden light from the corridor.

'Hello. What are you doing here?' Luke said softly.

She held out her hand.

'Come with me,' she said, her big, brown eyes the mirror of her mother's, looking up at him with urgency.

Luke frowned, but took her hand.

'Hurry!' Meg said, as she trotted down the main street towards the pub with Luke in tow.

Luke saw the cattle first, singed and footsore, ambling about the lawn behind the pub. Then, on the fringes of a crowd of townspeople, he saw Kate from the store holding two horses. A chestnut and a grey. Emily's horses! His heart began to race. Meg squeezed his hand as she looked up and smiled at him. Then he knew. He knew at the heart of that crowd he would find Emily. Emily was alive!

He swooped Meg up and carried her over, pushing through the people, and stood before Emily, breathless. He set Meg down, cupped Emily's face tenderly with his hands and looked deep into her eyes.

'You!' he said.

'Yes, me.'

He stooped down and kissed her so gently, so lightly, like a butterfly passing over her skin. Her lips were red-raw, her skin burnt and blistered. But she was alive. She was here with him.

They held each other, and Emily felt more butterflies tumble and turn inside her.

Their peace was shattered as the media stormed them, cameras flashing in their faces, microphones pressed far too close. The thrill of the scoop stripping away any kind of courtesy as the journalists fired questions in a frenzy.

'How did you survive?'

'How long have you been travelling like this?'

'Did you think you were going to die?'

'Do you have a message for the Victorian Government on alpine management and fires?'

Emily turned to the city media pack and, as best she could with her stinging eyes, looked down the barrel of one of the cameras.

'You don't need me to deliver a message. It's written all around us, in what's left of the land and the wildlife.'

As she turned and stepped into the warmth of her family, and Luke's arms, Emily wasn't to know that her image and her message was about to be beamed to the world.

As they walked along the main street Emily felt her father's hand on her shoulder. 'I think we'd better get you to the hospital.'

Emily shook her head.

'No way, Dad! No more hospitals! I'll stick with Evie's remedies.'

The family looked at each other, their faces falling. Someone had to tell Emily. But Emily caught their looks and smiled sadly.

'I know she's gone.' Again she felt her family fold in around her with love.

'How do you know?'

'I just know,' Emily said.

Settled on Bridie's couch, Emily watched as her family rushed to fill a bath for her and fetch her drinks and food. In the back garden Luke and Sam were tending to the horses, who now stood resting beneath a shady walnut tree. Bob was offering Rousie a fat steak on the porch.

Meg and Tilly sat with her on the couch and Emily draped her aching arms over them, just as Evie had done on the day of the fires. Emily rested her head against them alternately, breathing in their smell, kissing them over and over with her painful swollen lips.

'What happened, Mummy?' Tilly asked.

'You don't want to know,' Emily said. 'Let's just say I'm having a bad run with trees!'

'Tell us, *please*,' Tilly prompted again.

'Not today, darling. One day soon I'll tell you. Just give Mummy a rest now.'

Emily lay back and shut her eyes, conjuring up the vision of the giant burning gum that had crashed down in the winds gusting through the river bed. She had been about to hobble the horses and lead them into the deep hole of the river bed before returning to the bunker. But as she picked herself up from where she had fallen, Emily found the sparks, smoke and dust of the falling tree had blinded her.

Thankfully, when the tree fell, the horses had shied but not bolted. She grappled to find Snowgum, and held tight to her reins. She knew she had to stay with them. Blinded, she had no way of finding Luke. Shivering from the memory, she opened her eyes and reached for Meg and Tilly's hands.

'Thank God I'm home!'

'Bath for madame,' came Bridie's singsong voice as she held out a robe.

In the steaming tub, as she washed the soot from her tender skin, Emily's hands shook. The shock was settling in. She could still feel the fire around her and her conviction that she would surely die. She had clambered up on Snowgum and the mare had set off at a jog amidst the roar of the fire in the mountains above. At first Emily panicked, trying to rein Snowgum towards the deeper hole, but the mare resisted. Eventually she heard a voice in her head saying 'trust'. She let Snowgum have her head.

She could hear Bonus limping along behind them in the river bed, calling out madly if he fell behind. Her lips were so parched she couldn't whistle Rousie – she had no idea where he was. She had lain flat to Snowgum's neck as she trotted along the river bed, water splashing cool on Emily's legs as the fire raged above them. Low-cast branches scratched her back. Falling embers burned her skin.

Emily had no idea how long they travelled like that. She just felt Snowgum moving beneath her as she pressed her face into the mare's hot, sweating neck. She could smell her damp Akubra smouldering and hear Snowgum grunt with effort as she stumbled over boulders in the river bed. Emily clung so tightly to the reins her fingers curled and cramped as if in a death-grip.

Gradually the bush around them quietened. The wind settled. Still, Emily could not see. The mare stopped and dropped her head. She heard Bonus come to stand beside her and let out a slow snort. He too was easing himself down for a rest. When the horses began to doze, Emily knew they were safe.

Still blinded and lost, Emily knew Snowgum would eventually take her home. She tried to call Rousie but her throat was so swollen she could not speak. Soon, though, in the deadly hush of the burned bush, she heard a crack, a crash, a splash, then miraculously a woof. Rousie was bringing the cattle along to her! Emily could hear them crossing the river. Goosebumps trailed from her legs up to her scalp.

'Good boy,' she croaked. 'Good boy.'

Then in her mind, she began to call up her girls, 'C'mon, c'mon, c'mon!' Her beautiful, beautiful cows were with her still.

Bridie knocked and came into the bathroom.

'Okay?'

Emily nodded as Bridie tenderly pressed a cool cotton pad on her eyes.

'Ouch!'

'Sorry.'

She settled back into the bath.

'Want to tell me about it?' came Bridie's voice, sounding strangely far away in the tiny steamy bathroom.

Emily shook her head.

She didn't want to recall out loud how she had slid from Snowgum at the riverside and stooped to wash her face. The water was thick with ash and she could only just peer out from her swollen eyes. As she bent over the river and swirled gluggy grey-and-white powder, a pattern formed. Curious, Emily stared at it. She gasped when she saw the image. It was Evie's face. She reeled backwards, slumping to the ground with the sudden, horrible realisation that Evie was gone.

'Oh, God,' Emily's voice cracked. 'Oh, God, Evie, no.'

She had hunkered on the riverbank in a ball and howled. Rousie had come and lain next to her and she had pulled him to her and held him for comfort.

In the cottage, Emily sat in a fluffy white robe after her bath, her family all around her, Luke by her side, when their conversation was interrupted by a sudden burst of wind. It blew the door open with a terrific bang, sending Bridie's cat tumbling from the couch and Muff barking at the leaves that skittered over the lawn.

'What was *that*?' Sam said.

'It was just Evie,' said Meg. All eyes turned to the little girl as she nonchalantly continued to eat cashews from a bowl. 'Evie and Jesus Christ.'

Epilogue

At the mountain cattlemen's get-together at Rose River, Luke and Emily lay sweltering in the afternoon heat of their two-room dome tent as they watched insects crawl on the roof. Luke interlaced his fingers with Emily's and looked into her eyes happily. She sighed, enjoying their siesta, listening to the constant thrum of a generator nearby and the giggles of Meg and Tilly who lay beside them.

In the river next to the tent, kids screamed and splashed. They heard the deep *plop* of a heavy rock as it was tossed and swallowed up in the swimming hole. Then the generator coughed itself out of diesel and the silence that followed was blissful.

On the other side of the tent, they could hear Snowgum and Bonus chewing chaff steadily, squealing every now and then as they hunted the girls' pesky ponies away from their tucker.

Above the tent, birds moved busily in the leaves of the riverside gums and the river bubbled over rocks beside them.

Rolling over onto their stomachs, Emily and Luke looked out through the gauze from their tiny shell of privacy as riders on fit stockhorses ambled past, pausing to offer their horses a drink at designated spots along the river. Some horses had kids on ponies in tow, like little round dinghies trailing behind bigger boats. One big black stockhorse was so impressively fit and sleek, Emily's gaze lingered on him and the rider.

'Do you wish you were in the race tomorrow?' Luke said.

Emily shook her head. 'Not at all. I'd rather spend the Cattlemen's with you!' She nuzzled into him.

Emily thought back over her day. For the first time ever, Luke had set up a VPP display for the two-day get-together. It was not so much an information booth as a place where information could be freely exchanged.

Old, bent-kneed cattlemen shuffled up to tell Parks staff about bothersome patches of weeds. Could something be done? Young men came forward to report sightings of deer in areas they'd never been seen in before. Others came to say they worried about the lack of burning along rivers, where delicate populations of galaxias that lived in the shade could be at risk. Could a cool burn be arranged? After some initial prickliness, both sides had begun to listen to what each had to say.

Luke and Emily were on the stall the entire day. Meg and Tilly came and went on their ponies, begging money for ice-cream or chips, with their little entourage of friends in tow. And as the day wore on, Emily could see excitement building at the potential of a new partnership.

A year ago, this exchange would not have been possible. But

the devastation of the fires had forced a rethink. Old mindsets had to go. Already a contract was on its way from the VPP to employ Emily and another high-country family to graze cattle in the Wonnangatta National Park for fuel reduction. The mountain cattlemen had also been asked to be part of grazing trials on some of the burnt country as it recovered.

The turnaround in attitudes was incredible and happening so fast. But Emily knew she was being guided from above. As she dozed in the tent she daydreamed of Evie. Evie had talked about death and how souls and love were eternal. She'd said death was not such a final thing as people would have you believe. Wasn't that what Emily herself had found a year ago, when she had left this earth? She was jolted awake by Tilly. 'Mummy! Look!'

Outside the sun was disappearing behind a high wall of clouds that hung together in great swollen clusters, like fat grey balloons poised to burst.

'A storm!' the girls said excitedly, clapping their hands and bouncing up and down on their knees.

'The ute windows!' Emily said, ducking out from the tent, Luke following her.

They wound the windows up as the wind moaned in the trees. Horses were shifting about, working out which way to place their rumps against the coming onslaught. Emily felt warm turbulent gusts of wind on her bare limbs. Huge, fat drops began to thud to earth, hitting blades of grass like bombs in a London blitz and belting the dust on vehicles into muddy rivulets. The storm flung tarps about so they whip-cracked in the wind. Card tables were turned topsy-turvy, spilling sauces and salt shakers. People ran for cover.

Emily bent down and checked Rousie under the float. His ears were pinned down and he looked miserable.

'C'mon, fella,' she said. He hunkered his way out, tail between his legs. She unclipped him and invited him into the tent.

'Give him a cuddle, girls,' she said to Meg and Tilly.

'Can I put him in my sleeping bag, Mum?' Tilly asked.

'Maybe not. Just wrap him in a towel. He'll like that.' She had to shout above the wind that boomed in the tree-tops surrounding the valley. 'Luke and I are just going to tie the tent off tighter, then I'll be back.'

But the girls didn't answer. They were already offering Rousie a muesli bar and putting Meg's Winnie the Pooh coat with the fur hood on him. He looked very pleased with himself.

The rain hit like a fire hose and within seconds Emily and Luke were drenched. People scurried for cover all around them, but they stood in the torrential rain, arms around each other. They lifted their faces to the sky. Raindrops fell from heaven into their laughing mouths, and a blissfully warm wind on their bodies made them feel alive.

Emily and Luke kissed. Emily felt a rush of gratitude for this man in her arms. For his amazing energy, his spirit, his knowledge that the land was sacred. He belonged with her in the mountains. She leaned her head on Luke's chest and listened to the steady knock of his heart and knew that their love was eternal.

*

Later, when the clouds had cleared and stars shone in bright swathes across the mountain sky, Emily looked heavenward as she spun about, dancing with Luke as Sam played with his band from the back of a semi. Above them on the hillside moths danced in the gleam of the generator lights that lit the bar area and people milled about, gathering before the makeshift stage. Thinking back to the last mountain cattlemen's get-together Emily shivered. How far she had come.

There she was, with Luke, her daughters, Bridie, Rod, Bob, Flo and Baz. All of them rocking to Sam as he belted out new songs in celebration of the cattlemen and their life on the mountains.

Amidst the rabblerousing crowd of blokes and chicks in hats and singlets, the Flanaghan family stomped their boots the hardest and sang the loudest. From the crush of boozers and boppers, Emily gazed up at Sam. Beneath the spotlight he was the image of country-cool. A cluster of young girls at the front were calling out Sam's name, but there, on the side of the stage, stood Bridie, her hands resting on her swollen belly. She was radiating even more beauty now that she was pregnant.

Every now and then Sam would turn his head slightly and give her a quick glance, a wink or a smile. Beside Bridie stood Bob, an earpiece jammed in his ears, ready to run on from back stage to check amps, feeders and foot pedals. He gave Emily the thumbs-up and she returned the gesture.

Luke spun Emily around and she held his hands and looked into his shining eyes. He nodded his head, a big grin on his face as they took in the comical sight of Baz getting down on one knee in front of Flo, a bit drunk and wobbly, but nonetheless offering up a plastic ring from a six-pack of stubbies.

Then Emily watched as Rod danced with his granddaughters, the love and laughter between them shining brightly. The future and the past of the mountains embodied in them all.

Emily gazed up to the stars and thought of the two people she knew would be watching them tonight from above. Evie and her mother, Susie. She saw the brightest star wink, and suddenly Emily realised they were one and the same. The splicing of two souls. Her guardian angel, her mother, come to earth in the form of Evie.

As Sam's first song ended and the crowd cheered, Emily felt a rush of pure joy at the wonder and mystery of life. She thanked her stars she had seen the face of death in the horse race all those months ago, and that had opened up her mind and heart.

Her brother grabbed the microphone from the stand. In his fancy alligator-skin cowboy boots he stood at the very front of the stage. Everyone fell silent as he set his feet apart, his hands falling by his side, a beautiful smile on his face. Sam looked straight at Emily and spoke clearly into the microphone.

'This next one's for Evie,' he said.

Afterword

It was Ian Stapleton's book, *From Drovers to Daisy-Pickers*, that gave me the courage to write a novel based on my family's eviction from the mountains. I'd like to share a section with you now. It makes me cry every time I read it. Thank you, Ian, for allowing me to reproduce it here.

> As I write this book, the Victorian Government has just announced that it will not be renewing the grazing licences held by any of the families whose leases lie within the Alpine National Park. This decision effectively brings an end to 150 years of grazing, and has of course delighted some people, whilst devastating others. Some say it was inevitable in a changing world. But, regardless of your views on the relative impact of grazing and the role of the mountain cattlemen, few would surely not be saddened to see so many of the family names that have become synonymous with the mountains for so long, be hounded en-masse from their traditional High Country haunts. So many of them have been such tremendous contributors to life in the mountains, and such wonderfully colourful characters to boot. They leave behind not only their famous huts and names of many landmarks, but also a fabulous collection of stories and memories that will always be part of our mountains. Like so many others, I have been blessed with their friendship and support, and I only hope that books like this can help to dispel the prevailing urban myth that these families are being driven from the mountain in some sort of shame or disgrace. Our generation will never know the impact of another 150 years of ski village expansion, tourist development, road building, National Parks and bureaucratic management will be, but it would be enlightening indeed, to be able to briefly wind the clock forward 150 years for just a quick glimpse into the future, before too many hasty judgements are passed.

Bibliography

While a little family folklore has crept into *The Cattleman's Daughter*, this novel is not an historic or present-day account of the Treasure family. The Flanaghan family, the government organisations and all the characters, events and shenanigans in *The Cattleman's Daughter* have been made up by me. However, I have used my own experience at protest rides through Melbourne and Wonnangatta, and droving cattle on the Dargo High Plains as inspiration. Another 'real-life' event is the mountain cattlemen's get-together, which happens every January in Victoria – see you there! Other sources of research are:

Attiwill, P. M. et al, 'The People's Review of Bushfires, 2002–2007, in Victoria: Final report'. The People's Review, 2009.

Brown, Terry, 'Mountain folk gather to the fray'. *Herald Sun*, 10 June 2005.

'Call for Action on Fire Management'. *Bairnsdale Advertiser*, July 2008.

'East Gippsland Fires: A retrospective'. East Gippsland Newspapers, 2006/07.

Environment and Natural Resources Committee, 'Inquiry into the Impact of Public Land Management Practices on Bushfires in Victoria'. Parliament of Victoria, June 2008.

Grand, Danielle, 'Plea for big attendance at city rally, "Back Us"'. *Weekly Times*, 8 June 2005.

Hay, Louise L., *You Can Heal Your Life*. Hay House, 1984.

Hicks, Esther and Jerry, *Ask and It Is Given: Learning to manifest your desires*. Hay House, 2004.

Holth, Tor with Jane Barnaby, *Cattlemen of the High Country: The story of the mountain cattlemen of the Bogongs*. Rigby, 1980.

Leydon, Keith and Michael Ray, *The Wonnangatta Mystery: An inquiry into the unsolved murders*. Warrior Press, 2000.

Marino, Melissa and Garry Tippet, 'Alpine Grazing: 500 horsepower in support of the lows in the high country'. *The Age*, 10 June 2005.

Memoirs of Charles Langford Treasure, family collection of writing, provided by Ken Treasure.

Roberts, L. (ed.), 'Black Friday, 1939' from The Gap, 1969.

Stapleton, Ian, *From Fraser's to Freezeout: Colourful characters of the Dargo High Plains*. Ligare Printer, 2004.

Stapleton, Ian, *From Drovers to Daisy-Pickers: Colourful characters of the Bogongs*. Ligare Printer, 2006.

Stephenson, Harry, *Cattlemen and Huts of the High Plains*. Viking O'Neil, 1980.

The Voice of the Mountains: Journal of the Mountain Cattlemen's Association of Victoria. Mountain Cattlemen's Association of Victoria, 2007.

Tomazin, Farrah, 'Minister may yet give in to the cattlemen'. *The Age*, 10 June 2005.

2006 Emu Committee and the Gippsland Grammar Foundation, *Is Emu off the Menu?* E. Gee Printers, 2007.

69 Days of Fire: A Gippsland community perspective.

Acknowledgements

There are so many people to thank for the journey of this book, and if I've missed you, I'm sorry – I'm trying to brainstorm without Bundy! Just know I am grateful.

Deepest thanks to my editor Belinda Byrne – big sister and best friend. Thanks to Ali Watts, for giving me wings with your feedback! To my other Penguins, Sally, Dan and the crew, thank you. To my literary agent, Margaret Connolly, you are my safety net, mentor and dear friend. To my webman, Allan Moult, thanks for thinking pink! Thanks to the Tasmanian Writer's Centre for renting Kelly Street cottage to me at the crucial stages of this book. Thanks to my Hobart writer girlfriends for ongoing inspiration, and to Mev and Sarah – your love and friendship are a constant. Thanks to the Woodsdale Women, Levendale Ladies and Runnymede Rum'ens for giving me a life rich with laughter. (Sorry about the prank calls!) To Kathy Bright, thanks for teaching me so much – about God, the Universe and Everything – and inspiring the character of Evie. Thanks to the Tate family for taking me trucking – a day that sparked the idea of our fodder fun factory. I'll never forget those saggy silage bales, Ben! Thanks also to Roweena for minding the kids at crunch time. To KJ, for looking so inspiringly gorgeous in your ambo uniform. To Luella, for waddling with me until we both learned to fly. To Manty, my text buddy and third musketeer. Thanks to Heidi – my special phone-a-friend. To my Richmond team of oomphers, Judy, Danny and Helen, thanks. Thanks to Lou Loane for Emily's inspirational underpants collection (Tractor Fat Inc). To Margareta, you shine like a star for me, thank you for your early feedback on the manuscript – I'll be sure to do the same for you. Thanks also to Kathy, Jess and Pru. Thanks always to the Williams family, Maureen, Tubby and Jake,

Grant and Brodie (a la Beauty in the Bush) – you are my biggest support and I couldn't do any of it without you. And now to my treasured Treasure family, you are the reason I've written this book. Thanks especially to father-in-law, Doug, for the use of your MCAV speech within this book and to the Gippsland crew: Mary, Anna, Paul, Kate, Ben, Fee, Ken and Lynette, Linette, Christa, Rhonda, Bruce, Alan and the entire clan. Thanks to the cattlemen's daughters, Lyric Anderson, Kate Treasure, Kate Stoney, Anna Treasure and Rose Faithful, for being beautiful girls and giving me the basis for Emily. To Marc and Andrea, Rod and Leeanne, Sharon and Rob, your help during visits to Tassie made all the difference at tricky times. Thanks to the MCAV for ongoing support. My gratitude to Parks Victoria, Heyfield – especially Mick – and Department of Environment and Sustainability, Bairnsdale, for help with research for the novel. I hope this book helps to create a new page in the history of the mountains. To my Tassie clan, Miles 'the rock star' Smith, Kristy and Val and Jenny, again eternal gratitude. To my darling farm animals – especially Edith, Rousie and our Hereford bovines – thanks always for your inspiration. The biggest dose of gratitude to my husband, John – thank you for sharing your family's life on the mountains with me and for letting me leave so often for 'planet novel'. To my little one, Rosie, thanks for inspiring the character of Meg. You are a gift to the world. To Charlie, thanks for loving your mummy so much – you are a cattleman and a character in the making. So thank you, dear family and friends, for giving me the riches of life in the form of love, laughter and chaos. And thanks to Ian Stapleton, who is generous, humble, yet great. Ian, your life and your writings are inspirational. Your wisdom highlights the balance needed not only in the mountains but in life. You gave me the conviction that this story needs to be told.

Abundant thanks, love and gratitude to the following team who helped create our beautiful new book covers: horsemasters and shoot directors Heath and Krissy Harris of Harris Entertainment, the Hawkesbury River Saddle Company, photographer Peter Stoop and Kirsten Stoop, Girls Girls Girls trick riders/models Cody Wilson and Christy Connor and 'hot ute' model Jake Whiting. Thanks also to our gorgeous 'random ring-in' models Bridie and Matt, Kimberly and James, and gorgeous horse educator and model Adam Sutton. And not forgetting the wonderful horses, including Riley and Roger and their mob and Levi. Thanks also to Glenworth Valley Station, Steve Richards and Ruby the Kelpie. You are all real-life heroes and heroines and your inner beauty shines through to the outer! And thanks also to the Penguin design team for believing in this wild and exhilarating ride!